Praise for Lane Robins
and *Maledicte*

"A darkly original world of doubted gods and declining civilization. Robins is a fantasist with a future."
—*Publishers Weekly*

"*Maledicte* is a genuine page-turner with some tricks up its sleeve . . . as dashing as a swashbuckler and twisted as tragic opera."
—*Locus*

"A spirited, complex melodrama. At heart, Lane Robins has created an old-fashioned tale of revenge . . . [she] is a writer of genuine ability."   —scifi.com

"Jacobean-style fantasy . . . A strong-willed debut."
—*Kirkus Reviews*

"Machiavellian characters, erotic tension, sharp and witty dialogue, an up-tempo pace, sinister supernatural forces, and a melodramatic plot that twists and turns until its touching conclusion . . . [Robins is] a talented, up-and-coming author."
—Fantasy Book Critic

"*Maledicte* is as diabolically intelligent as it is nefariously compelling. It's a modern day *Count of Monte Cristo*, with vengeance, retribution, justice, and redemption . . . soon to become a contemporary classic."   —RomanceJunkies.com

"Great action and excitement. If you like your fantasy dark and bloody with intricate plots, this is the story for you."   —Coffee Time Romance

By Lane Robins

MALEDICTE

KINGS AND ASSASSINS

KINGS AND ASSASSINS

KINGS
AND ASSASSINS

Lane Robins

BALLANTINE BOOKS

NEW YORK

A Del Rey Trade Paperback Original

Copyright © 2009 by Lane Robins

Published in the United States by Del Rey, an imprint of
The Random House Publishing Group, a division of Random House, Inc., New York.

DEL REY is a registered trademark and the Del Rey colophon is a
trademark of Random House, Inc.

Library of Congress Cataloging-in-Publication Data
Robins, Lane.
Kings and assassins / Lane Robins.
p. cm.
"A Del Rey Books trade paperback original"—T.p. verso.
ISBN 978–0–345–49574–7 (pbk.)
1. Courts and courtiers—Fiction. I. Title.
PS3618O3177K56 2009
813'.6—dc22
2009001348

Printed in the United States of America

www.delreybooks.com

2 4 6 8 9 7 5 3 1

Designed by Stephanie Huntwork

For Cathy and Dick Robins,
the best parents a creative-minded kid could have
Thank you

·ACKNOWLEDGMENTS·

This book would not have seen the light of day without a small army of support. Thanks are due to the Wednesday Night Write Group—Barbara, Erick, Nate, Rob, and Shan—who heard far more of the plot wrangling than they deserved; to those who gave me valuable feedback: Larry Taylor, Luisa Prieto, and Jane Gunther. Thanks also to Caitlin Blasdell and Liz Scheier for their patience and support.

TRAITOR

*A*T THE SPIDER HEART OF Murne's radiating streets, the king's palace overlooked the city, its three wings jutting away from one another in uncomfortable points. The palace had been built in stages, generations apart. Dark granite blocks comprised the oldest part, a warrior's palace with arrow slits instead of windows: the palace of Thomas Redoubt, the Cold King, who had claimed Antyre for its own country, wresting independence from Itarus with the aid of Haith, secretive god of death and victory.

When the Cold King vanished into the walls of his own palace, leaving only the bodies of his family—wife, son, an unmarried daughter—behind, the claimant to the throne built a new edifice entirely, separate in style and space, leaving a sward between the two palaces. The new king built the antithesis of the Cold King's haunted granite corridors, a sunlit series of pavilions with wide corridors and wider windows, laid nacre over every upright surface, marble over the floors, and gilt across the ceilings.

The king enjoyed the sunlit views for less than a year after its completion. The ambitious Lord Ixion from the House of Last, made good use of the windows, clambering through, sword in hand, and left the entire royal family gutted, the marble floors awash in blood.

Ixion, though aware that the country was nearly bankrupt, built his own palace, an awkward bridge between the two styles. His was constructed of sensible brick, wood, and lath and plaster; and though the windows were wide, they could be barred and shuttered. A practical man's palace, and it had served the family well. Six generations and the House of Last still held the throne.

It made it all the more galling that Janus Ixion—current Earl of Last, the king's nephew, two steps from the throne, and resident of the palace—had been consigned to living quarters in the Cold King's wing, along with the other undesirables.

Of course, it was more galling still to be waiting on the attention of another undesirable, deposited in a visitor's salon like a recalcitrant child.

Janus rose from his chair, shivering as the warmth of the leather peeled away from his back. He poked idly at the low-burning fire, and twitched when the door opened behind him, let a quick swirl of cooler air spark the flames higher.

He didn't turn around. He didn't need to. Only one man could make free of these rooms: the Itarusine prince ascendant, Ivor Sofia Grigorian.

"My pet, I asked you here to play cards, not act the housekeeper. You should have asked a servant to stoke the fire for you," Prince Ivor said.

"And shiver while waiting for your man to do what I could do myself?" Janus jabbed at the scant pile of logs, satisfied when one of them crumbled into ash. It was absurd how cold the old wing was; it approached summer outside, but inside it was as if Ivor had brought the cold of the Itarusine Winter Court to Antyre alongside his servitors and guards.

"Ever precipitate," Ivor said, his tone indulgent as a fond uncle's.

Janus turned to accept the glass of Itarusine brandy the prince handed him, a drink unpopular in any rooms but these, which for the duration of Ivor's tenure here, were considered to be Itarus.

Janus took a thoughtful sip and reseated himself. The leather chair was still warm, still shaped to his broad shoulders, and welcomed him back. "Cards," he said.

"Is it so odd?" Ivor said. "We played many such games during your years in the Winter Court."

Janus frowned into the warm amber depths of the brandy, watched it wave against the clear glass like fire licking ice, and bit back comment. Many such games indeed. Prince Ivor was a true son of the Itarusine court, and nothing was ever as it seemed with him. Sit down to a game with Ivor, and rise poorer in coin; position; and, all too often, life expectancy.

Playing any game at all with Ivor was dangerous, but not playing . . . well, that was worse. Ivor saved his most inventive schemes for those who thought to escape them. Even now, his dark eyes lingered on Janus, daring him to make his excuses and leave. A perfect brow arched, glossy and dark against his pale skin.

Ivor looked every inch the aristocrat he was, the most-favored prince of Itarus, well dressed, elegant in his silk cravat and lace cuffs, but there was nothing of softness about him. His eyes, mouth, and hands were hard.

When Janus had first arrived in the Winter Court, a Relict rat dumped among the aristocracy, Ivor had unaccountably offered himself as a mentor, teaching Janus the best ways to survive in a court given over to bloody-bladed politics. Later, of course, once Janus had thought more on it, he realized Ivor had seen a useful pawn going to waste, and that his "training exercises" often removed those obstacles in Ivor's path.

Janus closed his eyes, sought peaceful darkness, then opened them, letting his gaze fall on a dusty frieze: an army in marching ranks with Haith at the rear of the column, His heavy hood obscuring His face.

Janus felt obscurely comforted. He might be living one level up in the old wing, surrounded by remnants of an earlier, unmourned age, but at least his rooms had been cleaned properly.

Ivor's seneschal tapped on the half-open door, ushered another man in; Janus felt his wary lassitude fail him. The blond fop, Edwin Cathcart, Lord Blythe, balked in the doorway at the sight of Janus, equally appalled; and Ivor raised a glass to them both, a wicked smile curling his lips.

Two black-clad servants, directed by the seneschal, followed Blythe in, grunting under the weight of a broad, carved table. The seneschal laid a swath of indigo velvet over it, bowed to Ivor, and ushered the servants out.

Ivor fanned the pasteboards, a gleaming run of painted feather, scale, sea, and flame, a riot of color against the inky velvet, and said, "Now that the players are here, shall we begin?"

A SUDDEN DRAFT MADE THE lamplight flicker, a breeze strong enough that the air coiled into the glass chimneys and battered the flames. Smoke sifted up in spidery trails, adding the sharp scent of burning wicks to a room already hazy with smoke. Janus fought down the undignified tickle in his throat that wanted to turn him red faced and spluttering. Were they not closeted in the old wing of the castle, he would demand a window be opened to let out the smoke, but the arrow slits and tight-mortared stone hadn't been designed with comfort in mind.

"By the gods, Blythe, isn't it enough we had to endure Challa-combe smoking those foul cigarillos at the table? I thought you too proud to ape a commoner." Janus laid down his card with a decided snap. The seven of earth, a spray of blood-red roses across a stone floor. His new card was earth again but more suited to the rest of his hand, the jack of earth, a man in a coffin. He filed it beside the jacks of air and fire.

Blythe's narrow lips tightened around his pipe at being compared to King Aris's common-born spymaster, but he made no retort, instead folding his hand. Janus believed the man was constitutionally unable to think at all. It made it all the more peculiar that Ivor had invited the young fop to play with them. Unless Blythe had invited himself, the Duchess of Love's stalking horse, in an attempt to curry favor with Ivor.

Janus washed the crackle of tobacco fumes out of his throat with a swallow of brandy.

"Perhaps he merely hopes to confound us with smoke," Ivor said. "Maze our vision, and so gain an advantage. He needs some aid at play—surely you agree with that, my pet." He flashed a quick, saturnine grin at Janus.

Blythe found his tongue and said stiffly, "I wonder you invited me to play at all, if it was only to treat me to insult." His pipe stem, held between clenched teeth, cracked, and the barrel tipped, shedding sparks and dottle. He slapped quickly at his chest and cravat, leaving tiny singe marks in the fine lace and brocade of his vest.

Janus traded bad temper for a quick and silent snort of amusement. "I wonder myself, but the ways of Itarusine princes are mysterious indeed."

Though he saw Blythe's choler rise, a hot flush on thin cheeks above the elaborate knots of his cravat, Janus's attention was all for Ivor, watching that tiny quirk of a smile, blossomed and gone, and entirely malevolent. It reminded him of a night spent in the Winter Court in an accommodating lady's boudoir. Janus had raised his gaze from the sweat-damp juncture of Marya's neck and shoulder, her hands still clawing at his back, and found Ivor watching, sleek, still naked from his turn in Marya's embrace. He had reached out, rested his hand on Janus's nape, a warm, possessive touch, even as Janus gave his final attentions to Marya with a shuddering gasp and groan.

The pleasure, Janus knew, wasn't for watching the act itself but at Janus doing something well.

Seeing the same pleased smile on Ivor's face over their shared complicity in Blythe's setdown unsettled his nerves. He felt a ghostly hand touch his skin, the weight of memory. When Ivor was this smug, trouble was sure to follow.

"But three is the ideal number for a game," Ivor said. He poured Janus another generous measure of brandy; Janus resolved not to drink it.

"If only two are seated," Ivor continued, "then they must be opponents by default, no matter their inclinations. But three—three allows men to choose alliances as they may."

"Allows you to work together to lighten my purse, more like," Blythe muttered. "If you find my smoke, my presence so objectionable, I could think of other places to be, Last. Were I you, and wed to such a tidy handful as Psyke Bellane, I'd find better pursuits than sitting to games with your fellows."

Janus sighed, and sipped the brandy more slowly this time. Blythe was an idiot and the comment wasn't worth a reply. His marriage might be a matter of politics instead of passion, but Psyke and he dwelled together respectfully enough. Janus turned his attention back to the pasteboards in his hand, waiting Ivor's turn.

He felt as if he'd been waiting for Ivor to show his hand all evening.

The prince was more than a simple foreign delegate, more even than the newest Itarusine auditor come to ensure the treaty between their two countries was upheld. Ivor might be a loyal son of Itarus, but his ambitions were bigger than playing warden to the Antyrrian finances; Janus had no evidence of it, but in his bones, he felt Ivor had the same prize in mind as himself: the Antyrrian throne. But their reasons, Janus thought, were utterly at odds. He knew his own: to see Antyre brought out of the stagnation it had been forced into by the Xipos treaty and by King Aris's neglect.

Ivor's reasons likely centered around his drive for power.

Ivor smiled, and set down a card of his own, the queen of air, Black-Winged Ani, the goddess of love and vengeance; all Janus's musings derailed on a sudden wave of pain and anger.

Maledicte had been gone nearly nine months, borne away by Ani's hatred of cages and Maledicte's own frustration with being locked away at Janus's country estate, a treasonous secret.

Janus set a silver coin, the Antyrrian luna, into the center of the small pile, and laid out his cards. Ivor dropped an Itarusine coin onto the cloth, and fanned his cards with a showman's gesture. A losing hand. One he would have won had he kept the queen of air.

Blythe, annoyed at being ignored, relit his pipe with deliberate emphasis, and said, "I suppose you might shun your wife's company at that, though. It would be all manner of awkward were you to seek her and find her bed already filled. Aris seems quite taken—"

"Aris is our king," Janus said. He collected his winnings, the pasteboards, tucking Ani's card into the rest as if it meant nothing to him at all. "Respect is owed him."

"Nicely won, my pet," Ivor said. "When I recall your first attempts at the game, I grow amazed."

"There is nothing amazing about progress," Janus said, more shortly than he had meant, but he grew weary of Ivor's teasing. Instead, he shuffled the cards neatly, dealt them out, noting that Ivor and he had nearly equal piles of coins, even five hands in, while Blythe's had dwindled.

Blythe dragged his chair closer, scattering ash from his clothes onto the velvet, eager for another hand. Janus eyed him and sighed. "What I find far more remarkable is the *failure* to improve."

"Agreed," Ivor said. The hand played out, but after the second round of bid and show, Ivor put his palm over the pile when Blythe would have added his coin on the third. "Our round, I think, Blythe. If Janus doesn't hold the suite of high fire, collected entirely from your carelessness, he is not the man I thought him."

"I suppose you would know," Blythe said.

Janus eyed the cards in his hands, the red wash of flame in all its guises, and tried to ignore Blythe. His temper, sparked by Ivor's trick with the queen card, was souring by the moment.

Blythe's tone shifted uglier as Ivor shut him out of the game. "I had heard, after all, that most of your games with Ivor were more intimate than this. Perhaps your wife is not the only one to seek companionship outside her marriage; but at least, if she is indiscreet, *she* cannot be considered disloyal to the crown."

Janus sucked in a furious breath but restrained himself. He was a king's counselor, albeit one in some disgrace, and he had a reputation to uphold. Still, he wanted nothing more than to break his goblet, then use the sharp edge to carve out the man's endlessly offensive tongue.

"Do you intend to provoke him to a duel, Blythe?" Ivor asked. "Do you believe the duchess's support allows you to make such insinuations? I warn you, it does not. Should Janus accept the challenge, I will act his second with pleasure."

Blythe's hands on the table clenched. There was a brief spurt of panic in his eyes that Janus enjoyed. He had had enough of the lordling's blatant dislike, and the idea of a duel was sweet. It would be sheer butchery though, no challenge. Edwin Cathcart, Lord Blythe, was a slight young man, prone to talk over action, and even that was clumsy in execution.

Maledicte, Janus thought, would have delighted in destroying him. First, Mal would have shown him what it meant to have a rapier tongue, and then he would have followed it with the blade, until Blythe's flesh was as flayed as his sensibilities.

Janus lowered his head, fighting that sudden sickness in him, the churned grief and anger that Maledicte had fled his side.

"Well, my pet, will you duel?"

Blythe's lips trembled briefly before he regained his confidence. "You wouldn't dare. You might be a counselor, Last, but Aris watches you most carefully. Your behavior must be above reproach."

Ivor laughed. "I believe he thinks he's confounded you."

Janus bit one of the coins; the color seemed off, but the gold softened well enough, and he tucked it away. "Blythe, you forget where we are. In this court, in this time, my behavior only need *seem* above reproach."

Blythe spluttered, but after a moment, finally proved he was capable of learning: He stayed silent, merely tucking his much denuded purse back into his sleeve.

That draft touched Janus's neck again, the sense of movement where there should be none. Janus turned, and be damned to losing whatever unspoken game was between Ivor and himself. Something was happening. Ivor fairly buzzed with it, like the sky before a storm; and faintly, faintly, carried on the drift of smoke, Janus thought he smelled blood, tasted it in the lingering tang of metal in his mouth.

"I need to be going," Janus said. He rose, and collected his coat, laid aside when the room finally grew warm.

"Stay for another round," Ivor said. The tone was a command, and Janus bridled under it.

"I think not," Janus said. "Blythe can continue to amuse you, as he's done so ably all evening. I have morning calls to make, and it's nearer dawn than sundown." Standing allowed him to see the bedchamber beyond, the source of the drafts and proof of it: One of the ornate bed curtains still wavered, as softly as the tide coming in. But there was nothing else, no one to see, and nothing at all to explain this knot in his belly, the sense that matters were changing too fast. After years of Maledicte's unpredictable company, when his temper could turn from sweet to murderous within moments, Janus had developed a barometer for the unseen currents beneath events.

"So unfashionable," Ivor mourned, "and so energetic, also. So unlike your countrymen."

Ivor was false tonight, Janus realized, playacting the part of the spoiled prince fomenting unrest and spreading dissension. It was a simulacrum of his usual self, a measure of his attention being elsewhere; beneath it, something burned with the careful intensity of a well-laid fire.

A rap on the door distracted them, and Ivor's seneschal, Dmitry, opened it on Ivor's irritable call. "Come in!"

"The Duchess of Love," Dmitry said, and let Celeste Lovesy sweep into the room. She directed a genteel nod and a polite smile first at Blythe, then at Ivor, but she turned her black-clad back toward Janus, refusing even to glance at him.

Janus felt the weight of her hatred against his skin, and while he wished he had his coat on so he looked more reputable, he cared very little for her scorn. There had been worse directed against him when he was only a child—and an unwanted child at that, a city stray in the slums known as the Relicts.

Blythe, he thought, was a spoiled fool and the duchess was desperate indeed, if he was the caliber of her allies. Given the displeasure on her face at the sight of Blythe's ash-dusted linens, the absence of coin before him, and the temper still bright on his cheek, she might be thinking just that.

"Edwin, your wife is looking for you," the duchess said. "I doubt she'd be pleased to find you in such company." A wintry smile for Ivor seemed to say that she didn't mean the prince, of course; all her animus was saved for Janus. "I suggest you tighten your grip on your purse; rats are proven thieves, and this old wing is full of them. Aris is not as decisive as he should be in rooting them out."

Janus grinned at her. "Our king is tenderhearted indeed. Why else surround himself with useless remnants of a gratefully forgotten generation?" His gaze skimmed her gloves, heavy with crystals sewn into the fingertips, dangling in a dizzying array of flashing light, emphasizing that this was a lady, and one not accustomed to labor, a style twenty years out of fashion.

As if an antiphon, Ivor drawled lazily, "Tenderhearted enough to leave his throne to a prince born witless and useless."

If the duchess had swelled with outrage at Janus's words, at Ivor's description of Prince Adiran, she grew so red with rage that Janus said, "Careful, your grace, your husband died of an apoplexy. Surely he'd wish otherwise for you."

The duchess's first shrill words drowned under the stuttering toll of a deep bell pulled to life by a hand unaccustomed to the task. The duchess silenced herself, and the silence spread out from her, a fragile thing echoing with the possibility of being broken again. The bell rang again, the sound gaining strength. The death bell.

Ivor glanced at the clock on the mantel, frowned, and when he realized Janus was watching him, turned it to a smile. "I wonder what the fuss is about."

"As do I," Janus said.

Then Janus was off, out into the hallway and into a near nightmare rush of guards and soldiers, a confusion that was all too reminiscent of the night the palace had been roused to hunt Maledicte down. Though then, at least, the hunt had moved to Janus's plan, whether they knew it or not. This . . .

Anxiety laced his stomach, turned the brandy sour—this was Ivor's puppetry in action, and there would be blood at the end of it. Any doubts he had that this was Ivor's doing fled when Ivor chose to stay behind. Itarusines were notoriously inquisitive: It kept them alive in their bloodthirsty court. For Ivor to wave him off with a casual hand meant he had no need to see what had happened. He already knew. He stopped a guard, claimed the man's pistol: This was no night to be vulnerable.

In the distance, Prince Adiran's mastiffs howled, urgent, hoarse calls more noticeable in the echoing spaces between the tolls of the slowing death bell. It rang a final time and the dogs fell silent with it. Janus felt the fine hairs on his body stand upright.

Mal, he thought, on a wild uprush of pleasure. Maledicte had returned, and brought Black-Winged Ani with him, as sulky and reluctant as ever, but caged. Janus knew the sensation of the god's presence as well as he knew the touches of his lover, and the halls were tinged wild with god power. But even as he thought it, his certainty faded. Maledicte was gone, and this was Ivor's game.

The echoes of the shouting soldiers lingered in the halls, hasty confirmations that Aris had slipped, unseen, from his quarters and couldn't be found.

Janus watched a quartet of gray-clad soldiers trot by, pushing past the servants. They headed toward the heart of the palace, the king's residence, and Janus chose the opposite direction, heading for the source of the bell.

The chapel was the first structure to be built by Thomas Redoubt; and history declared that, on completion, the Cold King had chosen to sleep at the feet of the idol of Haith. After his death, the room had fallen from favor, too steeped with the man's chilly presence. Subsequent kings had preferred the city's main cathedral, at least until the gods had taken themselves away.

Janus kept his footsteps quiet on the stone stairs, the borrowed pistol warm in his sweating grip. At the base of the stairs, lights beckoned him onward, the multiple flames of gas lamps lit in a customarily dark hall. As he neared the chapel, neared the susurrus of voices, he saw a fan of blood drops, spattered widely and smeared where a soldier's footsteps had hastened through it.

A sword, Janus thought, *and an old one*. Not the narrow rapiers now popular in the court, but a thick, wide blade with a heavy hilt that trapped gore and spread it. A blade like that was common in Itarus, where the cold made thinner weapons brittle. He had one himself, having been trained in swordplay abroad.

A woman's gasping breath caught his attention, a hiccup of sound that might be a voice giving in to tears or hysteria. He stepped into the doorway, saw Captain Rue of the Kingsguard turn to face him, eyes widening. "Last."

The blue-clad kingsguards wavered for a moment but parted before him, revealing the death Janus could smell in the air.

King Aris was dead, and violently so, his chest riven open, and his blood spilling darkly over the stone floors, trapping lamplight and giving back shadow. Janus's breath lodged in his throat, snagged on a cry of wild outrage. Not this. *Not yet.*

The delicately boned woman cradling the king in her arms looked up at Janus's gasp; her tear-blurred blue eyes grew wide, her mouth opened, and his wife cried, "Murderer!" at the sight of him.

PRETENDER

· 2 ·

ANUS LEANED BACK AGAINST THE cold stone jamb, numb with shock, listening to the echoes of Psyke's accusation ring off the looming idols and slowly disperse. When Captain Rue failed to act on Psyke's cry, Janus let out a breath, and let his attention filter outward.

The dusty chapel was overfull of people and voices: the hushed back and forth between the king's guards; Psyke's broken weeping; and, beneath it all, a tremor—the lingering shiver of the summoning bell and Aris's last, dying breath.

Once Rue had loosened Psyke's grip on Aris's body, he organized the bloody scene into something approaching order with a ruthless hand and a voice that he never needed to raise. Janus found enough rationality left in him to think that Rue was stronger than he first seemed, a young man in an old man's role.

A kingdom for young men, he remembered Aris saying. *The old men grow bitter and twisted by war and old enmities, but youth . . .* Aris had touched Janus's fair hair in benediction. *Youth is our only hope for the future.* It had felt like unconditional approval, the first he had ever earned, and it was meaningless, a sour reward, the words of a man groping desperately for hope. Ivor's grudging praise had suited him far better.

Psyke yelped, and Janus narrowed his eyes at the guard hauling her to her feet. "Watch your grip," he snapped. "The lady is not used to rough handling."

Rue intervened, drawing her up gently, though her body swayed and buckled at the knees.

"Downey, Miles, aid Lady Last, to Sir Robert's offices." Rue passed her over to the guards who hastily holstered their pistols. Psyke had given over to weeping; though Janus, watching her flushed and shocked face, thought the tears equal parts dismay and rage. He shared that sensation. Aris's death changed *everything*.

Janus had depended on Aris's surviving months yet, if not years, granting Janus the time to convince the king that Janus's plans for Antyre's improvement were sound, that Janus could slip them from the Itarusine noose without bringing them to war again.

Damn Ivor and his games—

"My Lord Last, if you will follow her and wait for me. Tell Sir Robert what's occurred. We'll be bringing His Majesty with us."

Janus watched Rue remove his cloak, lay it out, and, with another guard's aid, shift Aris's corpse onto the blue cloth.

"My lord," Rue said, rising and catching sight of Janus still there. "Your lady awaits you." There were hard glints in his eyes, either suspicion or anger, and Janus shook himself. No need to make an enemy of Rue, not over this. Not when Psyke seemed to be enemy enough in her own right.

Murderer, she had called him.

Janus nodded his acknowledgment of Rue's command—it was nothing less, no matter how it was couched—and set off for the physician's offices, unsurprised to find a handful of guards falling in behind him.

THE PHYSICIAN'S OFFICES CONSISTED OF two outer rooms— the cluttered apothecary where Sir Robert saw the servants who fell ill and a rarely used surgery—and the man's personal quarters beyond. The guards, after depositing a nearly limp Psyke on the chaise, found themselves jigging in an attempt to avoid oversetting the workbench, jostling Psyke, or interfering with the entrance of Janus and his entourage. Sir Robert was standing perfectly still in the midst of chaos, his nightshirt peeking out beneath his frock coat. "The king, dead?" He said it as if he had said it several times before, and with as little recognition of the fact.

"Yes," Janus said.

At the sight of him, Psyke began shouting again, a muddled slur of words half in Antyrrian, half in a language Janus didn't understand, though he caught their gist. *Murderer.*

He stepped aside for Rue and the grisly bundle clenched taut between two straining guards. The gray wool had darkened, and at the lowermost point blood strained through the dense cloth.

Sir Robert woke to action at the sight. "Bring him in here," he said, gesturing to the surgery chamber. "At once."

"There's nothing to be done for him," the gray-bearded guard said. The man, red smeared to the wrist, glared at Janus. Here at least was one who took Psyke's raving to heart.

"There's cleansing to be done, then," Sir Robert said, "his body made presentable."

"There's information to be gathered," Rue said, nearly at the same moment.

Sir Robert's face paled at the reminder that this was no dreadful accident but regicide.

"My lord, you'll wait?" Rue said while the physician summoned his assistants out of slumber and into nightmare. His apprentice, a sleepy-eyed, stubble-faced youth, was dispatched to tend to Psyke.

Janus nodded once, holding Rue's gaze with his own. Rue needn't worry. As much as Janus wanted to storm the old wing, shake the truth from Ivor, and then kill him, he knew that could wait. Ivor, ever confident, would wait, enjoying the chaos he'd created.

Psyke's sobbing breaths gave way to another shriek. Janus, nerves on edge, jumped, hand flying to his borrowed pistol. The remaining guards put their hands over their weapons.

Rue, about to close the inner door, said, "Lord Last, will you spare my guards' feelings and let them hold your weapon?"

"No," Janus said. "Not when the king has been killed. Not when there might be a plot against the entire royal family." The pistol wasn't much, when all was said and done, not if the guards chose to heed Psyke's words and execute him on the spot. A pistol gave him one shot only, enough to kill the first guard, perhaps seize his sword. . . . Janus had done lethal damage with less in the Relicts.

Rue made no reply but closed the door behind him.

Psyke, proving she had been heeding Janus's words, gasped, gained coherence. "Adiran! Who's watching the prince?" The vivid panic in her eyes faded to a more normal terror.

"Captain Rue sent another squad to guard the prince," the bearded kingsguard said. "And the dogs are there." He had taken advantage of the basin the physician's apprentice had brought and was cleaning the blood from his hands. Despite the confidence in his voice, his hands shook.

"It won't be enough," Psyke said, "not against him." Her hand darted out, lightning fast, and slapped the apprentice as he bent over her arm. The thin metal lancet rang across the stones, came to rest at Janus's feet.

The apprentice, his hand still tight on Psyke's wrist, said, "You're hysterical. . . ."

"And there's been enough blood spilled tonight without shedding mine," she snapped. She jerked in his grip, but he held fast.

"My lord," he entreated. "Aid me?"

Janus met Psyke's eyes, and the shivering calmness in her gaze fractured into near madness again. "I think not. Bleeding is an unclean practice. I'll have none of it. Give her a potion instead."

"Poison instead, you mean," Psyke spat. "Silence the only witness to your crime."

The apprentice ducked his head, pretending he hadn't heard the Countess of Last accusing her husband of treason, and bent to mixing a posset for her.

Rue, coming out of the inner room with a face white and set, knelt before her. "Psyke," he said, and the presumption of her given name on his lips drew her attention. "Psyke," Rue said again, and Janus belatedly recalled the rumors that said Rue had once courted her but, having no fortune and no future, been turned away.

"Ask her your questions if you must, though her mind seems to be wandering through impossibilities," Janus said. "Either way, stop making eyes at her."

Phlegmatic Rue blushed, a red stain there and gone.

The door to the hall opened, bringing in the king's other counselors, the financier Warrick Bull and Admiral Hector DeGuerre, distress in duplicate.

Rue held up a hand, forestalling their agitated questions with a series of grim answers. "The king is dead. Murdered. In the old chapel. The assassin escaped but not without witness."

"Witness?" DeGuerre asked. His eyes lit on Janus, surrounded by wary guards, hand still resting close to his pistol, and said, "Who?"

Bull, quicker on the uptake, or less blind to women, joined Rue at Psyke's side. "Is it true, Lady Last? Did you see who was to blame?"

Psyke nodded, her lips quivering. Her voice was composed, though her hands, still bloodstained, wound 'round each other like serpents. "Janus," she said. "My husband, the Earl of Last."

The resultant hush was broken by DeGuerre turning on Janus with the full force of a one-time admiral on battle-strewn seas. "Then why stands he here? Guards! Seize—"

"No," Janus said. His eyes were all for his wife, for the strange light in her eyes, the way she huddled in on herself. "She's mistaken. Or maddened by this death, one piled upon others in a single year. Her mother, her sisters, her friends—all dead at mad Mirabile's hands."

"I am not mad," Psyke said. "I know what I saw."

Bull said more temperately, "Will you tell us where you spent the evening, my lord? We require facts and not speculation."

"I played cards with Prince Ivor Sofia Grigor—"

"With our country's enemy? Do you have witnesses to this? Or should we presume the prince aided you? He claims friendship with you, does he not?" DeGuerre said.

"Two witnesses, actually," Janus said. He inclined his head briefly toward Bull, whose expression had eased at Janus's quick answer. "Blythe graced us with his presence, and I'm afraid we lightened his purse for his pains."

DeGuerre growled. "Games at a time like this?" He crossed the room, content that he had scored a point, and stood beside Psyke, arms folded.

Bull said, "Blythe is easily led. His words will lend no real weight to Last's claim."

"Then it's as well that our game was interrupted by the Duchess of Love," Janus said, aware of Rue's attention. He let his lips curl in a sneer. "She chose to stop in and treat us all to a lecture on gaming, the nature of rats, and the king's notoriously soft heart."

Psyke whimpered, her hand clapped over her mouth, leaving dark smudges on her pallid cheeks. DeGuerre's hand fell protectively on Psyke's shoulder, and she flinched; the long rip in her sleeve that the apprentice had made preparatory to bleeding her parted, exposing a deep bruise spreading over her shoulder. "You're injured," DeGuerre said, gesturing to the apprentice.

The boy brought the posset over. It sloshed in his nervous hands and the scent of adulterated wine temporarily overlaid the heavy tang of blood in the air. Psyke pushed it away. "I won't take it. Not with him here."

"Send for them both," Bull said, "Lord Blythe and the Duchess of Love."

The inner door opened, and the physician stepped out, borne on a waft of blood and alcohol. "My lords," he said.

Rue said, "You've examined the body, Sir Robert?"

"I have," the physician said. He took in his apprentice, still hovering over Psyke with the posset in his hand, and said, "Be gone with you, lad."

The boy set down the cup, dropped a grateful bow toward his master, a more nervous series of head bobs toward the rest of the party, and fled.

DeGuerre took Psyke's hands in his. "She's chilled through. Need she remain?"

Such solicitude, Janus thought, *for a woman who told such wide-eyed lies. The very picture of innocent grief and pain.* He admired the theatrics, even as he worried about the results of her playacting.

"For the moment, yes," Rue said. "Your examination?"

Sir Robert looked at Psyke, and she raised her head to meet his eyes with weary contempt. "I saw it done, sir, I am not like to quail over the retelling of it. He was shot and then worked over with a blade. A thick blade."

"Gut shot at close range," Sir Robert said, "followed by saber. A foreigner's choice of weapon."

"No foreigner did this," Psyke said. She darted her gaze up toward Janus, and the open blueness of her eyes, the fear and pain, the bewildered betrayal in them confused him. Was this acting? If so, it was of a caliber to match the grandes dames of the stage.

The guards brought in Lord Blythe; the young man looked both furious and scared, full of fading bluster. Behind him, the Duchess of Love came in like mourning itself, draped in black bombazine and her jet-crystal gloves.

"King Aris is dead, they tell me," she said. "Is this true? Is Antyre without its king?"

"It is," Rue said. "Will you attest to—"

"Last claims innocence," DeGuerre said, interrupting, "though his wife claims otherwise. Last says you and Blythe will vouch for him."

Celeste Lovesy's lips tightened. She said nothing. Blythe coughed, and when all eyes turned upon him, he fell silent after another glance at the duchess. Her gloved hand fell heavily on his arm.

Warrick Bull narrowed his eyes. "Speak up, and speak truly. Were you playing cards with the Itarusine prince and Last?"

"Yes," Lord Blythe said, though the single syllable was grudgingly given. Janus felt a relief of tension he hadn't realized he bore. "From after dinner until the bells rang."

The duchess, when pressured, admitted that she had found both Blythe and Janus in Ivor's company with every appearance of having been there for some time. The words were dragged out in poisonous short phrases. Yes, she had seen him. Yes, there were glasses aplenty laid out, and most of a bottle of brandy gone. Yes, there were coins, both Antyrrian and Itarusine, piled up as if several games had been won and lost.

"The wounds were dealt unevenly." Sir Robert braved the glacial silence the duchess's confession had left in the room. "The shot should not have missed the heart at such close range, the saber wounds were awkward, as if the wielder used two hands to compensate for the weight of an unfamiliar weapon."

Bull and Rue shared a glance, before Rue spoke. "You believe the assassin an amateur?"

Sir Robert rubbed at the collar of his hastily donned smock that showed splashes of drying blood. "I only mean to say that I understand the Earl of Last to be experienced with both a saber and a pistol."

Janus tried to hide his surprise at defense from an unexpected quarter.

DeGuerre raised both hands, brought them down in a sharp gesture of exasperation. "And so it begins again. Janus profits, and yet . . . he cannot be blamed."

"He is," Psyke said. "I saw it myself." She drew her arms tight about herself, rocked in her seat, nearly pitching to the floor. "It is the same as before." She laughed, the sound strained and terrible. "*Exactly* the same."

Rue dropped to his knees, "My lady—"

"No," she said. "I *saw* him. Saw him come out of the darkness, like a piece of darkness, death in his face."

"Who?" Rue said. "Who did you see?"

Psyke shivered all over; *cold*, thought Janus, *not fear*, though it played well to the room of men who didn't know what real fear looked like. "I saw him."

"Last?" DeGuerre said. "You saw Last himself?"

Psyke laughed again. "Not Last, but his hand. His evil desires made flesh. I saw Maledicte."

WHEN THE CHAOS CREATED BY Psyke's announcement had faded, Celeste Lovesy removed Psyke, weeping, dragging Lord Blythe in their wake. DeGuerre departed with a final, disbelieving glance toward Janus and a mutter about beginning funeral arrangements. Rue, Janus, and Sir Robert stood in a silent circle around Aris's body.

Janus touched the cold, still face once, and turned away, his thoughts churning like a whirlwind.

"Will someone tell Adiran? Will he understand?" He let the words free, empty things to hide his bewilderment. Had Maledicte done this? Killed Aris, the king he had been unaccountably fond of, and without even a word to Janus? But Ivor—Ivor had a hand in this, Janus was certain of that.

"He won't be told the entirety of it," Sir Robert said. "Only that his father has died."

Janus nodded.

"Sir Robert, his majesty had you to see Prince Adiran frequently of late," Rue said. "For any cause? Is the prince ill? We need him hale, more than ever now."

Sir Robert shook his head. "I forget sometimes, how gossip drives this court. Yes, I've been attending the prince. King Aris believed he saw improvement in the boy's state."

Rue hissed, a tiny, quick sound urging Sir Robert to belated caution. Janus chose to stay unoffended. Let Rue caution Sir Robert as he would. Janus could collect the information from a handful of voices, nurserymaid, pages, servants, guards. In the meantime, he worried about Psyke's words.

If naming Maledicte was a lie meant to wound, it was a careless one easily turned back on her. Everyone in Murne knew that Maledicte, the god-touched murderer, was nothing but a collection of bones fed to the sea; Janus had seen to that himself, burying the truth of Maledicte's escape with another man's body.

If Psyke spoke truth . . . No, Janus thought. Maledicte was gone. And did he return, it would be to Janus first of all, not to kill the king in the silence of an old chapel.

". . . Maledicte," Rue said and drew Janus's attention like a magnet. "You examined him, did you not? His body? Is there any chance Lady Last is correct?"

Janus turned away to hide the sudden startled heat in his chest and face, the racing of his heart. To consider the illogical, the impossible, to ponder ways it could be made less so, made Rue a dangerous man.

Sir Robert cleared his throat. "None at all. Lady Last is overset. Maledicte is dead—stabbed, buried, unearthed, and hanged for the crows to feed. Barbarous, but effective."

"He had a god's aid," Rue said. "Does death apply to one such as that?"

"You might recall, Captain," Janus said, his voice rough, "Sir Robert claimed the king's assassin a paragon of ineptitude. I assure you, even a year dead, Maledicte would have shown more skill than that." The look he earned from Rue was an ugly thing, but Janus didn't care. The memories Rue had stirred were ugly also. He felt physically sick. The scent of blood in the air, Janus swallowed, fought bile.

"Gods." Sir Robert shook his head. "Life immune to death. Rankest superstition. I thought better of you, Captain."

Janus pushed away from Aris's body, from Rue and the physician and the whole, bewildering mess, and headed for the door. One person held the answer he needed.

"Last," Rue said.

Janus refused to turn and meet those intelligent eyes. "Do you have further need of me, gentlemen? I'd like to see to my wife."

HERE WAS, THE YOUNG ASSASSIN thought, such a thing as being *too* well informed. Ivor had given her a map of the hidden passages which she had received gratefully, but he had gifted her also with far more palace legend than she wished to know, old deaths and disappearances; at this moment, she feared her fate would be to add to their number.

Lost in the darkness of the Cold King's private tunnels, her racing heartbeat and her panicked breath were the only sense that the world moved on, that time had not locked up about her, sealing her in the dark and dust. If only she hadn't lost her lamp. Sweat trickled into her eye, stinging, and she rubbed it away, transferring streaks of drying blood from her red-washed hands to her cheeks.

She fumbled her way to the wall. Her fingernails scrabbled at the tightly joined stones, collecting dust and dirt and old, dried mold as she fought to regain her composure, to find the way out. She felt one step from animal terror and that had to be avoided at all cost, or she'd run, mindlessly panicked, through the tunnels until she either brained herself on a protruding stone or ruined Ivor's careful plan.

It had been a simple enough task Ivor had given her: Use the palace's oldest defenses to kill its newest king. Simple instruction, simple plan, but the execution had been difficult. Her aim had been off—she rubbed at the straps of her eye patch resentfully—and she'd needed the sword. And all Ivor's training failed to prepare her adequately for the awkward weight of a man's body slumping over a blade embedded in his guts, tearing the blade from her grasp.

She had had to wrest it free, Aris groaning pitiably, his hands feebly grasping at her thighs, turning what should have been a neat job into a slaughter. Bad enough that she had to slice his throat to make him die when the bullet hadn't done it, when the gut wound hadn't done it. Worse was the sudden cold realization that he hadn't been alone. When his voice, his breath was finally, *finally* silenced, she heard gasping sobs beyond her own.

She'd whirled, slipping on the spew of blood and intestines beneath her feet, and gotten a quick glimpse of gilt hair, a face going to shadow in openmouthed terror, and then the Countess of Last vanished, seemingly dragged into shadow.

The blade had trembled in her hand, but she moved forward, hunting that pale hair. The chapel shook under the weight of a sudden distortion, as if the very stones had released a long-held breath. The hair on her nape rose; every muscle in her body shuddered, and she turned and fled.

As a girl living in the Explorations, she had attempted to steal away Miranda's husband, unaware that Miranda had once been Maledicte, Black-Winged Ani's chosen courtier.

The assassin lost her eye to Miranda's blade, lost everything else in the lingering shadow Ani's wings cast: her village burned, her parents died, and she had been harried from one false refuge to the next, until she learned the only way to shed Ani's attention was to shed herself.

She'd forfeited her wants, her past, and her name, ever aware that Ani listened for it still. A single recitation of her name and Ani's wings would close over her once more.

To be hunted by a second god—the thought was more than she could bear.

A glance back and a shifting shadow set her moving forward again in blind panic, her blade scraping lichen into a fall of dust that trickled into her boots and left a pale mark on the stone, a clear signpost to her direction. The rasp echoed oddly, bounced back at her, rippled along the walls, and settled like fog, hopefully as confounding to any pursuer as to herself.

Challacombe, the spymaster, hadn't been in her plans either.

She'd fled the god's approach, blundering back into the tunnels, and found the spymaster awaiting her, teeth clamped on his cigarillo, eyes furious, a pistol to hand. "Assassin," he breathed. "Who sent you?"

Filled by terror, she hadn't even paused, bulling into him, heedless of the pistol, the explosion held tight between them, and then she was past him, tripping over the lamp, spilling its oil into the thirsty dust, disappearing into the Cold King's tunnels gone stranger still in the darkness.

It had taken her three turnings with her breath coming fast, a ruinous stitch in her side, to realize that she had been shot. Not fatal, not even close to it, but it burned and hurt until she tightened the waistcoat brutally close over the wound.

The spymaster hadn't been so fortunate. She had left him behind, his blood slowly felting the dust beneath his corpse.

The god's presence filled the tunnels like the strange stillness before an earthquake, changing her path, tangling her in a spiderweb of blind turns and false exits. Her fingers, replacing her vision, fumbled desperately along the stones, hunting for the little carvings that mapped the tunnels, but found none. Her skin crawled.

Legend had it that the Cold King built the tunnels not to escape his enemies but in a vain attempt to protect his loved ones from himself. The Cold King, the first of the Redoubts, had taken the throne by force and by the will of a god. But alliances with gods were treacherous, and Thomas Redoubt . . . changed, found Haith's likeness settling into his skin, raising horns from his skull, raising scales along his skin, and leaving death and illness in his wake.

Superstition, Ivor had scoffed, a grain of truth distorted for better telling; and she knew that was true. But the assassin also knew how tenuous the line was between legend and actuality.

The god's presence found her again, swept about her like a whirlwind, raising grit and dust, but causing no more harm than stung skin and burning eyes. She cowered nonetheless, waiting. . . .

But after a long moment where all she heard was the frantic thud of her heart, she realized the god was waiting also, waking slowly, studying the world.

A ringing bell shook the walls: the chapel bell tolling, its vibration turning the tunnels into pipes, and the god's attention faded. She crouched and covered her ears until the echoes stopped.

She gasped, glad for the first time to hear the rasp of her voice, the angry thumping of her heart. She crept forward on hands and knees, and her shoulder brushed some imperfection in the stone. Her coat seam tore, and she reached out, nearly laughing. There it was, one of the directional markers, a sinuous stone lizard, feeling oddly alive beneath her trembling fingertips.

She followed its cue, making her way through the dark until a faint bleed through of light and the sounds of uneasy horses led her into the oldest stall in the palace. She waited for their curiosity to override their sense of duty, and crept out into the palace mews. The horses nearest her raised their heads and whinnied at the scent of blood.

In the torchlight, she found herself gore smeared, nearly head to foot. A quick casting about found a stable boy's cheap woolen coat laid over a bale of hay. She dragged it on, rinsed her face in a horse trough, scrubbing off the worst of the blood, before heading into the night and the docks.

She'd have to find a message boy to take a carefully worded missive to Ivor. Ivor's plans were thorough, his temperament nerveless; still, things had changed. It wasn't simply Janus he was challenging, and the court; there was a god returned to the city and what gods wanted all too often boded ill for mortal ways.

· 4 ·

ANUS STRODE THROUGH THE HALL at an unfashionably quick pace, blind to the luxuries that usually soothed him; the eggshell and gilt papered walls, the raised niches that once held small idols and now held a fortune's worth of spring roses in blue vases. Now he noticed only that the plush carpet was unpleasantly stained in a staggered, crimson trail, showing the path Aris's body had come.

Once outside the royal residence, the lingering scent of blood gave way to waxed flagstones and polished wood, and approaching him, the prince-ascendant, no doubt coming to offer his aid to a palace in chaos. Ivor smiled, that same complacent amusement he gave those whose job it was to entertain him. "A lucky thing you sought my company tonight," Ivor said.

"Your company changed nothing," Janus said, voice as brittle as his nerves. "They still suspect me, think it my plan if not my hand." Janus was in no mood to play the role so clearly outlined for him: meek with gratitude that Ivor's company had saved him from immediate arrest.

"Shall I vouch for your sterling character?" Ivor said.

Janus found himself more frustrated yet by the laughter in Ivor's eyes. He wanted Ivor to feel the same confusion, the same unfocused pain. He drew back his hand in a fist, all poise gone, reduced to the Relict rat who wanted to share his hurt.

Ivor seized Janus's hand before he could strike, using his calmer temper to gain control. "Oh, you know better, pet," Ivor said. "Temper leads only to mistakes."

"Let me go," Janus gritted out.

"Prince Ivor," Rue said, coming down the corridor with another squad of kingsguards behind him. "The palace is unsettled. It would be best if you returned to your quarters. The country cannot afford to have another Itarusine auditor killed on our shores."

Ivor stepped back from Janus and smiled at the captain. "I don't think there's any danger of that."

Janus bit back a growl, and watched as Rue and the guards managed to sweep Ivor up in their passage, asking questions about the servants Ivor had brought with him, allowing Janus to escape.

A familiar dark head passed, and Janus reached out, shoved Savne against the wall. The young courtier, an obsequious hanger-on of his, lost his breath and Janus took ruthless advantage of it. After all, it wasn't often that Savne could be silenced.

"Where is my wife?" Janus asked.

"Last—" Savne gasped, throat obstructed. The glossy dark hair, the dark eyes, the pale face flushing to red with the pressure on his throat—Janus released him, a little shaken. Savne was a poor imitation of Maledicte, and one made pathetic by being so deliberate, but even that false face made him ache with loss.

"Where is Psyke?" Janus said. "I know you're Lovesy's man. She escorted my wife where?"

"Just to her quarters, just that."

"Be more precise," Janus snapped. "If you must ape Mal, recall his words were never less than precise."

"Lady Last has been returned to her own quarters," Savne said, rubbing his throat with shaking fingers.

Janus swung away from him, making for the stairs to the old wing, and Savne called after him, "'Tis a pity her door is well guarded. Rue holds her in near as much regard as the king did."

"Fool," Janus said under his breath. Savne lacked even the meanest intelligence to fuel his spite. Psyke and Aris? Yes, the court whispered and gossiped over their closeness, but Janus knew better. Aris feared intimacy with women, feared another child born mindless. Psyke had been Aris's spy, now declared herself Janus's enemy, and that was a matter of far more import than whether or not she'd cuckolded him.

The chill of the old wing flowed down to meet him as he closed on the uncarpeted stairwell. He made short work of the stairs, and the palace servants that saw him made haste to clear his way.

Two blue-clad kingsguards, a young man and an older one, watched him approach with expressions veering toward dismay and panic. The guard was soft these days; the most seasoned had followed their maimed Captain Jasper into the ranks of the city Particulars, where they tried to discipline an increasingly troubled populace. The remaining guards were the lazy ones who wouldn't leave a familiar life for confrontations on the streets, the greenest of recruits, and the few paranoid loyalists who thought a threat to Aris would come from within the palace walls and not without. Janus doubted they enjoyed being proved right.

The young guard, showing more bravery than sense, made the mistake of stepping forward, hand raised to slow Janus. It was a moment's work to step into the man's reach; the recruit's hand went to his blade, but he was too slow or too uncertain to draw it. Janus pinned the guard's sword arm behind his back before the lad could finish dithering. Using the boy as a shield, Janus pushed the other guard back and slammed the door open to his wife's chambers, an incongruous clutter of pastel and gilt furnishings adrift in a granite cave.

An opened interior door granted him sight of his goal: Psyke sat at her dressing table like a statue. If she had been overwrought and frantic when he had last seen her, now she had plunged into despairing stillness. The only liveliness about her was her voice, issuing a series of commands to her maid. "No, Dahlia. I don't need to change my gown. I don't need an infusion of Laudable, and I don't need you."

Dahlia fumbled the pearlescent bottle, dropped it, staggered forward trying to catch it, and squeaked when Janus made his entrance, the guard struggling in his grip.

Psyke's stillness only grew deeper, an animal freezing before a predator's gaze.

"Get out, girl," Janus said. Dahlia, after a last look at her mistress, darted for the door, leaving the bottle rocking on the carpet. Janus shoved the young guard after her, and bolted the door whose latch, like all those in the old wing, would withstand armies.

Assured of their privacy, Janus paced the room, trying to outwait that furious pounding in his chest. Right now, he wanted her dead, wanted that delicate neck between his hands—it wouldn't take much effort. She was thin boned and slight, untrained in even the slightest defense, as helpless as a rabbit before a hound.

Psyke sat motionless, though her hands twisted in her lap, knotting and unknotting over the bloody patches Aris's death had left, and her eyes sought escape as fervently as any prisoner faced with the gallows.

"Tell me," he said, and the deep growl of his voice made her jump. "What wrong have I ever done you that you would tell such a lie?" It was hard to come at her obliquely when all he wanted to do was demand the truth: Had she truly seen Maledicte? But that question couldn't be asked, not without betraying the deadly secret he had kept for near a year: that Maledicte lived.

"Lies?" she said. "I told none." Her voice wavered, thin and reedy, uncertain. She turned her back to him, but in the age-mottled mirror before her, her eyes were resolute.

Janus let out his breath. "You should have held your tongue until you knew where I had been. If you hate me so much that you would see me hanged for treason, it's best to know my whereabouts before you make your accusations."

He approached her, felt stiff with controlling his rage, more a toy soldier than a man. Her eyes followed each step with rising worry; her hands fled her skirts, shifted to fiddle with the jumble of artifacts on her dressing table. A tarnished silver-backed brush, bristles nearly worn away; a child's locket; a scatter of stained ribbons. Not the usual clutter, Janus knew, but something closer to a shrine, the grisly mementos of her murdered family.

She shook her head, breaking the connection between their glass-caught gazes. Head lowered, voice small, she said, "Your where-abouts are irrelevant when you have a killer on a leash."

He reached out to shake the smugness from her mouth, the prim hatred from her eyes; and she jumped away, spinning, standing, nearly falling over her seat. She pressed her back to the wall, and her expression veered toward panic. He seized her shoulders, gratified that she shuddered beneath his hands.

"Your lie injured your cause as well," he said. "The entire court whispers that the witch Mirabile left you mad when she slaughtered your family. Do you think this lie did anything to counter it?"

"Careful," Psyke said, a weird wild light in her eyes. "Be cautious which weapons you marshal against me. If no one believes my words tonight, neither do they trust yours. There is no madness in me—"

"Appearances are everything in this court. Abandon your grief; wallowing in the past will only cause you misery in the present."

He reached for her again and she quailed; he caught her hands, dragged them down to her skirts. "Feel that?"

The cloth, stiff with blood, resisted their touch, crinkled against the weight of their joined hands. "Tell me, my sweet, how mad must one be before one refuses to change out of a blood-soaked gown. To accuse one's husband of regicide on no evidence at all?"

Her gaze shied from his, fell to the clotted stains, dark even against the dull navy of her dress. Her hands in his trembled and grew cold. "How mad," he whispered, "to not even notice that you reek of Aris's death?"

"A death you caused," she whispered, even as her weight folded inward, her legs giving out. Janus tightened his grip, dragged her to face him.

Her eyes were the blind blue of summer skies.

"Aris is dead. My king dead," she whispered. Her hands fluttered, tightened on his sleeves, so lost that she clutched him as an anchor.

He shook her off. "Aris *is* dead. Most inconveniently so." His tem-per swelled at the memory of Ivor's smile, and settled only when he thought Rue, at least, would be making the man's evening near as uncomfortable as Janus's promised to be. "Aris was a fool to hold his rendezvous with no one but yourself to guard him. Not even his hounds! The man *wanted* to be killed and, by the gods, someone obliged."

She slapped him. It wasn't much, a feeble blow, but the quickness of it, the angry glitter in her eyes, made him flinch. His enemy indeed.

"He was your king and your kin," she said, and the fury in her voice was the fury of generations bound by tradition and unthinking loyalty.

"And such kinship," Janus said. "To allow my abandonment, to turn my mother whore. Aris knew my father threw me away like refuse and said nothing until I was needed. Kinship means nothing to me but pain and rejection." He found himself panting, his breath hot as it rebounded from her bent head.

"So you destroyed it? When a country depended on Aris? You allowed your pain to rule you? Set your paramour upon a good man?"

"Enough, Psyke," he snapped. "No one will listen to you."

"I will make them believe me."

"Make them believe the dead walk? This is the age of reason, my sweet." Janus forced a contempt into his voice he didn't feel, *couldn't* feel. The age of reason, yes, but a reason under siege by sickness and starvation, beset by fears of war and an uncertain future.

"And a man that didn't die? Is that reasonable enough for you, my lord?" Her lips curved into a smile, but she couldn't hold it. They trembled and her next words were whispers. "I am not blind, Janus. Nor am I a fool. And bodies can be had for the taking. Tell me, my lord, whose blood did you spill to spare his? Another innocent's? Another good man's?"

She slumped, and he nearly believed her fatigue, but years of Maledicte's companionship had taught him caution. Still, when her nails slashed at his eyes, he was taken off guard. He ducked; her clawing hands caught in his hair, and he grabbed her wrists, grinding the bones tight. She thrashed against him, kicked and cursed in a way that he had no idea an aristocratic lady could.

He dropped them both to the carpet, jarring her silent, pinning her beneath his weight, thankful that she was so slight. Maledicte would have left him bruised at best, and worse—he'd suffered from Maledicte's love of sharp objects before.

"Tell me," he gasped. "Tell me what you saw."

"Maledicte," she spat. "Just that. All dark hair in the shadows."

Hardly conclusive, he thought. Men of Maledicte's coloring were rare in Antyre, being both dark haired and pale skinned, but common enough in Itarus. The assassin could be any of Ivor's men.

Sir Robert's words came back to him. An amateur with the blade. An inexperienced hand.

His breath let out all at once. Of course it wasn't Maledicte. Hadn't he said it himself? Maledicte was an artist with his blade. The realization that it hadn't been, *couldn't* have been, Maledicte twisted into equal parts relief and pain. If Maledicte *had* done it, killed Aris, risked Janus—at least that meant Maledicte had returned.

Psyke took a breath, twisted under him, mustering herself for another round, and he pressed her back more firmly, her skirt an ungainly tangle around his knees, flakes of drying blood sifting free about them. "Hush," he said. "Hush, or you'll have that fool guard in here to defend you, and I'm in no mood for that. My reputation's been blacked enough for one night; do you think I won't hesitate to add wife beating to it? I assure you, I will not—"

"Did you court Maledicte with such talk?" she spat. He rolled away as her words did what all her efforts hadn't—wounded him.

She lay sprawled, a discarded doll, and after a moment her hands crept up to cover her face. Her shoulders spasmed. Janus watched her cry, the wetness slipping out between her fingers, her face and neck growing pink blotches, wondering from what source the tears came. Had she loved Aris as well as been loyal to him? Was it grief or anger that fueled her?

Aris had expected too much of her—seen her intelligence and missed the gentle core.

Her breath grew rough, catching as her sobs continued. It grated on his nerves. Maledicte would never have wept. Maledicte would have lashed out with words, with blades, with anything to hand until his point was made. Psyke merely sobbed.

"You'll make yourself sick," he said. "You should care for yourself first. Mourn later."

Her sobs turned into hiccups; her breath narrowed and strangled, then the weeping began anew.

Enough.

Janus collected the Laudable bottle, shaking it firmly. He grabbed her chin, ignoring the teeth that tried to bite a finger too close to her mouth, and ruthlessly tipped multiple thick mouthfuls of Laudable into her. She gasped and swallowed; for a moment, he thought she would choke, but then her breath steadied.

"You didn't simply kill Aris," she said, her voice a rasp. "You destroyed a kingdom. Who will keep the Itarusines at bay?"

He hushed her with another mouthful of the bitter liquid, and though she spat some back at him, most of it disappeared into the pink recesses of her mouth.

"I didn't kill Aris," Janus said.

She turned her face from his, but her sobs didn't recur. "Better," he said. "I never guessed I had such a watering pot for a wife." Her skirts crackled against the carpets, left rusty smudges on his breeches, on his hands.

Aris's blood on my hands, he thought, *and all unearned.* There was something repulsive about it, about the smell of it, heavy in the room, warmed by their struggle.

She pushed him away as he reached for the buttons of her dress, ripping them free rather than unhooking them one by one; the damage the dress had gone through made it unlikely to be salvaged, even by the ragmen. "No," she muttered.

"Would you prefer Dahlia back, dripping tears all over you and clumsier than usual in her distress?" Yanking her to her swaying feet, he worked at the fabric until it gave.

"No," she said again. It surprised him, but perhaps the Laudable had taken effect, made her pliable. He didn't much care.

"There's the first sensible thing I've heard you say all evening," he said. Her dress hung open from neck to hem, but still clung to her undershift, the bloody stain soaked through and fading brown against the pale linen. He pulled the gown free, wadded it into a foul knot, and hurled it into the maid's chamber for disposal.

"Off," she said, squirming in distaste. Her hands skated over her undershift, recoiling from the blood-soaked linen. "Take it off."

"Do it yourself," he said. He pushed her back onto the bed, tossed her dressing gown after her.

"You killed the king, and you balk at stripping your wife," Psyke said, the Laudable loosening her tongue. "How—"

He yanked the laces down, and the draft on her pale skin shocked her quiet. "You sound like Mirabile, inciting men to mayhem."

Blood had seeped through the shift, touching her skin, small dark discolorations barely recognizable as such, but they corresponded to the sodden clothes above.

As Maledicte's name on her lips had wounded him, so Mirabile's on his wounded her, leaving her flushed, silent, and miserable. Janus paused, his hands hovering over the curves of her shoulders. He had seen the one bruise earlier, thought it blood smeared through her clothes. But it wasn't blood, not this high on her pale skin.

Her shoulders bore dark and ragged marks, bruised nearly to the bone, and the bare touch of his fingers made her flinch and sigh.

They weren't his marks; his bruises were still incipient, places pink and puffed. These were older. "Hmm. Whoever would have thought Aris to be so rough?"

Her gaze, avoiding his, fell on her own skin and the black bruising rising on her flesh, the distinct marks of large hands on either shoulder, swelling.

"You think Aris's grip was so strong? He couldn't even hold on to life . . . and this is everything of death." She laughed, high and wild, until he pushed her back into the mattress, and sealed her mouth again. She nipped his hand. He released her mouth, and she said "Murderer" on an outborne whisper. "Murderer." Her lips and breath were warm against his palm.

Her eyelashes fluttered as the Laudable took hold; her body fell into a languor he knew well, having seen his harlot mother succumb to it nightly. He raised himself away from her, and she hooked a hand on his shoulder and followed. "Will you kill me?" she asked. "I've accused you of murder, accused you of regicide. Now that I lack Aris's protection—you needn't pretend you ever cared for me. . . ."

"Had I wanted you dead, my sweet, dead you would be. Yet here you live, and well enough to vex me."

She touched his face gently; her eyes dazed but intelligent, questioning. Her face hardened as her emotions resurfaced beneath the smothering blanket of the narcotic. "Go away," she said. "Murderer."

"And abandon my wife when she's so beside herself? Trust your safety to a pair of kingsguards green and lazy? I'll stay. And, see, I'm so far from killing you, I'm offering to protect you." He grinned and she squirmed back against the bedstead.

"You protect yourself," she said, her words slurred and slow. "Rue might wait for evidence, but others would kill you given the opening, let matters sort themselves out as they might."

He twiddled the edge of the blanket for a moment, a little taken aback, and then found himself surrendering to a tiny laugh. "I do believe I prefer you on Laudable," he said. "You're far more interesting.

"There are those who want me dead, certainly. There are those who will think to use me as a placeholder to keep Itarus at bay, until I can be safely removed. And there are those who understand that to dispose of me is for Antyre to lose what little independence we have left. Aris's advisers may hate me, but they do need me."

Psyke groaned into her pillow, tossing her head. He wondered if it was the politics that displeased her so, or that she found herself unable to comprehend his words through Laudable's veil. Her eyelashes flickered; she rested her head on his thigh and fell asleep.

He touched the matted tangles of her hair, comparing it to her usual smooth coils, and found satisfaction in the physical disorder.

Psyke whimpered in the back of her throat, a muffled thing, her brow creasing, as if her worries were so vast as to chase her into Laudable's dreamless sleep. When a small hand sought his warmth, creeping toward him with the blind instinct of a nursing animal, he left the bed and settled himself at her dressing table, knees banging the gilt tips off the elaborate wooden crenellations dangling beneath. A woman's room this, and a small woman at that.

He tugged the drawers open, one after another, hoping to find something to ease his own tension: the Laudable was all gone and the drinks at Ivor's table seemed hours ago. Psyke's furious tongue and temper had been a surprise coming from a young woman who might as well wear a porcelain mask for all her placid perfection. Mayhap her furniture hid secrets as well.

The drawers disappointed him, yielding nothing more than the usual fripperies of handkerchiefs and lace panels, the brilliant parure he had given her on their engagement, discreet boxes of rice powder, milled carmine, and the tiny pot of eyeblack. A bottle of perfume came to hand, oddly sharp scented for a woman, mint and vetiver, nothing like Maledicte's sweet lilac, so rich a scent that it clung for days, and to bury his face in Maledicte's black curls had been like finding an unexpected garden at the start of spring.

Janus unbarred and opened the door, shouted out at the guard to bring him *Absente*, even if they had to roust every member of the palace staff to find him a bottle.

His darting gaze fell on Psyke again, the tidy tumble of limbs and long, pale hair; the stained shift and her bruising shoulder the only shadows on her. Psyke made another soft sound, a mutter that could be complaint or pleasure, and Janus's lips curled.

He hadn't expected her to be so . . . agreeable, even with Laudable's influence. To go from spite and blackest rage to yielding in his arms—

He traced the bruises on her shoulders, so much like handprints but longer, broader than his and chill beneath his fingers. Leaving that mystery, he reached out to touch her lips, parted and soft, and a tiny breath wisped against his palm on a stuttered sigh. Janus drew away, repelled.

The sound woke memories that bewildered him, of standing above a royal infant's cradle with a dagger in his hand. The actions he recalled perfectly, the simple thrust that ended the threat his half brother posed to him, the moment when Maledicte drifted in, all wild eyes and feathered wake, to find the deed accomplished. Janus had been decisive then, his plans crystalline, and they had played out as he intended.

He had felt no hesitation as he struck, felt nothing more than surprise when Auron bled out, the fine lace gown sweeping blood into its traceries; the infant earl was so entrenched in his mind as a symbol of what he deserved, what stood in his path, that he had nearly forgotten it was a living thing.

But blood was necessary, and hardly something Janus minded. Nothing of his memories explained why he woke so many nights with the sound of that child's soft gasp in his ears. It hadn't plagued him while Maledicte was his; the sound grew in the wake of his leaving. Sometimes Janus thought he had borrowed some of Ani's ferocity from Mal, cradled it as close as he had cradled his lover. Sometimes he thought Maledicte had been all his strength, and without him, he . . . weakened.

Even as he shied from the thought, he made himself consider it. It would explain much; tonight he'd been more a fool than a plotter, allowed Ivor to kill Aris and reset the board too soon for Janus's players to be aligned. And instead of plotting a way to steal back the ground he'd lost, he'd reacted instead of acted, played into Ivor's scheme, and even Psyke's words had filled him with terror and rage. But how to turn the tide once begun? Ivor was a difficult opponent; Janus would need an ally.

Fanshawe Gost, he thought, *the Kingmaker*. Aris had called him home from his long ambassadorship in Kyrda, where the man had aided an unexpected and unqualified heir to gain the Kyrdic throne. He could do the same for Janus.

The *Absente* arrived, and he took it without thanks, mind working on what would please Gost most. It galled him to go courting in this fashion, but Ivor, damn the man, had left him little choice. He strained the *Absente* through sugar and sipped. A vile drink, really, but for easing the body while keeping the mind active, there was no substitute.

WHEN HE CAME BACK FROM airy imaginings of himself king and Antyre prosperous, the false dawn was in the air, evident even in quarters without windows by the quiet scuffling of early morning maids beginning their day, the soft murmurs of the guards changing in the hall. A new day, then, the first without Aris, and the first for him to prove his mettle to the country he would have.

Ivor's plans be damned; Antyre was his.

Still, he thought, it had been too bad of him to loose his temper on Psyke. Though he no longer needed to keep her happy to soothe Aris, he still required a noble wife if he was to have any hope of the throne. Currently, she loathed him, her whispered *murderer* argued that, even if the lingering scent of her on his skin suggested otherwise. She had been won once, even if it was at Aris's command; he could win her again, turn her into an ally.

He collected the blankets, fallen from the mattress, and laid them over her. His fingers brushed her cheek, and it was cold; her lips, still parted, gave no breath to the air, and her breast, when he laid his hand over it, was as quiet as the tomb.

Janus recoiled. He reached out once more, placed his fingers against the thin skin of her neck, and found only stillness.

He remembered this surprise, death of a sudden. The Relicts had seen children die overnight from scratches, from whippings, from poisoned food left out as if they were nothing but rats. One night, he and Miranda had fallen prey to such—back when Miranda had still been Miranda instead of Maledicte and as such, vulnerable to poisons—and spent the dark hours in a panic, waiting for death to claim them.

Now a similar panic stalked him, trying to stir blood slowed by his consumption of *absente*. Psyke's death was near as devastating to his plans as Aris's had been. The second shock left him reeling, left him dwelling on the past instead of the future.

The Relict deaths had been scattered and random; there had been one kill where he and Miranda had hit their robbery victim too hard, and spent a month scrabbling away from the sound of the Particulars' bells.

There had been fights to the death with men who would have killed either of them for spite, for their clothes, for their accents, so far above the usual Relict rat's.

It wasn't until Janus had been collected on his noble father's command, whisked abroad for a quick polish of his manners in the

Itarusine royal court, that he had truly begun to understand murder, that it could have purpose beyond immediate satiation of rage or need.

Janus twitched to his feet when a bell rang distantly in the hall—some noble demanding attention at an unfashionable hour—and his troubles still looming.

Psyke was dead, and Janus the only one present. Janus, the one she had accused of regicide the night before. *Damn her anyway*, Janus thought—it had been her fault, goading him, and Celia's fault also, for her habitual need for Laudable, so common that he forgot what a normal dose looked like, and damn Maledicte for leaving him when he needed help most.

Blame, Janus thought, and like that, his nerves settled. Dahlia. The country clod of a maid. New to the court, clumsy, easily overwrought, and slow of intellect. She could be brought to believe she had mixed the Laudable incorrectly. Dahlia wooed disaster with her every action.

He settled himself onto the bed, though his heart thumped oddly—he had always left his victims before, not lain beside them, and Psyke's face, even in death, held trouble on her brow.

He willed himself toward sleep; he could feign it, but it would be more effective if Dahlia's cries woke him. That sort of sudden shock was difficult to counterfeit, and while Dahlia wasn't a critical audience, the guards would be.

Psyke's skin, waxy now, drew his fingertips. Maledicte had called her a pretty little doll wife, something to play with and discard. Janus hadn't ever paid her much mind at all. She hadn't ever been real to him before last night, when she unleashed months' worth of fear and temper on him.

Beside him, she gulped suddenly, the sound nightmare vivid to his ears. He jerked; she twitched as if she were hooked up to one of Westfall's engines, her spine attached to cogs and chains and gears. Her body arched and teeth gritted in her jaw. Her undershift slid off her shoulders, revealing knotted muscle and that black bruising like the marks made by a giant's grip.

Alive, after all, but the relief was tempered by something like terror in his veins. He was no child to mistake sleep for death, and this weight in the air tasted of the gods.

Janus scrambled off the bed as she began muttering in her sleep, not in Antyrrian, but the older language from time when Itarus and Antyre were one, the language of the dead. Her eyelashes fluttered, and Janus seized his coat and fled, unwilling to see what greeted him when she woke.

· 5 ·

$\mathcal{T}$HE KING'S LIBRARY HAD ALWAYS been a place Janus enjoyed, a place of purest pleasure; Aris's library was the project of generations, reflecting interests that spanned history, natural wonders, legends, geography, memoirs, and genealogies. Aris had added social treatises and tracts on engineering and medicine. It was impeccably organized, well maintained, and dusted once a week. It was also completely useless in Janus's current search.

He missed the library at Maledicte's Dove Street residence, the casual spill of pamphlets on poison and murder, the pornographic woodcuts, the histories of scandal and a hundred or more handwritten files kept on all the members of the court, details easily turned to blackmail.

Once Maledicte had given his servant Gilly funds of his own, the shelves had gained a collection of religious treatises, rare in this time when the gods had been presumed dead, when the intercessors had been abandoned in Antyre, killed outright in Itarus.

Those books were gone now, collected avidly by those people who had seen Maledicte in bloody action, or had been touched by Mirabile's madness, and knew the gods weren't gone at all. Janus would have paid dearly and gratefully for one of those tracts now and the answer to what had happened to Psyke.

He had lived with Maledicte for more than a year, had grown to feel Ani's presence in his lover, changing Miranda into something new, strange, and glorious. He had felt that same strange glory in the air last night, blooming through the dark halls where Aris died: the presence of a god invading the realm of humanity. The question plaguing him was, If not Maledicte, was it still Ani's wings overshadowing the palace? Or another god entirely?

Gilly, curse him wherever he was, would have known whether *all* gods raised the same tremor deep within a man's bones or whether this was a different god, focused not on Aris, not centered around the assassin's blade, but elsewhere. Perhaps on a woman who had woken from death as if it were only a deeper sleep.

Janus brought down another book on medicine; accounts of apoplexies that paralyzed men, mimicked death's stiff touch, and poisons that echoed death's effects. Hadn't he used one to spirit Maledicte's "corpse" from the palace all those months ago?

Stillheart was notorious for its deathlike sleep, the cold pallor of the grave it brought to flesh, but the poison was also rare. Psyke would have no chance at all to gather it; and, more to the point, the only poison she had swallowed last night was the Laudable Janus had fed her.

He set the book aside with a growl of irritation; his reach toward another was interrupted by a faint cough. When he turned, Evan Tarrant was awaiting his attention, hovering nervously in the doorway.

"Come in," Janus said. "Come in and close the door."

The boy nodded, trotted in with an eager obedience only slightly dimmed by the black armbands he sported. Officially, Evan was one of the palace pages, and as a new one and junior, the one most likely to take on the disagreeable chores. Unofficially, however, everyone knew Evan was the Earl of Last's personal page, and so Evan spent his days idling about the palace, waiting to carry Janus's infrequent messages. Janus found the boy's enthusiasm pleasant but bewildering. At fourteen, Janus's entire world had been about keeping himself and Miranda alive; this boy's cheery nature was as foreign to him as the trust in his eyes.

"I need you to go down to the docks," Janus said. "Try not to get in the soldiers' way and steer clear of the Particulars. They'll be combing the ships, hunting for Aris's assassin."

The boy nodded, his smile fading. "What do you want me to do?"

"You'll be doing the same," Janus said. "A single boy can see far more than a squadron of soldiers, especially a clever boy who knows the docks as well as you do. And one who still has a sailor's cropped cut. Report anything out of the ordinary back to me."

Evan said, "If I see the bastard what did it—should I call for help?"

"No," Janus said. Evan's pale brows furrowed. Janus had no intention of explaining his concerns to the boy—that if the assassin were caught, the Particulars, no friends to him, might encourage the assassin to name Janus as his patron. "Just send word to me. I'm going to give you coins—if you lose or spend them all on sweets, I'll thrash you—with which to bribe a ship's captain if it looks likely that the assassin is intending to set sail. If the matter seems urgent, send word to Delight and Chryses at Seahook."

Evan took the heavy purse with a widening of his eyes. "It's a fortune!"

"Hardly that," Janus said, but he said it without bite. Despite the boy's unaccountably sunny nature, Evan reminded him of his youthful companions, Relict rats who were dangerously envious of any wealth at all.

Evan shifted foot to foot, and Janus said, "What is it?"

"How will I know?" he said. "What's a killer look like?"

Janus sighed, fought the urge to tell the boy he was looking at one. "You'll be looking for someone who's trying to remain inconspicuous, a man or woman, likely to be Itarusine, without luggage, attempting to buy or barter passage out of the country."

Evan nodded, turned toward the door, and paused once more, to say hesitantly, "The pages are all saying . . . what about the prince?"

"Ivor's not like to be trying to escape—"

The boy interrupted, and Janus reminded himself to go over basic etiquette with him once again. "Not him. *Our* prince. He's upset, isn't he? I know I was when my ma died, and I was only five. Will you take care of him?"

Janus said, "He has guards to care for—"

"You take care of me—"

"I struck a bargain with your father. Do not think I am fond of children."

Evan said stubbornly, "Still, you're his family, aren't you?"

If Evan's father hadn't been so important to Janus's plans, Janus would have boxed the boy's ears. But Captain Tarrant was essential to the kingdom's finances and he doted on his son.

Janus settled for snapping, "Just go." He waited for Evan to be gone from the corridors, paced the library three times 'round, casting displeased glances at the useless books, and finally gave in. Why *not* go see his sweet simpleton of a cousin? Aris's stricture against it was as dead as he.

Aris had feared Janus meant harm to his son; as always, blinded by his own concerns, Aris had missed the obvious. Janus had nothing but the warmest feelings for the lad. How could he not? It was in Adiran's eyes, palest blue and utterly blank, that Janus had seen his future written. Until that moment, he had not thought of anything beyond claiming his father's title and land, of ensuring a future without want for himself and Maledicte. But Adiran changed that, his vacant eyes a spark to his ambition. Why stop at earl when he could have the throne? Only a fool settled for a mouthful of bread when he could have a feast with careful planning and effort.

Antyre needed him as badly as he wanted it. The country was stagnant, its most certain future a slow decline into insignificance.

But if Adiran was improving, then everything changed. If Gost, the Kingmaker, found Adiran a viable heir, there'd be no gaining his support; all Janus's plans would have to change.

IN HER DREAMS, PSYKE WANDERED the dusty tunnels again, creeping to her rendezvous with Aris, walking those secret passages carved through stone. Her skirts trailed after her, sweeping away the dust and leaving a spiderweb stream of blood, thin traceries of black in the darkness. She knew she walked in a dream, simply by that—when she walked the tunnels awake, she held her skirts high, and the dust rolled over her shoes like startled mice.

The lamp in her hand guttered and dwindled; she watched it with a numb horror. Left in the dark, the doors sealed tight—these tunnels would be her tomb.

"They were mine," a man's voice said, as dry as old bone, a mere frisson on the still air. "After my family . . . died, I sought the dark spaces and the cold silence drew on me until I lacked the strength to leave." A light flared, a smoky yellow torch, oil-soaked rag around wood, and Psyke shied.

"Have you never seen one god-touched before, child?" he said. He blinked mottled eyes at her, and adjusted the torch in its sconce so that it stood upright, sending thin trails of heat up a tiny shaft in the stone. His long fingers, clawed and scaled, rasped on the stone, through the stone, as intangible as the dream itself, and Psyke fought back the urge to run. She needed the light if she was to find the king; and this man, strange as he was, had offered her no harm.

"No harm at all to you," he said. "Blessed by the god."

"The gods are gone," she said. "Or so I was told and so I believed, until my family was murdered by those who claimed Black-Winged Ani's—"

"Shh," he hissed. A narrow flick of a tongue made it more serpentine than human, and she shivered. "When you speak Her name, you court Her attention. These corridors are safe from Her; She loathes the close and dark so greatly that not even Her children will walk these halls. Remember that, should She come hunting."

"Who are you?" she asked.

"Do you not know your king, child?"

"Never my king," she said.

"Perhaps not your king but decidedly your kin," he said. "I grow old, even in death, and my mind wanders. Would your king be the one bleeding below, wailing for his lost son? Or is yours the one fretting on blood and politics above the stairs? I believe them both yours. Which one are you seeking?"

"Aris," she said. "Aris." And dreamlike she sank through the floor, the torchlight fading in her vision, until she had returned to the gods' chapel.

"My son," Aris said, turning his face toward her, eyes blind with desperation and pain. "Take heed of my son."

She woke to her own voice, the vow quivering on her lips. "—will, sire. I will." She woke alone and to limbs that seemed weighted, as if the dusty stone of the chapel and the back passages had come with her, their chill grip lingering in her bones.

It was Laudable that slowed her blood, she thought, Laudable that Janus had fed her, and as she recalled him, so she felt his absence with a jolt of pure terror. Adiran!

Protect my son, Aris urged again. She choked on an inborne breath, found herself struggling for air, and gaping at the man seated at the foot of her bed. Aris, it was, but thinned and faded, a most melancholy ghost of a melancholy man. *Adiran,* he said, without looking up from the translucent bones of his hands, palms up in his lap, slowly filling with his own blood.

Janus will kill him to see his ambitions met.

Madness, she thought, her dreaming mind dragged into waking, grief playing with her mind as well as her heart. Aris sighed and on the breath faded completely.

She scrabbled out of the linens, dropped gracelessly to the floor when her knees buckled under Laudable's pervasive hold and her own fear.

She glanced up at the man by the door, embarrassed he found her in such disarray. "Challacombe. Is Adiran guarded?"

I did warn you, he said, still bracing himself against the wall. A lit cigarillo made a tiny flame near his thigh, burning red and redder as he let it dangle. *The face Janus presents is only a mask, but you gave him your heart along with your body.*

She was across the room before she knew it, numb limbs forgotten in reflexive outrage that he should speak to her so, but the blow she dealt him only bruised her own hand as it passed through his shadowed flesh and brushed stone.

Whimpering, cold to the bone, she backed away. Aris's ghost, she understood; it was the product of her grieving mind. This . . .

The assassin killed me in the passageways, left my body for rats. Yet Janus walks free. Challacombe disappeared as Aris had done, leaving only a lingering scent of smoke.

Psyke collapsed, stones clammy against her bare legs. Her head spun; what *was* this? Her shoulders burned and ached, and a moment half remembered washed over her: standing in the chapel, staring at the assassin's tumble of dark curls, and feeling cold hands pull her close, shield her in the scent of earth. The scent of the grave.

Challacombe's accusation lingered, settled in the crevices of her heart. It was true enough, she knew it by the aching sense of betrayal that stirred beneath her grief and guilt.

She'd wedded Janus to serve as Aris's spy, to pick out truth from pretense, and instead, she'd been lulled, first into relaxing her suspicion and then, damningly, into supporting him. Hadn't she argued just last night that perhaps Aris misjudged Janus? That as unlikely as it seemed, perhaps Maledicte had acted of his own accord without Janus's instruction? Minutes later, her king was dead at the hand of a courtier who had been buried months ago.

Janus profits when men die. It wasn't a ghost this time, only a memory. A phrase heard more than once, a phrase that Aris used against Janus's charm like a shield.

Janus profits when men die. She shuddered. One step closer to the throne.

Protect Adiran, Aris had pled.

The lingering lassitude in her bones, the sluggish pulse of blood and breath, gave way to fear-inspired haste. She scrambled to her feet.

If the guards, if even Janus's sworn detractors like the Duchess of Love had found him blameless of Aris's murder, then they had no reason to deny him the nursery.

Psyke's hysteria, her own weakness and shock, had betrayed more than her own respectability. She hadn't been able to explain herself last night, had only been able to hold on to the truth: Aris died and it was Janus's doing. Maledicte's hand but Janus's command. Rue had dismissed her first strangled explanations outright, and she had faltered to rabbit muteness when Janus arrived.

Her gaze flew to the bellpull, but Janus had dismissed Dahlia last night; and even if Dahlia did answer Psyke's summons, the girl's clumsiness and nervous questions would slow her rather than aid.

Psyke ransacked her wardrobe, seeking a particular gown. Another mourning dress, a dusty, dull navy with one singular virtue; it buttoned up the front. With the worst of the wrinkles shaken out, the dust brushed away, she set about dressing herself. Her fingers wanted to linger on each jet button, tasting the death of her sisters, her mother, her friends with each stone, but she had no time for old tears now. Aris's voice, that bled-out urgency, still echoed in her ears. *Adiran*—he begged. *Adiran*.

She pressed her feet into satin slippers and felt them sting like splinters. Kicking them off again, she rubbed her toes against the stone floor, felt the yawning emptiness of the intervening spaces and the chapel below in the sheltering earth.

The chapel of the murdered king: They'd call it that in years to come, she thought, long after they knew who had died and why. The Cold King was proof of that, his name near forgotten in the common way of things, but Thomas Redoubt had been her ancestor.

And, she realized abruptly, the scaled man who had guided her dream. His wing, his bones lost in it for all eternity.

Psyke yanked open her door, fled into the hall, away from her own thoughts and the ghosts that lingered at the edge of her vision. Aris, still entreating. Challacombe with his hooded eyes. Others yet lurking in the shadowy halls.

The hour was early yet, Psyke knew; the shocked quiet in the palace, the way the Laudable still clung to her, the crisp chill of granite beneath her feet—surely Janus would expect her to lie later abed. And even one such as he must balk at killing an innocent; if she hurried, she could station herself at Adiran's side, as much a guard as any soldier. If she had no weapons to bear but her rank and her eyes as witness, she would pit those against Janus's sword.

The nursery door was swinging closed behind the maid when Psyke reached it, five hallways and two flights of stairs later, out of breath and still bundling up the mass of her hair.

The guards looked askance at her disarray but stepped aside to allow her entrance. The nurserymaid looked up from the low table she was setting with child-sized utensils, and dropped into a hasty curtsy. "My lady."

"Elysses," Psyke said. "Where is Adiran?"

His absence was unusual. Twelve years old, and yet he lacked language or more than basic rudiments of intelligence. His dogs were more capable of learning lessons than Adiran. Still, the boy understood time well enough, and this was the hour when Aris came and ate breakfast with him. Usually, the boy prince would be hovering at Elysses's side, snitching bits of his favorite pastries.

"The window, my lady," Elysses said. Her gaze rested on Psyke's creased skirts, on the long tangle of her loose hair for a moment, fascinated with Psyke's unusual disorder, before she recalled the question. She gestured behind her, toward the draped window that overlooked the city.

Adiran had clambered up onto the narrow ledge, balancing unevenly against the glass. Psyke moved to pull him down, and Elysses said, "I wouldn't. He's been doing that ever since that damned . . . He must have seen him come in through the window." She shook her head, trying to loose the unpleasant reminders, hid in practicality. "He'll come down when he's hungry."

Maledicte again, Psyke thought. A weight in the palace, the shadow that they would never be free of.

The boy pressed delicate fingers above his head, tracing ripples in the glass, spreading his hands out like the jut of rising wings.

Elysses finished setting out the plates, and Adiran hopped down with an unsettling agility, pointing out that this collection of rooms was his kingdom and that he was the master of it.

Psyke clenched her jaw against sudden tears. How would they ever begin to explain the loss to Adiran, the sudden absence of his father? As if her thoughts summoned him, a faint gray smear shimmered in her vision; Aris settling into the rocking chair, watching his son.

Adiran balked at the table, studying the plates.

There weren't enough, Psyke realized. Aris ate with him; the table should be set for two.

Adiran backed away from the table, confused by an inexplicable change, and stopped before Psyke. His gaze was on her bare toes poking out beneath her skirts; a smile glimmered on his mouth. Then he raised his eyes to meet hers, a blue as bright as forget-me-nots, as a summer sky.

She wished they could stay untroubled, clear of pain; but even as she did, his eyes widened, filling with a grief so profound that Psyke was shaken to her core. While she tried to understand how this could be—how the child who knew nothing of reading nor of the ways of the world could read the death in her eyes—he opened his mouth and screamed.

6

ANUS LEFT THE LIBRARY, CATCHING Walker and Simpson arguing in whispers, heads bent together. They sprang apart, and Simpson's teeth clicked closed on the hissed end of Janus's name.

Simpson, Janus thought, one of his regular attending guards. And apparently one who thought Janus should be waiting out the hunt for the assassin in a cell.

"Where to, my lord?" Walker said, valiantly attempting to distract Janus from Simpson's words and the weight they left in the air between them. He fingered the scars on his face in a gesture Janus had learned was habitual when under stress.

"The nursery," Janus answered. Without waiting for their response, he headed for the carpeted stairs up to the third floor.

Janus had not been in the nursery since the night he murdered Auron, but as he approached it, he heard all-too-familiar sounds: a child shrieking, the dogs in full cry—a fury of snarling, snapping— and bleeding through it all, voices of two women near to weeping. Despite himself, Janus turned to sweep the hall with his gaze, half expecting Maledicte to burst from shadow, blade bared, for the thick-laid carpets to grow bloodstains again, for time to reverse itself.

The shadows of the men moved like the flutter of wings, and the fine hairs on Janus's nape rose like a dog's hackles. He pushed past the nursery guards, pressed open the door with a pounding heart, though he knew from their unhappy calm that the uproar inside was harmless.

The door slipped free from his hand, slammed back against the wall, shaking plaster dust loose and tipping one of Adiran's clockwork carriages over, setting the horse's legs to twitching spasmodically.

Three sets of eyes met his in varying shades of startlement. Hela, one of Adiran's two mastiffs, raised her head at Janus's sudden entrance, woofing softly to express her displeasure. Across the room, Bane, chained to the radiator, peeled back black lips and snarled. His ivory teeth slowed Janus's hasty steps; they glistened evilly and were larger than the pieces of whale ivory the sailors sold for lunas ashore.

Adiran hiccupped, his red-faced weeping pausing for a heartbeat, and then beginning again, though softer. The nurserymaid dropped her eyes immediately, hands fisting in the folds of her skirt, a handful of candies falling to the floor, and being gobbled up by Hela.

Psyke rose from where she knelt, trying to tempt the prince with one of several toys. Janus found his throat drying as she approached him, her steps soundless, oddly delicate as she evaded the broken pieces of some previously refused toy. Her breath was inaudible over the sound of Adiran's weeping, and Janus couldn't help but recall those long hours of the night when her silence had been that of the grave.

"What's happening here?" Janus said. He stepped back as she approached, his boot heels crunching on glass. She paused in her forward steps and bent to collect another toy. She brushed glass off its sides before answering him.

"The boy, my lord, is grieving."

"Does he even understand grief?" Janus asked.

She reached out to stroke Adiran's matted curls, and he shrank back, crying more shrilly, in a tantrum unlike any Janus had imagined the boy capable of.

Adiran let Psyke press a toy into his clenching hands, a wooden ship, carved, painted, and gilded. He held it for a moment and then hurled it. Across the room, the nurserymaid yelped and ducked.

"Enough!" Janus said. His head was aching, trying to decide if grief was a sign of increasing wisdom or not—after all, dogs had been known to pine themselves to death over a lost master and no one considered them rivals to man. "Don't just stand there and weep, girl. Fetch Sir Robert to give the boy a potion."

"Do no such thing, Elysses," Psyke said in immediate contradiction. It startled him, though it shouldn't have. She had made her position clear enough when she accused him of killing Aris, but he had eight months of her quiet passivity to unlearn.

"He'll make himself ill," Janus said.

"Better that than to swallow anything you offer," Psyke said. Janus took a step back at the cold knowledge in her expression.

She turned back to Adiran, shaping her expression to sweetness, her voice to light. "Here, Adiran," she said. "Take your toy." The boy scuttled back from her, grabbing tight to Bane's heavy chain and leather collar, baring his teeth at her, his eyes swelling shut with all the tears he'd shed.

Janus said, "Seems to me it's you who are upsetting him, not Aris's absence."

He glanced back toward the low table, saw the plates laid out, and thought, grief or not, intelligent or not, Adiran understood time and absence well enough. Janus grasped Psyke's shoulders, felt her go as rigid as a corpse in his hands, and moved her bodily from his path, remembering belatedly the wounds on her shoulders. She, no doubt, would think he had pressed upon them with careful deliberation. So be it.

"Adiran," Janus said. Bane snarled, deep and low, a rumble that made itself felt in Janus's bones. He moved forward cautiously, and put one hand on Bane's withers, gambling that time spent feeding the hounds treats would garner results now. His other hand fell gently on Adiran's narrow shoulder. The boy let out a tiny moan and fell into Janus's side.

Psyke made a sound of outraged protest that brought a smile to his face. There were many things Adiran couldn't learn, but Aris had taught the boy about family. And before Janus had fallen from grace,

Aris had brought Janus to the nursery often, teaching Adiran to trust his cousin.

Janus released Bane, who growled halfheartedly but licked at his palm in passing, and took Adiran up into his arms. The boy clung to him, thin limbs tight around his back and neck, his sobs dying as Janus awkwardly rubbed Adiran's shoulders. He'd seen Aris do so before, and Adiran reacted much as the dog did, relaxing against his will. It was a good thing the boy was so small—his arms and legs were awkwardly long as it was. Janus rocked in place, afraid to step forward and trip in the tangle of the boy's dangling legs.

"Put him down," Psyke said. Her eyes were huge and shadowed in her face, bruised looking, as if Adiran's affection toward Janus injured her.

"And start the weeping again? Perhaps your nerves can stand it. Mine cannot." He shifted his grip on Adiran, rearranged the boy, and began walking toward the center of the room and the low table there. "If my presence disturbs you, you may leave. I am quite competent to care for one boy."

Psyke's response was lost to him; Janus passed the glass-paned doors to the inner bedroom, and saw Auron's crib still standing there, the wood varnished where blood had been spilled.

Mad, he thought, Aris had been mad to keep this reminder in place. Adiran raised his head when Janus paused in his steps; his frail neck twisted as he looked to see what Janus saw.

He sighed hugely and murmured something in the childish glossolalia that passed for the majority of his speech.

Psyke's lips firmed. She came closer, reached her arms out to take Adiran from him, and the boy recoiled.

"No!" he cried. "No!" and buried his hot-cheeked, wet face into Janus's neck, new tears seeping into his cravat.

"Seems he's made himself clear," Janus said. "Guards, would you escort Lady Last out?"

Psyke shook her head at once. "No. I'll see myself out, if I must. The guards will stay and attend to Adiran's safety."

"You don't trust me? My sweet, I'm devastated," Janus said, trying for insouciance, and yet—the growl came through. Her lies could have cost him everything. He could imagine the whispers now, "Even his *wife* thinks him a villain. . . ."

In the corner, Bane raised his heavy head, pricked his ears. The chain holding him jangled; he paced to the end of it and echoed Janus's growl, facing Psyke.

Her cheekbones tipped red. "I am neither a dog nor a fool to be easily misled by a superficial charm. I know you for what you are."

"As I know you now," he said. "I trust we are both enlightened." He set Adiran down at the table, urging him to his routine.

Psyke turned on her heel, her skirt flaring out to reveal shoeless feet beneath the heavy wool, as if she had rushed to Adiran's side as soon as she had awoken. Or as if she no longer felt the chill of stony floors.

Adiran paused in his desultory forking up of boiled egg mash and venison. He watched Psyke leave, the guards opening and closing the door for her, and tugged on Janus's sleeve.

Janus bent his head down, the better to hear the boy prince's whisper. No random collection of sound this, but a single questioning syllable. "Dead?"

He shook off the chill the boy's clear voice left and sighed, "Adi, such is life. Everyone dies or leaves you. Best look out for yourself."

IVOR TOOK CARE HUNTING HIS prey through the palace, using the skills of a lifetime spent in court, passing a few minutes of gossip here with that courtly sycophant Savne, listening quietly to Admiral DeGuerre as he spoke with Bull, ostensibly waiting his chance to express the Itarusine court's sympathy, and finally, heard one boyish page fretting to another that Last and his wife were in the nursery, trying to soothe the prince.

The placement was unfortunate; it took him some time to find a page harried enough to allow him entrance to the private floors of Aris's residence, long enough that he found his quarry coming to him instead.

All good things, he thought, and tried to make his smile pleasant instead of wicked.

The Countess of Last rocked back on her heels, and displayed an unflattering and entirely impolite suspicion.

"Prince Ivor," she said, and though etiquette demanded an acknowledgment of his rank more sweeping than her bare words, she withheld it from him in an insolence he thought better suited to her husband. "What brings you here?"

"My lady," he said. "I came to bear condolences to the crown prince on behalf of my country. Quite pointless, I understand, given the boy's circumstances; still, basic courtesies are rarely unwelcome."

She flushed, taking his words as a reproach for her rudeness, and he noted it—new to insolence and not native to her nature. He wondered if she had learned it from Janus or if she was recalling it from some other source. In all his studies of the Antyrrian court, he hadn't paid much attention to Janus's wife, taking it for granted that the gossip had sketched her correctly, a sweet, unquestioning woman, intelligent but not clever, Aris's favorite of the court women and his eyes upon his troublesome nephew.

Ivor's own spies assured him that after the death of her family, she was like to avoid confrontation at all costs, to plead for peace over bloodshed; in other words, a woman much like Aris. Ivor had never considered that she might be witness to the assassination, or that she would attempt to use the same against her husband. His interest had doubled overnight.

"I wonder at you pushing in to disturb a family in mourning. A note would have sufficed," she said. The words came out stiffly, oddly spaced as if she had to work to offend, had to draw again on the pool of something other.

Instead of doing as she so obviously wished, taking affront and leaving, he curved his lips into a smile. "You have spine behind your sweetness," he said. "I suppose it should come as no surprise. After all, you have witnessed some truly terrible crimes, or so gossip gives me to understand, including Aris's murder—"

"I will not discuss that with you." Psyke turned to walk away from him, then balked, as if belatedly realizing that to do so would allow him free access to the halls behind her and the nursery.

Ivor let his smile broaden. No, she was no practiced schemer. Her every thought betrayed itself in the sway of her body, even if her face remained a mask.

Ivor would have gambled a pouch of Antyrrian sols that she confounded Janus. While Janus had been in Itarus, letting Ivor teach him how to be something more than a Relict rat, he had spoken often of his fierce Miranda. Focused entirely on the girl he had been forcibly parted from, he never paid the type of attention he should have to the noblewomen of the Itarusine court. More, Janus's obsession with Miranda had led Ivor to a truth Janus would no doubt prefer buried.

Maledicte, the effeminate courtier who, by all accounts, had captured Janus's attention the very moment he laid eyes on him, who had him running tame by his side, in his bed within a night . . . Maledicte could only be the Relict girl, Miranda.

And it followed, therefore, that Maledicte had eluded death as easily as Miranda had eluded her original fate in the Relics. After all, the body hung above the gates had been male.

Ivor stepped to the side as if to pass Psyke by, brushing close enough to taste her scent in the warmed air between them, pungent and earthy, like clay brought into the sun. She jerked away from him, breath quickening, her pulse beating in the hollow of her throat.

"You feel threatened," he said, "here in the heart of the palace?"

"Aris is dead," Psyke said. "Why shouldn't I feel fear?"

Ivor leaned against the flocked wallpaper—a style ten years old and worn beneath his palms—and smiled lazily at her.

"How highly you prize yourself. A wife is a small thing, easily set aside and forgotten. A king, however . . . only death will see him gone."

The woman paled, licked her lips, a pale pink tongue touching skin one shade lighter. Ivor's smile grew; whether Janus admired her or not, she was a sweet piece, all rose and cream and gold, the very epitome of an Antyrrian maid. Her words though, her words were as cold and hard as jet. "I never said I feared for myself."

She glanced back over her shoulder at the shadows draping the nursery door.

He used a booted foot to press himself from the wall, stalked her in a graceful circle, watching her turn to keep him always in her sight. Once, when his boots came too close to her skirts, she twitched them back, giving him a charming view of pale arches and a bare stretch of heel and toe.

"No," he agreed. He raised a hand, watched her eyes grow wary as his touch neared her face, but this time, she refused to flinch or back away. He let his fingertips fall lightly over the curve of her cheek, found it as cool and smooth as ancient marble. "No, I see that. I should have expected nothing less from one who escaped Mirabile's trap."

At the mention of Mirabile's name, her eyes darkened. "She dallied too long," Psyke whispered. "Gloated too much, and I . . . fled."

"You showed remarkable sense for a woman," Ivor said, meaning it. He knew men who would have shown less intelligence, men who would have gone after Mirabile with a blade and met a gruesome end. "Which surprises me the more that you showed so little yesterday. Accusing your husband of treason was not only rash but ill-advised."

Psyke's chin firmed. "I had to speak," she said. "He killed Aris as surely as if he wielded the blade himself."

Ivor let out a breath, fought the urge to smile. *This* was why he had hunted her, *this* was what he had needed to hear: How had she managed to witness Aris's death without falling to his agent's sword?

"Did you see it happen? See his stalking horse so clearly that you could name him one of Janus's men?"

The stiffness of her body shifted in an instant from rigidity to something softer, leaning toward him. Her gaze traced his face, gauged his interest, his sincerity, and found it satisfactory.

Ivor bent his brow into deeper earnestness, when he badly wanted to smile. She burned to tell him, her very body vibrated with the need to relive the murder, to be reassured that she had done right, that she was not to blame. *A woman's weakness*, he thought, *to care so desperately about the opinions of others.*

Some of his amusement must have leaked through, because she drew back. "You needn't think I'll tell you anything I haven't already told Captain Rue."

"But *I* might believe you." A gamble, a large one, but she had the air about her, that bruised outrage.

She came closer still, her head barely reaching the level of his heart. He took her elbow in his, guided her down the hallway, away from the nursery she wanted to defend, finding a quiet spot near the main landing. She came quietly, docile enough now that she was promised a listening ear. "I thought Janus your friend," she said.

He lowered his voice, made it intimate, and watched her fidget. "Had I time, my sweet, I would tell you such tales of Janus in the Itarusine court as to make your blood freeze. Your husband is that most dangerous of creatures, a savage beast with an agile mind."

"Yet you spoke to his innocence," Psyke said. "I cannot trust your words or your intentions."

Ivor shrugged, insouciance in the shift of his shoulders, as if he had no real interest in what she might say. Her need for an audience, he thought, was strong enough for him to allow a touch of contempt to lace his voice. "I only spoke truth," he said. "You did not, and yet I am the one to distrust? You accuse Janus of regicide when he was so distinctly elsewhere. Tell me, did you truly witness the crime, or did you merely seize the moment with the impetuousness and arrogance of an Antyrrian noble, sure no one would dare contradict you?"

The flush rose in her cheeks so fast that her hands flew to cover them, as if she felt the rage and embarrassment might welt her skin. She shook her head once, twice, as if she were shaking his words away. Her hair, only loosely pinned, slid free.

Bare feet, worn navy gown, loosened hair; Ivor wondered how roughly Janus had treated her last night to set her fleeing her quarters without even a care for her appearance.

"It was foolish," Ivor said, "to make an enemy of Janus."

"It would be more foolish to keep quiet and see Janus profit when Aris died." Her reply was immediate; her eyes ablaze with fury.

"Then share his description with me, with the guards. Steal that profit from him." Ivor gave her his most vulpine grin. "And spare me the indignity of Rue's men searching my wing three times over now, hunting some cause to blame Itarus. My father would dislike that, and the treaty that binds our countries in friendship—"

"Friendship," Psyke said. "When you bleed us dry—"

A page scuttled by, his tight-drawn shoulders and lowered head a tangible reflection of their raised voices. Psyke turned from Ivor abruptly toward the stairs.

Ivor pulled her back, hands wrapping easily about her narrow waist. "Who did you see that made it evident Janus was behind it?" He breathed the words into her ear, felt her tremble, rage and fear commingled, and almost envied Janus this wife who felt so much. "Who did you see that made your Captain Rue think you a liar or a madwoman? Someone, perhaps, you had thought dead. . . ."

Another gamble this, but a smaller one. After all, Ivor knew the assassin intimately, and knew what Psyke must have seen, if she had seen anything at all: a dark-haired courtier wielding a blade like a vengeful spirit.

"I saw—" Her voice wavered, faltered.

He released her, though he stayed skin close, resting his weight at her back, the plummet of the stairs before her. If she needed leading, he would clap the bridle on.

"We heard tales," he said, and every word he uttered was true. "Tales in the Itarusine court of a certain courtier. They said that Black-Beaked Ani Herself took action in his cause. They said also that Janus killed Her avatar with a single blow. In the histories, Ani is not driven back so cleanly. It seems . . . possible that he survived. Ani's determination is the stuff of legend."

"His body was displayed above the palace. The crows ate his flesh," Psyke said, but her words were empty of belief. Her hand reached out to the banister; she tightened her grip, the dark wood as ruddy as blood against her pale fingers. He overlaid her hand with his.

"And Janus—did he grieve? When the crows devoured his lover? Or did he continue as before, a man unacquainted with loss?"

"Why?" she said. "Why do you care? Itarus can only benefit from the confusion and chaos here."

"Believe what you will," Ivor said. "I can weather your distrust and your fear. It is not undeserved. My reputation is more based on truth than slander, and it is a violent one. But do not allow your distrust to taint your vision. Ani's wings are far-reaching; Janus guided Her once to his purpose, clearing lives from his path: his father, his father's wife, their child. Now Aris is dead at a shadow's hand. *Janus profits when men die.*"

"*Maledicte,*" she whispered. "I saw him. His hair loose and wild, wrapped in shadows, his blade leading him into the dance."

Ivor hid his amusement. Black hair, shadows, and a blade, and she cried Maledicte! Had his little assassin been red-haired, dressed in white, likely Psyke would be gibbering about Mirabile instead. Fear made people a pleasure to manipulate. "So tell me, how did he let you live?"

Psyke shivered; her arms came up to clutch her shoulders. She ducked her chin into the shelter of her arms and stayed silent for a very long time. Long enough that it took an act of will to keep his expression just so: a smidgeon of concern, and a blend of interest and belief.

"Maledicte didn't see me," she said. "I hid in the shadows of the altar. I hid while Maledicte killed Aris. I saved myself and Aris died while I did nothing."

Her breath was fast, her voice hoarse, and her lashes damp, but despite her fervor, her tone lacked conviction.

Ivor felt his interest kindle higher. His assassin might be young and new to the work he had asked of her, but she was dedicated and loyal to him. Nothing should have spared Psyke from his assassin's blade.

7

ANUS, IN THE CHATTERING COMPANY of the high court, followed the palace servants through the moss-laden cemetery, trying not to slip on the green-slicked stones. Outside the distant gates, carriages disgorged more of the nobility than he recognized. Admiral DeGuerre walked alongside him in thoughtful silence, thinking on Aris, or simply attempting to recall the proper etiquette for a king's funeral. With the gods gone, funerals as a whole had fallen out of fashion, save those times when family felt the need to see their dead safely interred or when death granted an excuse to socialize. Challacombe's body, found in the tunnels during the hunt for the assassin, had been interred without witnesses beyond the gravediggers.

The usual political ritual—a laying out for weeks, so that the people could visit the dead king and mourn—had been dismissed immediately. No one wanted to open the palace grounds to the public, not with the assassin still more shadow than flesh. So the funeral plan had begun at once, word spreading outward on genteel invitations and a distressingly abrupt notice in the broadsheets when the palace secretary ran out of time.

It lent the entire matter a regrettable air of spontaneity, as if the nobles, bored, scrambled to attend a last-minute ball, those in Murne counting themselves luckier than their country cousins who would miss it entirely and have to make do with secondhand gossip and newspaper reports.

Janus found it all incomprehensible; as he had when he first attended the Winter Court, he found himself watchful and quietly confounded.

On Janus's left, Bull and Lord Blythe paced him, equally silent, though Janus thought Bull was visibly uneasy at Blythe's presence. Warrick Bull was a consummate politician, well aware of public opinion; Blythe was repellent, an obvious schemer, but very well connected. To deny Blythe pride of place in the procession would have turned the duchess against Bull.

The procession should have been family first—Adiran, Janus, and Psyke, before the other counselors, DeGuerre and Bull—but Adiran had been left behind in his nursery, safe with his dogs and nurserymaid. And Psyke . . . his so-sweet wife had made her opinion of him too clear for comfort, choosing a place in the procession beside his most vocal detractor, the Duchess of Love.

Procession—Janus spared a sweeping, contemptuous glance at the scatter of aristocrats—procession was far too orderly a word for this movement. During his years in Itarus, he had seen processions with the finesse of military drills, the nobles moving to one purpose, their focus ahead.

Here, the young pallbearers grumbled under their breaths as they carted Aris's coffin uphill toward the mausoleum, superstitious whispers that traveled much too well in the still air. The ginger-haired lad, fingers white around the handles, went so far as to claim the heaviness of the coffin was due to the soul clinging to the body until his murderer was caught. His companions stifled him with hisses and appalled glances.

It hardly mattered what they said, Janus thought, not when the aristocrats straggled behind, gossip slowing their steps, and cried for their servitors to dart back and forth from the carriages, ferrying cast-off cloaks in a day gone unseasonably warm, bringing cooling fruit drinks from the hampers or warming spirits from flasks. Even the death of their king couldn't dampen their frivolity.

Why should it, when they presumed nothing would change, that nothing *could* change? Their lives were comfortable; the strictures Itarus laid over Antyre spared the aristocrats. Aris had seen to that, finessing the Antyrrian audits; the kingdom bled, the commoners bled, but the aristocrats . . .

They reached the end of the stone walkway, penetrated deeper into the green heart of the palace cemetery. It, like the rest of Murne, crept toward decay. The hillside cathedral had been given over to Parliament, and all the pews had been thrown into the cemetery grounds, scavenged over years, but shards of wood still studded the pitted grounds in unexpected places.

No one attended services now, no one would, even were the building reclaimed and intercessors found to hold them. But the graves were untended also, ivy eating away at the stones where the salt air had left white stains and etched holes in the marble.

As they reached the mausoleum, Janus stumbled over a hummock in the grass, a mole furrow or interloping root, and his mood, already bleak, soured. Lady Secret laughed at him from behind her black fan, unafraid and unapologetic. She whispered in her escort's ear; and while Janus watched her, DeGuerre took shameless advantage of his distraction.

As the pallbearers set the coffin down before the mausoleum, Admiral DeGuerre rose to stand on the crumbling marble dais where the intercessors had stood before the gods took themselves away. Without waiting for anyone's attention, he began speaking.

A man of Aris's age, gray hair in short ringlets and wearing a coat better suited to the winter months than to this early spring, stepped up beside Janus. Admiral DeGuerre, glancing at his slowly growing audience, nodded to the man with approval. Janus was heartened to see that this new attendee did not return the approving nod. The man's confidence, the elegance of his clothes, his apparent chill on a warm day—all argued that this was Fanshawe Gost, the new head of Parliament, the Kingmaker.

The admiral spoke of Aris's intelligence, his kindness and humanity, and Janus thought the admiral defanged. This man, speaking in platitudes and oh so carefully turned phrases, had been one of Antyre's feared naval officers—Demon DeGuerre—and had been whittled to what? A man whose war was lost long ago and who was left mouthing another man's words of peace. Aris had much to answer for, not least the gelding of men of war.

Fanshawe Gost said, voice low so as not to be heard over DeGuerre, "I recall my father's interment. Then praises were sung to purpose and layered about with his flaws, so that the gods might recognize him as he traversed their realms. This empty flattery—"

"There is nothing of use in it," Janus said, abrupt and uncivil though he knew he needed to woo Gost. He felt sometimes that Maledicte had been his shield; with Maledicte to speak venom, Janus had no need to do so himself. With Maledicte gone . . . his anger burned hot and close to the surface, smoldering like a fire on a summer's day. "There is nothing of future in it, no guidance for those left behind. Only a smug maundering on the past."

DeGuerre's smooth platitudes were interrupted by a hoarse voice laden with the mangled drawl of the street. "Niver min' the dead king. Who's the heir?"

"Not the simpleton," another voice protested. "Not when Itarus slavers at our shores . . ."

The nobles were no longer the only ones at the boneyard. Beyond the palace soldiers, the lines of the Particulars, the citizens of Murne crowded to watch, and the yell had come from somewhere within the push and falter of the people. Guards rested hands on pistols.

"Never mind that," another voice called. This one was crisp and tight, an actor's voice, pitched to carry. "Who killed him? The Itarusine prince assassin or the murdering bastard? Which one of them's the assassin?"

A group of rats picked up the question, answered it with the maddening chant passed on in the streets. It had been a rope-skipping song, Maledicte's bloody exploits simplified. Now, it had altered.

> Maledicte's gone; the rooks don't fly,
> yet through the kingdom sounds the cry:
> The bastard profits when men die.

Janus relaxed his jaw, eased his shoulders. Meaningless words. Nothing more.

Admiral DeGuerre continued as if he had never been interrupted, though his hands twitched. Janus imagined him on deck of his ship, and knew any sailor who had committed such a sin would be sorry soon after.

"Better a murderer than a fool king." That same hoarse voice, full of vicious contempt. Janus narrowed his gaze, pinpointing him at the head of the crowd. The man was distinctive, a hawk-faced blond in a butcher's leathers. Beside him, a slight, dark-haired man nudged him, hands brushing. The blond looked down at his hands and grinned wolfishly.

Janus took a discreet step back; Gost echoed him, and the rock fell far short, rattling off one of the old stone monuments.

"You notice the citizens," Gost said. "A welcome trait in a noble."

"I notice trouble," Janus admitted, "and try to predict foolishness."

The soldiers had gone after the stone-throwing pair; the crowd booed them and closed ranks so that the soldiers had to force their way through for what would be wasted effort. The mood was ugly, though the nobles seemed unconcerned.

"So you think on the future."

"I quite dwell on it," Janus said. Gost's solid clap on his shoulder startled him; he looked over to see the man grinning at him, teeth white in a tanned face.

"Good man," Gost said, "but thinking's only part of it. There comes a time when one must act."

"I'm not feared of that, either," Janus said.

"Then you'll round out a triad of regents quite nicely. DeGuerre's experience, Bull's financial sense, and your youth and ambition."

"Adiran is heir, and I am blood kin," Janus said. "DeGuerre is an old man who's forgotten glory, and Bull—Bull's too preoccupied with his banks and making his fortunes to be a support to Antyre."

"You think you should be king?"

"Regent," Janus said. "And why not?" He was pushing, knew he was, but self-confidence was easily turned to charisma. If Gost were the man the reports painted him, he would be more dismayed by false modesty and attempts at manipulation. Janus would play this game with all apparent openness and win Gost to his side.

Gost studied him for a long moment, leaned back, and surveyed Janus as if he were a piece of land. "Do you think you're competent to rule this country?" Gost asked. It was the honest inquiry in his tone that soothed the hot roil in Janus's belly, kept it from erupting into intemperate words.

"I've been trained. I've studied economics, history, the sciences—"

"I commend you for it. It shows an interested mind. But studying for a bare handful of years is a far cry from practical experience."

"If I was expected to learn sooner, perhaps you and your aristocratic friends should not have allowed Last to spurn my mother. Or retrieved me when it came clear that Adiran was damaged. Aris should have forced Last to retrieve his bastard then. I will not apologize for my past."

Gost said, "For a man who dwells in the future, thinking overlong on the wrongs done you in the past is a sign of frustration, futility, or—most damning of all—doubt in your own purpose."

Janus brought his head up, looking for the condemnation in the man's eyes. There was none. Only a strange gentleness. "Allow yourself to be guided, Janus."

"By you? By DeGuerre—that desiccated sailor? Or Bull, who sees all problems in financial terms? Or perhaps you mean Adiran—"

"Lower your hackles," Gost said. "Your lack of training has already raised comment. I understand you couldn't read the latest missive from Parliament and Aris had to translate it for you."

"It wasn't in Antyrrian," Janus said. "I'm not illiterate." But Gost's words woke that same sick sensation in his belly as he had had then, looking at the incomprehensible letters while DeGuerre and Bull took up pen and ink and added comments in the margins. He had felt as useful as Adiran, playing quietly in the corner of the king's study.

"High Antyrrian," Gost said, "a language used these days exclusively for laws and sensitive material. Or to put an ambitious man in his place. I imagine that Ivor Grigorian could read it. Perhaps even your lady wife? Her father used to boast quite unbecomingly about her intelligence."

"I can learn it," Janus said.

"You will," Gost said. "But you will always be two steps behind. Let DeGuerre declare a triad of regents. Give yourself time to grow."

"We cannot afford a rule by committee," Janus said. "Not now, when Itarus stoops like a hawk. The prince ascendant's presence is proof of that. We need a single figure, one who can rally the people, who can save Antyre."

"Even from itself?" Gost scoffed. "The aristocrats may be swayed only so far by pretty words and a commanding manner. The poor are not swayed at all by such. They cannot, after all, eat words or promises."

"I have more to offer than that," Janus said. "Have you heard of Westfall's engines?"

"Heard enough to know that they are torn down as often as they are erected."

"The antimachinists say they fear our engines will eradicate even the few jobs remaining. Though they lay claim to preservation, their aim now seems simply to provoke disorder," Janus said. "I've a man in their ranks, and he believes the antimachinists are being manipulated. He feels the antimachinists can be brought to heel if the leaders are identified and removed, when the remainder see that we can recover our country's strength and their futures. Once the antimachinists have settled, the poor will follow."

Gost shook his head. "Perhaps you should study more philosophy. Change is always unwelcome."

Another stone came their way, followed by a shout of "Murderer!" The soldiers at the perimeter wavered, torn between fruitless pursuit and standing their ground.

Gost watched the stone slip through the grass at their feet and tumble slowly downward until it rolled against the Duchess of Love's carriage at the base of the hill. Beside it, Psyke and the duchess watched them. Janus followed Gost's gaze, stone to carriage to wary faces. The Duchess of Love tugged Psyke further back into the security of the carriage.

"I'll look at your engines," Gost said. "Show me what you believe to be Antyre's future. But I tell you now—if you wish to be a power in this country, you must prove yourself innocent of Aris's death. The people are no longer willing to accept usurpation by regicide. Your reputation works against you. Your misalliance with Maledicte—the rumors of it reached as far as Kyrda. You have enemies aplenty, remarkable for one so young, and it seems that your wife is among them. That is she, is it not, with the Duchess of Love?"

"Ivor Grigorian had Aris killed, not I," Janus said.

"Inconvenient then, that you were with him when Aris fell. Rue and Jasper are blanketing the city looking for the agent he used, but this city is a warren and the ship captains are easily bribed to take unlisted passengers. Nor does that account for the fishermen's dinghies that put out to sea with no fanfare at all."

"But they're also easily bribed to share information. If one knows the correct people."

"Do you?"

Janus smiled, liking the flash of approval on Gost's face. "Quite well."

Gost smiled. "I had heard you were the one running the privateers."

"I am. Unless you're speaking to the prince ascendant. Then, I deplore the piracy in our waters."

Gost's pleasure had not gone unnoticed by the Duchess of Love; her lips below her half veil were pinched. At her shoulder, Psyke watched him, her customary mask of pleasant amiability missing. He had not seen her smiles, false or otherwise, since the evening before Aris's death.

She had barred her door to him the past two nights—and given the events of the first, he couldn't blame her. Still, it made his skin itch to think of her, alone in her rooms where Rue had found an unwatched exit into the tunnels. No wonder she had been able to rendezvous with Aris unseen except by rumor.

Captain Rue had closed off the tunnels as best he could, but it was only a matter of installing bars across doorframes; the Cold

King's tunnels had been carved from the stone themselves. Collapsing them would result in the fall of the old wing; and it would take weeks, if not months, to bring in enough rubble to fill them to impassability.

A sudden shout brought him back to the here and now, and he stepped to the side without much thought, noting idly that someone in the crowd, obviously better off than the rest, had hurled bread. The low mutter turned inward; the crowd pushed back in among itself. Fists were raised.

"This bodes well," Gost said.

"Only for the surgeons," Janus said. "How much longer does DeGuerre intend to keep us here? The crowd grows more agitated with every moment."

The Particulars, less confident than their palace brethren, raised pistols and swords; a few unfortunates, the lowest in rank, raised old pikes.

Janus shook his head sharply. Enough. He pushed past Gost, climbed up beside DeGuerre on the dais, still prosing on, and said, "End it. Now. Or you'll have open rebellion on your hands."

DeGuerre's face mottled red, and he pulled his arm free of Janus's hasty grasp. "Do not presume! I am not my sons, to listen to your commands."

Bull laid a hand on DeGuerre's boot top, smudging the fine gloss with sweaty fingertips, and raised his face, his brow deeply furrowed. Behind him, Blythe dithered, trying to shelter in the lee of a towering headstone.

Bull said, "He's right, Hector. Look at the crowd. Let's be done with it and move on before the carriages are endangered."

"Before we have to fire on Antyre's citizens," Janus said.

DeGuerre bristled, chose not to end his speech with any grace, instead dropped off the dais, leaving Janus a clear target of the crowd's attention.

"Murderer!" A voice went up, shrill as a woman's, and Janus turned to see a dark-haired head ducking away from his gaze.

The crowd echoed it, once, twice, and Janus raised a hand in time to catch a thrown stone. It stung his hand, raised welts and painful memories of Relict warfare, but he took care to show nothing on his face.

"The king is dead," Janus said, pitching his voice to carry. "If you want the country to follow, continue on your path. The Itarusines await on the edges of the harbor. Give them a reason and they will enter. Their prince is within our borders. A riot endangers him and brings his fleet in.

"Continue as you are, and you'll have more of a fight than you wish," Janus said. "Or you can show respect for the country's loss in silence and allow us to bury our dead."

Janus climbed down from the dais without any hurry, refusing to let the crowd think he was afraid, though his skin crawled beneath the weight of the dangerous gazes, only some of which were directed at him from within the mob. The Duchess of Love's expression was positively venomous, her mouth pinched shut, her hands so tight on Psyke's arms that Psyke's face was white with pain.

Gost helped Janus down the last two steps, shielding his body with his own. "You don't lack audacity or decisiveness, do you?"

"I'd be no good to the kingdom if I did," Janus said. "Aris thought too much, felt too much, and dared too little. Look where we stand now."

Janus waved impatiently to the lurking gravediggers, and Aris's funeral ended as shoddily as it had begun, with the coffin tipped into the earth and dirt shoveled hastily after.

· 8 ·

SURPRISINGLY IT WAS WARRICK BULL who, entering the king's dining room, flung the newspaper down before Janus at the breakfast table, and offered to give him the name of his solicitor. "It's libel, Last, and I hope you won't stand for it."

Janus pushed the paper aside after a quick glance, wondering if Bull's apparent outrage on his behalf masked the desire to see Janus's expression when confronted with the sketch on the front of the broadsheet.

"A cross letter does appear necessary. After I've eaten." He folded the paper over, fastidiously tearing away the corner that had landed in the butter dish, and applied himself to his toast before it could grow any colder, pretending the color hadn't risen to his cheeks.

Janus was late to the table; it was nearer noon than daybreak, but he had woken late in the dark quarters of the old wing. Woken unpleasantly at that, from uneasy dreams wherein Ivor and he played endless hands of cards over a swath of rippling velvet with tiny ships as currency.

The broadsheet shifted, threatened to flip open, and Janus laid his saucer upon it. He had seen the image previously; Evan had brought it to him, hesitant and drooping like a dog tucking its tail, while Janus was still in his dressing gown. The sketch was Poole's, even if his iron nerve had failed him and he had sent the drawing to the paper unsigned.

Poole had given up his usual quick caricatures in favor of something ripped from a penny dreadful. A squint-eyed man wearing a crown peered into the shadows where a cloaked swordsman was stepping out, blade extended, dripping gore. The caption beneath, lettered in a hand entirely different from the usual script, read *I am the Last thing you will ever see.*

"It's actionable, Last," Bull said, slapping his hand down on the table with force enough that Janus's tea slopped and seeped into the rough paper. "Do nothing and the public will wonder why you allow such libel to stand. It argues you fear losing your case, that there may be truth in it."

Janus cast a quick look at the guards, wondering if he could have Bull thrown out of the breakfast room, at least until he finished his meal. Regretfully, he decided the ensuing fuss would do as much to keep him from peace as Bull himself.

"Really, Warrick, have you *looked* at the sketch? It's designed to be a snare of exactly that sort. The illustration isn't signed, and the lettering beneath . . . it's not the usual writing. I drag the paper into the courts for satisfaction and Poole will say it's an imitation of his style, and not a good one; the editor will have been elsewhere when this edition was set, and the caption artist will be long gone."

Bull's gaze was downcast, fixed on the paper as if he wanted nothing more than to unfold it and rest his eyes on the sketch once more. Janus wet his throat with a mouthful of cool tea, and continued, "All I would accomplish is busying myself with legal woes, keeping this unfortunate image in the public's mind, and wasting my time when it could be turned to far better effect elsewhere."

He took another look at Bull's reddening cheeks, and said, "Perhaps that was the intent. To busy me with things inconsequential."

Bull coughed. "I won't say you're wrong." The admission surprised Janus, made him more suspicious than ever. He had known Bull disapproved of him, but hadn't realized the man had any skill in cloaking deceit in truth. That was a talent worthy of Ivor. "It still can't be left to stand. What will they print next?"

"What would you have me do?" Janus said. He pushed his empty cup aside. "Poole is in Stonegate prison already. Killing him would only lend credence to his illustrated ravings. No, I'll bide. Poole's a poor entertainer these days, harping on one old tune. His audience will grow bored."

"Bored? With Aris's murder?" The new voice was entirely unwelcome. Janus pushed away his plate with an ostentatious sigh.

"Is it too much to ask for a meal to be taken in peace?" he complained. "I swear, I ate more peaceably in the gutter."

Admiral DeGuerre balked as Janus had thought he might. The benefit of a scandalous upbringing and a reputation for being touchy about it was that dropping it into conversation left awkward silences perfectly designed for unhindered exits. Janus rose from the table, caught a smile on Bull's face, and hesitated just that moment too long.

DeGuerre reined in his irritation and demanded to know where Janus thought he was going. "Sending messages to your privateers, I suppose. Spending your time with those deviant twins."

"We are not father and son," Janus said. "I've heard you say it several times over. So my direction can be of no interest to you. I'll return by nightfall. Do try not to make decisions without me."

DeGuerre said, "You overreach yourself, Last."

Bull agreed. "If the good admiral and I agree on a course of action, your opinion is unneeded. It's a simple matter of mathematics."

"This is not Parliament," Janus said, "nor is this an egalitarian land, despite the violent attempts of the antimachinists to make it so. My blood counts for more."

He left the room, Simpson and Walker dropping into step behind him, and found Gost poised to enter. "If you've any real appetite, best seek other environs. The company in there will turn your stomach."

Gost grinned, a boyish thing in his lean and otherwise austere face. He lingered in the hall, as perfect as any portrait, his dark frock coat a sharp line against morning sunlight and the ivy-patterned wallpaper. Reluctantly, Janus acquitted the man of posing. It was only that Gost walked the palace halls in total ease, regardless of the twenty years spent elsewhere, while Janus still startled at servants appearing of a sudden and begrudged his shadowing guards.

"Bull and DeGuerre, I presume. Give them more of a chance. Hidebound men may take time to come to the point, but they often have one worth hearing." Gost turned toward the door; a gray-clad servant reached to open it.

Janus forestalled him, saying, "I've had months of listening to them and watching Aris daydream his way through their speeches. You may recall DeGuerre as he was. Currently, he's more concerned with his rank, such as it is, than with the kingdom."

Gost nodded slowly. "You may be correct. I left Antyre shortly after the war was concluded. Aris felt we needed a strong presence in the other courts to keep Antyre from becoming a country diminished to insignificance by the Xipos treaty. I spent five years in Dainand, returned to Antyre to broker the marriage between Aris and his Itarusine bride, and sailed to Kyrda. The DeGuerre I recall was a man of purpose."

"He's spent the intervening time on gossip and petty bickering. He and his cronies spend hours sitting in their clubs, drinks at hand, complaining about the slackness of young men."

Gost's mouth tightened, two white lines bracketing his lips. "These are men who fought valiantly during the Xipos War and saw their efforts go to waste when Aris surrendered. These old, useless men sitting in their clubs may find new life now that Aris is gone and the power is shifting. Wouldn't you prefer allies to enemies?"

"I know where I stand with enemies," Janus said. He had meant it to be just another cynical remark, leavened perhaps with a dash of humor, hoping to bring Gost back to good spirits. He hadn't expected it to come out as it had: raw and entirely too revealing. He shrugged one shoulder, a vulgar motion covering a more vulgar display of weakness. "I'm afraid I must leave you. I have an appointment."

"With your engineers? Your machines?"

"The very same," Janus said. "Would you care to join us now? Take a look at what minds not gone fallow can create?"

Gost smiled. "Would that I could, Last, but I've a meeting with your old men. But allow me to set a demonstration time for you, and I'll ensure that not only am I there but Bull and DeGuerre. Perhaps a tangible display will go a long way toward allaying their doubts."

Janus nodded, quite pleased. "That would serve admirably well, sir."

"In three days' time, then? I'll determine the place."

"I'll mention it to my colleagues," Janus said. "They might have situational requirements."

Gost stopped Janus in his forward movement with a quick hand; Janus evaded the touch without thought.

"Have a care, Last. The streets are unsettled. Can you not attend your business through a proxy?"

"There's the beginning of the end," Janus said, "when it takes an act of bravery to take to the streets. Show a hound fear, Gost, and it's more like to bite."

"True enough. I will believe you, since it's your wife put to the test. She left the palace with only two guards in addition to the coachman and tiger, and if a delicate woman like her is un-afraid . . . she shames us all."

Janus's ill humor returned. Off to see the Duchess of Love. Ever since Aris's funeral, the duchess had laid claim to Psyke's compan-ionship with an assiduousness that wouldn't have been out of place in a courting lover. Psyke, when pressed, had evaded Janus's ques-tions in a manner that made him more wary than ever. Nothing in-nocent hid itself but lived in the open air.

He nodded once more at Gost, and said, "I'll not keep you any longer, sir."

Long strides took him out of the pleasant surrounds of Aris's central wing and back to the Cold King's hallways; behind him, the stone floor reminded him of his following guard's presence—their boot heels thumped after him as steadily as an echoed heartbeat.

Two guards still stood at his wife's chamber door, and Janus paused. "Is the countess within?"

Marchand, the older of the two, responded, "She's not stirred, my lord."

The younger guard, the one Janus had manhandled previously,

stood straighter as if, this time, he meant to be successful in barring Janus's way. Janus throttled the urge to rise to the challenge; there was no need to fight to enter an empty room.

But did Marchand and the boy know it? Was Marchand's assertion an outright lie? Janus headed farther down the dimly lit corridor. Lying to a lord carried a stiff penalty, and for a lie so easily disproved? No, Janus thought, despite Rue's efforts at closing them, Psyke must still be using the Cold King's tunnels, keeping ahead of Rue's men, perhaps even undoing their labors, the better to allow herself to stealthily conspire with the duchess.

She probably knew the tunnels better than Rue, never mind that it was his duty. He was new to the position, after all, and Psyke was fond of history in all its guises. It had been work enough to keep Maledicte hidden from her at Lastrest, once her sensible nature had sent her hunting answers to the harassment Mal visited on her. The only successful method of distraction had been the coaches Janus arranged between Rosany's Booksellers and Lastrest. The coaches had increased in frequency, bearing old, dry tomes, until Janus had been able to track his busy wife by the scatter of opened books and the scent of old vellum.

A door shut ahead of him; his attention sharpened.

He narrowed his gaze, picked a black-clad courtier hustling away from his room, dark head bent, trying for stealth. A hopeless task given the glimmering silver embroidery in his coat and the heavy wave of lilac scent the man favored.

Savne again. Janus would have to dump all the opened wines and spirits in his room and inspect his bed for tampering. Arsenixa sprinkled over bed linens had accounted for the death of at least one ambitious princeling in the Winter Court. Janus had no illusions that the Antyrrian court was more civilized.

"Savne," he said. The slender young baronet stopped in his tracks, his loose queue of messy black hair slipping free.

His expression shifted rapidly from sheer terror to a false civility and innocence. "Oh, my lord. How you startled me." A certain determination reached his eyes, and Janus gritted his teeth in pained expectation.

"Oh, my lord," Savne said again. He dropped his voice, an excuse for sidling closer, for resting an insinuating hand on Janus's arm. "I was just looking for you."

As Janus tensed, the man backed away, the memory of being pushed into a wall obviously still fresh. But he soldiered on, keeping his tone falsely intimate. "Is there anything I can do to help you through this most difficult of times?"

Maledicte would have laughed at the man's antics, so much a parody of a seduction. Maledicte would have laughed, and then when Savne stiffened in offended dignity, would have used the man's own posture to draw a blade in a perfect line from chin to crotch.

"Yes," Janus said. "I'll be moving to the central part of the palace. I mislike the idea of Adiran surrounded only by guards and no family. Arrange for it."

"Would you like the king's suite of rooms?"

The man had no subtlety at all. Janus decided he was more offended by that than the clumsy attempts at seduction.

"I hardly think that would be appropriate," Janus said. "My father's suite will do nicely. It will need to be aired, though, if I'm to sleep there this evening. I'm afraid you'll have to hurry."

Savne nodded again, hiding his face behind the sweep of his hair, and thus his emotions. Janus waited for him to reach a decent distance, and then hailed him again. "Oh, and, Savne. If I recall correctly, my father's rooms connected to a smaller suite, often used for his paramours. Would you air those also? I have a need for them."

"My lord?"

Janus strode toward him, enjoying the way Savne's body tensed. He leaned close, as inappropriately close as Savne usually favored, and fed his fingers into those dark curls. "My lady wife, you understand," Janus whispered as if he feared being overheard.

Simpson and Walker shifted uneasily, a betraying scuff of fabric, a gloved hand brushing a beaded hilt. Janus forced himself to forget them.

Savne's neck was corded tight beneath his gloved hands. Janus let his fingers tighten, felt Savne's throat swell as he swallowed.

Janus stepped away and said more plainly, "Dwelling in the old wing has worn on her excitable temperament, weighing her mind with melancholy and ghosts. I think her outlook will improve with the change of rooms. See that her belongings are transferred to the suite attached to mine."

Janus left the man without waiting for his acknowledgment. The work would be done, though Savne would have to chivy the servants ragged to do so. There were benefits to being wooed with such motives as Savne had: The man needed to get close to Janus to please the duchess; he could balk at nothing Janus asked. It gave him a courtier who, if not loyal, at least aped it well enough to make no practicable difference in the smaller tasks. Better still, by setting Savne to such thankless tasks, Janus spared himself the ill will of the palace servants.

Maledicte had never quite understood that—that there could be layers of satisfaction within a simple manipulation. Maledicte had been too fond of using his wit as if it were an extension of his blade, never content unless his victims bled, and never mind that they were useless ever after.

But this . . . done and well done, he thought. Psyke would find her access to the old tunnels gone. Savne would have a task to keep his spying hands busy. And Janus would be in the thick of things, not easily excluded.

Let these aristocrats try to shut him out; while they wasted their efforts, he would take steps to ensure they could not ignore him— and damn Ivor for forcing his hand this soon.

In his rooms, Janus pulled on a greatcoat more nondescript than his usual stylish wont, despite Padget's protest. His valet's objections faded when Janus tucked a pistol into a deep pocket and, collecting his two guards, faded back into the city's streets. He bypassed the stables and carriages, strode out onto the rough oyster-shell drive, and then onto the cobblestoned streets.

He retraced the funeral course, noting that much of the black draping was already gone from the poorer windows, but not from any grand denial of grief, or political disloyalty, no matter how Simpson grumbled it was so. Rather, Janus thought, it was simple penury and a season unseasonably chill. The lower classes of Murne would be blanketed tonight in mourning cloth and clad in cut-down and hastily resewn fabric by daybreak.

The kingsguards might complain about a lack of respect and worry about the national appearance, but Janus saw little difference between pennants flying and black armbands, and a populace clad in stolen blacks. Aris surely never had cared enough about the doings of his people to object to them in death.

Janus turned his steps south toward the scented lanterns of Sybarite Street, just being lit against the earliest taste of twilight; the guards grew uncomfortable, their boot heels shuffling as if they bent their heads close to confer, their pace suffering for it. Janus allowed himself a grin, imagining them foreseeing the scandal sheets full of his impropriety; that in the same week his uncle, his *king*, was laid to rest, Janus worked his leisurely way through the brothels. It would be one way to shift the focus from that unfortunate illustration, though a method Bull wouldn't approve. Nor Gost, either.

It wasn't in him to tease the guards long. He, after all, had no desire to see his name belittled. He turned his steps, heading down toward the older section of the city, the empty manor houses near the quay, and his destination.

"Sir," Simpson said. Janus ignored him until the man said, "My lord," instead. Another skirmish won.

"Yes?" Janus asked promptly and as perfectly civil as if the man had only now spoken.

"Where do we head? If it's beyond Sybarite Street, we should summon more guards. Your safety—"

"Scared of the Relicts?" Janus said. "And you both armed with pistol and sword. Be easy. The neighborhood we go to is not dangerous, merely dangerously unfashionable."

Simpson subsided, and Janus kept his face pleasant with some effort. No wonder the Relicts continued to rot away, if even the guards were feared to go there. That would have to change, Janus thought, and soon. There would be no part of his kingdom he would be unable to rule, no pockets of savages where the only rules obeyed were those that guided beasts: fear, hunger, survival.

He turned his steps westward, toward the district where the

wealthiest of merchants had once lived. Seahook Bay, a sharply curved shoreline of toothy, jagged rocks, which sailors swore were the shed teeth of the serpent god, Naga, it was all but inaccessible from the water. After a few calamitous attempts to build a pier over the rocks, the king of the time, Aris's grandfather, had decreed it unsuitable for a port and concentrated on the expansion of the southern harbor. The merchants, the *wealthiest* merchants, had been less persuaded; and numerous small boats had wrecked on the shore, scattering goods the merchants hadn't wanted to pay tariffs on.

The house Janus made for was the southernmost house, and the one closest to the encroaching sea. The stables had crumbled into the water some time back, and spurred the abandonment of the house. Any closer to the Relicts, and the manor would have been filled to bursting with life; poor families, runaway children, thieves, and other assorted riffraff. But in this particular instance, the abandonment was superficial, the gates were locked tight, and the grounds secure against any would-be squatters.

Janus, at the front gates, turned to face his guards. "Wait here."

"Your—"

"Wait here," he repeated, and reluctantly they stepped back. He might trust them with his life, or at least feel confident he could fight them off successfully; bringing them into his secrets was another thing entirely. Janus unearthed a key from his pocket, an overlarge handful of wooden haft and metal teeth. He inserted it into the lock, and turned it. As the gates rattled into life, pulling back with a mutter of clicking clockwork, Walker jumped and swore, his broad country accent deepening the oath. Janus stepped through, turned a dial, and the gates rolled shut again.

He walked up the drive, boots crunching on shale and shell, and could smell the sea as he approached the house, the sea and more— a subtle taste he had learned to recognize as worked metal and grease, solder and tallow. Behind the house, on the sea, a pale glimmer of a sail caught fire in the setting sun.

Reliable man, Tarrant, Janus thought, before turning to head into the house proper. He let himself through the front door, noticing that the piles of books and journals on the stairs had grown more precarious and that the dining room table, seen through a door propped open with an oblong piece of brass, was littered with papers and pens and glasses.

Drawn in by hopes that matters had progressed further than he had been told, Janus flipped through illustrations of clockwork engineering, a giant pincer of a machine, a chain and winch, and several crossed-out sketches of a frame that had, by the acrimonious and heavily underscored comments in the margin, failed to support them.

"Chry?" the low voice came, and after it, a figure in long skirts. "Janus. We didn't expect you this evening."

"Delight." He nodded in greeting, then said, "I have an appointment with Tarrant, but even without one, I would have come. I'm sick to death of the court."

"Unfashionable words," Delight said. He smiled a little around the cup of tea he had carried out with him; his lips left a red blush on the china.

"Unfashionable household," Janus said, returning the smile to keep any sting from the words. Seahook was not only an ill-favored house in an unpleasant neighborhood, but Delight himself was not the sort to brighten an aristocrat's gathering, not in his skirts and lacy bodices, his rouged lips and blacked lashes.

Delight—Dionyses DeGuerre—had been run out of court years before Janus had arrived in it. It wasn't much he and his brother Chryses had done; they had chosen to attend a notorious gathering, the seasonal courtesan's promenade—the evening fantasia in the well-tended public gardens of Jackal Park when only the courtesans and their chosen escorts were permitted to attend. Chryses had desired to view the season's new beauties and convinced Dionyses to play his female host, allowing them both access to the harlot's court.

The ruse had worked, but Janus had difficulty imagining Delight a successful woman—though he supposed the man had been youthful, willowy, smooth-skinned. From what Delight had said, he had made a more than passable pretty, so much so that Chryses, dizzy with a surfeit of flirtation and drink, turned his attentions to the lady at his side.

Delight, loath to be unmasked and evicted, pushed Chryses off with a laughing promise of *later, later* . . . when presumably they would be less sotted with spirits and sensuality, and could laugh over the mistake.

Only being as this was Antyre, where scandal was eagerly sought, the twins had been recognized by someone willing to spread the tale, putting the most shameful interpretation on it. And as was often the case, the greater the scandal, the greater the listener's willingness to believe. The twins woke from their carousing and found society had closed its door to them. They had lost their homes and their futures: Dionyses had lost his bride-to-be.

It had been the first genuine moment of awkwardness between Delight and Janus, when Delight mentioned that he envied Janus his wife. That Psyke had been promised to him since birth, their estates and families long allied.

Delight's choice to continue wearing the guise that had seen him cast from court bewildered Janus, but it was old bewilderment.

A near year of acquaintanceship had inured Janus to Delight's vagaries, and soothed the faint irritation that though Delight chose to mimic a lady, he made no real attempt to pass as one. Maledicte had been more thorough. But then, Mal had reasons beyond simple spite.

"Do you have time before your meeting with the good captain?" Delight set his teacup down on the pile of books, adding another ring to the stains already present.

"Some small time," Janus said. "The guards will be restless soon." He grimaced. "They're feared of the streets."

Delight blinked slowly at him, his mouth pursing, then said, "You brought guards here? You've spent the past months slipping their lead before you came here. I began to feel like your mistress or your moneylender."

"Before, they reported on my doings to Aris. Aris is gone, and their reports are split among Rue, Bull, and the admiral, who bicker over what they mean. Besides, as I've been accused of regicide, I prefer their company to my own, lest I find myself tried and executed on the streets. Still, you needn't feed them tea. No sense in them becoming too welcome."

"I'm sure if I offered them tea, they would feel anything but comfortable," Delight said. "But look here—" He started rifling through the papers, frowning and muttering as the plans he wanted eluded him. He paused a moment, looking at the sheet in his hand, then fumbled for his charcoals and scrabbled a series of notes in his cramped handwriting.

"Tarrant's waiting," Janus said. "Show me on my return. And, Delight, we need to make a spectacle soon. Gost has expressed interest in a demonstration. Three days hence."

He nodded absently, and Janus sighed. Brilliant, the both of them, Westfall had been right about that, but Janus would trade a small piece of that brilliance for a gift for organization. He left Delight shifting papers from one pile to the next, and stirring his cooling tea with the charcoal pencil.

Janus took the back way down, the rickety stairs that Chryses had shored up with leftover copper wiring and random patches of wood and metal sheeting. It still swayed in the sea breezes, gave him a dizzying view of the rocky beach below. Janus wished, not for the first time, that Tarrant was a little more accommodating and that it was Tarrant's weight on the stairs instead of his. But Tarrant was a sailor through and through, held the land in the same distrust that most farmers held the sea. It served the kingdom: Tarrant had no desire to give up his ship, and he had been the first to cut sail and run rather than turn his ship over to Itarus. It served Antyre well enough, allowed Tarrant to become a weapon against Harus that couldn't be traced to Aris.

Disarmament had been the second article in the Xipos treaty. The first, of course, had been a tithe that Antyre owed Itarus, a full 30 percent of the country's profits.

If Aris, that peaceable scholar, had died in the war, how different Antyre would be.

Janus made it to the bottom of the stairway and saw the dim, shuttered light that let him know Tarrant was already ashore, the narrow dinghy anchored precariously on the one flat spar that reached out toward the distant ship.

"Ixion," Tarrant said, as he approached. "I thought it would be the admiral for sure, with Aris's death so recent. Have to say I wasn't looking forward to that meeting. Ol' Demon's never forgiven my turning pirate. He thought I should have done the same as he, sunk my girl and become a landsman."

"DeGuerre does seem the unforgiving sort. Besides, he's the last man I could send through Seahook's doors. Were I unable to meet with you, I'd send Delight." Janus sat down on the rocks out of the sea spray but close enough for speech. Tarrant was a shadow in the darkness, a man both nimble and bulky. The lantern hanging from a raised hook on the dinghy's prow gave Janus the flash of yellowed teeth in a gray-streaked beard.

"So I'm to keep on, then? I'm not recalled? Good thing, as it happens. You know you've got a dozen or more Itarusine vessels lurking around the sea borders? Not merchant ships either. Took some careful sailing, I tell you, to come this close to shore."

"Unsurprising news but unwelcome," Janus said. "Itarus will be quick to act on the chaos of Aris's death. With no heir officially named—"

"Well that's you, ain't it," Tarrant said. "You're not telling me you'll let that idiot child have the throne."

Such rough support, Janus thought, and wished he could believe it. Tarrant was a man used to dissembling, a good naval man turned privateer at his king's bidding.

"It's a matter for Parliament and the counselors to decide." Janus chose the perfect truth and let all the rest of it remain unsaid, that he intended to make himself the only viable choice.

"I need supplies. I'm nearly out of shot, and the men will mutiny if the larder's not refilled. Permission to keep some of the captured goods for ourselves?"

"Just don't get caught selling them," Janus said. "And if you sell them ashore, make sure none of the goods end up on the Itarusine tithe ships. They'll be hunting supplies also, and I don't like to think what Ivor would say if he found his ships were buying the same merchandise twice."

Tarrant gave him a wry salute and took a long sip from his flask, offered it. "Drink?"

Janus took the flask, raised it up, sniffed, and smiled. Itarusine brandy. He took a grateful swallow, letting it warm the chill from the sea air's kiss.

Tarrant shifted on the strand, pebbles grinding beneath his weight, preparing to go, and Janus found other words tumbling from his mouth, low and urgent. "That other commission I asked of you? Any word?"

It was madness to even ask. It had been anger and grief that had driven him to ask Tarrant the first time, careless words that could doom his reach for the crown. Madness to remind Tarrant of it, yet Janus couldn't help but ask.

Tarrant said, "Precious little," as if he didn't understand how badly Janus needed to know. Discretion or sheer uninterest, Janus didn't know which, and it woke him sweating some nights that he had handed Tarrant such a weapon. But it had always been a failing of his, this inability to let go of something that had been his. To let the past fall gracefully away.

"Your dark-haired youth, scarred at cheek and chest. Sounds distinctive enough, 'til you go and mix in with Itarusine born crews, all crow black and battered. No woman either, tall, dark haired. I assume the scars are the same? And that it's your youth attempting to escape notice?

"Women are rare on ships, at least those that travel more than the distance between Itarus's court and our own. I've heard no gossip about one such."

"There might be a man acting as companion," Janus said. He grudged the words.

"So you said before. Blond, a servant."

"He, at least, should be easy to find," Janus said. "He fancies himself a sailor, and has no reason that I can see for hiding himself away."

"By your indulgence," Tarrant said. "If he knows you at all—well, he might guess at the murder in your eyes and keep his passage quiet."

Janus said, "He only need fear me if he still travels with my black-haired boy, and you've heard nothing? I was certain that they were headed for the Explorations."

"There's your problem," Tarrant said. "The Explorations are full of folk who just wanted to start anew and are willing to pay for the privilege. Gossip only goes so far, even between crews. Your need for discretion hampers me. If you permitted, I could send word ashore to the settlements in the Explorations—"

"No," Janus said.

Tarrant nodded, but there was a certain knowledge in his eyes that Janus would eventually ask for that, as inevitable as a drunkard returning to the tavern. An amused curl took his mouth; he said, "At your leisure, then. I'll be waiting."

Janus couldn't allow that smugness to prevail, nor could he afford to antagonize Tarrant. Fear, he thought, was not an easy currency here. Tarrant would strike rather than bow his head. The best Janus could do was remind him that Janus wasn't the only vulnerable one.

"Your son is well," Janus said. "Settled nicely in the palace and at my side most days."

Tarrant nodded, his voice gone rough. "Piracy's no life for a child. But you tell him I think on him."

"I will," Janus said, and let the matter drop. No need to belabor something they both understood. Instead, he took out the pouch he'd prepared for just this meeting, containing a scatter of currencies and gems such as a pirate captain might be expected to carry.

Tarrant tucked the money pouch Janus handed him into his rope belt and said, "I'd best be going. Tides wait for no one. If you have further instructions, you can leave them for me with the *Gazelle*, as usual. But it may be a fortnight or more before I collect them."

Janus helped him maneuver the dinghy out into the chill water, watched the man push off from the jagged rocks with confidence and long practice.

He climbed the stairs again, more quickly now that he had the tide raising the breeze at his back. He shivered, wet with spray, and when he reached the house, he saw that Delight had had a moment's thought to spare from his notes. A collection of towels and warmed water waited him.

He made use of them, chasing the chill from his hands, wiping the salt from his face, smoothing the damp-born curl from his hair before returning to Delight and the parlor turned tutorial hall.

Chryses had arrived from his spying among the antimachinists, clad in an open linen shirt and hemp breeches, his hair darkened to brown with dirt and sweat and dye. Delight curled beside him, sitting closer than the books piled on the settle required, and sipped his tea.

Chryses scribbled notes on paper with a rough-tipped nib whose sound reminded Janus of mice scratching.

More supplies, Janus thought. Chryses was as rough on his possessions as Maledicte, and Janus grew weary of interpreting blotched and blotted writings.

"Janus," Chryses said. He made to rise, hampered by the welter of Delight's skirts and his own obvious weariness. "How goes it?"

"I spoke to Gost," Janus said, was rewarded by Chryses's exhaustion sharpening to full wakefulness.

"Oh? And what did the lord of all our hopes and futures have to say?" Delight said. He slouched against the high back of the settle in a way that would have had the ladies of the court muttering imprecations on his upbringing.

"Delight," Chryses said. "Gost can—"

"I know," he said, "but I don't like our futures riding on a man known to be a stickler and a prig."

"Better that than one of the useless, uninterested lords," Janus said before Chryses could. "Gost has offered us a platform and a chance to prove our engines to him."

"So gracious of him," Delight said. His mouth turned down. "Does his support truly mean so much?"

"Only the difference between me taking the throne by force or with grace and the will of the majority," Janus said. "An important distinction, I think you'll agree. Celeste Lovesy is my most vocal opponent, DeGuerre a close second. Given time, I can deal with Celeste. Gost, on the other hand, may sway your fath—"

Delight held up a hand; Chryses rolled his eyes. "You avoid his name as if it were the plague, Di."

"He didn't disown *you*," Delight said. "Or do you forget—"

"The admiral then," Janus interrupted. Their squabbles, once rare, had become increasingly more common and more vehement, the stresses of the circumstances wearing on them.

"If we turn Gost to our favor," Janus said, "the admiral will follow."

Chryses paced across the room, threw open the double doors that had led once to a ballroom, and now to the heart of their workshop. The scent of metal and oil overwhelmed the sea fog. "Choose as you will," Chryses said. "Which machine will you rest our future on?"

9

ELIGHT FOLLOWED JANUS AND CHRYSES to the back of the house and through the great double doors. They were oak, darkened with age and exposure to the salt air, and Georgie, their assistant who was equal parts engineer and artist, had carved into them a rough likeness of Weeping Espit, that reluctant patron of creative endeavors. The salt-damp air condensed sleekly in the lines of her robes and her face, and ran wet on high tides. Beyond the door lay the ballroom, overlooking the encroaching sea.

No one danced here any longer; the tiles were buckled where the foundation had shifted with the falling away of the cliff. Now the ballroom was full of hulking metal shapes, drafting tables, and a near constant eddy of paper. The scent of salt warred with that of charcoal and grease, of gas lamps burning at all hours.

So as they entered, Chryses merely turned the key on the nearest lamp, collecting it in their travels through the ballroom. Janus walked as fastidiously as a cat, Delight thought, moving without apparent effort among metal works, wooden frames, and assorted tarpaulin-covered shapes. He paused at the first table, to touch the machine there.

Delight was rather proud of that one. It lacked the grander purpose of their best designs, but it worked reliably and meant money for those who owned it. The small mill was a series of cogs and gears and graduated rotating stones, capable of grinding even the coarsest meal to a fineness that the noble markets would pay highly for, and did so without effort by man. For the farmers who saw their best grain shipped to Itarus, a mill such as this would allow them to make a living off the lesser grains.

Still, Janus passed it by, and Delight wasn't surprised. The mill was useful, but to collect Gost's approval they would need something completely new.

Chryses said, "No, not the mill. Perhaps the shipbuilder, if Delight can weight the arms *properly.*" Delight's attention roused to irritation. He pushed a hank of hair from his face to snap at Chryses, but stopped at the expression on Janus's face. Chryses had taken him by the sleeve, was guiding him around the room as if he were a recalcitrant child; and his hands, covered in dirt, were passing the smudges on to Janus's sleeve.

Delight decided he didn't need to say anything. Given the clear displeasure in every line of Janus's body, he wasn't inclined to hear anything Chryses had to say.

"We have too much labor and not enough jobs; Gost won't be pleased by a machine that encourages the situation to worsen. In any event, our country's shipbuilding skills are not in question." Janus took a tarpaulin off another pile and wrinkled his nose at the sharp alcohol reek beneath. "A still? Do tell me *this* isn't behind your inspiration. Gost's already made it clear he thinks this country needs less drinking and license."

He dropped the tarpaulin back over the mechanism. Delight hid a smile; from the distaste in his voice, one would think Janus an abstemious sort, but he'd shared *Absente* with the two of them often enough, let his eyes go soft and dreaming, building their future in words.

Chryses, always smart, never wise, answered back, voice hot with irritation. "Never mind the still, with regards to the shipbuilder, you miss the point. We have an abundance of labor to be sure, but it's all unskilled. Those with the skill are too busy working to teach. The shipbuilding machine would allow them time to teach the brighter of the unskilled."

"And the rest become crews to staff the ships? No, Chryses, we have enough of our people leaving Antyre for lives abroad. We want something to convince them to *stay*, to convince Gost that we can salvage a future."

"It's a security matter, as well," Delight said. The two of them turned angry glances on him, and Delight busied himself with tying up his skirts, tucking the long hems into the garters beneath his knees. He smoothed his stockings and caught Janus watching, gaze gone puzzled instead of angry, and smiled. He wandered into the hall proper, closer to his brother and Janus, and keeping careful distance from the edges of the machinery. Skirts were a problem but one he had chosen to live with. "Could we risk that the Itarusines would not benefit also? Tarrant tells me that Itarusine sailors have been promised a bonus for any ship plans they can gather."

"Tarrant told you this?" Janus asked.

Delight quirked his lips. "He's been a-sea for quite some time. I think he forgets who and what I am. When he offloads material for us, and takes on our cargo, he often stays for tea and flirtation."

Chryses shook his head. "Be careful, Dionyses."

Delight felt himself surge into the anger Chryses could provoke so easily these days. Words hovered on his lips, accusations whose time for speaking had passed years ago; *Whose carelessness was it that saw me disowned, that put me into this costume?* But that wasn't entirely true. Delight had chosen to keep the skirts at first in answer to the scandal sheets that had dubbed him DeGuerre's Delight; now he kept the skirts to build a layer of obfuscation between his brother and himself. Chryses spent his days in the antimachinist crowd, spying on its charismatic leader, Harm, who claimed his terrible scars were the result of one of Westfall's engines. With company like that, it seemed best that the engineer known to be creating the machines be as distinctive as Chryses was nondescript.

Janus coughed and brought his attention back to the problem at hand. "What about the communication device? Gost's been abroad for a long time, understands better than most the importance of quick information."

"No progress at all," Delight said. He grimaced. "The flashes of light reach farther than flags, but it is still hampered by the same problem. If there's no one in the line of sight, the message drops. It works well enough for inland villages, but you wanted it for the sea. Perhaps . . ."

He fumbled in his pockets for the charcoal again, then recalled he had left it beside the mill. He moved off to collect it and heard Chryses's half-mocking, half-fond mutter, "Head full of inventions, that one."

Chryses stroked a line along an exposed piece of brass tubing, waiting to be cut. "Whatever we choose, it must be sturdy, flame-proof, and easy to defend. Harm's no fool. I've learned that he watched you talking with Gost at the funeral and has spent the past few days urging the antimachinists to be ready to act and act decisively. They think, not unreasonably, that this is the best chance to make their opinions known to the new leaders. They hope DeGuerre and Bull are less supportive of our machines than Aris, Westfall, and you."

Janus bit his lip, obviously annoyed. "This city turns on an engine of gossip. Chry, do you have any inkling where the antimachinists will choose to strike?"

"The demonstration you give for Gost seems likely. Best not have it here, or we'll be burned out by nightfall."

"Gost said nothing about a public event," Janus began, but Chryses's laughter stopped him in mid-speech.

Mistake, brother mine, Delight thought. Janus had a temper at the best of times, and as his frustration soared with each obstacle, it only increased. To laugh at him, flick him on his pride—well, Janus was a young man, after all, and prone to acting on instinct. But he was also thoughtful and dedicated to the kingdom in a way that so few of their leaders were. Hadn't he heard Janus worry aloud about a population growing ever more split between starvation and gluttony? About a country growing ever more stagnant as the doers and thinkers sought their fortunes in the Explorations, where their profits would not be taken by Itarus?

Hadn't Delight watched as Janus tried vainly to rouse the city Particulars into rebuilding the Relicts instead of simply controlling them?

"Of course the demonstration will be public," Chryses said. "How else will Gost gauge the public interest? What else could counter public opinion of you as a murderer when your own wife spoke against you?"

Delight's breath caught. Mewed up in Seahook as he was, he was the last to receive the gossip. He had seen the illustration in the papers, of course, but... "Did Psyke truly speak against you?" he asked.

Janus growled but made no denial. Delight swallowed. If Psyke believed it to be so... *Could* Janus have done it? They'd heard him rail against Aris often enough, calling him a blight, an obstacle to progress, a scholar whose curiosity had been eroded by despair.

Janus was capable of murder, that Delight knew for certain. Hadn't he disposed of the antimachinist who had followed Chryses home, dispatching the man with a single blow of a wrench snatched up from the nearest table before Chryses and Delight could do more than gape? Janus had picked the man up, heedless of blood, and dropped him casually off the edge of the cliff, following him down more sedately on the stairs, to kick the ruined body into the sea.

"Look, Last," Chryses said now, heedless of the man's temper—as if he hadn't watched murder done or never dreamed that wrath could be turned their way. Chryses, Delight thought, was short-sighted and overconfident. Always had been. "I say use the cannons. The remodeled cannons are... showy, and the admiral would approve. We have a full complement of them. A bit of target practice would be spectacular, make Harm and his bullyboys think again about fighting us. It might even make Itarus think twice."

Chryses grinned with easy malevolence, and Delight read the truth of it. Chryses was tired of spending his days playing spy among those who would destroy everything he chose to create.

"No," Janus snapped. "The cannons are for the privateers, and can we afford to have questions raised when Tarrant starts using them?"

"It would be worth it—aim one above the crowd, scare the antimachinists into obedience."

"And have Itarus take notice of our manufacture of weapons?" Janus said. "No, Chryses. Show some sense."

Chryses turned his back, shoulders tight, the very picture of a man muttering imprecations under his breath.

Janus said, "Best not get in the habit of arguing with me. If our plans come to fruition, I will be your king; and while there's always a place for counsel, the decisions are ultimately to be mine."

Chryses whirled on him; the bronze scales behind him rocked and clattered to the floor, spilling gunpowder. "We help you because we helped Westfall. We help you because you promise us a better life. Do you think I enjoy this? I was brought up in the court, had an estate to inherit—one of such size that it took a horse all day to traverse—and now I spend my nights in this pantomime of a court and my days in the company of *rabble*, trying to keep abreast of their intentions. You came from nothing to riches. It's harder in reverse."

Delight moved forward hastily, too hastily; his skirt, even looped to knee height, caught on a pile of levers, tore, and sent him and the metal spilling across the floor. Neither Janus nor Chryses noticed, too intent on each other.

"Sacrifices need be made for a cause," Janus said. "Weather this discomfort now and have—"

"*Sacrifices?*" Chryses said. "Your sacrifices have been conveniently lacking. You live at court, you keep your estate. *You wed Psyke Bellane.* Where's your sacrifice? You don't make sacrifices. You offer others up. Like your lover, Maledicte. Did he believe in your better days?"

Janus said, "Mal trusted me to do what needed to be done."

"Done to death. Did he trust you when you drove your blade into his heart?"

Even Chryses paled as the words left his mouth, suddenly conscious of having gone too far. Janus moved like a lick of flame, hands tight around Chryses's neck. Both men were panting with rage, though Chryses added pain and effort to his breathing.

Idiots, the both of them, Delight thought, and coughed as he rose. He found an empty teacup and spoon, and picked them up, stirring the spoon as he moved forward. The simple, peaceful sound made them both jerk, release each other. Chryses inhaled greedily and rubbed his throat resentfully.

Delight came closer, hoping Janus couldn't see his fingers were tight around the cup, the nervous tremor of his lips stilled between anxious teeth. Delight tried a wavering smile. "I do apologize for my brother. As you say, he lacks good sense."

Janus merely nodded, but the redness on his cheeks seemed less about rage now and more about embarrassment.

Chryses coughed a little and spit red-tinged phlegm at Janus's feet. Delight scowled. "Please, Chryses. The house is ruin enough."

Delight passed the empty teacup to Chryses, who stared at it in sore-throated betrayal, and said, "You never did know when to leave well enough alone. You think on a machine for Gost, and let me talk with our lord and master here."

Delight reached up and tucked a lock of his brother's hair behind his ear; coarse with dye and rough handling, it clung to his fingers, and turned the moment into a caress of a kind they hadn't shared since that one ruinous night. He jerked away.

Delight wrapped his hand around Janus's elbow, succeeding despite Janus's instinctive flinch, still trembling with nerves and temper.

"Forgive me," Janus said. His voice was husky; his head drooped. Delight, after a panicky moment of indecision, put his arms around Janus's shoulders and drew him close.

"Of course," he said. "But your temper will bring you to regret one day, when you kill someone that you need."

Janus shuddered in his arms, hesitantly leaned close, whispered. "Too late for that advice, I'm afraid." Delight touched his hair, stroked it once, and then Janus was pushing away. A chink of glass hitting metal drew both their attention. Chryses let the bottle down from his mouth, and without a word, passed it toward Janus.

Delight nodded when Janus, seemingly unaware of it, glanced at him for . . . what? permission? encouragement? Janus tilted the bottle and took several long pulls of Chryses's homemade brew without more than a grimace.

"Peace between us," Chryses said, though his voice was sullen yet.

Janus nodded, and Delight felt the long-held tension in his body subside. His skirt quivered along the torn section; his muddied stockings drew his gaze, and he bent to rub at them. "Ten lunas gone," he said.

Janus laughed, coughed, and laughed some more. Chryses's face darkened, taking personal offense at Janus's laughter. *No sense,* Delight thought again as Chryses stormed out.

"Laugh too hard and I'll send you shopping for me, and wouldn't that set the cat among the canaries. The Earl of Last buying stockings."

"Don't be ridiculous," Janus said. "I'd send Savne."

Delight had to laugh himself. Janus had described Savne so often and so unlovingly that Delight could imagine it well enough.

He ushered Janus back to the study, pushed aside a stack of papers in front of a cabinet, and unearthed a bottle of Antyrrian whiskey. "Here," he said. "It'll soothe you better than that rotgut Chryses brews."

Janus took the dusty bottle, but made no gesture to drink from it, merely turning it in his hands.

"You should be careful of Chryses," Delight said. "He holds grudges, and I believe you need us more than we need you."

Janus raised his head, infuriated anew. "Your country needs a king. It has no need of a fop who prefers women's clothing."

"So moody," Delight said. "I suppose it's a function of your youth."

"Or perhaps it's a result of my plans being constantly overset or challenged," Janus said. "I swear this kingdom wants nothing more than to be annexed by Itarus."

Delight paused in putting the whiskey away to pour himself a glass. "Are things so disordered as that?" He sipped; he didn't allow himself much in the way of spirits at all. Drunkards made dangerous engineers.

"Could it be anything else?" Janus said. "I needed Aris alive. Failing that, I needed my wife not to accuse me of his murder. My chances dwindle and yet, I must spend time I cannot afford attempting to prove myself innocent of regicide. I'm not at all certain such proof is attainable, unless Ivor's pet assassin can be found and be persuaded to speak out against his master. I have doubts either one will be an easy task."

Delight set down his glass with a decisive clink. "Let Rue worry about Aris's murder. It's his duty, and Rue is a man who loves his duty. You can trust him—"

"When Bull owns him and the kingsguards? Bull is no friend of mine."

"Are you certain?" Delight asked. "I rather thought he was. Though perhaps he's been put off by your temper since Aris's death. When you first came to us, you wore a pleasant mask of civility. What happened to that?"

"It was a mask," Janus said. "They wear, they crack, they fall to ruin."

"That's when you tie the straps tighter and soldier on," Delight said. He swished his skirt over Janus's boots briefly, making his point. "Until your task is done. This is a court of artifice—"

"I know," Janus said.

"You *forget*," Delight said. "Play your games as bloodily as you need but keep a civil tongue and *smile*. At the very least, the ladies will nag their husbands to support your pretty face."

Janus's neck tightened. "Not with Psyke and Celeste Lovesy spreading slander."

Delight sat behind the great desk, traded his glass for a pen, and sketched tiny gears and chains thoughtfully, a ship, a fallen crown, a woman's long hair. His hands stilled. "You say Psyke blames you?"

Janus sighed. "She witnessed the crime. Aris died in her arms."

Delight's lips felt tight, numb. "Poor girl."

"I might have felt pity if she hadn't accused me with all the fervor of a broadsheet sensationalist." Janus dropped into a chair on the other side of the desk; it creaked beneath him.

"Psyke is not imaginative," Delight said, feeling his way gently into this conversation. He had no desire to provoke Janus into another tantrum. It was healthy for neither of them. Still, he couldn't reconcile Psyke with Janus's description. "Or used not to be. I always found her a most rational being."

Janus twitched; his eyes widened and then hooded again. *Oh, Delight* thought. *Janus didn't know they were acquainted.* Sometimes Delight forgot how recent an arrival to the court Janus truly was.

"I saw nothing rational about her," Janus said, "only hatred and rage."

Delight shook his head. "No," he said. "People do not change so much as that. Her feelings may be dark and furious, but her mind is a reasonable place."

"People change in deeper ways than you might think," Janus said. Something in his voice echoed with exhaustion. "Maledicte was not always as he was. It was Ani who shaped him."

"Do you really believe in that archaic nonsense?" Delight asked. "They're wonderful tales, morality plays of a most dubious sort, but nothing more."

Janus shook his head. "Now who's naïve?" he muttered. "I am a logical man, Delight. You know as much. My interests are in the sciences, in the mysteries that can be solved. If I tell you that Psyke's behavior has altered in a profound fashion, you may trust it is so."

"The king died in her company. Reason enough for moodiness," Delight said. His tone or expression must have been forbidding; Janus merely shrugged and let it go. With, Delight noticed, a particularly false smile.

"Will you do one thing for me?" Janus said. "You're better placed than I for research." He shrugged. "I can't even take a meal in peace."

Delight fought a smile; sometimes Janus was more boy than man. "If I can."

"Research the gods for me. Turn your mind to Them. I have questions regarding—"

"Of course, my *lord*," Delight said, letting aggravation and acid etch his tone. "Because I have so many hours free where I'm not attempting to create machines that may save our country's future—"

"Chryses has time to infiltrate the antimachinists *and* to aid your engineering—"

"Less and less," Delight said. "This is the first night he's back before the false dawn—"

"Do as I say," Janus snapped. "Any god but Ani. I want their signs and portents."

Delight bit back his retort; that fixed tension in Janus's jaw was beginning to return. He gentled his voice, "I wouldn't know where to begin, Janus."

"Rosany's Booksellers," Janus said, surprisingly prosaic. "I understand they have a back room for such things. I have an account with them. You can send one of your assistants if you're too shamed to be seen buying religious tracts." That pale blue gaze dropped, traced the line of torn skirt and ruined stocking, and Delight sighed.

"If you insist. Will you tell me why?"

Janus shifted uncomfortably in the leather chair, poked at the gap where Delight had taken wadding from it in a sudden need for such to apply oil to a recalcitrant set of gears. Janus sighed, leaned his head into his hands and peered up with one, tired blue eye. "Something stirs in the palace. I would be ready for it."

"If you're hunting gods," Delight said, "you'll be wasting your time and mine."

Janus sighed again. "Let's not discuss it further." Though it was couched as a request, there was no doubt Janus meant it as a command.

Delight nodded; Janus was tired, Aris was dead, and the Itarusine prince made himself at home in the palace. Likely Janus wasn't thinking clearly. Delight decided he'd send Georgie or Whitsonby, whichever one of their aides came earliest, to collect a handful of tracts to give Janus on his next visit. Likely by then, Janus's common sense would have returned and he'd chuck them straight into the fire. "To business, then. I think the steam-powered boat might be prepared."

At Janus's skeptical look, Delight said, "It hasn't exploded for a week now."

"The last time you tested it?" Janus said.

"A week ago," Delight admitted. "But I've a new idea that should solve the difficulty. It would be something new, and something that can't be seen as a violation of the treaty."

Janus nodded. "I'll leave it to you and Chryses. Find me something special to show Gost. I won't be able to help much. I cannot be away from the palace too long, not while Ivor dwells within the walls."

Delight leaned forward, hopeless curiosity rising in his breast. "Is the prince ascendant truly as terrible as they say?"

"Ivor? He's everything charming," Janus said. "Right up until the moment he steps away from your corpse."

10

PSYKE IXION, COUNTESS OF LAST, was perched on a nursery stool, too low even for her comfort, watching Prince Adiran play with lettered blocks, when the Duchess of Love ran her to ground.

At first, Psyke failed to recognize her as anything but another of the shadowy figures that trailed her and breathed cold words into her ears. But the nursery attendant dropped a hasty curtsy at this black-clad visitor, and when Psyke raised her bare feet from the stone floor, Celeste Lovesy stayed, while the other shadows vanished.

Whatever madness plagued her, Psyke thought, it was remarkably consistent. Let her skin touch anything of earth—stone, soil, wood—and ghosts lingered in her sight. Yet to divorce herself entirely from the earth caused her inexplicable pain. She rocked on the stool, its legs wobbling beneath an adult's weight, and she set her feet down again.

Aris's shade returned, though the others—faceless entities nebulous enough to actually be shadows were it not for the lack of light to cast them—had faded away. Nearby, Adiran pushed blocks together with a careful determination that was new, sorting them instead of simply piling them one atop another.

"Psyke," the duchess said, but all Psyke's attention was on Adiran, on the blocks that were slowly spelling out *papa*. Sir Robert had been in the nursery earlier, testing the boy's reflexes, his responsiveness, and pronounced the boy's condition improving. Psyke saw evidence of it herself. What neither the doctor nor her own observation had gathered was any reason *why*.

The duchess pinched her arm, the crystal-tipped gloves sharp and painful even through Psyke's thin, wool sleeve. She jerked her arm away, rubbing the tiny injury and noting that Adiran had paused to watch them warily.

"Do come along," the duchess said. "I wish to speak to you in more congenial surroundings."

"Adiran should not be left alone—"

"There are guards aplenty," the duchess said. "The boy will bide."

Psyke cast a last glance about the room, at the boy huddled into his tight, defensive knot, arranging blocks as if the words formed could protect him—*papa, papa,* and some blocks newly lettered in a childish hand when the illustrated blocks had lacked the proper letters—and at the dancing shadows through the window, birds darting and swooping, their nest disturbed.

The duchess snatched at Psyke again, and Adiran tensed, his soft mouth tightening into an unhappy frown. Psyke rose to her feet, brushing her skirts, and followed the duchess out of the nursery, rather than upset Adiran.

Expecting Celeste to guide her into one of the many empty rooms along the hallway, Psyke found herself stumbling instead down the main stairs, past the throne room and antechamber and outside into the pillared arcade. She blinked in the daylight, the crisp spring air with a few lingering hints of smoke from the cool night previous.

Psyke leaned back, breathed deep, but the sun and the sky failed to lift the weight on her skin. Her shoulders ached dully, as if the black bombazine she wore were heavy enough to bruise her flesh. The duchess's carriage waited; the duchess, handed up into the coach, tapped her foot once. Psyke straightened her shoulders, and took the coachman's hand.

The coach moved slowly through the crowded streets, giving Psyke a view of the public's mood. The wealthy merchants waiting to see the regent or regents—or whoever they could voice their worries to—had faces writ with confidence or concern. The general rabble of pickpockets, gamesmen, and harlots preying on the crowds were all focus and determination: Who knew when such ripe pickings would walk the streets again, and so distracted? But there were a disturbing number who left the carriage's path wearing masks of quiet fury. Men who looked like displaced farmers. Beyond them, jostling and picking fights, were the young men of several classes who had nowhere to direct their ambition in the overcrowded city.

Aris had tried to quiet this aimless hunger in recent months by allotting each ship that sailed for the Explorations a handful of open berths, a spur to those seeking life and profit elsewhere. It had been one of the few points she and Aris had quarreled on: What kingdom could benefit by its people fleeing it? But Aris had only accused her of listening overmuch to Janus, and dismissed her concerns.

The jolt and clatter of the coach wheels smoothed to a hum as the coachman guided the horses into Garden Square, where the pavement was smooth as tile to provide a gentler ride for those of the most genteel blood. Psyke, looking curiously about her, saw mossy stone walls behind the homes, hiding the elaborate private gardens that gave the square its name and the cachet of the most sought after residences.

How often had Psyke heard her mother say that if only they lived in Garden Square all her daughters would be wed and wed well, that there was nothing for eliciting proposals like a young girl in a bower of roses. Gwena, Psyke's youngest sister—brittle tempered, always quick to defend herself from slights, imagined or otherwise—had retorted that the young ladies of Garden Square had more than a backdrop of flowers to their advantage—they had extraordinary dowries, and if their mother would be so kind as to oblige—

The Lovesys had held ownership of their Garden Square manor for six generations. Amarantha Lovesy, Celeste's daughter, married so briefly to Michel Ixion, the former Earl of Last, had brought nearly thirty thousand sols with her to the marriage, as well as several priceless pieces of personal jewelry. Psyke knew the amount of the dowry exactly; Janus had told it to her once, giving her an explanation for Celeste Lovesy's hatred that had little to do with Maledicte or Amarantha's murder.

Greed, Janus declared, was the duchess's driving force, not grief.

After all, at Amarantha's death, and the former earl's death, Janus had inherited it all.

Psyke's fingers clenched on her skirts, remembering with a cold shock that in her jewel box, she had Amarantha's best parure. Janus had brought the set to her, its necklace composed of elaborate links of alternating sapphires and pearls.

He'd left it for her, awkwardly, in the first days of their marriage, with a comment that they suited Psyke far more than they had ever suited Amarantha, whose beauty, he claimed, was too hard for bright stones. Psyke had been appalled at the tactlessness that gifted her with a dead woman's most recognizable jewels and at the furtive pleasure she felt that Janus admired her at all. The pleasure had lasted until she realized the other set famously worn by Amarantha—gold pieces with onyx and ruby—Janus had gifted elsewhere.

Now Psyke gritted her teeth, feeling the fool. The onyx and ruby parure, or what was left of it, had resurfaced the day they moved from Lastrest, the country estate, to the palace. The stones had been pried out, the gold twisted and broken by a too-hasty hand and discarded in a linen room. With Aris's death fresh in her memory, Psyke redrew the past. Janus had given the parure to Maledicte—a bizarre gift for a young man, but Ani was crow enough to be fond of glitter. Psyke groaned, and Celeste condescended to acknowledge her presence for the first time in many minutes.

"Whatever is it that pains you?"

"Maledicte dwelled at Lastrest and I didn't notice. I could have stopped it all. If only I'd been less blind, Aris might live." She rolled her head, fought tears.

"Don't dramatize yourself, girl," the duchess said. "Maledicte is dead."

"Maledicte killed Aris."

The carriage halted at the Lovesy mansion, and the coachman came to open the door. The duchess said, "We need to refine your strategy. Maledicte's name is good for waking fright in those too dull to be roused any other way—"

"It's true," Psyke said, though the passion was already gone from the retort.

Celeste merely sighed. "What does it matter whose hand it was; Janus is to blame. That we can agree on. Your husband is all things malignant, and worse, he has been very industrious. Petitioning Parliament for funds for his disgraceful privateers, his silly experiments, food for the rabble. I never thought to find myself grateful for an Itarusine presence here, but without Prince Ivor, Last would be further ahead in his plans."

"Ivor's no gift," Psyke said.

"Don't be argumentative," the duchess said, finally allowing the coachman to hand her down. "It's unbecoming."

Left with only Celeste's retreating back, Psyke hesitated in the carriage, irritated and contemplating commanding the coachman to drive her back to the palace. The coachman coughed, an arm outstretched to take her weight. "Your hand, milady. The horses wait on you."

She scrambled out of the coach, feeling like a debutante who had just fallen headlong over her hem before an audience. Stone chips stung her feet. The duchess had whisked her away from the palace so swiftly, that Psyke had forgotten she had spurned her slippers.

As Psyke trotted to catch up with the duchess's longer strides, the woman turned a brittle smile on her. "Without Ivor to goad him, to distract him, Janus might pay more attention to Bull and DeGuerre. As it is, he has merely dismissed them as weak, apparent from the manner in which he deals with them. But should he gain some sense—both men are easily wooed. Admiral DeGuerre, for one, is watching Janus most carefully—always jealous that the title went to his brother's family. Janus could own him simply by declaring the Marquis DeGuerre's exile permanent and the title passed to the admiral's side of the family."

"Aris is dead—murdered," Psyke said. She walked past overgrown climbing roses that snagged her skirts. She paused to free herself from the thorns. The roses were white, mostly withered, and scentless; the thorns pricked her fingers. "The admiral would not collude with a regicide simply for a title."

Celeste swept through the doors opened by two curtsying housemaids. "Don't be naïve, girl; you are too old for schoolgirl dreams and in too important a position. Men have always bartered with their enemies when it suited them. Aris's court has been static and small natured, ambitious men locked into petty struggles. His death opens the door for change. Fortunes rise or fall in times such as these."

Psyke was silent, thinking about it. She turned automatically toward the open parlor door, caught in years of tradition. An afternoon call, no matter the circumstance, meant the parlor and tea, perhaps a stroll in the gardens after if the weather was particularly fine. Celeste reached out and took her arm, cozed it against her side. "The dining hall upstairs, please. I have something to show you.

"I think our time to stop Janus is limited. Did you mark Gost and Janus at the graveyard together?" At Psyke's nod, Celeste continued. "Gost can increase Janus's power immensely."

"He's been out of the court for years," Psyke said, but the flash of angry disappointment in Celeste's eyes made her stop, pull her arm free, and think. She traced the carvings on the banister, imagining the elaborate curlicues as Janus's plans, twisting behind the scenes. "Gost might support Janus simply because he . . . doesn't know Janus," she said, "only the rumors, which are easy to discount for a man who is notoriously fond of fact."

"Exactly," Celeste said. "After ten years among the ascetics in Kyrda, turning their frivolous child prince into a man of well-restrained power, Gost has been vocal about disliking what he's seen on his return. A court in twilight, fading away. We must show Gost that Janus's schemes are flawed, dangerous, and that Janus is the spit of every wolf that threatens our kingdom."

"How?" Psyke said. "Gost tends to impatience with females."

They entered the dining room, and Psyke's question fled her mind. Suddenly she was no longer sure she wasn't lost in another vivid nightmare. The Duchess of Love bestowed a benign smile on her, and moved to the table and the thing on it.

Her gloved hands, jet crystals dangling from the fingertips, made tiny, melodic chimes as she stroked the tabletop, over the skeleton that was laid out as tidily as if it were nothing more than a place setting. The linen tablecloth browned where the sodden bones pressed and the marrow leaked.

Psyke pressed her shivering back against the doorframe for support. Her shoulders throbbed, and there came an instant of silence that engulfed her body, leaving her stranded in a space as soundless as the grave. She thought she heard a tiny, pained whisper rising from the bones before Celeste's voice broke through, as calm as if the table were set for dinner. "Now that the gods have returned, if one can so judge by Ani's presence in Mirabile and in Maledicte, we shall have divine aid in ridding our kingdom of the blight—"

Psyke found her voice, or what was left of it. She said, "You can't mean to call upon Ani! It was Her doing that Maledicte became a threat at all."

"Calling on Her would be inappropriate and, as it stands now, unnecessary. We have other means at our disposal."

Psyke held back, wanting to leave, afraid of the fervor in Celeste's eyes. A breath of air, a draft in the pleasant room, made Psyke feel as if someone had come to stand beside her. She wished someone had so that she could turn, shelter her face in a strong shoulder. Avoiding the bones decaying on the table, her gaze sought refuge elsewhere but found no relief: the sideboard held knives and age-spotted tracts with lurid covers of men dying in agony.

"Come, come," the duchess said. "Come see, here is your fear undone—Maledicte gone to mortal clay—and we will use it against his own lover."

Closer to the body, a smudgy shimmer seemed to rise from the bones, like a ripple of air on an overhot day. In contrast, the cool draft moved more silkily about Psyke, resting against her skirts and ringleted hair without disturbing them. That whisper came again, borne in her bones and blood.

"It's not Maledicte," she said, her voice a distant surprise even to herself. "It's witchcraft you've planned, bones that have been touched by the gods to power your spells, but this—this was just a boy."

The history of flesh coated the bones even as she spoke—a young man, peak faced, with dark hair, a gaping wound in his chest and surprise in his expression. Having dressed his bones in flesh, she undressed his past piece by piece. A city lad, prone to consumption, like his mother, like his father, and sold to the country—

For his health, a shadow breathed in her ear, a cold, furious whisper. *Or so they told him.*

—and farming was hard, so hard, too hard, and there were riches back in Murne, so he packed his best shirt, stole a pair of good breeches from the farmer, and sought the city again. The ships caught his eye—

No intelligent captain takes a boy like that on, the voice continued, *too sickly, too pretty. It's nothing but trouble.*

—and no one wanted him except the brothels, so he learned to shrug the pain and shame off; with enough cheap *Absente* to drink, he learned to like it—

A familiar story and save the ending, too dull to be borne, the voice whispered, insinuating. *His looks attracted the wrong man, and he found a blade in his heart. He found a lord asking for him, a shining man with blond hair, eyes bright blue.* Psyke disliked the arch amusement of this ghost, a voice familiar but unrecognized, tried to shy away. Her face felt hot, her skin cold. Her mouth was as dry as if she had been eating clay.

Pain burst against her arm, the sharp edge of crystals pressing into her soft skin. The images, the whispering ghosts, blew away like smoke, taking all that knowledge with them. She blinked at the duchess standing beside her and repeated the only thing she knew. "It's not Maledicte."

The duchess's hands tightened again, and Psyke thought the crystals must be causing Celeste pain as well as they gouged her fingertips. The woman's lips compressed as tightly as her grip. "These are the very bones that hung above the palace. I paid the guards a fortune to divert them from the grinders and the sea tides. They are Maledicte's—"

"They are the bones of a prostitute, likely murdered so that his hair, his bones could be sold to decadent noblemen and women as gruesome conversation pieces. Here, my dear, you must see . . . the very bones of Maledicte, the murderer. . . ." Psyke said, acid mockery scouring her throat. She yanked her arm out of the duchess's grasp, heard the fabric rasp free. "They have no power over him at all."

The duchess stared at her in such a way that Psyke thought if she were the woman's daughter, she would have had her ears boxed. "You have always been a fanciful girl," she said, though their worlds had never mixed. Still, it was clear that the duchess had a marked preference for her own assumptions. "There is a time and place for stories, but you have long outgrown it."

The duchess swept over to the bellpull, and gave it a firm yank. When the maid appeared, she kept to the doorway as if she couldn't wait to be dismissed from the room; skeletons, Psyke thought, were no doubt an inexplicable change in their routine.

"Bring us fresh water," the duchess said. The maid bobbed her head and disappeared without a word. She tapped her hand against her skirts, a rustle rasp three times, and a scrabble of nails on wood responded, as her little lapdog leaped off a chair and came to her.

The duchess placed the little dog on the table; it squirmed and wagged its stubby tail, climbing over the bones until she urged it to lie down.

The maid returned with a crystal decanter on a tray, two goblets, and a tiny bowl. At the duchess's imperious nod, she put it down on the table, though the tray rattled as she reached the bones.

The duchess reached into the rib cage of the skeleton, removed a small piece of chalk. "It's been resting in the place of his black heart," she said, "and should be quite steeped in poison by now."

"It's harmless," Psyke said, but she watched as the duchess tipped the chalk into the decanter, removing her glove and tossing it away as if it had been contaminated. She swirled the water, raised it to cloudy sediment, seemed bewildered that there was no quantifiable change—*rank superstition*, Psyke's father would have said, and the chill of disapproval in his voice marked the return of the cool weight at her back.

That other voice, the one Psyke knew she would recognize if she only allowed herself to, sneered and said, *Wrong materials. She might as well spit in it and expect her own hatred to do the job.*

The duchess poured the water into the crystal bowl and set it before her dog. Psyke drew back in surprise and distaste. The pained satisfaction on the duchess's face said the lady expected the poison to work; she would prove Psyke wrong though it would cost her a beloved pet.

The dog lapped, splashing water over its fuzzy muzzle and across the linen cloth. When it was done, it leaped down and frisked about the duchess's feet, worrying at the beadwork on her skirts.

After several minutes, the duchess reached down with a hand that shook, and collected her dog to her breast. She smoothed its cotton-fluff fur with her bare hand; it chewed on the crystal-tips of her glove and growled.

Psyke found herself talking again, channeling that sneering, unwelcome voice. "Witchcraft was your only plan? Hardly what I would expect of a lady of your stature. Are your wits all geared to the lesser battles of bad manners and scandalous dress? No stomach for striking one's enemies head-on?" The voice faded away as rapidly as it had overtaken her, leaving her dizzy and faint. She leaned her weight on the back of a carved chair, her fingers stroking the soothing scrolls of painted wood until her heart slowed.

"Mind your tone," the duchess said, though it was pro forma and had no real heat behind it. She rang the bell again, and when the maid reappeared, she said, "Dispose of that." The sweep of her hand encompassed the mess of water, the crystal decanter, the bowls, and the skeleton itself.

The maid looked dismayed and no wonder, Psyke thought, faced with such a chore, but the duchess began speaking again. "If guile will not serve us, we will have to act directly, and that is a more chancy prospect. Your husband is not foolish enough to leave us an easy avenue of attack."

"Need we attack him at all?" Psyke asked. "Captain Rue will find proof against him, and the court will judge him. We only need keep him from killing Adiran—"

The duchess's face froze into a mask of perplexity and disapproval. "Vacillation is a sign of a weak mind, Psyke. I am perfectly capable of judging him, proof or no proof, and I would think you able to do the same. Judge your husband by the caliber of his enemies— right-thinking men like Hector DeGuerre, like *Aris*—and by those he deems friends, killers like Maledicte."

Psyke frowned, let her gaze fall to her skirts. Was the duchess right to act so swiftly? Psyke thought of Adiran in the nursery, of

Janus discovering the boy's unaccountable improvement, and imagined the bloodshed that would result.

"You have a plan?" Psyke asked. She felt oddly disloyal, and chastised herself for it. Janus might have been kind to her in the past, gentle with her, but it had been a sham, a pretence to distract her from the truth that Maledicte lived. Janus had killed her king, had lied to her, had . . .

Killed her, a shadow whispered. Psyke shuddered but remembered those strange, cold dreams, and the effort it had taken to wake.

". . . will continue my research," the duchess said, her skirts flaring as she turned away from Psyke, leaving her with the nagging sense that she had missed her cue. "If these bones played me false, well, there is another to be unearthed. In the interim, I suggest you gentle your husband, so that, like my pup, he will take poison from your hand." She collected one of the philosophical tracts and left the room.

Psyke followed, but diverged from the duchess's path to tell the duchess's coachman to return her to the palace. Once safely enclosed and hidden by the black drapes covering the windows, Psyke let her posture slump, her tears rise. Janus was a threat to Adiran, to the kingdom—his ambition trumped any ideals he spoke. He had to be stopped. But, oh, she hated the duchess's eager grasping for the gods and their cast-offs. Psyke had seen the gods at work, seen Mirabile, aided by Black-Winged Ani, murder her friends, her family.

Psyke believed the problems of men should be solved by men.

She leaned forward and put her face in her hands. She had wanted the Duchess of Love to agree with her, to aid her against Janus; she had that now, but the taste of triumph was bitter.

11

PRINCE IVOR SOFIA GRIGORIAN HAD intended to make another attempt on the nursery but found himself turned back by a guard at the base of the stairs. Rather than cause a scene, Ivor merely shifted his goal, heading for the open pavilions where the nobles gathered and gossiped. Mid-afternoon and the scandal was being passed as freely as the tea and cake. Rumors blew on the breeze, brushing against eager ears and dispersing as quickly as they had come.

Ivor sat down in a low chaise near a wide window overlooking the gardens, smiled at Lady Secret, sitting nearby like an overblown peony. Fifteen minutes later, Ivor was coaxing out the rumors he wanted to hear most, the ones centering on Prince Adiran.

The stories overlapped, contradicted, built on one another: *The boy was witless and always had been. The boy had been shamming for years, dilatory by nature. The boy had been hidden, Aris's secret weapon, or victim of Aris's paranoia. The boy was recovering, through Sir Robert's medicine, through Aris's tender care, through intervention by the gods. . . .*

The rumors spun endless variations on a single tune: The prince might be fit to rule.

Ivor found it hard to accept; he had seen the boy. The prince had been brought down to dinner often enough, as if he were a son to be proud of, instead of weak and soft and simple as an infant.

Grigor would have made quick work of any son born so flawed. The icy waters that surrounded Itarus were a boon to families who wished such burdens gone discreetly.

But the Antyrrian softness benefited him. Without Adiran, Aris's death would have put Janus squarely on the throne. With Adiran ... well, Janus was forced to play Ivor's game, a tangle of politics, politesse, and power.

Ivor hid his smile—the lord on his right was bemoaning a lost wager—by studying the glossy tiles at his feet, a mosaic of a sea serpent speared by Antyrrian sailors.

Janus Ixion thought himself clever, thought himself worldly and competent. Perhaps by the standards of the Antyrrian court he was. But Ivor had been playing this game far longer and his stakes were equally high: if he rid Antyre of Janus, there was a throne to be won.

Quick footsteps pattered over the tiles, the soft pad of smooth-soled shoes, and Ivor turned in time to see a palace page bowing before him. "Prince Ivor, I've a message. . . ."

The quick tumble of dark hair; slim, pale neck; and a single piercing eye, black as a raven's—Ivor's breath caught, for once startled out of his poise. Though his throat felt dry, his hands were steady as he sipped his tea. "I'm sure it can wait," he said. The page nodded, and faded away. The nobles about him, gossip hounds all, had never bothered to raise their heads.

Had Janus been here ... Ivor's teacup chattered quietly as he set it down.

He forced himself to participate in another round of gossip—this centered on the Countess of Last and her erratic behavior—though he wanted nothing more than to leave, to chase the page. But nothing drew attention so much as a man attempting to avoid it.

Recovering, he made his farewells, and sought a less traveled corridor to have the inevitable conversation in. As he passed the audience hall, where petitioners usually waited to speak to the king, the page fell into step beside him, a slim, gray-clad shadow.

Ivor ducked into the nearest private nook, one of many arranged to be convenient to the audience hall for the times when a petitioner might find himself suddenly needing new information, yet reluctant to cede his position in line. As long as a man didn't dally in the nook, his place would be waiting, held by a palace servant.

The room was near as small as a servant's bedroom, though considerably better appointed. A single brocaded chair devoured most of the space, and Ivor sat in it, the fabric rasping against his clothes, his skin.

The page drew the curtains closed behind her.

"I cannot afford to be seen with you," he said. "Be quick with your explanations. I thought you a-sea by now."

She leaned on the wall opposite, though in such close quarters it meant only that she leaned her body away from his; her ankles in neat palace slippers, rested between his own. Overall the poise bespoke her comfort with him rather than her obedience. When her first words, then, were not her excuses, but rather discursive commentary, he was not as surprised as a prince should have been.

"I think you forget who I am," she said. "There's no wrong done in a page speaking to a noble. Even a noble like yourself."

"You are no page, no matter how well you wear the guise." The small spots of ink on her gloves took the temper from his response. For her to go to that extent, to ape not only the clothes of a page but also to take on some of the hazards of always being handed parchments wet with ink, reminded him of her devotion to duty. She would have a reason for lingering in Murne.

"True," she said. "Nor am I a guard, a maid, or a merchant making a delivery, though I have been all of those today. A palace is not an easy place to remain unseen, unless you give them something to look at."

"Oh yes," he agreed, all silken anger rising. "And to be all those things when you wear an eye patch—how unnoticeable is that? When Rue searches for my one-eyed valet who flirted with a stable boy on our arrival."

"I did no such thing," she said. "As for the guises?" She shrugged her head forward, slipping back into the page's subservient hunch in answer. Her hair covered much of her face, and he sighed.

"Guard wore a helmet," she said. "Maid a bonnet, and the merchant? Well, he was quite a *dashing* merchant and wore vast quantities of feathers hanging low from his cap."

He gritted his teeth, and she stepped away from the wall, coming forward and settling in his lap. After a quick glance at the closed curtain, he rested his hands on slim hips. "You cannot afford to be seen. There was a witness."

Her confidence faltered. She licked her lips, bent her head in true discomfort. "There was," she whispered. "I saw her briefly, before it all changed. Ivor, you must be careful."

"Of Lady Last? She saw you, but her own fears took root and so she saw the one you resemble so greatly. Mal—"

His assassin placed a quick, hard hand over his mouth. "No. Say no names associated with those above and below. They take an interest."

Ivor felt his heart skip a single beat, a visceral reaction to the obvious fear in her voice. He drew back, freeing his mouth; her nails scraped lightly across his shaven cheeks. "They? Go on."

"I saw Lady Last." She continued, her voice going quieter and quieter until he was listening with his forehead pressed to hers, as if her meaning could be carried to him by vibration. "She stepped into shadow and one of the five gods woke and embraced her. She disappeared before my eyes."

"And you're sure your dread over the task didn't influence you to fear immortal judgment? You made rather a mess of things, I understand. Not least by your continued presence here."

"I did go down to the sea, I swear on my unspoken name, I did. But I had to rid myself of Challacombe first, and the god confounded me so that the tunnels twisted. By the time I reached the port, my fisherman was gone, and the docks were crowded with the Particulars and kingsguards."

The young woman rubbed her arms briskly, as if she felt that morning chill again, the brisk sea air.

"So I came back to your side, fearing that net more than the palace. Everyone knows an assassin must flee. . . ."

Her composure faltered, her manner with it. No longer a coquette, a page, or invisible servant, she pressed her face to Ivor's neck. He petted her hair absently.

"I cannot keep you here," Ivor said now, thinking of possessiveness and the flaws it created. "No matter what guise you wear. Captain Rue's guards are everywhere, and Lady Last shows a distressing familiarity with the back ways of the palace, depriving you even of those hiding places. No, we need a safer harbor for you, a position, and a—"

"No name," she warned him. "No name at all."

He shook his head at her. "I'm not like to forget that. But there's a grand difference between not having a name and playing an incognita."

She thumped her head on his shoulder. "You make my head hurt. Let me stay, be your valet, unseen in your quarters."

"When the kingsguards take every opportunity to enter? No, I have a new ally in mind, and you will go to her. The Duchess of Love hates Janus so greatly she will turn no aid away if she thinks it will rid Antyre of him."

He stood, forcing her from his lap; she kept possession of his arm, her fingers tight against the fine wool, creasing it.

"*Please*," she said.

The clinginess displeased him but it wasn't unexpected. Ever since he'd found her, the sole survivor of a burned-out Exploration village, she'd followed him as faithfully as a hound.

He shook his head, removed her grasp from his sleeve. "You know I cannot."

"It was hard," she said, all bravado stripped clean. Her voice wavered. "It was so hard." The assassin folded herself into the deep creases of the curtain like a child finding solace from a nightmare; her hair clung to the nap like spiderwebs, left trails of shadow behind.

"You succeeded. Do not doubt yourself now." Paper rustled in the crease between arm and seat, and Ivor teased out a piece of waxed paper, frowning at the fragment of crimson sugar caught in it. Adiran was partial to such sweets which left his lips painted with dyed sugar, but Ivor hadn't thought the boy roamed so freely.

"The pistol failed me and all I had was the sword." Her breath rasped, on the verge of tears, and Ivor gritted his teeth. "For all your instructions you never warned me how it would feel to drive metal through—"

"There is no warning adequate to that task," he said. "The deed is done. Forget it, lest you grow overwrought."

When she looked inclined to nurse her hurts, he said, "Lady Last allowed her emotions to overcome her sense and what has it gained her?"

She shifted forward, drawn into question and answer, as he had intended. "Gained her . . . She made a mistake. She let old fears resurface and thought me Maledicte."

"A costly mistake," Ivor said, "and one that turned the pursuit on Janus. Psyke's mistake aids us." He took her hands in his, drew her close again, rested her head against his chest, played out schemes in the tangled strands of her hair between his fingers. "Her aid, inadvertent as it is, could shift against us. Psyke concerns me all out of proportion."

"She woke a god," she said, words muffled not only by the layers of cloth she breathed them into but by her caution.

"Which one? Blood, death, betrayal, despair; all of them wake for such. And the rooks—"

"The rooks fly about the palace," she finished. "Black-Winged Ani's eyes."

"As you are mine," he said.

She tapped the patch over her eye with a rueful humor. "But flawed."

He raised her face to his, kissed her lips, her cheek, and mouthed the leather that shielded her ruined eye. "You see clearer with one eye than many do with two. You, after all, have learned how to see beyond expectation."

She preened beneath his attention, his praise; her back straightened, the miserable tension in her face eased.

"Go then, join the duchess's household. Watch over our disconcerting Lady Last." He tweaked a long lock of her hair, and said, "Best wear a veil."

She stepped away, straightening her crumpled page's tunic, sleeking her hair to fall just so, shaking the personality from her bones until she was only another invisible servant scampering off on some urgent chore.

Ivor followed after a discreet few minutes, well pleased with himself. Who would have thought that having his assassin fail in her escape would prove so useful? With her in the duchess's house, he would hold his people in the palace, in the aristocratic circles, and in the streets. The Antyrrians feared his fleet? Let them. He had a small army already on their shores.

IT WAS FULL DARK AND past his stated time for return when Janus and his guards arrived back at the palace. As a sop to Simpson and Walker, who were uneasy at traversing the darkening streets afoot, Janus had hailed one of the coaches that traveled between the better-heeled districts and the more dangerous streets that promised the very best in vices.

The hired coach released them at the near edge of the palace, the coachman's pallor a clear sign that only now did he realize who his passenger had been: the palace's murdering bastard.

Janus paid the coachman and moved toward the dark gardens, following the lure of gentle fragrance and the softness of lawn underfoot, the guards reluctantly behind him, though Janus caught Simpson's exasperation before the man masked it with obedience.

The garden walk took him near the nobles' ballroom, unlit for the first time since Janus's return to Antyre. It seemed that even the frivolous nobles drew the line at dancing when the king had been murdered.

Janus wondered how long their restraint would last. As long, he supposed, as they could applaud themselves for it.

He veered away from the walk that led past the ballroom's balconies, through the king's maze. The night was full enough of memory; every step reminded him of the night he'd found Miranda turned Maledicte, not waiting for Janus to find her but coming to meet him.

Delight and Chryses reminded him too much of what it had been like, to be in unity with another person. Quarrelsome or not, they returned to each other again and again, and Janus envied them that. He'd had that once.

His path toward the rear of the palace woke a challenge from a kingsguard more alert than others. The young man tapped his sword hilt against the stone balustrade, the sound alerting the other guards, but more discreetly than the rasp of a drawn sword would have done. Janus paused in his path up the wide, shallow stairs to note the young man's face. A bit more clever than the rest.

The guard's query was half begun when the lamplight, bleeding outward, illuminated Janus and his escorts, and the young man turned his challenge into welcome. "My lord."

Janus nodded, and entered through the wide glass-paned doors into Aris's study. The warmth of the room enveloped him, making him belatedly aware that the evening had been chill. For a moment, he was caught up in a bone-deep gratitude that he knew a home out of the cold; even if they treated him with suspicion, no one denied he had the right to be there.

Janus poured himself whiskey, a bare splash against the crystal tumbler. Simpson and Walker were replaced, their shift done, and two new faces came to stand on either side of the inner door into the palace.

"Wait outside, please," Janus said. The guards nodded and vanished.

Janus set down his drink with a last, appreciative touch to its heavy crystal rim. He trailed his fingers along the wood of the desk, admiring the sheen, glossed with the weight of age, of five kings who leaned over it to work on matters of state.

A lamp dangled crystals around its central core, refracting light in tiny shards across the carpet and dancing in the empty fireplace. Two prisms had been unhooked, lay loosely on the desk, their surfaces smeared by sticky fingers. Janus picked one up, matched the smears to the ones on the candy dish on the edge of the desk. Janus recalled Aris sitting at the desk, Adiran lying on the thick carpet beyond, eating toffees and fur in equal measure as he interspersed candy nibbling with petting Hela.

Janus felt his lips twist. Adiran hadn't been out of his room since Aris's murder, victim of Rue's new caution. Janus thought they might as well let the boy breathe fresh air; Aris's death was proof enough that assassins could lurk anywhere.

Janus took out the tiny key he kept secured inside his waistcoat. He wasn't certain that Bull or DeGuerre knew he had it, though they had expressed irritation with the results more than once.

The key slipped easily into the locked tray of the desk and Janus pulled out the day's correspondence—loose drafts of statements directed to the Parliament and a thick sheaf of paper written in High Antyrrian with his name, worrying and identifiable, in the midst of unfamiliar words. Worse yet was Bull's comment in the margins, laconic: *Let 'em whistle for it. We continue as we are.*

Janus folded the sheets over, tucked them into his pocket just as a scratching came, mouselike and low, on the door. Evan followed the sound, ducking his tousled head beneath the guard's arm.

"No one said you was back," Evan said. "But Walker's in the kitchens, making eyes at his girl, and so you had to be here."

"Or they'd murdered me in the streets," Janus said.

Evan checked in his path to the desk, visibly judging Janus's mood. A smile brightened the boy's face as he recognized Janus's dry humor and came to stand beside him.

"I'm s'posed to get you to your rooms."

"I'm familiar with the palace," Janus reminded him and Evan grinned, white teeth in a red-cheeked face.

"Well, then you'd better hurry. That valet's having nine types of fits and you're gonna be late for supper."

Janus fluffed the boy's hair. "One of the benefits of being blood," he said. "Cook'll wait on my arrival. I'll be unpopular, but I won't go hungry."

He caught Evan's sidelong glance at the candy dish, still half full, and gave Evan a few pieces. "Didn't I give you a full handful earlier this week?"

Evan shrugged.

Janus smoothed the boy's tufty hair, tilted his face up to him. "What, did you find a maid or bootboy to share them with?"

Evan blushed, a deep mottled embarrassment, and more, the first honest discomfort Janus had seen. "Who *are* you sharing with?" If the boy who understood no barriers, no rank, was conscious of wrongdoing . . . "Evan?"

"The prince," Evan said. Janus imagined Ivor stooping down to take Evan's outstretched hand, selecting the best piece of candy with careful deliberation, and listening to the boy's chatter with an attentive ear. Evan had his own uses to a man who collected gossip. But surely Evan had more sense.

"I'm sorry," the boy said. "I know I ain't supposed to talk to him, but he talked first. I've got no manners, I know it—get yelled at enough for it—but he's *royalty*, I had to say somethin' back, didn't I?"

"What did he ask you?" Janus knew the boy was right, but anger still laced his voice. "What did you tell him?"

Evan took a step back. "He asked me for candy, and his dog licked my fingers."

"The dog—the prince? *Adiran?*" Janus had forgotten again. To Evan, there was only one prince.

Evan nodded. "I gave him candy, and he gave me this." He reached into his pocket, a little awkwardly, torn between finding the item and taking his eyes from Janus. Palace pages were accustomed to casual buffetings from irritated lordlings, but the boy's caution offended Janus. He hadn't ever laid a hand on the child.

The boy finally succeeded and pulled out a battered feather from his pocket. He looked at it in some dismay; its confinement in his clothing had damaged it. Janus plucked it from his loose grip. The rachis broken, the barbs turned stringy, there was still no doubt. Janus held a rook's feather in his grasp.

He let it fall, and seized Evan's shoulders instead, guiding him over to the chair beside the fire and pushing him into it. The boy's feet dangled; he shifted uneasily.

"Tell me exactly what happened when you met Adiran walking the halls. Tell me what you saw."

12

*E*VAN SHIFTED AGAIN ON THE chair, slipping on the high peak of the over-stuffed seat, and Janus gave him a footstool to brace himself against.

His reward was an uncertain voice, thinned with discomfort. "I told you."

"Adiran was in the halls? Unguarded and alone?" Janus sat on the edge of the footstool, the better to watch the boy's expression. He didn't think Evan would lie to him, but Janus was a man who hedged his bets as best he could.

Evan nodded, seemingly glad of an excuse to drop his gaze from where Janus held it. "The papers tell truth, don't they? The prince ain't . . . right. But he's not so bad as they make out."

"Papers sell better at extremes," Janus said, "but that's a lesson for another time."

He ran Evan through his story again: the two boys meeting, Adiran drawn close and out of shadow, no doubt intrigued by the rare sight of another boy in the quiet halls, the oddly clear request, *I want some candy, please*—had he ever heard Adiran speak a full sentence?—and the incomprehensible trade of a feather for the toffees.

Where had Adiran obtained a feather? It had been new, or Evan's face wouldn't have betrayed concern at its rumpled state. When had Adiran begun to understand the concept of trade?

Under questioning, Evan admitted to accompanying the prince on his perambulation until they'd made one full circuit of the upper floor and returned to the nursery.

"The guards there?"

"Sleeping," Evan said, and his voice dipped, knowing that something had been very wrong and very unreported. Janus wondered if Rue had heard; Rue would be his ally in this. Adiran was far too vulnerable and valuable to be allowed to walk the halls alone, hound by his side or not.

The clock struck, tolling nine times, and returned Janus's attention to the here and now. It also brought the unwelcome realization that there was a distinct line between being tardy and being unforgivably rude.

Evan squirmed and said, "Can I have my feather back?"

Janus picked up the draggled feather and handed it to the boy, though he was oddly unwilling to do so. It felt like proof in his hand, but proof of what? Ani's interest in the kingdom? Or something simpler, sweeter: a tangible sign of friendship. That envy touched Janus again; and this time, reluctantly, he named it loneliness.

Evan, biting his lip, did his best to smooth out the barbs, the damage done by the sojourn in his pocket, and Janus, who remembered all too well the pain of broken treasures, held his hand out again.

He melted a bit of sealing wax—crimson shot through with gold dust—and repaired the cracked rachis. Evan smiled, and Janus felt obscurely happy at the boy's pleasure. But then, Evan's problems were small and easily remedied. If only Antyre could be so easily repaired, or people's hearts turned.

The boy's pleasure was soothing but meaningless; there was no wisdom or power behind it. Tarrant's boy was bright enough, a clever monkey, but hopelessly innocent. *Fourteen*, Janus thought, *and a privateer's son should argue otherwise*, but Tarrant had chosen to keep his son sheltered. When Janus was Evan's age, Ivor was teaching him the proper way to hold a blade and to converse pleasantly while poisoning someone.

"Evan, do you know if Lady Last returned in time for dinner?"

Evan nodded. "She's eatin' in her rooms. She . . . didn't look so good, sir."

Janus muttered, "You should have seen her the other morning." But the memory that brought with it—Psyke gray, her skin stiffening with chill—made him greet Evan's confused "Sir?" with "Tell Cook I'll be dining with the countess in her quarters."

Evan tucked the feather away in an envelope Janus liberated from the desk. As an afterthought, Janus scrawled his name across the end of it, so that should Evan be caught with it, he wouldn't be suspected of pilfering expensive stationery. "If you see the prince out again, direct his path to me if I'm in the palace. Otherwise, seek Rue."

Evan trotted off, the envelope with feather tucked neatly into the inner pocket in his jacket. Distracted, trying to figure out how a squad of guards fell asleep all at once without outside intervention, and yet no harm had come to the prince, Janus made for the old wing and found his rooms stripped, stopped at Psyke's and found them emptied also.

A quick bark of rueful laughter touched him. Perhaps he should have had Evan lead him to his quarters after all. Savne had done as Janus asked and that eased some of the knot of trouble in his chest. Janus wanted to believe it was a portent of things to come.

He backtracked his way through the quiet halls, past the closed doors, into the dining hall, hearing DeGuerre's voice raised in sharp protest, probably at Bull's newest expenditure reports; the man was determined to keep the palace finances afloat, even if it meant removing luxuries from the dining table. Janus, who thought the Antyrrian food too fussy, too many flavors fighting for notice, rather enjoyed meals since Bull had begun supervising the cooking staff's expenditures.

DeGuerre, on the other hand, opined if he wanted to eat like a commoner, he could go down to any tavern. Janus wished he would, wished DeGuerre would see what the general public considered eating well; the man might learn to be appreciative after that.

Janus left the quarrel behind, glad it had nothing to do with him for once, and sought his new rooms. Once he had sent Padget, still fussing, off for the evening, his rooms were everything pleasing. Where the old wing's walls were stone, sheathed in threadbare tapestries, the central wing offered creamy plaster and wallpaper, the granite floors traded for plush carpets and allover warmth. The fireplace was ringed 'round with a mantel and hearth, instead of being a stony, dark pit crusted with embedded ash and icons of old gods.

Someone had taken advantage of the mantel already; a folded letter waited for him. Janus broke the seal, a crest unfamiliar to him—a spreading oak with deep roots—and found himself screwing the stiff paper into a knot a moment later.

Chryses had been right, damn him, and Gost was hasty; the demonstration had been arranged and in the most public place imaginable.

> Your young engineer, Chryses DeGuerre, agrees that the central docks would be an ideal proving ground, allowing you space to both display and defend your engines.
> As you are so sure of your ability to win the public, I thought to take advantage of it. I sincerely hope your words were not idle boasting.

Janus threw the letter into the fireplace, and turned away. He couldn't even object. For the demonstration, they needed water deep enough to float steel to display Delight's steam-powered boat. And better the ocean than setting the palace servants to filling the old and empty fountains that ran the edges of the garden.

Doing such would turn their demonstration into a toymaker's display. The nobles might approve, but it would be another social event, much like Aris's funeral; any solemnity would not only be lost but trampled underfoot. Still, Janus would have preferred a discreet demonstration in a quiet cove, with an audience they could trust not to throw rocks.

Perhaps, if this display met with reasonable approval, Janus would build a demonstration hall for intelligent and inquisitive audiences, who might genuinely want to be educated in the wonders that a rational mind could create.

He dropped a lit match onto the crumpled paper in the fireplace, turned, and caught the reflection of the flare in a row of crystal carafes on the dresser opposite.

Janus ran his fingers along the carafes offering him his choice of liquid refreshment, including the temptingly opened bottle of *Absente*, transferred from his previous quarters; a few swallows of that and the edge would be gone from his day. It would be foolish though, to trade wariness for languor, when he meant to dine with his sharp-witted wife. He recorked the bottle.

The bottles would be better emptied and refilled under his watch before he drank from any of them—he was not Maledicte, not proof against poisoning—but their presence was welcoming nonetheless. A tray full of goblets, crystal and metal, all etched with the Last hourglass crest, made him sigh.

So ostentatious, and so foolish. An invitation to poison, but his father wouldn't have cared for that, confident in his name and power. He had been an excessively proud man, so much so that even after fifteen years and three wives dying in an attempt to give him an heir, it still took a command from the king for Last to reclaim his bastard son.

"We taught him that pride spared him nothing, didn't we?" Janus murmured, remembering that blackest of nights on the dock when he and Maledicte had cut the man down.

A swath of heavy, blue curtain drew his attention; it was on the wrong wall to veil windows. He pulled the curtain back, collecting a sparse handful of dust—it seemed he wasn't expected to pass this fragile barrier—and found the gilded door to the connecting rooms. He pressed the handle, expecting it to be locked, but it opened, sent him into the quiet rooms beyond.

Moving through the sitting room, and into the private rooms beyond, he found Psyke seated before her dressing table, gazing blankly into her mirror. Evan had been right in his assessment. She *didn't* look well—her shoulders rounded forward, all proper posture fled, her skin seemed gray with either fatigue or pain. Even as he watched, her hands flew up to cover her ears. She shook her head, once, twice, and murmured, "Enough of this nonsense."

"I quite agree," Janus said. "You spend too much time with Celeste; her spite will make you ill. It spills out and taints everyone about her."

Psyke jerked, nearly fell from her stool, hands flailing and knocking a tiny perfume vial over. It cracked and the oil seeped out, chokingly strong and smelling of funeral rites, myrrh and moss and something sweet laid over foulness. Janus rubbed his nose, opened his mouth to complain about her choice of scent and found himself distracted by her bare toes, peeking through holes in her stockings.

He knelt beside her, seized her left ankle in his hand, his fingers enveloping the dainty joint with ease. The silk was ruined, its soft ivory stained and splattered, and the sole—he traced a finger beneath the arch of her foot, ran it toes to heel, and felt only tender skin. "Have you been dancing so fervently on my grave that you've worn your slippers through? Your celebration is premature."

She shook her head. "My time is my own." Her voice was ragged, but not as hostile as he had expected. It was nearly breathless.

"Not when you spend it with my enemies, sweet." Her skin was chill beneath his fingers; he traced the sweep of her ankle up beyond her heel, up until the flesh warmed beneath the thin wrapping of silk. She shivered, her eyes darkened, but in welcome or distaste, he wasn't sure.

"If I thought that, I would forever dine alone," she said. "Surely, you wouldn't want that on your conscience? Your young wife become a recluse?"

"I'd bring you books," he said, "and you could read your afternoons away. You used to do so and come to my bed with ink stains on your fingers and lips. Surely that was a more pleasant way to spend your time?" He stretched up on his knees, stroked her hair back from her face, her shoulders; the strange dark bruising still clung to her skin, the marks of hands other than his own. She closed her eyes against his touch, the gentle exploration of a type they hadn't shared since their return to the palace.

"Would that I could," she said. "But I find it hard to recall past pleasures now." She shifted from his touch, but slowly. The blueness of her eyes caught him unaware, pinned him. "Times change, and pleasures must be forsworn in the name of duty."

"Stick to pleasure," Janus suggested. "Duty treats you ill." He tugged the thin wool away from her shoulders, kissed the edges of the bruise, tasting smoke and musk, and something *other*. He shivered; it tasted oddly like old books and knowledge, not so much a flavor as an impression.

Her hands settled on his shoulders, balancing herself as he pressed closer, and the gentle weight reminded him of their first night together, bonded as man and wife, and never mind that he was bound already—by blood, loyalty, and the past—to Maledicte. Or that Psyke was bound to Aris, in much the same fashion, by the blood of her slain family, by her loyalty to the crown. Their first coupling had been careful and wary, the movements of two strangers who had little in common and uncertain interest in finding such.

"It's often the nature of duty," she said. "But if a task is unpleasant, does that mean it should be shirked?"

Janus pulled back from his exploration of her skin, though his body protested the space between them. Still, her tone had been so honestly questioning, he wanted to see her expression. It was strained, a little desperate, and he felt it echo in his own chest. He stood, idly straightening up the tipped perfume vial, and wiping his fingers with a handkerchief.

"I have done many unpleasant things out of necessity and in the name of survival," he said. "I've waylaid sailors on the streets and beat them senseless for what poor coin they carried. I've eaten scraps stolen from dogs and seabirds, netted dead fish, and made sickening meals of them."

"You've killed men," she said. Her lips tightened.

"I thought we were speaking of unpleasant tasks," he said. "Yes, I've killed men, and enjoyed doing so."

Her breath caught, a painful gasp in her throat.

"That," he said, "does not include Aris, by the by."

"Your father?" she asked.

"Nor him," he said. "Maledicte had that privilege. Still, you were asking about duty, I believe, and not for a list of my varied misdeeds. The truth is, my sweet, the more I attempt to do in the name of duty to Antyre, the more people despise me."

He heard the frustration in his voice and shut his teeth on further words. Psyke would report to the duchess, who would be pleased to hear of his failures. But it galled that even simple tasks such as sending food to the poorest denizens could not be accomplished without all parties involved treating him with suspicion: the nobles he solicited for funds, the Particulars he asked to oversee distribution, the Relict rats who hid rather than face armed men.

Did no one see that poverty was a danger of its own? The hungrier people were, the more likely they were to grow dangerous. Time passed, and soon no amount of charity would restore them to peace.

"My duty," she murmured, interrupting his cycling thoughts, "was to Aris."

He knelt beside her once more, folded the layers of her skirts upward, fine-brushed dark wool and pale linen slip. She stiffened, but made no attempt to stop him. "To the man? Or to the memory?" Janus asked.

"Before you lecture me on holding too closely to the past, consider yourself," Psyke said. "Or will you lie and tell me you've forgotten Maledicte."

He paused, hands curving around her thigh. "Perhaps not," he said finally. "But at least no one doubts my sanity. There are rumors that Aris's death has turned your mind."

"Rumors you planted," she said.

"You're the noble lady who's chosen to gad about without shoes, as if you were a savage from the Explorations," he said. He found the tops of her stocking, unbuttoned the garter, and peeled the silk away. "You blacken your own name without my aid."

"I have larger concerns than gossip," Psyke said. "My motives are far different from yours."

"I suppose you think it so," he said. "But I ask you to consider the methods you will employ. I imagine the Duchess of Love to be indelicate in her stratagems. She must be, to upset you so. Does she plan to assassinate me outright? Or something more, perhaps see Adiran killed and me blamed. . . ." He stifled Psyke's retort with a quick kiss, her breath misting against his lips, a lick of a heated tongue.

He pulled away and continued. "She is quite capable of such, I assure you. Her hatred outstrips her love for the country. Have you learned that yet?"

He studied her expression for any signs that he might be verging on truth. But her face held no expression at all, had fallen back into the formal mask of composure that he had first mistaken for a widespread lack of intelligence among the noblewomen of the Antyrrian court.

She shook her head abruptly, her hands clenching in her lap as if she had only just managed to keep herself from repeating her earlier motion, covering her ears. Her lips moved, twisted, spit out silent words he couldn't interpret. He felt that same withdrawal in himself that he had felt when confronted with her waking from the dead: that cautious pause to reassess an enemy once he had accomplished something unexpected.

Psyke seemed not to notice his hesitation, and having won the argument with herself, pressed into his arms, tilting her mouth up to his in clear invitation. He bent to accept it, her mouth moving against his, drawing him closer, hands fisting in his coat, ruining the crisp line of the wool. Was this what drove her tonight? Not desire but the same thing that drove him to her rooms, loneliness and the urge to leave the incomprehensible mysteries of politics and enmity aside? Or was this an attempt on his life in some subtle fashion; women of the Itarusine court had been rumored to coat their skin with poison and encourage lovers to have their fill.

He licked a delicate stripe from her collarbone to the fast-beating pulse in her throat, but tasted only warmth and the lingering residue of myrrh in the air. She arched herself against him and he drew her up, drew her closer, nothing loath to lose his own troubles in something so simple and pleasant.

The door opened behind them, and Janus growled. Psyke stepped back as her lady's maid entered, guiding another maid carrying a heavy tray. The maid curtsied awkwardly and set down the food in the sitting room, then vanished. The scent traveled toward them, as did Dahlia, though Dahlia hesitated in the doorway.

Janus said, "Don't dither, girl. Come help your mistress out of her gown."

Psyke's lips curved. Dahlia came forward, visibly reluctant. Janus thought it at his presence until he saw her hands shake as she pulled the first pin from Psyke's hair.

Janus leaned against the wall, and watched, oddly fascinated by this routine. He couldn't imagine Maledicte standing still for a dresser; he barely managed to do so himself. Psyke had been doing so since birth.

Dahlia undid the tiny buttons along the back, frowning briefly at the strained loops where Janus had forced the fabric from Psyke's shoulders. Overall, though, Dahlia worked with more haste than was seemly, letting the gown fall to the floor rather than catching it and waiting for Psyke to step out of its confining loop.

Psyke undid the first lace on her chemise, half turned so she could watch Janus as she did so. When Dahlia rose to help her remove the chemise, Psyke stopped her. "That's all for now, Dahlia. You may go."

Dahlia nodded, snatched up the dress, then dropped it over the nearest hook, and fled, her duties barely begun.

"What have you done to her?" Janus said. "She was always inept, but now she's both inept and frightened. If you're beating your servants, you might make sure the results are—"

"She blames me for her recurring illness," Psyke said. Her chin tilted upward; her expression challenged him. "She finds my presence tends to exacerbate her symptoms. She fears me."

Janus let his lips curl into a mocking grin worthy of Maledicte. "Fears you?" He circled her, all tousled blond hair, creamy linen, and that one stocking-clad foot. "You look like a girl's doll done hard by."

Psyke laughed, a bit brittle. "You're the one who plays with me. If I'm damaged, who bears the blame?"

Again, that tiny frisson touched him. The rumor he had alluded to, of Psyke's madness, had not been an invention meant to wound. Her own actions had seen to that on the night of Aris's death. But for the first time, he wondered if there was some truth to it.

Rationally, he knew madness was the likely answer, that she had been fed a surfeit of death, and found it indigestible.

Irrationally—he kept remembering the feel of a god in the air, Psyke's unaccountable waking from death.

"Not I," he said. "You know me well enough to know I value my possessions, having had so few until recently."

She tilted her head, and said sweetly, "You valued Maledicte so much, you ran him through with your blade, then imprisoned him in your country estate. Or was he never your possession? He left you, after all."

Janus grabbed her, slammed her back against the wall, and Psyke laughed. "I was so frightened when we were wed. I'd never known men beyond a single kiss, and then there you were, my husband, my enemy, my duty. . . . You treated me gently then."

Janus breathed hard for a moment, trying to put away the red tide before his eyes. Her hand curled around his forearm, scratching lightly, and he turned his gaze downward. "Don't fret," she said. "I'm sturdier now. Well able to withstand you."

She reached up and pulled his mouth toward hers, her lips hungry, her tongue questing; and he let all his immediate questions go as his skin woke to need, woke to its own loneliness. The sudden urgency of it made him pause, made him cautious, but Psyke writhed in his arms, and his body yearned in a fashion entirely uncharacteristic of him.

Loneliness, he thought, *and best stamped out with Psyke, here and now, than fall prey to it later.* He drew her over to the bed, finished unlacing her chemise, removed that final stocking, and she twined her arms around his neck. "You feared to unwrap me the other night, my murderer."

"Not feared," he growled. "Never feared." He pressed her into the mattress, the clean, sweet scent of rosemary rising from the linens. She clawed at his back, making him rise, and she reached for his buttons, pulling his shirt off with as much haste as Dahlia had taken with Psyke's gown. His cravat and collar stayed behind, choking him until he removed them himself, flung them to the floor. An imaginary Padget wailed at him, and Janus bit back an oath. If he was concerned with what his valet would say, he was coming perilously close to being just another aristocrat.

Psyke's hands worked at his breeches with a bewildering boldness, her lips bitten and reddening. Janus helped hasten the task, and then they were pressed together again, their bodies working against each other in concert, trying for mutual satisfaction all the more elusive for the unlikeliness of finding it.

Janus gasped as Psyke sank her teeth into his shoulder. He was no innocent, no stranger to women's bodies, but Psyke was fast becoming like no woman he had bedded before. Not a clueless sycophant or a bored aristocratic lady, not a prostitute—all of whom had seen only his superficial self, his title, his wealth, his golden looks.

Psyke saw deeper, saw as deep as Mal had, but where Maledicte was his conspirator, Psyke was his enemy; and still she took him in, her hips shifting to meet his, deepening their connection, her nails crosshatching the ridge of his spine, her breath ragged in his hair.

The sting of her nails, the sharp edges of her teeth against his jaw, made him ponder poison even as he stifled his moan against her skin, nuzzled sweat from her cheek. Would such explain her unusual boldness? Had Celeste sent Psyke to bed and kill him?

She shivered against him, echoing his shudder. He grabbed her hands, tasted each of her fingernails, finding only salt and the faint hint of his own blood. No poison there.

Psyke whimpered into his shoulder; he worked a hand down between their bodies and turned that whimper into a soft wail and a long series of shudders.

Entangled by her sudden pleasure, he plummeted quickly after and disengaged himself. He lay beside her, and she drew the sheet over herself.

The aroma of their dinners cooling made his stomach growl, and he rose to investigate what the kitchens had sent, judging the state of Cook's aggravation by the complexity of the dishes: stew meat and bread meant they might as well be chastened children. But the chafing dishes revealed tiny roasted hens, so delicate that the bird came apart in his hands, the juice dampening his skin with salt and oil. He licked it away, curling his tongue into the crevice between thumb and forefinger, feeling as feral and as hungry as he ever had in the Relicts.

Psyke joined him, draping her dressing gown over her shoulders and fastening the buttons herself. "Your breeches," she said, "are on the floor."

He tugged the sheet from her bed, wrapped it about himself partially to annoy her, partially because his breeches were too tight to promise comfort at the moment.

She made a face, but no further comment on his manner, and he was oddly grateful. Meals in the palace had turned into rather an ordeal. If he could get through even one in peace, it would be a pleasant change.

Psyke nibbled at her own fowl with hungry unconcern. Her right hand disarticulated it, wing from breastbone with aristocratic ease and a single gilt-tipped fork; her left held paper spread open on the low table.

Janus felt his temper spike uncertainly. She was poring over the letter he had liberated from the study.

"Can you read that?" he said.

"Can you not?" she replied. "The Ixions have always been trained in High Antyrrian."

"And the Bellanes?" he asked. "What need had your family to learn the king's language? Did your family aspire to the throne?"

Psyke sighed. "My family *was* the throne once. Did you study only recent history?"

"I was rather pressed for time," Janus said. "Keeping myself alive in the Itarusine court was a bit more involved than I had bargained for. Then I returned home and found things even more complicated."

Psyke made no comment, but instead began to read aloud:

Inasmuch as Aris's murder has left the people unsettled and his assassin still free, we suggest that to soothe public unrest, the following measures be taken:

That Janus Ixion, bastard nephew to the king, be taken into custody until such time as his guilt can be proven.

That Adiran Ixion, heir to the throne, be given into the Duchess of Love's

care, since the palace nursery has been proven unsafe once before, resulting
in the duchess's grandson's death.
That the counselor Warrick Bull step down, and allow Edwin Cathcart,
Lord Blythe, to step in as regent, choosing his own counselors.

Psyke said, "Need I continue?"

Janus laughed. Blythe was an idiot and a transparent one, a lord with an overabundance of self-importance and no common sense. He said, "Did Blythe sign it himself? The duchess won't like that. Him laying out her hand so soon."

"It's unsigned," Psyke said. "Coward, I suppose. A rare sin you lack."

"Careful," Janus said. "That ran perilously close to approval." He reached out and tugged on one of the long tangles of her hair, idly sleeking it with his fingers. She brushed his hand aside, and bent back to her meal, her dressing gown sliding over her pale skin.

"Will you tell me," Janus said, "who marked your flesh?"

Psyke set down her fork with a noticeable clatter; her hands shook, and she tucked them beneath her dressing gown, as if the room had suddenly grown chill. "I crawled beneath the altar to get to Aris, and rose too soon. There's no great secret there. The deepest of hurts linger as the pain works its way to the surface."

"I'm familiar with such injuries," Janus said. "We fought with stones in the Relicts."

She rose and faded back into the inner bedchamber without another word.

Janus applied himself to the second covered dish, found it was rabbit wrapped in pastry and very tender. No wonder DeGuerre had complained; rabbit was a commoner's dish, suitable for grounds-keepers and staff, hardly the thing to grace a noble's table.

Janus reached over and collected the letter again, trying to make sense of the words and the meaning Psyke had ascribed to them.

Let 'em whistle for it, Bull had written. As well he might to such a litany of ridiculous requests. But to write that rejection, not beside the paragraph with his own name, but Janus's, the only request anyone was like to consider . . .

For a moment, Janus wondered whether Bull could be trusted. Hadn't he offered advice earlier? Or he could be setting up an elaborate charade meant to lead Janus into trusting him. And that was all presuming Psyke's translation was truthful.

Janus put his chin in his hands, missing Maledicte, the comfort of knowing who his best ally was. A rustle behind him made him turn. Psyke stood in the doorway. "Come, see how well you can bruise me." She dropped the gown, let him admire the red bloom of his bite mark on her neck, and disappeared into the room.

He took the time to secrete the letter away again—perhaps Delight could read High Antyrrian; he seemed prodigiously well educated—and then followed his wife.

13

A FINE SPRING DAY, THE newsboys proclaimed as they progressed, pleasant enough that Last's mad start at the docks should be well attended. Janus, jostled between Fanshawe Gost and Evan Tarrant on one coach bench, with guards lining the outside, thought the weather not as fine as the criers declared, though attendance swelled as if it were. In older times, the people gathered for hangings, too, with every bit as much interest.

He reassured himself. He and Delight and Chryses had argued, but the steam engine they showed today would impress the sea-dependent city, show them a quicker way to sail, and one not reliant on the fickle wind. Best yet, it wouldn't profit Itarus in any way: the treaty was about tithed funds and goods, about keeping Antyre defanged.

The crowd gathered, pressed back by sheer number until some of them found that having their curiosity assuaged would in no way make up for standing so close to the rubble that marked the edge of the Relicts. Those lingering there would see nothing but their purses picked.

Westfall's cronies were on the docks, an assortment of aristocrats and well-heeled merchants, watching with interested eyes to see what Janus had done with their funds, with Westfall's reputation. They stood closest to the docks, recognizable in their serviceable clothes in practical colors, dun and cream and gray, though still of cloth finer than most people would ever see.

They leaned up against the old iron cannons gone white with salt, old sentinels for a war long lost, and watched Delight, skirt clad, barking orders at two young men forcing a laden cart slowly toward the clearing guarded by several smocked men.

If Westfall's followers watched in interest and hope, there were others that made the kingsguards draw closer to the noble coaches and lay their hands on their weapons.

Anger and dissatisfaction turned down mouths and shuttered eyes. Patched jackets, sleeves rolled up, bared arms corded with muscle, wiry with hard use.

"Antimachinists," Evan spoke, his clear tenor startling in the otherwise quiet coach. Fanshawe Gost shifted, his eyes flicking over Janus as if to ask was it usual that his servants spoke freely in his presence. Completely heedless of the surprise and disapproval, Evan continued, "They're troublemakers and I don't like the look in their eyes. Mutinous, if we was on board ship."

"A wise child," Gost said, after a moment during which Janus failed to chastise the boy. "The country is much like a ship, and we must pull together."

Janus let out a breath so he didn't argue with the idealism Gost revealed there. He chose instead to be pleased that Gost showed some symptoms of egalitarianism; the more Gost showed himself interested in men's capabilities, the more likely he was to throw his support behind a clever and determined bastard.

Evan grimaced. "Then the country's been scuttling herself, and ain't that a pretty thing to think."

"Evan," Janus said, a halfhearted warning. His attention was all for the tarpaulin-covered cart. The burdened horses were sweating, their hides lathered with effort and the stress of the shoving, roisterous crowd. Whitsonby and Georgie, two of Delight's most reliable assistants, rode in either side of the cart, pitchforks in hand. Currently, they were using the smooth end of the handles to encourage curious people out of their way, to keep their hands, and protests, at a distance.

Janus narrowed his gaze, stepped out of the coach for a better glance—he hadn't thought the engine could be laid so flat. If they'd taken it apart completely . . . well, their unwelcome audience might grow weary and wander away while it was reassembled or they might treat the demonstration as a most unsatisfactory entertainment and hurl missiles.

"There have always been reactionary elements in society, the ones who cling to the past, to the traditions even when they benefit no one," Gost said. "Think of them as the fuel that keeps clever men's minds active. Without them, we would merely—"

"Without them, more'd get done," Evan said. His pointed chin stuck out mulishly. "Beggin' your pardon, but it's true. An' they're only getting worse. Used to be they were countryside only, breaking the spinning engines, breaking the mills. Used to be they threw rocks or burning garbage to express themselves, and scattered when they saw the guards come."

"And now? Do tell me," Gost said. His hands tightened on the gloves held in his lap.

Janus thought he saw Evan's point. *This* crowd of people pushed their way to the front, heedless of the Particulars in their midst, the mounted guards with pistols in their sashes, watching from above. And when shoved, they shoved back. Horses shifted and snorted uneasily, small continuous bursts of respiration as if the city itself breathed in anticipation.

"Now, they're organized. Now the blighters have guns instead of rocks."

If the boy wanted Gost's attention, he had it. The man's dark eyebrows arched. "Pistols are expensive."

"My da said they started off the leftovers of soldiers that King Aris left jobless when the war ended."

"Your father?"

Janus shifted his weight on the carriage's doorstep and diverted Gost from his question. "Seems reasonable enough to me. Cared for, the weapons would last."

Evan was more valuable than he might appear, and Janus wasn't minded to hand the key to Captain Tarrant's obedience over to anyone, even a man who would be a formidable ally.

"You assume they'd have reason to care for them," Gost said. "The war was decades ago, and people's memories are short."

"Not in my experience," Janus said. "Grudges are long. These men are soldiers' sons, brought up poor, brought up with nothing but a sense of what they're owed, what their fathers were denied."

"My da says they want blood and don't much care whose. Like your mutineers who think any rule's better'n this. My da says they're no better than Relict rats."

Janus reached through the window and cuffed Evan gently. Tarrant's son or not, he didn't care for comparisons being drawn between the city's agitators and himself. The boy subsided.

"You're here to watch, to learn, and, if needed, run messages between myself and Delight, not ramble on as if you're in the kitchens."

"No," Gost said, "I find myself interested in the boy's speech. I find myself shamefully surprised that a child cares for politics."

"Ain't politics," Evan said, though he said it quietly and with a sidelong glance at Janus, ensuring that he was allowed to speak his mind. His warning given, Janus merely nodded. "It's just the way things are. Best to know who's got the power, and who wants to take it away."

"I wouldn't worry yourself about that rabble," Gost said. "Pistols, they may have, but I sincerely doubt any of them could find the funds for the shot. Your surname, boy?"

Janus twitched, suddenly and uncomfortably reminded of Ivor's first question to him, that probing desire to know *will this person be of any use to me?*

"Evan Tarrant, sir."

"Your father's the . . . privateer?" Gost hesitated briefly, before judging the boy wouldn't have heard the contempt often attached to that word. It was a delicacy Janus approved. Evan was an amiable boy, and kept so, would be a useful tool, while sullenness would lead to the same seething resentment that plagued the city streets.

"My da works for the king," Evan agreed easily enough. "Didn't want me along 'cause it's risky work."

A shout interrupted them and Janus found himself sharing the step with a small serious boy. Evan wormed his way out past Janus's arm and said, "It's that feller Harm. I shoulda known. Mr. DeGuerre said things got worse when he took over the antimachinists. He ain't no soldier's get. He's Itarusine."

Gost said, "Harm's an Antyrrian name."

"He's not dumb," the boy allowed. "Not to walk around on our streets with a foreign name, telling our men what to do."

"And he's in charge of the antimachinists?" Gost smiled down at Evan and Janus felt himself bristling, all his attention drawn from the pushing and shoving crowds, the cart still making its way through the horde. Evan was *his*, rats take it, and if Gost wanted a spy, he could find and nurture his own.

So possessive of what's yours, Maledicte whispered, haunting his memory.

"Partly," the boy said. He preened a little under Gost's attention. "There's factions."

"There are always factions," Janus said. The shouting grew louder, picked up other voices behind it, and was overridden by the Particulars' bells as they moved in to squelch them.

Evan pointed at the cart, which had cleared the last obstacle. "Oh look," he said, "it's starting."

Janus stepped down, setting dust stirring beneath his feet. Before he could reach Delight, Evan hopped out after him and seized his arm.

"Mr. Gost says will you wait in the carriage, please," he got out on one breath. "Says the crowd's too risky to put you at its heart."

Another glance around: the antimachinists beginning their tedious chant of "Break it down, tear it down, burn it down." The mounted guards drew closer, and the crowds nearest them cried out as iron-shod hooves shifted, scraping shins and crushing bare feet.

"Going to be a right spectacle. But Mr. Gost is right. We're close enough." Evan's eyes were cheerful, his cheeks flushed with excitement, too young to understand how dangerous a riot could be.

Gost was right. The Last coach was in the first ring of spectators, a bright gem as blue as the sky above the ocean. Janus's gaze, traveling seaward, granted him the view of a ship at the horizon, flying Itarusine sails. One of Ivor's fleet, keeping itself busy by patrolling the territory they wanted to claim for their own.

Delight spotted Janus and leaped off the tarpaulin-covered cart, his homespun woolen skirt nearly catching on the cart wheel, his long red braid flaring out like a thrown torch; Georgie and Whitsonby objected as the covered objects slid with Delight's hasty exit. Janus shook off Evan and went to meet him.

Delight joined Janus and said, "All this spectacle. All this anticipatory censure . . . Reminds me of my first presentation at court." His mouth twisted into something not quite a grimace, not quite a smile. He hooked his arm into Janus's as if they were merely two friends out for a stroll, as if Delight weren't dressed like a woman, and a lower-class washerwoman at that.

Janus sighed and said, "I'd worry less if it were. Both the Antyrrian court and the Itarusine are easily swayed by style. Gost, on the other hand, wants substance, so do *try* not to be flippant with him."

As if his words had summoned the man, Gost came through the aristocratic side of the crowd, stern in the face of a dozen social smiles. He dropped a polite nod to Janus, then in Delight's direction. "Last. The coach? You are too careless with your person. Ma'am."

Delight, caught in years of habit, curtsyed, then scowled, and stomped back toward the cart. Gost's bewildered eyes lingered on the snap of Delight's skirt resisting the long strides Delight took. "One of your . . . engineers?"

There was no point in dissembling when Gost could take the note of Seahook's lease and see who held it, or when Delight cut such a figure. "Dionyses DeGuerre, the admiral's son. And, yes, he is one of my engineers."

"Is he possessed of his reason? Why would he choose, of all days, to wear such preposterous attire?"

Janus found himself bridling unexpectedly. "I haven't felt the need to inquire into Delight's private actions. As long as he builds what I need—"

"And you were trained in Itarus? You spurn information?" Gost didn't need to say more, or even turn a direct glance Janus's way.

"I've all the information I need. Enough to know *Delight* is worthy of my trust," Janus said.

"As you please," Gost said. His eyes stayed on the swaying woolen hem of Delight's dress, frowning. "Is that Chryses DeGuerre?"

Janus blinked, first at the ease of recognition in Gost's voice and then in dismayed realization that the man was right. Chryses made his way through the crowd, a noble's greatcoat, embroidered and tucked at the waist, thrown on over his laborer's wear, and joined the engineering apprentices by the cart. Chryses slapped the side of the cart; Georgie jumped down to join him, and Whitsonby began to unload the first covered object into their arms.

No friendship weakened the instant misgivings he had at Chryses's presence. Their argument at Seahook had proven that Chryses's sentiments were directed toward immediate profit; Janus had trusted Delight to lead his brother into sense. In a crowd full of antimachinists, Chryses's arrival was both an act of betrayal and a disaster.

Chryses had accused Janus of selfishness, but what else could this be but selfishness of his own? Chryses was weary of playing the spy, spending his days with the antimachinist agitators, his nights bent over plans, and so he broke cover in the most overt fashion possible.

Given the incongruous size of the covered objects, Janus wasn't surprised to see the new cannon unveiled instead of the tiny steamboat. Furious, but unsurprised. He moved forward, and Gost caught his elbow. "Something amiss, Last?" His lips turned slightly upward, a grimace against the sunlight or a delicate indication of amusement.

Janus said, "You knew this would happen. You expect me to fail. *You've met with Chryses.*" The letter Gost left had said this, and Janus cursed himself for a fool for not understanding that it meant Gost had met with Chryses, perhaps even the same night Janus and Delight had waited for him.

"Calm yourself," Gost said. "I am no more fond of failure than you."

"Release me," Janus said. Gost's hand tightened on his elbow, shot pain through the joint, and turned Janus's objections to a hiss.

"To enact a scene before the assembled court and public? I think not. Does a king rush around like a child in a temper? Show your mettle. Allow your men to do as you directed."

"Disaster—"

"Disaster either way," Gost said. "I watch you. You are a clever young man, but much too self-satisfied, prone to temper when thwarted."

Janus pulled free, took two strides forward, then forced himself to a halt, breathing harshly. There were only two types of words that were so unpalatable: absolute truth and absolute lie. Gost's words rang against the fragile parts of his mind that woke him at night with doubts, with the enormity of the task facing him. Difficult enough to bring himself out of the gutter, trying to raise a kingdom back to glory. When the people who should care most were actively hindering him?

Janus found himself shaking with anger and dread, his arms tight wrapped about his chest as if he were a chastised child again, seeking the only comfort he could find.

The second cannon was on the ground. A mutter of interest rose from sailors among the crowd as they began to catalog differences between the new cannons and the old ones bolted to the docks. Admiral DeGuerre, speaking with Warrick Bull, stiffened and stared.

Delight stretched, rubbing his back after the cannon was set down, and smiled in Janus's direction; Delight's smile faltered, no doubt at Janus's expression. He leaned close to Chryses, gesturing concisely, that near sign language the twins used with each other, and Chryses shook Delight off.

All Chryses to blame then, Janus thought, and Delight fed some line about Janus's changed opinion. Chryses rolled the cannons side by side, and waved at Georgie and Whitsonby, who began haranguing the crowd as if it were market day and the cannons nothing more than merchandise. In the bay, an old dinghy drifted slowly out to the mouth of the harbor, having been pushed into the current by Whitsonby. Janus followed it with his gaze and bit back a groan. Beyond it, in the distance, the Itarusine sail flared, moving closer—the last people he could want as witnesses.

The antimachinists had traded their shouts for whispers. Perhaps they didn't see the cannons as kin to the hated engines that threatened their livelihoods. Or perhaps they were simply waiting for the right moment; the wary hunger in their leader's face argued such. Harm stood tall and still, his hands clenched tight on each edge of his jacket, focused entirely on the cannons, while Delight's apprentices shouted hoarse praise for the new cannon, extolling the strength and distance attainable.

Focused *almost* entirely on the cannons; Harm's gaze flicked to the crush of aristocrats and settled, for a telling moment, on Prince Ivor Grigorian.

Whitsonby stepped back from one of the old cannons that had been roughly scraped clean, signaling ready. Its fuse lit, the cannon went off with a roar and a plume of acrid smoke; the ball, sent hurtling outward, fell far short of the tide-caught dinghy.

The crowd laughed and jeered; Chryses held up his hands, flashed a bright smile before turning his attention to the new cannons—thinner, lighter, mounted on wheeled platforms, and oddly decorative. Delight's trademark, that twist of brass curling around the base.

Janus found himself wishing for a misfire, for the months of work to come to nothing. A failed experiment would be the source of a thousand jibes and scorn, would hamper Janus's movement through society. The aristocrats preferred a villain to a fool. But to succeed?

Ivor clapped politely as the second cannon was wheeled into position, the clamp locked on the platform's wheels. Janus hated that Gost was right; he wanted nothing more than to wrest Chryses away from the cannons and into the arms of the muttering antimachinists.

The fuse lit and smoldered; the second cannon fired and the sound of it silenced the crowd. Where the first cannon roared, this one howled—the sound of a whirlwind grinding ground. The old dinghy's side exploded, a plume of water rose like a pale, enveloping shroud. When the spume faded, splinters rode the waves while the dinghy sank as if Naga's coils had crushed it.

The crowd erupted. One man, sounding more like a child than an adult, cried, "Again! Again!"

Chryses laughed, bowed, playing to the people, playing to his father's disapproval. Harm had disappeared, Admiral DeGuerre's face was grimly set, and Ivor Grigorian looked as if he shared Chryses's triumph. It was that smugness that shattered the last of Janus's control.

Without meaning it, Janus found himself across the intervening space, knocking the long match from Chryses's hand as he reached to light the fuse of the reloaded cannon.

"You *fool*," Janus said. His hands were tight on Chryses's neck, and his own throat was sore with the only restraint he could manage, keeping himself from shouting. "Do you understand what you've done?"

"Showed Gost what we're capable—"

"Showed *Itarus* the weapon that's meant to put holes in their ships. Given Ivor a perfect reason to act the auditor and censure us. Or do you forget we're under treaty with them, our country a slave to their wishes? Our purpose, Chryses, was to build a future, not flaunt our disobedience. You wanted your father's attention? You have it. What you've lost? My trust and that of the antimachinists. What do you think Harm will do, knowing now that you're—"

"He always knew," Chryses said. His voice was tight. "My name is known. He thought me disowned, disgruntled, seeking vengeance. He will still think it."

"When your demonstration was so arguably a success?"

Chryses laughed at him. "When you're so obviously unhappy with it? I believe Harm might be more convinced of my allegiance than before. If you send me back to play spy, he'll likely raise a toast in my name."

Janus found himself thinking quite calmly that if Chryses could say such irritating things then he, Janus, wasn't holding tight enough. He remedied that, watched Chryses go purple and blotched.

Then there were hands over his, two sets. One pair was work roughened, frantic. Delight's voice was a running, distressful murmur in his ear, alternately berating and soothing. The second set of hands was gloved and impartial. They pinched the nerves in Janus's arms, and when his hands palsied, pulled them away from Chryses's throat.

Gost stepped back as Chryses dropped; Janus panted, his hands twitching.

"Antyre and its peoples are overfond of violence," Gost said. "Your demonstration only exacerbates that. I had higher expectations of your engines, Last. I had higher expectations of you. A king should have better control of his subjects and, most important of all, of himself."

With that, Gost walked away, back stiff and straight, gait relaxed as if he were simply taking his leave of a garden party, leaving Janus behind in the chaos.

Chryses stumbled to his feet, aided by the wary apprentices. Delight pointedly kept his hands on Janus's arms, both a quiet restraint and a reproof to his brother, a visible choice of whose side Delight had taken.

Janus wished it mattered to him that Delight was his, but Delight's company was as scandalous as it was helpful. A clatter of carriage wheels diverted him, gave him a glance of Psyke being driven away. He expected her to look triumphant at his failure, but instead her gaze was inward directed and deeply worried.

KINGMAKER

· 14 ·

PSYKE HESITATED AS SHE ENTERED the Duchess of Love's dining room and saw a new set of bones awaiting her. The bones before had been distressing, so enormously out of place in the duchess's home, but Psyke had named the woman's attempt at witchcraft desperation, the actions of a powerful woman who suddenly found herself powerless when it most counted. But this—

This smacked less of desperation and more of deliberate wickedness. If only it weren't so necessary. Nights spent listening to Aris's ghost reliving his murder had worn her nerves until she felt that Janus's death might be the only thing that could grant her rest, be it just or unjust.

A dark-gowned woman, slim and veiled, jerked at the duchess's snapped command and continued sifting dark, clotted powder into a tiny vial. Holes marked the long bones of the skeleton's legs and arms, and Psyke, trained in at least the preliminaries of human biology, connected the two. Bone marrow; the stuff of life and the malignant heart of a dozen poisons.

Psyke's attention wavered when Mirabile ghosted up beside her, a phantasm of sound and scent more than vision.

She brushed by Psyke, indignation lending her weight and heft. For a moment Psyke saw the drift of soiled feathers and white silk, as if Mirabile, in death, still wore the costume from the night she went mad and murderous. Mirabile whirled, granting Psyke a quick glimpse of reddening eyes, a crow's beak, before fading back to a spiteful voice. *Does it please you to see me thus? My bones laid out for your purposes? The power I fought for, scavenged?*

"It's foul," Psyke answered without thought. Her other ghosts were never so direct. Never so prone to talking to her. Instead, they spoke elliptically, nearby, like gossip overheard. But Mirabile, as she had in life, made her presence felt.

"It's unpleasant to be sure, but so many of women's tasks are," Celeste said, pausing in her instructions to the veiled girl. "All you need do is slip this into his food—"

"I will not," Psyke said, and it was her own voice, not Aris's complaint or Mirabile's spite. Just her own, quiet and steady, drawing the line she chose not to cross.

"It's no less necessary than disposing of a rabid animal. He will destroy everything he touches."

Psyke shook her head. "And if Janus dies before we have a strong replacement, Prince Ivor will step in. The country—"

"The country," Celeste said, "fawned over Maledicte and Janus while they destroyed my life. You will do as I say."

"No," Psyke said. "I came to you for your aid in finding evidence of Janus's wrongdoing, not to dabble in witchcraft and treason."

"If you truly believed that, you would have gone to the city Particulars, to the guards and soldiers. Take the poison. Remove Janus."

Psyke took a step away from the table, leaving Mirabile's ghost behind, a swath of fading mist embracing her own bones.

The veiled girl spoke, startling Psyke, who had thought her nothing more than another of Celeste's servants, but that she would interrupt the brewing quarrel argued otherwise.

"Lady Last," she said. "Think on this, if you will. These bones, Mirabile's bones, are contaminated so thoroughly by the god that they can cause death. What do you think has happened to Janus, who embraced his god-touched lover so often? Can his soul be anything but corrupt? Would you have one such on your throne?"

Psyke let herself be diverted by the veiled girl's accusation. "There's no evidence at all that Janus is corrupt in any fashion more than human. There never has been. Aris charged me with finding such, and I found nothing beyond arrogance."

"Corruption may run deep," the girl said. "Such things are often hard to find, like rot moving through wood. By the time it's discovered—"

"It hardly signifies," Celeste said. "Whether he is corrupted by Ani or not, he must be removed."

Psyke shook her head again, distaste and doubt warring within her.

The duchess sucked in a quick, furious breath and said, "Go wait in the drawing room, think on the wrongs Janus has done you, me, the *kingdom*, and when you've come to sense, I'll bring you the poison."

Psyke left the two women, would have left the house entirely save that the coachman refused to take her without the duchess's command. So Psyke waited in the shrouded drawing room, the drapes still pulled tight, locking death and grief inside. A maid tiptoed into the room, whispered a slur of questions in a frightened country accent that could have been anything from an earnest wish as to her mistress's doings or a query as to Psyke's preference in tea.

I'm thirsty, Mirabile complained, *and hungry. I miss tea cakes.*

Psyke shook her head. "Nothing, thank you." Mirabile hissed in frustration and faded. Psyke sat on the divan, wishing her nerves could be put to rest. It was hard to find the center of calmness that was the foundation of a lady's poise when she felt she was either cursed or mad, when her allies were discussing witchcraft as the best method of removing her husband from power. Her father would have called it treason.

A man's voice came to her ears, a whisper as faint as the brush of a cat against skin. *My wife has always been a most fearsome enemy.*

Psyke rose and turned hastily, skirts hissing against the upholstery, and caught a shiver of movement, the portly shade of the Duke of Love fading away before she could decipher his intention. Were his words warning or praise?

Her shoulders ached coldly. She stretched them as best she could, given the constraints of fashion—tightly-laced corset and the close-fitting silk bodice. Rising, she rubbed at the bony knobs of her shoulders, finding them both oddly numb and tender where those strange bruises lingered, the all-too-tangible reminder of Aris's murder.

She shuddered, remembering the cold grip that had both sheltered her and forbidden her to die for her king. Psyke pressed into the soft embrace of the heavy, black drapes, parted them to the daylit world outside, so far from her trouble. If she had died then . . .

She leaned her cheek against the windowpane, letting its coolness wick away the need she felt for hot tears. An equally cold touch, delicate as a fallen petal, landed on her bared nape, and left a tiny spot of chill dampness behind. Her eyes flew open in shock, her fingers to her neck, testing the contours of what had felt, undeniably, like a kiss. The coldest and most hesitant kiss she had ever imagined, but tender, nonetheless. As tender and sweet as the first kiss Janus had pressed to her skin.

In the glass, dizzying her with the shifting intricacy of its reflection, something, someone stood behind her, close enough that she should feel a breath. But there was nothing. No living sign at all— no breath, no warmth, no heartbeat. Not even one of her ghosts; it lacked the tattered glamour of Mirabile's gown, the faded gilt of Aris's bent head. Instead, something vast stretched out behind her, eclipsing the rest of the room. Shadows layered on shadows, and within them, the expectation of eyes, a face, not quite human. It recognized her gaze and bent its head, the heavy cowl hiding its face, its demeanor . . . expectant.

Psyke shivered, her hands on the glass sweating, her breath thin and hard to draw; her eyes fluttered shut, rather than see what courted her so.

Give me your—

The door opened behind her, and a fierce hiss of shock dissipated the cold caress, the dry whisper as if they had never been, as if she were as mad as she feared. Psyke turned, found the dark-veiled woman standing within the doorway, a velvet pouch in her hand.

"Lady Last?" she said. "Are you well?"

Psyke nodded, but her voice came out as small as a child's. "I'm cold."

The woman nodded as if it were only to be expected. She set down the pouch, tugged the bellpull, setting off a distant jangling.

When the maid appeared, the veiled woman said, "Tea, please. With honey. A dollop of brandy would not be amiss."

The maid bobbed an uncertain curtsy, openly torn between bridling at another servant ordering her about and understanding that the veiled woman was Celeste's compatriot.

"Thank you," Psyke said, and stepped away. She wrapped her arms about herself and rested her hands over the marks on her shoulders. "I'm sorry. What was your name?"

"Currently, I have none," the woman said. "To avoid attention, you understand."

Psyke didn't, but the woman's voice was so expectant, she found herself nodding as she had as a debutante, being agreeable instead of informed.

"Though I deny you an answer, may I ask a question of you?" the woman said. She waited, the black silk veil swaying gently in and out on the tides of her breath, for Psyke's second nod.

"Did you summon Him, or did He come to you of His own accord? It's only I have never heard a whisper of how the first might be accomplished. Haith is unlike the others, quite shy of attention."

"Haith," Psyke echoed and felt the echo move beyond her, a quiet scent of cold dirt, tinged with stone in the air.

"Yes," the woman said, her tone sidling toward offended. "I am a scholar of sorts, you understand. My interest is hardly prurient. I survived a god's wrath once, and seek to prevent Her attention from falling on me again."

"I—" Psyke committed the sin of a careless debutante, beginning to speak with her thoughts muddled and unclear, leaving her grasping for any words at all.

"Girl," Celeste said, passing by the room and detouring in it. "Haven't you given Psyke the poison yet? Time moves on, and we need to move with it, ahead of it, if we are to catch the bastard unawares." The maid came in behind her, laden tea tray in her hands, and Celeste's attention veered. "What is that? We have no time for niceties. Take that back to the kitchen. Psyke, the carriage awaits."

Psyke dropped into a curtsy; the veiled girl did likewise.

Celeste nodded once, well satisfied. She collected the velvet pouch and handed it to Psyke. "The poison has been ground fine for you. All you need do is add it to his wine. As his wife, that should be within your meager talents."

Numbed by the girl's assumption of the god's attention, and by her own frightened conviction that the girl was correct, Psyke let the duchess fold her fingers around the pouch. If the god of Death walked behind her, what was a single drop of poison? If Death walked with her, then her very presence was poison.

"Your concern is unnecessary," the veiled girl said. The shadows shifted over her hidden face in such a way that Psyke became convinced the girl smiled. "Lady Last is a fearsome creature in her own right."

15

ANUS ROSE FROM HIS SHEETS, heart hammering, skin slicked with sweat. Despite the heat of his room, the coals in the hearth left to smolder, he stirred up the fire, fed in another log with shaking hands. Another nightmare, he thought, surprised. So this was what people feared, this heart spasm and breathlessness, the sense that he had been fleeing his enemies through the night.

A nightmare, he thought, was a hideously unpleasant experience, even as he gave up the idea of returning to bed. Instead, he collected his dressing gown, drew it tight around his waist, letting the heavy brocade absorb the sweat.

He hadn't thought nightmares could be anything much. After all, when Miranda woke from hers, all she could murmur by way of explanation were tales of violence or fear, and wasn't that the meat that filled their days? But this had been insidious, mixing old troubles with new, so that he hunted Maledicte while Ivor fired the new cannons, engulfing Murne in smoke, flame, and destruction.

Firelight washed the papers on his escritoire; he contemplated another pass through the High Antyrrian grammar book he'd acquired, or even another look at the tracts Delight had had Evan deliver, though likely those were the source of his disjointed dreams.

The tracts had arrived on the heels of the canon debacle, Delight's wordless apology. Janus hadn't had time to read them in depth: each moment he stole for his own interests came at the expense of progress with Bull and DeGuerre. Each hour he spent away, he spent two hours finding what the other two counselors had agreed on in his absence.

For all the palace's grandeur and space, Janus was beginning to feel it an elaborate menagerie. Even when the cages were opened, there were leashes of ritual and requirement. Hard to imagine he might have been more free when he and Miranda roamed the streets, masters of their world, controlled only by their impending starvation.

A sound roused him from his contemplations to full awareness in the space of a jolted heartbeat. He drew his lips back.

In this menagerie, some of the denizens fancied themselves predators. He stepped out of the firelight's reach, into the shadows of the curtained windows.

The furious whisper outside the bedroom door stopped, and the doorknob twisted as one of the guards bypassed the lock. Janus slipped out of his dressing gown, unwilling to have the heavy cloth hampering his legs, then headed for the sheathed sword he kept beside the bed.

The kingsguard Marchand entered first, not an unwise precaution; they assumed Janus, if woken, would be eased by the presence of a familiar face. They were wrong. His sword, still out of reach by his bed, Janus seized the poker and brought it 'round, crushing Marchand's hand and knocking the pistol free.

The pistol hit the wall and discharged, the report and Marchand's mingled cry sounding as one. Janus pivoted, struck again with the hot poker, hitting the man's upper arm, spinning and burning him at once. Marchand crashed into the fireplace hearth and out again, his uniform smoldering; he moaned, curling around his burned flesh. The room grew darker as the brief flare faded.

Janus heard the second man approach, a hasty footfall between Marchand's moan, and traded the poker for his blade, dropping the empty sheath onto his bed. The man, a stranger to the palace, showed shock when Janus parried, and at that moment Janus knew it hadn't been Ivor who hired them. Ivor knew that Janus was more than passingly familiar with a blade, having trained him himself. The Duchess of Love, then, or perhaps Harm, the antimachinist. As Evan noted, the antimachinists had grown bold.

Janus shifted his feet, giving himself space; his attacker, eyes still adjusting to the dimness, thrust again. Janus heard the blade catch on the drape surrounding his bed, and grinned. His blood ran hot, and he imagined Maledicte cheering him on, though he would have made mocking comment about the swordsman's abilities, which Janus had to admit, were lacking.

What had his enemies done? Handed the first man they saw a blade? Janus ducked another inept slash, took the man's overextended arm in his free hand and pulled. The man fell forward, dropping his blade in a vain attempt to catch himself, and Janus swept his saber through the back of the man's neck, the wide blade nearly severing the head from the body.

A faint gasp turned him; he moved silently and quickly, blade extended. He swept back the heavy blue drape, then halted, his blade a bare inch from Psyke's white throat. She shivered; his blade traced the movement. She swallowed but made no outcry, no protest, and he lowered the blade, noting as he did so, that she clutched a man's dueling pistol in her hand. It fed his fury. Had she thought to aid his assassins?

Her gaze fell from his, and, as if it had been the bridle to his temper, he lunged forward, pinned her against the wall. She felt cold to his heat, her bones as fragile as a bird's. Deceptive, he knew now. She had strength aplenty.

"Did you bring the pistol to complete their task? If so, best screw up your courage, and aim it someplace other than the floor." He ran his hand down her arm, reaching for the pistol.

She squirmed forward, using an agility he hadn't expected to escape his grip, darting forward into the center of the room as instinctively as a wild creature who craved room to bolt. Janus caught her arm before she got three steps away, letting his blade drop, the better to seize her. He tucked her tight against him, her back against his chest, and raised her hand in his, the pistol shaking in her grip. This close, he recognized the weapon. It had been a recent gift to Aris; a pistol so decorated with gilt scrollwork and colored enamels, it looked more a toy than a tool. Janus had thought it a subtle insult, mocking Aris's inaction, but the king had accepted it with courtesy. And apparently gifted it to his wife. Protection, of some sort—perhaps for Psyke's wanderings through the tunnels, or perhaps . . . as protection from her husband.

"Do you even know how to fire it? It's a very simple device," he whispered. "A child could kill with it. . . ." She shuddered in his arms; the fine, pale hairs on her nape rose, prickled against his lips. He nipped the top bone of her spine, fought the urge to bite down hard and deep, to see if her blood was as chill as her flesh.

"You aim it—" He turned her body to face the traitorous guard, Marchand, still moaning, struggling to regain consciousness. Janus stroked his fingers over hers, pressing down, pointing the weapon at Marchand. "And hope it doesn't explode in your face."

The pistol went off with a roar and a flash, almost stifling the cry she made, sweet to his ear. If she thought to deal death, this might cure her of the desire. Her arm, pressed against his, jumped and trembled. The pistol fell from her grip, dropping to the floor. Janus felt poisonous amusement as he released her, and she sank to her knees. "There, you've saved the gallowsman his trouble. Or had you another target in mind?"

Psyke panted, gone wordless. When he bent to kiss the top of her head, the acrid scent of black powder rose from her hair. He stepped away and reached for his dressing gown.

She rolled up to her hands and knees, retching.

"Oh, don't do that," Janus snapped. The room was miasmic already, the scent of gunpowder and blood, the stench of funeral pyres. Janus, irritably, kicked the guard's singeing hand away from the hearth. The thin line of lace on his sleeve smoldered still, raising thin wisps of smoke chalking the shadows of the room.

Janus flung open the windows and let the night air in. The coals, guttering red, flickered and brightened, casting golden light over the corpses on the floor. Janus leaned against the window frame and sighed. The successful rebuff of his enemies, the first touch of the air cooled his skin and his temper. He found a smile on his lips and felt a brief, nearly physical shock when he turned and didn't find Mal grinning back in shared triumph. This one was his alone.

Psyke had curled inward, her face pressed into her hands. When he crouched beside her, reached past her to reclaim his sword where it had fallen, she raised her gaze and recoiled at finding herself so close to the blood-clotted blade.

"They attacked you in your sleep," Psyke said. She wiped at her mouth. The hectic spots of color in her cheeks began to fade; she fumbled to her feet, toward her rooms. Janus's words halted her.

"Did you expect otherwise? You are naïve," he said. "As for myself, I have been expecting something of this nature once it became clear that, rumors or not, I am not destined for the gallows. I simply hadn't expected the attempt to be this clumsy. Disappointing, as I'm sure you'll agree."

"No," Psyke said. "No, I'm not disappointed. Assassination and murder are distasteful ways to remove one's enemy. A coward's way."

"*I didn't kill Aris*," he said.

"He's dead, by saber and by pistol, and here I see you familiar with both. A northern saber carved out his heart, an uncommon tool in Antyre."

"Not uncommon for a man to cling to the weapon he learned with," Janus said. "Not uncommon at all to think an Itarusine might choose such a blade to strike with. Why blame me, sweet Psyke, when Ivor makes a far more likely foe?"

"Ivor has an alibi," Psyke began.

"As do I . . ." Janus grated.

It made him wild; did no one see? Did they all prefer the known villain, the small villain? Was it some bizarre Antyrrian pride or the well-vaunted ability of the public to deny what was real?

Look outward first for danger. The Relict rats had muttered that instead of their prayers. Known dangers—squabbles over food, over allies, over coppers—were less threatening. After all, the rats might all fight for the same prize, but they at least shared belief in its value. An outsider—the Particulars, a robbed merchant—might not, might destroy the prize in their attempt to get at the rats. Ivor was no different. He didn't value Antyre beyond the power the throne offered.

Janus drew her toward him, her cold hand in his, determined to win her this time. "Ivor Grigorian killed Aris. His father lives on and on, his brothers circling like wolves, and Ivor hungers for his own throne, one not torn apart in the struggle for it. It was Ivor's man that struck, not mine."

"Even if you are innocent of Aris's death—"

"I am," he said.

"Do you think that absolves you? To be blameless of this one death when so many others can be laid to your name?" Her lashes, tangled gold, shielded her gaze, but Janus, watching closely, knew her attention was for Marchand and the splintered hole in his vest.

Janus growled. "They entered with intent to kill me. Self-defense is no crime."

"The others?" she said. "How many enemies you must have if you would cry self-defense for all of them."

"Kritos. Vornatti. Last. Maledicte would have killed them regardless. You cannot lay them at my feet."

"And Amarantha? Her coachman? The *child*? Would Maledicte have killed them without your command?"

"Ani drove him more than I ever did," Janus said.

"Ani feeds on jealousy and anger. Amarantha married your father, not you. Her murder was political, not a matter for either Mal or Ani, of benefit only to you. And the babe, the infant earl who supplanted you for the title you hold now—"

Janus looked at his own hands, recalling how the simple weight of his blade had done the work for him, sinking through Auron's tender skin.

Psyke's trailed-off words belatedly caught his attention, and he looked up to find her backing away, her mouth working, a new and terrible knowledge in an expression already burdened with too much truth.

She drew in a steady breath and froze like prey before the hunt, hoping to be unseen.

A pale tongue wetted her lips; her voice was thin edged but un-afraid when she spoke again. "I own Auron's death struck me as peculiar at the time. If Maledicte had killed the babe, why leave Adiran alive and witness to it?"

"Why dwell on it?" Janus said, surprised that he managed to sound so uninterested when his heart beat so fast. What the assassination attempt hadn't accomplished, his wife had. "The past is past. You might make yourself useful and ring for Rue. I'd like to have the bodies cleaned away before they start to—"

"The past informs the present and the future," Psyke said. "How can I believe your protestations of innocence, when you killed Auron yourself?"

His breath snagged, made him cough, taking in great gasps of tainted air. He dropped his dressing gown, reached blindly out for the breeches in the airing cupboard. "Risky accusations," he said, "if I am the murderer you claim me to be." He dressed hastily, keeping her in sight.

She flinched when Janus stalked past her and reclaimed his blade. Her hands flew up, as if they could shield her heart.

"Are you afraid," he asked, "or do you merely simulate it? You didn't die of poison. Will a saber do it?"

"Try it and see," Psyke said, and it wasn't her voice at all, but something else, a whisper that raised thunder and shadows in the room, drowned the fire glow, and put them both into darkness.

Into that charged darkness, their doubled, panting breath, came a single prosaic hammering on the door. "My lord? My lady?"

Rue opened the door when they made no response, spilling torchlight into the room; Janus lowered the blade, still wary but unwilling to be caught holding his diminutive wife off as if she were more a threat than the assassins who had tried for his life.

16

AWN CREPT IN TOO SLOWLY for Janus's nerves. After Rue had turned Janus's chambers into a hive of kingsguards and servants, Janus had been sent off to bed in Psyke's quarters like an overtired child. Psyke, gone pliant and sweet in the company of the guards, came after him, her eyes glazed and nearly as vacant as Adiran's, exhausted or in shock.

She curled up on her mattress, finding the spot she had left less than an hour ago, sighing into it as if it were still warm, going boneless into sleep or death. It raised all the hairs on his nape and kept him wakeful through the rest of the night, listening to her alternate between deathly silence, even her breathing gone, to fitful mutterings spanning several languages.

Had his childhood instincts held sway, he would have fled the palace and disarmed the snare he felt closing about him by taking himself from it. But those days were past, and he could not afford the luxury of leaving the field. If he left this battle, he lost; Antyre lost. He knew that, saw that, more clearly than perhaps any other, save Gost.

Janus had seen Antyre from gutters to gilt, and spent years in the Itarusine court, learning the measure of Antyre's beloved enemies. For all that confidence though, he felt more and more as if he were a boy shouting at the adult world to pay attention to him.

As Last's son, as Maledicte's lover, he had been someone, someone scandalous, tinged with danger and the rise to power. With Aris alive, Janus had been a source of wariness in the courtiers and lords who debated his position. But with Aris dead, and so suddenly, the only respect Janus gathered was the respect granted a killer who looked to be escaping the noose.

But who had sent the assassins? Blythe disliked him enough to see him dead, but the fop couldn't suborn a paid whore, much less a member of the Kingsguard. Bull, who owned the guards, was an easy answer; but if Bull wanted Janus dead, his guards would have appeared with trumped-up excuses and a writ of execution. The Duchess of Love or Harm still were the most likely suspects.

Psyke roused all at once; she scrambled from the bed in wary silence at still finding him in her quarters. She disappeared into her dressing room, discreetly tucked behind another narrow drape.

A vase teetered, rocked by her passing, and Janus stilled it, wrinkling his nose at the cut flowers gone rank. In the hallway, two maids spoke in low voices, moving from room to room, bringing fresh water and linens. Janus thrust open the door, startled them to silence, and handed the nearer one the vase. "Dispose of those, and find Dahlia. Her lady is waiting her."

"Dahlia's ill," the maid said, her shoulders touching the stone behind her as she stepped back.

"Then find a replacement," Janus said, and shut the door firmly. Dahlia was hopeless. Dahlia had allowed Psyke to creep out and meet Aris secretly. Too young; too callow; and, worse than both of those, too stupid. Janus despised stupidity; everything else could be taught. Still, it was intriguing. If Dahlia was ill, perhaps Psyke's assertions were more than delusion.

One of the religious tracts had mentioned illnesses accumulating about Haith's avatar, a collective of death. Janus had taken it for hyperbole, but perhaps it was based in truth; his wife surrounded by the dead.

Psyke burst into rapid speech, shrill, a little frightened. "It wasn't my fault, Marchand. My hand on the pistol, but his guidance. And you were hardly blameless. Assassination's a chancy thing, and death can be dealt either direction." She paused as if listening to a response; Janus drew in a careful breath, understanding that Psyke thought the shut door had heralded his departure.

His wife talked to herself, spoke sometimes in her sleep; he had known so, but this—this tasted of madness. Or something more. A collective of death? Janus crept closer.

"It's all very well for you to say, but it's still treason. There is, after all, a good deal of difference between proof and punishment. Assassination is not the same as execution, and you know that. You swore an oath to protect. You violated it for a promise of coin from a dubious source, and, worse still—"

Splashes sounded, the quick tide of someone washing her hands and face in jerky movements. "Worse still," she hissed, "you admit you took money to cloak another assassin in Kingsguard colors, money that might as well have been stamped with the Itarusine glacier. The money, the weapon, the direction . . . all from that Itarusine agitator whose name is too aptly chosen to be anything but deliberate mockery."

"Harm, the antimachinist, paid Marchand to kill me?" Janus said, and there came a crash, as if the water basin had been knocked over.

Psyke whirled, pulled the curtain back to gape at him, standing in the dressing room doorway.

"Don't go silent now," Janus said. "I found your words most illuminating, even if your source is suspect."

She tilted her chin, drew her water-spattered nightgown about her, and brushed past him. He caught her arm. "Psyke."

"What would you have me say? That Marchand was so offended by his untimely demise that he came to file a complaint like some petulant customer?" Her tone was offensive, and Janus smiled. So like Mal, cloaking truth with audacity and rudeness. His smile faded—her words cloaked with truth? All her mutterings not madness, but an overheard conversation with the dead?

She turned away, her gown staying put in his hand, sliding away from her skin, baring shoulders gone black.

They were the marks of heavy hands, but no human left marks that grew black, then turned to something other. He touched her left shoulder, traced the long shadow, ridged beneath his fingers, the rasp of scales. In the tracts Janus had read, a god's touch might manifest so, altering the body of their worshipper. Hadn't Maledicte, at the very end, sprouted feathers, black against his white skin? This looked like more of the same and if so, allowing Psyke to remain his enemy was no longer an option; he needed to win her away from the duchess.

"Why do you praise Aris so?" Janus said, voice rough. An awkward question, but not incendiary, and something he dearly wanted an answer to. "He was a deadly king for this country. Nothing but a fool."

"As much a fool as you must think me. You will not cozen me," she said, and he slid his palm over the petals of her lips. Edged pearl flashed, set his fingers dancing away, nursing the tiny hurt where she had bitten. A bead of blood rolled up to the surface of his skin, etched two fingerprints with crimson.

She slowly slipped free from his grasp, scale giving way to sleek skin beneath his fingers. Psyke left the nightgown in his possession, walked away from him, leaving only the warmth of the silk falling through his hands. He cast it aside, and followed her. "You listen to the dead but can't be bothered to listen to me?"

"The dead, at least, are honest," she said, and while the easy acceptance of his accusation made his stomach clench, he still found a rebuttal for her.

"They can afford it; they are long past the point their enemies can damage them."

Psyke stepped into a black gown, drew it against her bare skin like any harlot, in that much of a hurry to escape his company. Janus caught the loose tapes at the back, and when she twisted to look at him, merely said, "Dahlia's ill. Again. You might cede to the inevitable. My hands, or wait even longer in my company."

Janus brought the gown up, covered those hard, rough spots on her shoulders, using the edges of his hand to test the width of the taint.

She sighed, and Janus busied himself with rows of tiny jet buttons, his bitten fingers leaving a few smears of blood on her white back.

"Your beloved Aris," he said, "allowed the Relicts to molder for generations. What king permits a section of his city to rot, breeding villains, poverty, and plague, and makes no attempt to repair it?"

The tassel of her braided hair, a welter of snarls, scented faintly of blood and powder, brushed the backs of his hands as he worked, stung his face as she swung 'round to protest his blackening of Aris's character. He pressed a kiss to her mouth, a more civilized way to silence her than a hard hand clamped tight, and turned her back around.

"Aris was a good man," she said.

"Good enough to watch his brother throw his pregnant and noble-blooded paramour into the streets and make no objection," Janus said. "A good man overall though, given his rank, his expectations. But as a king? What will history praise him for? For surrendering to Itarus when the cost of lives grew high?"

"More people suffer now—hunger, fear, uncertainty—under the Itarusine treaty rules than died. War kills soldiers. The treaty starves infants and women, turns soldiers to forgotten toys and our future to ashes. Aris was a scholar, well versed in history; he knew the cost, but his tender heart couldn't allow the war to continue."

"People were dying," Psyke said.

Janus turned her to face him, and whispered close, hot in her ear. "We would have won, Psyke." She pulled back to look at him, blue eyes sober and calm. Listening, he dared hope that her reasonable mind could sort truth even from a distrusted speaker. "Each winter that the battle dragged out brought us closer to a victory. It was a seaman's war: our ships were superior, quicker to be replaced, and Itarus froze each winter, locking them in, leaving them with supply—"

"I know the history; I lived it," Psyke said. "I watched my father leave and never return, watched as the royal house diminished from six to two. War is about more than strength and logic, Janus. The country couldn't stomach the grief."

"Couldn't stomach the change," Janus countered. "Aris gathered his apathy from Antyre itself. Its own worst enemy. The war bit into the nobles' lives and so had to stop before the season could be disrupted again."

"Will you bring war back on us?" Psyke said. "Is that your idea of the future, why you treated us to the spectacle at the docks?"

"I don't want war. But neither do I think Antyre should cower, afraid to grow, afraid to breathe, for fear of Itarus's displeasure."

"A schoolboy's idealism," Psyke said.

Janus laughed. "I was born in the Relicts, trained in politics by the most ruthless Itarusine prince ascendant—do you believe idealism is a fault of mine? Antyre must change or die. Aris was content to let us fade."

Psyke shook her head, but it was a quick, aborted gesture; her eyes were sad, as if she would like to debate the point but couldn't, trapped in her own memories of the king.

"Adiran is a sweet child, but he cannot claim the throne. To rule by committee is a fool's game. Help Antyre, Psyke. Help me. Cast your support with me. The past is only peopled by death and despair. Aid me, any way you can," he said. He stroked his fingers over the marks on her shoulders; she arched into him, lips parting on a silent moan.

"At the very least, don't hinder me," he continued, pitching his voice to show nothing but earnestness and entreaty. "Allow me to bring Antyre into the future, help her prosper and grow. After that, if you still wish me gone, you're welcome to try."

She shivered against him, close enough that his breath ruffled back to him when he sighed. She turned, mutely presenting the last space of bare skin to be buttoned away.

He stroked his hand up the delicate knobs of her spine, let his hands sink into the warmth beneath the tangle of her hair, before pressing the last tiny buttons into their matching loops. "Your plans for the day?"

She smiled at him, slow, sweet, uncomplicated, the very picture of demure trust. "I thought to see to Adiran's needs, and then Celeste is sending her carriage for me."

Hot fury spiked in him; he swallowed it, though it burned his throat and belly; and her face paled, arguing against his complete success. But he refused to revisit last night's confrontation. Psyke was dangerous enough as a noblewoman and wife; last night she had been something far more deadly. If it slumbered now, coiled within her skin, he chose not to wake it.

"Take a guard," Janus said. "If things are so unsettled that Harm will strike within the palace—"

"Will you suggest a guard I can trust?" Psyke said. "Or should I take your boy Tarrant and save you the trouble of spying on me?"

"Do as you will," he said, pulling away. "Give Celeste my warmest regards and tell her I remember her."

"I'm sure she'll find that . . . comforting," she said, wrapped in an armor he couldn't penetrate with words.

He let her go, sick with frustration and for the first time contemplating that as bad as his position was, it could be worsened. The gods seemed minded to play with Antyrrian souls of late; Janus meant to see they caused little harm. As much as Ani had been a boon, granting Maledicte immunity to hurt, She had also been a curse. *The gods,* Janus thought, *should have no place in mortal deeds.*

Janus returned to his own rooms, grimly pleased at the bloodstain beside the bed and hearth, signs that he had had his moment of triumph amid adversity, and rang for his valet.

Padget sighed when Janus ruined the line of his best coat by strapping his blade to his hip, but made no comment. The man learned. So did Janus. His blade would be at his side from now on, no matter the comments it occasioned.

He sent a page with a message to Ivor, requesting a moment of the man's time. A letter awaited him spattered with transparent grease marks around the seal. Chryses or Delight undoubtedly, and when Janus broke the seal, he found a tight smile on his face. Chryses, in the aftermath of his disobedience, was not so sanguine as to his continued employment with Janus, though he cloaked it in a too-careless demand about Janus's next wishes. Janus could almost hear Delight's exasperation with *his brother, the idiot.*

Janus bent to the letter, crossed the sepia pen strokes with blue ink and sent Chryses back to spy on Harm. Dangerous, yes, but

Chryses had seemed certain he could gull Harm. If the antimachinist was, as Psyke seemed to imply, an Itarusine agitator, Janus needed the information. He folded the paper over, melted the old wax, and dribbled it over the edge.

Another page, unluckier than most, and well aware of it from the huffy sigh barely suppressed, was dispatched to the streets outside the palace and to Seahook. Without waiting longer for a response from Ivor, Janus headed toward the prince's suite. Visiting Ivor would fuel gossip; best it be done before the rest of the palace awoke, and Janus knew Ivor well enough to know the man was awake with the dawn. The prince had a ferret's obsessive interest in everything to do with power; if anyone could guide him to what . . . possessed . . . Psyke, Ivor could. The difficulty came in getting an answer without betraying how much Janus needed one.

17

A SMALL PARADE TRAILED JANUS down the stairs and halls of the palace. Six guards traveled in Janus's wake, studying one another as warily as they studied him.

Assassination attempts always complicated matters. The guards' uniforms, overnight, seemed to have sprouted minute but meaningful differences; three of the guards sported a black-edged ribbon twined about their sword hilts.

Janus hoped the ribbons weren't the marks of those loyal to him: How infuriating to have defenders unable to free their blades from the tangle of ribbon and sheath. On the other hand, if they were his enemies' marks, well, how kind of them to tag themselves so visibly for him. He would have to see whether Evan Tarrant appeared beribboned or not. In the interim, he thought of them all equally as unreliable allies, much like the gang of children he and Miranda had led in the Relicts.

As they clattered down the last flight of stairs, the guards' boot heels noisy on the stone, they were met by a squad of the palace soldiers, set to watch Ivor Grigorian, and Janus stifled a sigh. He had known his visit to Ivor would be a matter for gossip, but with as many witnesses as he had gathered, and with the ribbons' rapid appearance a clear sign of exactly how quickly word could spread within the palace walls . . . well, he had hoped for more time.

He thought briefly about turning around, but caution and cowardice were two separate traits; caution was acceptable, cowardice was not. Janus tapped on Ivor's door. Dmitry opened it to him with a bow, a smile, and a murmured, "My lord, good to see you again," before ushering him into Ivor's private dining room.

Ivor, seated at one end of the long table, let his pen fall, and raised a smile with an ease that Janus could only attempt to imitate. "My pet, how considerate of you to save me the time otherwise spent assuring you of your welcome." He folded the note, added a careless splash of wax that nonetheless sealed the note with exactitude, and stamped it.

He tapped the edge on the desk, testing that the wax had firmed, and passed it, plus a sheaf of others, to the manservant.

Janus couldn't help but eye the correspondence with suspicion, thinking of Itarusine agitators beneath his very nose, of assassins paid in foreign coin. The expression on Ivor's face—calculation and amusement—stifled Janus's desire to confront the prince ascendant regarding Harm. Ivor expected him to do so, and Janus had had enough of performing as the man wished.

"You're turning into your father," Ivor commented. "All pinched-face disapproval and suspicion. It doesn't suit you, pet. It augurs anxiety and self-doubt."

"For you to correspond so much argues your unhappiness here. Perhaps you should ask Grigor to recall you."

"Come now, you know better. Vying for a throne requires constant vigilance and effort." Ivor stretched, long and lean, as smugly content as a cat, the type of self-aware pleasure that sent debutantes into ecstasies of speculation over what secrets such a smile held.

Janus could think of one reason for Ivor to be so satisfied: if he had made progress in his plans.

And what was he to take from that assumption? That Ivor had nothing to do with Harm's attempt on Janus's life? If Psyke's words could be trusted, and Harm was indeed the instigator . . . then perhaps Ivor and Harm were two separate agents of the Itarusine court, and Antyre was in more difficulties than Janus had dreamed.

"I begin to wonder why you came at all if you have nothing to say,"

Ivor said, still draped across his chair, as confident as if it were a throne and Janus his supplicant.

Coming here had been a mistake, Janus thought, but there was no retreat. He squared his shoulders and said, "You once told me there comes a time when respect demands honesty instead of fencing with words."

"Between equals," Ivor said. "And friends. Are we either of those?"

Janus dropped onto the chaise beside the breakfast table, looked at the remains of Ivor's meal, chose a pastry from a plate, and picked at it, sorting shreds of spiced game from the crust. His stomach growled and he ate, irritated at the waste of food.

A rough hand stroked his hair, crown to nape, and he jerked. Ivor sat beside him, and sighed. "Such a difficult pet, always reverting to the wild just when you believe him tamed."

Janus chose not to reply; sometimes silence was the safest retort.

"Surely you didn't come here to cadge scraps from my plate? Tell me, what can I do for you?"

Janus said, "No barter, no consideration? You simply want to know? You've gone native, Ivor." He found a ginger amusement in the slight stiffening of Ivor's posture. Something had struck more closely than Ivor would care to admit. Something like his desire for the Antyrrian throne. Janus's amusement faded.

Ivor saw a chance for a throne with only a few men standing between him and it. Janus, a handful of Antyrrian lords, and an idiot child—far better odds than Ivor faced in Itarus.

"So tell me, pet, how I can aid a man who once controlled a god, even secondhand?" Ivor took a sip of cooling coffee, grimaced, then pushed the cup away. "I wonder what it is about Antyre that directs women to pacts with the dead gods."

Janus slumped. Outmaneuvered, his interests apparent to Ivor, likely before he ever arrived, he admitted, "Psyke is no longer what she was."

"People alter their habits, their wants. Women more so than most, being fickle at heart. Still, as one who lay with Ani, I suppose I must believe you. Do you seek to use another god? I wonder if you could. Psyke, unlike your Maledicte, bears no love for you."

"Perhaps not," Janus said. His tone was sullen, and he knew it, felt the petulant cast of his mouth. His stomach churned with temper. "But she fails at hating me. I've seen hatred in men's eyes, and she lacks it."

"Indifference or duty can kill as neatly as hate; you should be aware of that. Or did you hate those political enemies you killed at my command?"

Janus shook his head, unwilling to revisit the days at the Winter Court when he had let Ivor dictate his actions.

"I suppose much depends on which god it is." Ivor looked speculative and pleased with the puzzle Janus had given him. "If Baxit chose to bestir Himself, Psyke would be a creature of logic and indifference, perhaps capable of claiming Antyre's throne for herself, could she be bothered to care."

"No," Janus said, though the thought was unpleasant and showed Psyke in a new and disturbing fashion. More like, Ivor meant to divide Janus from any aid Psyke could grant, were she so inclined.

Ivor shrugged. "Please yourself."

"I intend to," Janus said, and they shared an honest smile, the pleasure of two men who knew themselves to be in control of their destinies.

"So, Espit or Naga?" Ivor said. "Despair or greed? If Naga had His coils about your lady, His greed might prove troublesome. But I see no sign of His presence in her."

"She picks at her food," Janus snapped, "like one who's never known want or hunger."

Ivor pushed his breakfast tray back toward Janus, and said, "Should I call for more? You've obviously missed your meal."

Janus shook his head, belatedly embarrassed at his outburst. Ivor pulled the bell cord and when his seneschal appeared, said, "Please ask the kitchens for another breakfast. And a new pot of coffee."

Ivor stifled Janus's protest. "Please. It's only my duty as a host. Nothing more. And you'll recall I breakfast uncommonly early. A second breakfast would not go amiss on my plate either. Espit, you think?"

Janus allowed himself to be drawn back into speculation. "Espit is the most truly dead of the gods, the only one who went gracefully, according to the legends."

"As you say," Ivor agreed. "I cannot imagine Psyke strong enough to lure Espit from Her chosen grave. Unless your lady's with child?"

"I think not," Janus said. His heart gave a sudden lurch. Himself, a father? It would be disaster. With a child of his blood, Psyke could position herself well. Even Gost, his dubious ally, would turn to Psyke and an untainted child to turn into a king or queen.

"Death and the beauty, then," Ivor said.

"Haith," Janus said. "The god of death and victory." It fit with the little he had been thinking before, the sketchy details he had gleaned from the tracts Delight had sent. He licked his lips, a revealing habit he had thought conquered years ago in the Relicts, when his mother, Celia, had used it to gauge when he was lying.

It went unnoticed by Ivor, his attention gone to the opening door and the trays the maids brought in. The scent of fresh bread and the pepper-spiced meats came in before them. Janus, who often found the food in Antyre too fussed for his tastes, nearly salivated.

"Lovely," Ivor said. "Makes me hungry again, myself."

Janus allowed the maids to serve him; there was no point in denying himself simply to spite Ivor.

"Come back to Itarus," Ivor said, his forkful of pastry held abeyant. "Grigor rather admired you."

Janus smiled. "As if Grigor's attention is something to be courted. It's as dangerous as it is to be desired. You agree, or you wouldn't have come here to play auditor." He picked up his pastry, sans fork, crunched into it. Flavors exploded over his tongue, memories of three years of breakfasting with Ivor, plotting strategy and murder.

Ivor collected the broadsheet laid beneath the covered plates, opened it, raised eyebrows, and set it down.

Janus felt wariness seep back into his bones, pushing away the dangerous comfort he felt in Ivor's company.

"Death is a reclusive god and difficult to court," Ivor said. "I know of only one who succeeded. Your Cold King, the first of the Redoubts. The battlefield poets had praised him in verse so greatly that Haith heard his name echoing below and rose from His sepulchre to see such vitality for Himself. Redoubt stood, surrounded by dead soldiers, facing his enemies all about him, and laughed.

"Haith interceded, though no one recorded how, only that once Redoubt stepped out of His embrace, he walked through the streets, and all who opposed him died. I notice that Psyke's maid has taken ill. . . ."

Janus poked at pastry crumbs, refusing to be drawn into speculation.

"So sullen today, though I suppose that's only natural, given the broadsheets. Poole goes too far, I think. I own amazement that you've not killed him yet."

"Poole?" Janus said, the word slipping free. The name tasted foul in his mouth. "What's he done now?"

"Done as he always has," Ivor said. "Made mock. You've not seen it?"

The broadsheet left smudges on the linens when Janus snatched it up. The cheap ink bled on his fingers—a second printing, if it was still wet—and what could Poole have drawn to have proved so popular?

Janus had become accustomed to virulent screeds on his viciousness, the accusations of regicide, but the actual image made him flush with humiliation and fury. *Assassin*, he could bear. *Viper in the court, a wolf in the fold;* these were images he was accustomed to, and, if forced to be honest, images he rather enjoyed. Dangerous creatures were always worthy of admiration. But this . . .

The sketch showed him as a petulant boy, yanking Chryses's arm beside the cannon, crying, *Again! Again! Make it go Boom! again!*, looking nearly as witless as Adiran. At the edges of the sketch, Gost and DeGuerre shook their heads, while Ivor, drawn wearing bestial furs and a beard, grinned. The cannonball, Janus noted, stove in the side of a boat called *Peace*.

"It does divert your mind quite wonderfully," Ivor said. "Your wife is no threat to you, no matter that you fear her. Poole, on the other hand, or rather those behind him—"

The paper tore beneath Janus's hands; given that his poise was so obviously shattered, he took childish satisfaction in ripping the rest of it to bits and flung the confetti in Ivor's direction. Childish, yes, but his blade was across the room, the seneschal moving discreetly between Janus and his weapon, and Ivor was, after all, a foreign prince, and untouchable. Despite claims made otherwise, Janus had no desire for war; while he wanted Itarus's shackles taken from Antyre, there had to be less damaging ways to see that done.

Ivor kept his smile, and, as Janus regained his composure, collapsing into the mess he had made, Ivor's smile only deepened. "Oh, I've missed you, my pet. Be my right hand. I'll give you more power than the Antyrrians will ever allow you."

"And see Antyre fall? The throne is more than a prize," Janus said.

"Prettily put," Ivor said, "but spoken to the wrong audience. I know you, know your nature. People rarely change."

Janus said, "But they can learn what matters to them. I can make this country better, stronger, return it to glory."

"You can't," Ivor said. "While that fool child lives, you'll rise, at best, to regent, and find your every decision debated, your plans stymied on all fronts. But come aid me as you once did, and I'll see you rewarded."

Janus flicked bits of newsprint from the table in silence. Ivor was likely correct. Adiran blocked his path, a symbol too easily used by the duchess, by the Parliament, by the counselors. If Janus couldn't supplant the boy prince, the future—his and Antyre's—promised nothing but a series of battles, some won, others lost.

He licked his lips, and Ivor said, "Janus . . ." his tone pleased, confident.

Janus raised his head, met Ivor's eager gaze, and banished all friendliness in the man's face, real or pretend, with a few, simply stated words. "I'm Antyrrian, Ivor, to the bone."

· 18 ·

As Janus left the old wing of the palace, he found Evan Tarrant pacing outside, casting fulminating looks at Ivor's guards. "I'm his personal page—" The boy broke off, his anxiety switching to a quick grin at the sight of Janus. Janus had the uncomfortable thought that this boy might be one of the few people in this city that would smile at his appearance.

The boy's anxiety returned; he fidgeted in a manner unbecoming to a member of the palace staff. "Sir—"

"Not here," Janus said, snatching the boy's sleeve and turning him like a wave collecting driftwood.

The boy's stumbling gait smoothed as he caught up to Janus's quick pace, and trotted alongside him. "It's Gost and DeGuerre, sir." His voice, breathy, was pitched for Janus's ears and so Janus let him continue, bending to accommodate the boy's piping voice. "Admiral DeGuerre got a letter from Prince Ivor and then he and Mr. Gost shut themselves up in the king's study."

"Are they still meeting?" Janus asked. He cast a glance at his guards, following as faithfully as his shadow.

The boy nodded, and Janus clapped his shoulder. "Thank you, Evan. You've done well." Beneath his grip, the boy squirmed, pleased to be praised and careless about showing it.

Janus headed to the closed double doors of Aris's study. Janus nodded at the guards outside, a clear sign that he expected to be let in; after a moment, one of the guards opened the door for him. His sword hilt, Janus noted, was not beribboned.

Gost and DeGuerre stood on either side of Aris's desk, leaning over it, the crowns of their heads nearly touching. When Janus entered unannounced, their expressions commingled aggravation and outrage.

"I'm sorry to intrude," Janus said, "but as this is the king's study, it can hardly be a personal problem that DeGuerre sought you out for, and if it involves Antyre, well, I knew you'd be wanting me."

DeGuerre bristled. "Wanting you! If it weren't that Adiran were . . . as he is, I would see you whipped from—"

"Words, hastily said, take far more time to forget," Gost interrupted, taking off his spectacles and folding them neatly into thirds. "Janus, you were with Ivor all morning, did he tell you nothing of this?" he asked, gesturing at a sheet of vellum on the desk.

Janus, who had spent all of his childhood untaught, nonetheless suddenly understood all Delight's extravagant dislike of being called on the carpet by his various tutors. He raised his chin and said, "We discussed other matters."

"Useless," DeGuerre muttered.

Gost frowned; it aged his face from merely distinguished to something approaching old and weary. He said, "Well, as you're here, come and see what you have wrought."

As such had been his intention, Janus made no demur, but stepped obediently to the desk. Gost spread out the letter. This was a letter meant to intimidate, Ivor at his most official. From the weight of the vellum, nearly as thick as cloth, to the precision of letters and spacing of the lines, every word was as elegant as a well-kept blade.

"Don't know why you bother, Gost," DeGuerre said. "The boy can't read it."

"I haven't been a boy for quite some time," Janus said, finding something he could protest. The rest was regrettably true: another letter written in that damnable High Antyrrian.

"Your display at the docks was nothing but boyish temper and pride," DeGuerre said, and Janus's mask of politeness cracked.

"Is it you I have to thank for Poole's lovely sketch? I might remind you, it was *your* son who—"

"I have no son," DeGuerre said, voice overriding Gost's quiet reprimand.

"My father felt the same way once, and he had need of me nonetheless."

"Your father died of it—"

"Your sons may do the same," Janus said. "While you sit, secure behind your walls, Chryses walks among the antimachinist agitators. While you find fault, Delight builds machines—"

"Delight is nothing of mine and Chryses is, and always has been, a fool."

"Fools? They *act* to save their country while their elders fuss and fret. Aris used to harp on the need for young men; I begin to understand," Janus said.

"Aris," Gost said, "is irrelevant to the matter at hand. Last, shall I translate the letter for you? Or would you prefer to bicker longer?"

"Translate. If you would," Janus said. He forced a veneer of civility over his frustration and rising temper. In this situation, Maledicte would have seized the fireplace poker and burnt out their mocking eyes; faced with a language he couldn't read, Maledicte would ensure they couldn't do so either. But any violent act Janus chose must be for better purpose than simple relief.

Gost coughed, and Janus met Gost's all-too-knowing gaze. Kingmaker, they called him, and while Janus mocked Gost's reputation, he knew the man understood ambition and hatred.

"The letter is, as said, from Ivor in his position as treaty auditor. He has made a list of demands in reaction to what he deems a 'most troubling call to arms in the very heart of the city.'"

"Call to arms, indeed," Janus muttered. "Why must everyone persist in assuming I want war when Antyre lacks the resources to fight one?"

DeGuerre's automatic rebuttal stalled on the man's lips. He

looked . . . thoughtful, and Janus wondered why this one throwaway complaint might do more to prove his intentions to DeGuerre than a workshop full of plans.

Gost said, "We also lack the resources to pay the fine Ivor asks. Ten thousand sols from each of the families involved."

DeGuerre's expression grew cold again and Janus sighed. Gost had appalling timing.

". . . As well as a fine from the kingdom itself, matching in total the penalties assessed on the families. Ivor also requires immediate surrender of the new cannons and shot, so take pleasure in that at least; Ivor was favorably impressed by your designs."

"The money is nothing," Gost said. "One more hardship piled among others on Antyre's back. Ivor's next demand is ruinous. He requires us to allow his ships entrance to our waters, our harbors, the very heart of our country. One moment of arrogance, Janus, and you see our shores invaded in the name of peace."

"A moment you forced. If you'll recall, I wanted to halt the demonstration," Janus said. "But it won't come to that." They turned equal expressions of skepticism on him and he gritted his teeth. Was he the only one who made plans at all? Two days gone from the catastrophic demonstration and he had dismissed nearly as many plans as he had imagined.

Gost sighed, and sat down behind the desk, steepling his fingers and resting his chin on that uncomfortable point.

Janus said, "We are in the same position we were before. Ivor's letter is nothing more than a letter of intent; he polices the treaty, but Grigor is the only one who can adjust it."

"I fail to see why that is a matter for celebration," DeGuerre said. "Grigor is as eager as Ivor to devour Antyre. All it allows us is time to rail against our fate. Perhaps if we make it clear that you and yours acted against the kingdom's wishes, Grigor will forgive—"

"You would risk everything on Grigor's mercy? I am not such a fool," Janus said.

Gost leaned back in the chair, propped his feet up on Aris's favorite footstool, making himself entirely too comfortable. Aris used to sit thusly, watching Janus, Bull, and DeGuerre debate, before making his decisions.

Janus thought Fanshawe Gost just might have been making plans of his own, while wearing the mask of a false friend.

"Time can be an invaluable ally, if one knows how to use it," Janus said, turning to DeGuerre. The admiral's hands were shaking with agitation, and Janus acquitted him of not caring about the outcome. It wasn't cowardice that set him worrying about soothing Grigor but genuine concern for the country. "And we do have time. A fortnight minimum—time for Ivor's report to reach Grigor at the Winter Court and return."

"And you have a purpose for those scant days?" DeGuerre asked. Hope glittered in his eyes.

"First, find Aris's assassin. If we use this time to prove Ivor guilty of Aris's murder, we can counter their claim that it was Antyre who broke the treaty."

"*Will* we find proof of Ivor's guilt?" Gost murmured.

"Sooner than you'll find proof of mine," Janus said. "Though it would be easier if we had some method of keeping Ivor's attention elsewhere while we attempt to net him."

"The money!" DeGuerre said. "It can come from the funds for your precious privateers. If we hand that over—"

"If we hand over the funds, all at once," Gost interjected, pinning DeGuerre with a disappointed look, "it will become apparent we've been falsifying the books for years. We'll be in worse straits than we are now."

Janus said, "The money is hardly our first concern. Nor will it be Ivor's concern. We must prevent his fleet from touching ashore, prevent their soldiers from setting foot in our streets."

"Without arming the people?" DeGuerre said. "They'd be cut down, slaughtered all."

"I don't want war," Janus repeated. "If I wanted war, I'd have murdered Ivor and sent his head back in a tax chest." Janus smiled at both men, letting them see that, yes, he could do such a thing, and without qualm, even to a man he felt a reluctant fondness for. After all, they persisted in thinking the worst of him anyway; he had nothing left to lose.

"How do you intend to stop them, then?" DeGuerre said.

Gost said, "You think you can prevent their landing and keep the peace? How?" His eyes narrowed, and Janus decided then and there, that his plans would remain his own. There was too much hunger in Gost's face, in the clutch of his hands on the armrests of his chair.

Janus allowed himself a vulgar shrug, enjoyed the way both men twitched in instant disapproval, and made no answer beyond that.

Predictably, DeGuerre spluttered at him, words made incomprehensible by his agitation.

Gost, in contrast, settled back again, that shadow of suspicion hooding his eyes. Janus turned his expression as blank and as guileless as he had done during his first days in the Antyrrian court, and smiled.

He had no intention of sharing his plan with Gost. He had been gulled by the man, and it rankled. Though Janus distrusted altruism on principle, he had believed in Gost's offer of aid, forgetting that men who played games with power were uniformly ambitious. The result of such carelessness? Gost's first suggestion of aid had led to the demonstration at the docks.

No, Gost was no ally, but another like Ivor, one he must take by surprise.

DeGuerre left the room with an ill-mannered slam of the door that set the dust on Aris's bookshelves falling like ash.

Gost said, "You make an enemy of one who might otherwise be an ally."

"Do you speak of yourself or of the admiral? I prefer his honest frustration and temper to your more calculated words." Janus sat in the chair opposite Gost, stretching his feet out before him, and studying the shine of his boots. His hand dropped to his hip and rested there, above his sword hilt.

"Your father did you a grave disservice when he chose to have you schooled in the Itarusine court. You exhibit the worst of their manners—insolence and distrust." Gost's face betrayed no sentiment other than a faint, fatherly disappointment. A practiced liar indeed.

Janus nearly laughed, freed by the realization that if Gost was an enemy, he needn't court his approval any longer. "It wasn't schooling he sent me there for but disposal, a way to placate Aris's demands for my reinstatement as father's heir and to please himself. The Itarusine court's notoriously dangerous. Unfortunately for my father, Ivor found me useful, Aris recalled me home, and well, we know the rest."

"You slaughtered your father," Gost said, "and fed him to the sea."

"Not I," Janus said.

"Your lover," Gost said.

"Unproven," Janus said. "Though I will admit Mal's desires sometimes exceeded sense."

"Indeed," Gost said. "It seems to be a flaw of youth." He rose and left Janus in possession of the king's study.

Janus's satisfaction faded between one heartbeat and the next. All very well to name Gost enemy, but the recognition of it didn't make the man any less powerful. Gost commanded respect; held a fortune earned in Kyrda's court, safe from Itarusine predation; had the friendship of the Kyrdic king; and, if DeGuerre and Bull supported him, owned the majority of the Kingsguard.

Gost might even have been behind the attempt on his life. Janus had only Psyke's word that Harm had been behind it, and how could he trust the word of a woman who spoke with the dead and counted the Duchess of Love among her friends?

Janus leaned forward, elbows on his knees, and tangled his hands in his hair. Enemies on every side, yes, and he was accustomed to that, but never before had he needed to turn them to allies. Even having Maledicte by his side would fail to help toward that end.

Turn the knife outward. It had been all the advice Mal had ever given him. Advice that had served them so well in the Relicts. It was the same thing now. Stop hurting himself with doubts.

Stop his enemies, yes, but recognize that Ivor took precedence over the rest. Ivor commanded a near army of loyal men, brought to Antyre with him, in the very walls of the palace, playing at being simple servants; he owned men in the streets, Itarusine merchants who were likely more than they appeared. But Janus knew Ivor and the Winter Court, and knew they were not without fears of their own.

Janus's idea turned and twisted in his mind as he added and discarded elaborations, hunted for the perfect plan. He collected the broadsheet lying over the arm of the chair, folded it back to the caricature, and thought of Poole, in his privileged prison cell, high above the crowded and diseased lower levels. There was the place to start.

BEFORE LEAVING THE PALACE, JANUS thought to visit Adiran, see how the boy fared. After the tantrums had ceased, he'd heard nothing from the nursery save gossip.

The guards outside Adiran's door made way when Janus approached, ushering him in, then, as he passed, Janus heard one of them heading away from the door, undoubtedly notifying Rue of his visit.

The low table was set for lunch and Adiran looked up from his plate, leaning away so the maid could finish cutting his meal into bite-size pieces. She set the fork into the boy's lax hand.

Adiran smiled, wide and sunny, and Janus joined him at his low table, fishing in his pockets for a sweet.

The nurserymaid said, "Not 'til after he eats, my lord," then paled and removed herself from his reach.

Janus laid the waxed twist of paper on the table, and Adiran peeled it open to reveal a crimson chunk of rock sugar.

"Thank you," Adiran said clearly.

Janus blinked. Courtesies were rare in Adiran's world. The boy was only tangentially aware of people at all, though Aris had worked with him. Perhaps it was simply table etiquette, drummed in by rote practice; the maid seemed unsurprised, even as she disapproved.

"It's a single piece," Janus said, "hardly enough to ruin his appetite."

"His appetite's not good," she said. "He doesn't do enough to wake it."

"I suppose not," Janus said, after some thought. Done with his candy, Adiran reached for a piece of venison, and the maid coughed.

Janus caught the boy's hand, and held out the fork. "Use this," he said.

Adiran took it, though he sent Janus a glance much less sweet than usual. He poked at the meat with the fork clutched tight in his fist, little bursts of frustration.

"I can watch him." As the maid hesitated, he said, "Or do you think my manners so barbaric I cannot even instruct a child. . . ." He let his tone grow sharp and cold, watched her pale.

"Of course, my lord," she said, dropping a curtsy and taking herself out of the room.

Adiran watched her go, and dropped the fork, plucking the meat from the tines and eating it defiantly from his fingers.

Janus laughed, and let the boy eat as he would. Intelligent or not, the boy did have a will of his own. Gost, no doubt, intended to use it to prove the boy was fit to be king. It was what Janus would do, if he felt inclined to hide his goals: Pretend the boy had recovered well enough to rule but keep him confined and pretend to receive direction from him.

Janus snitched a piece of the venison, ate it, and watched Adiran eat the rest of his meal faster, protecting it from Janus.

When the food was gone, the boy pushed his way into Janus's lap and started rooting through his pockets. There was no more candy to find, but Janus let the boy collect the tiny dagger he carried in his waistcoat, a last-ditch weapon should his sword be taken from him. Adiran tilted it back and forth, watching the shine of the blade in the room. "Would you like it?" Janus asked. "It's not a toy, but you have enough of those."

Adiran stopped fidgeting and tilted his head up to meet Janus's gaze. Completely still, completely silent, those blue eyes watched Janus with a strange intensity. "It's only a thought," Janus said. "Even toys might pall if that's all you're allowed. Though best not to let your maid see it. Consider it a birthday gift. Likely your first."

Adiran laid the dagger on the table, walked his fingers up the blade, leaving fingerprints on the steel.

"Do you want me to tell you a story, Adi?"

Still looking at the knife, Adiran nodded, the reflection of his eyes blurred shadows in the blade.

"When I was your age, I had a birthday as uncelebrated as yours. Yours is tainted by the death of your mother. Your father mourned her loss so much that even though he loved you, he couldn't celebrate your birth. Typical of Aris, if you ask me. In my case, though, there was no celebration because my mother wished I had never been born. When I turned thirteen, Miranda kissed me. Not in play, not to make mock of our whorish mothers. But because she loved me.

"I miss her, Adi. I feel incomplete without her." He pressed his face into Adiran's knotted curls.

A dark weight rose up through him, the cold chill of Ani's voice not as he had always imagined it, harsh and cold, but a childish treble that stung his ears deep inside, made him clap a hand to them, expecting blood.

Then you shouldn't have used her. Betrayed Her.

Adiran's hand fisted around the dagger's hilt.

Janus pushed the boy from his lap, snatched the dagger from his hand, breathing hard and fast. Adiran blinked at him, quiet and entirely too watchful, a predator's eyes in a boyish face. But the intensity of his gaze faded. Adiran yawned and held out his hand for the dagger.

"Please?" he said.

Janus kept the dagger close for a long moment, then passed it over, along with its sheath.

Janus sat down again, numb. The boy's intelligence was no greater than before, though Gost might find it so, did Janus choose to acquit him of duplicity in the matter. It was simply that Adiran was no longer alone in his soul. As much as Janus wished to deny it, he could not. As Maledicte had been a composite personality, comprised of Miranda and Ani, so Adiran grew into something more. Something new and dangerous, though right now, with Adiran leaning up against his hip in sleepy contentment, it was hard to believe. Could the boy, flawed as he was, even hold the god's attention?

Vengeance, Janus thought bleakly. *Love and vengeance and a beloved father murdered. Ani would take notice.*

The double doors to the nursery opened wide, giving Janus a glance at a squad of guards, with Rue at the head, the mastiff Hela at his side.

Hela jerked out of Rue's grasp and began to bark, deep furious notes that filled the nursery. Rue gestured sharply and a guard dragged Hela back into the corridor, still barking and growling.

Rue bowed briefly to Janus and said, "Might we speak?"

"Of course," Janus said. He gave Adi a gentle shove toward his toys, and followed Rue into the hall.

Hela had calmed, and was being led away on a heavy chain. Rue watched the guard go and sighed. "Bane's already been transferred to the stables. I had hoped Hela would stay manageable."

It was Adiran, Janus thought. The dogs knew, sensed the god's presence lurking within the child, knew and hated Her.

"The guards believe Maledicte left a taint in the room, and that's why the dogs bark and growl so, where once they loved to be."

Janus bridled, but Rue's face was only quietly thoughtful; in fact, when he saw Janus's expression, he shook his head in apology. "I'm sorry. You cannot like hearing such rumors."

"I've heard worse," Janus said. He felt oddly anticipatory. Since Aris's murder, Rue had been occupied in chasing a killer most likely long gone, in separating rumor from truth and fears. That he spoke with such civility to Janus argued that perhaps he accepted that Janus was innocent of regicide. But then again, Rue had been polite during the worst of it, when the smell of Aris's blood still soured the air.

"I would ask a favor of you, sir," Rue said.

Janus raised a brow, leaning back against the flocked wallpaper of the hallway. It rustled against his sleeves, whispering like the scratching of rats. The muscles in his back tightened, though he endeavored to be still.

"Adiran is the prince of the realm," Rue began. "The last of the blood—"

"Hardly that," Janus said.

"Legitimate bloodline, then," Rue corrected himself. "As such, his life is not his own. For the good of the public confidence, I ask you to stay away from the child."

Janus had expected something of the sort from the moment Rue mentioned Adiran's rank. It was enough in itself to make him bridle, the idea that this guard thought to tell him what to do. Coupled with his sudden and new awareness of Ani's presence, it seemed unwise to leave Adiran alone to listen to Black-Winged Ani.

"I think you'll find that I'm the only one who can understand him," Janus said.

"He has the nurse to see to his needs; and, as he is, he has no desire for more."

"Are you so certain?" Janus said. "Adiran's wits improve, thus making him capable of boredom and discontent."

"Your concern does you credit. I will ensure that the nurses report any of Adiran's progress to you."

Janus bit back any further argument. This was a battle that could be fought later; it was insulting but hardly injurious. "If it will help reassure the people in these uncertain times, I can do little else but agree."

He nodded stiffly at Rue, got a nod in return, and stalked away, trying to keep calm. It shouldn't rankle so much; Adiran, after all, was nothing to him. Nothing but his only family.

Janus pulled his temper in tighter, and thought, as his mood had gone so foul, perhaps now would be the ideal time to visit Stones.

STONEGATE PRISON LOOKED MUCH AS it had on Janus's last visit, an edifice of leprous stone, flaking under the pall of soot, riddled with dark slits like rents in an old shroud, and as quiet as a tomb. Appearances, though, Janus knew, were deceptive. This peace was as false as a courtesan's smile, and hid the same sort of ugliness: disease, murder, madness.

Inside the walls men, women, and children were packed as closely as animals in market pens, punished for crimes that the noble class committed often and without retribution.

It only took a few owed sols to send a merchant or working-class man to Stones, ensuring the ruin of their health and status. The nobles, though, were extended credit until there was no hope of repayment; ironic that a good portion of the debts that destroyed the merchants were caused by the nobles who couldn't be bothered to pay their bills on time. Or at all.

As his carriage neared the prison, the wheels stuck and churned, the gravel drive unraked and in humped furrows. After the third such jolt, Janus tapped the roof of the carriage. "I'll walk."

The horses drew to a halt, and Janus stepped out. The air was foul, and he pressed a sleeve to his face, feeling oddly as if the past had impressed itself upon his present. Hadn't he and Miranda watched Kritos come out of this very same carriage, hand up to ward off the stink of the Relicts? Had he been so long away that he had become unable to bear the stink of unwashed men?

The wind rose, coiled miasma about him, and Janus coughed until his gorge rose. This stench had little to do with life and everything to do with death. He stepped out of the shadow of the carriage while the guards' horses bridled and danced, and looked again at Stones.

The narrow strip of gravel leading up to the barred front door was on firm soil, rutted and hollowed and uncared for, but firm. The rest of the courtyard—the dirt was turned and turned again, rich loam showing through, studded with flies rising in small buzzing spirals like smoke.

Simpson's and Walker's familiar faces were grim, repulsed, and Janus nodded at them. "Inside's like to be worse," he said. The wind shifted; Simpson gagged audibly, and nearly set Janus to doing likewise.

"My lord," Walker said, his face pale beneath the disfiguring blotches on his cheek. "There's plague inside. The charnel pits are full, thus the ground turning. The very air is riddled with disease."

"Your concern is noted," Janus said. He assumed the man feared for his own well-being and not Janus's. The scars on Walker's face were old echoes from the man's battle with a past plague. Janus had a matching array of scars tucked beneath his arm where blisters had burst as a child, though his scars were far lighter. Ella, Miranda's mother, for all her sins, had had a deft hand with folk medicine.

Janus might fear a relapse of the plague himself had it not been proven to him that for those who survived, the plague's grasp grew weak on them ever after. A later bout of it during his time in Winter Court had left him unmarked, though others died.

Janus continued on his way, though Walker was right: the air was weighted with disease, so strong a presence that the air seemed smudged by it. Walker conferred briefly with Simpson, and Simpson went back to stand guard over the carriage and coachman. Not an illogical assignment, Janus reflected. Times were uncertain; his carriage might be attacked for any number of reasons from penury to politics, while he would be safer than usual inside a prison. His enemies preferred to strike in the dark and from behind.

Walker hastened to Janus's side. "My lord, may I ask your business here?"

"No," Janus said. He narrowed his eyes at the first dim stretch of the tunnel entrance, trying to recall his prior visit. Then, he had been focused on retrieving Mal.

The halls were dark, dirty, and narrow; the ground beneath his boots soft with dirt and spilled blood; and the stink seemed embedded in the very stone. Janus took his sleeve from his face, forced himself to breathe it in. Wasn't this the stench of his childhood, the odor of poverty without pride or expectation? Wasn't this what he intended to eradicate from his kingdom?

"Such a sour face. Is my prison not to your liking, my lord?" Damastes growled when Janus entered the head jailer's chambers. Janus wove his way through the man's rooms, crowded to the ceiling with a collection of bribes and favors that encompassed everything from jewelry to furniture, and drew up a seat before the man's desk, a delicate pièce of furniture in the latest fashion, all gilt edges and painted wood. A dish of herbs burned sluggishly, the scented smoke pushing back some of the prison stench.

"The prison's fine; it's only the wrong people are in it," Janus said.

"Come to take someone else out, my lord?" Damastes asked. "Last time, it was the courtier Maledicte. I was surprised to not find you here in his place, after what he did."

"Perhaps you should be more cautious with your tongue, man," Janus said. "You address a peer."

"Ha," Damastes said. "A jumped-up bastard—" He broke off to cough, a long, liquid sound that told Janus exactly why Damastes felt so free to disparage him. The man was dying.

Best to business, then. Janus took out the parure he had thieved from Psyke's chambers; he doubted she would miss it, having re-coiled from it when he offered it to her, but she might object to the use he had for it. Sudden bright motes danced in the close room as the diamonds and gold threw back the light. "You have jewels aplenty, I am well aware. But I also recall you had an aristocratic sensibility. The stones are worth a fortune, but the provenance . . ."

"The Lovesy parure," Damastes said. "Given to Amarantha Lovesy, who wed your father and who died by Maledicte's hand. These are gems with history." He wiped his mouth on a silk handkerchief, spotting it with a smear of watery blood. He reached out for the necklace, then hesitated, his strange stone-colored eyes glancing at Janus. "What do you want for it?"

"Poole," Janus said. "To treat as I see fit." He brushed at the dust clinging to the overtasseled lampshade, setting the fabric wavering, releasing the scent of old flame.

Damastes sat back without touching the necklace, though every sinew in his body yearned toward it. "You overpay. Something that is uncommon both in the general and in the specific. What aristocrat ever looses his grip on coin without need?"

Janus let the necklace lie. "My wife displeases me, taking up with unpleasant company. Why not be rid of her jewelry?"

Damastes laughed, then choked. The handkerchief came into use again, and longer this time, came away wetter and darker. He dropped the sodden cloth, reached out and drew the necklace to him, tucking it beneath his brocade vest with the greedy savor of a child hiding away a sweet lest he be expected to share. The bracelet and earrings followed, finding a new and unlikely home in the jailer's clothes.

Janus rose to go, and Damastes said, "Will you kill him?" Before Janus could confirm or deny, Damastes went on, "If you do . . . take his body elsewhere for burial. We're awash in corpses here."

JANUS TOOK THE NARROW STAIRS to Poole's tower cell; a litany of cries and curses trailed up from the common cells spurring him upward. A tight grin touched his face, banished before he tapped on Poole's half-open door.

"What is it?" Poole snapped, without looking up from his desk. His untidy hair and lean fingers were constantly in motion as he sketched figure after figure, and pushed his graying hair, far too long for fashion, from his face. On one of the sweeps, he caught a clear glimpse of Janus and his fingers stilled. He dropped his charcoal; it splintered on the flagstones.

"You," he said. He leaned back in his chair, plush velvet and leather, and lit a cigarillo with the same nervous gestures that seemed more habit than actual emotion. "Come to threaten me? Bribe me to stop my inks?" Charcoal dust smudged one eye socket and the bridge of his thin, beaky nose.

"Would it work?" Janus said, honestly curious. He had always wondered if Poole were purely a scandal chaser or a man of genuine feeling.

"I stand by my art," Poole said. He reached past the rat's litter of scrap paper on his desk and dug out a monocle, screwing it into the smudged eye socket, adding another sooty print to his cheekbone.

"I'm glad," Janus said.

The monocle shifted abruptly, nearly falling loose, though Poole's face otherwise betrayed no surprise. "Really? I hadn't thought you a man appreciative of the art of truth."

"I'm not appreciative," Janus said. "Don't mistake me, Poole. And your truths are only half-truths at best. You belabor old wounds and wake new ones."

"I speak for the common men and their fears," Poole said, polishing his monocle with feverish intensity.

"You care for them? For their needs, their wants, their pains?"

"More than you do, for all that you were born one of them."

Janus grinned. "Then you'll be pleased that I've come here to help further your understanding of the common man." He pushed aside a sheaf of papers, lip curling as he uncovered one of Poole's earlier sketches of the dock debacle, and leaned against the exposed corner of the desk.

"Help . . . ?"

"You see only the poor, suffering men with hearts of gold and an earnest desire to prosper. I think you need to see the other side—

those poor who would rather drag everyone down to their level than raise a hand to help their neighbors. The mothers who sell their children to feed themselves. The men who take their frustrations out on women's bodies or find solace in drink or drugs until they end up dead and decaying in the streets."

"That's the Relicts," Poole said. "Those who bide there are nothing but animals."

Janus reached across the desk, collected a bottle of whiskey and the glass beside it, pouring himself a splash just to watch Poole bridle at Janus's easy assumption of his belongings. "Tell yourself that. Why not? It's what the aristocrats say so they can despise us without any such inconvenience as conscience. It's what allows the struggling middle class to stay calm, instead of murdering us in our sleep. After all, they can always reassure themselves that the Relict rats have it worse, reassure themselves that they are prospering. They are, in comparison. Of course, starving dogs are prosperous in comparison."

"Aris sent the Particulars to clean the Relicts of such influences."

"Oh yes," Janus said, "and perhaps Echo, for all his sins, had the right of it. He didn't target the current blackguards and whores, let them kill each other off. Echo concentrated on the children. Do you know how many of us his men sent to the sea or saw beaten and jailed for no more a sin than a theft of food?"

Janus found his breath coming fast, his hands tightening on the glass and the bottle, remembering Miranda crying as their friends were lost to Echo's bells. He shook his head. "But we are talking of your future, not my past. Gather your paper, your inkwell, your charcoal and quills."

"You've paid for my release?" Poole gaped like a fish, long limbs gone slack and spindly in surprise. His monocle dropped to his breast, and he didn't pay it any heed at all.

"Ease your mind. The world is as you understand it, and I am the monster you call me. I've paid for new lodgings for you. You'll enjoy your stay in the central cells, down with your poor, misunderstood common man. When you've seen enough, write me."

Poole's face, pale already from the long confinement in Stones Tower, grayed; he looked his age for the first time, his fervor faded to an old man's fear. "You're a cruel man, Last, and foolish. When my patron hears about this—"

"How will he hear?" Janus said. "Will you write him? I warn you, the only letter that will leave this place will be the one with my direction upon it. Best save your paper."

Janus oversaw Poole's transfer from the relatively cozy room high above the stench and clamor of the central cells, and watched with a smile when Poole gagged visibly as the big broad doors swung open, revealing people all going rigid in the sudden light, more like startled vermin than humans.

"Back," the guards yelled, "back up."

They gave Poole a none-too-gentle nudge inside, suggesting that Poole, during his stay upstairs, hadn't managed to make allies of the guards.

Ill considered of him, Janus thought, but that was Poole. For all his claim of protecting the common man, he was as willing to overlook the ones who served him as any aristocrat. The doors slammed shut behind him, giving Janus a last glance of the man's rigid spine, his arms clutched tight around his handful of paper.

Janus tipped each of the guards involved with a luna, collecting their smiles in return, before seeking out Damastes again. The man hastily tucked the earring away from where he had been studying it in a rare shaft of sunlight.

" 'S funny," he said, once his treasure was hidden again. "Your father was the one who put 'im here. Now you've consigned him to the death Last didn't."

"I don't want him dead," Janus said, unwilling to bandy words. "Part of the payment is to keep him alive but miserable."

"You really are a right bastard," Damastes said, raised his hands in automatic apology. "Wasn't meaning nothing by it. Not your birth, anyways." The man's gray eyes were sly, making mockery of his apology, but Janus ignored it; he'd heard worse.

He stepped out into the daylit yard, eyes watering again as the scent of new graves assailed him. *Three days*, he thought. He gave Poole three days before the man sent either a letter or word, well within the time Janus needed.

Janus raised a hand, and the carriage was brought around. He collapsed into its fragrant interior; the scent of wood polish, cedar, and lavender was a balm to his senses after the reek of Stones.

"My lord?" Simpson asked. He coughed into his gloved hand and looked as horrified as if he had found his skin blistered with plague marks.

"Return to the palace," Janus said. "We're done here."

OUTSIDE THE KING'S STUDY, THE noonday sun lit trees thick with rooks. Janus eyed them warily, searching for some sign that they had purpose beyond simple animal need for shelter, and finally drew the curtains back, darkening the room back to predawn light.

"Are you listening, Last?" DeGuerre asked. The tone of voice left no doubt he thought the answer no.

"Always to you," Janus said. It was truth; DeGuerre might be a conservative thorn in his side, but he had a powerful following. The fact that DeGuerre took his truthful response as a veiled insult only made it more appealing. "Shall I repeat it back like a schoolboy? You believe Bull and I are overreacting to the unrest in the streets, that it is only the usual malcontents voicing their unreasonable demands for jobs, for shelter, for food, for a life not lived in desperation."

Gost, sitting behind Aris's desk, having assumed the position of authority with a slick ease that made Janus itch to have him thrown out of the room, derailed DeGuerre's protest with a quiet "Hector."

Bull sighed and spoke before anyone else could. "Egalitarianism aside, I stand by my findings. Murne is overcrowded, the city streets full of those who seek a life more profitable than the farming communities outside."

DeGuerre said, "Only proves my point. Malcontents all. They come from farms where there's both work and food."

"There's work enough for entire families, yes, but not food enough—not when a third of their crops goes to Itarus and the rest is sold to merchants who have little money of their own. Is it any wonder they flock to Murne? Or sell their children?"

"A pretty drama for the serial sheets," DeGuerre said. "Every story is a stage tragedy."

"It's true," Bull said. "Farmers have always sent their children into Murne to find jobs. Only, in recent years, there have been no jobs to find."

"Itarusine merchants don't hire Antyrrian brats," Janus murmured. "What was Aris thinking to allow so many of them to profit here?"

DeGuerre looked as if Janus had stumbled upon a question he had asked himself more than once.

Gost tapped the ink bottle with a lazy hand, his nails clicking against the glass, drawing their attention. "I believe Aris saw it as his own quiet war of attrition against the country that held the reins. He assumed that their interests were more personal than political. A reasonable enough assumption. Men are driven by their own urges, not abstractions. You must admit it in yourself, Last. You wish to be king to please yourself, first and foremost."

DeGuerre's gaze, softened in thought, narrowed again as distrust bloomed anew in his heart. Gost smiled, that paternal smile that hid nothing but smug self-satisfaction.

"Aris was naïve if he thought the Itarusines would shift allegiances," Janus said. "Grigor supports their endeavors financially, or did you think it coincidence that while Antyrrian merchants struggle under the weight of an aristocracy that thinks it good financial sense to shirk their bills, the Itarusine merchants prosper? Aris didn't welcome émigrés. He welcomed spies."

"I suppose Ivor shared this information with you," Gost said.

DeGuerre, like a trained dog, began muttering.

Gost, Janus thought, needed to be silenced, but he doubted a friendly request would suffice. Dagger, sword, a hired footpad on a dark road—it begged for blood.

DeGuerre's rant wound down with a last, familiar splutter. Janus didn't bother listening. DeGuerre was bluster and bluff, prone to speaking wildly while his actions were the very model of caution.

Bull said, "Aris knew they were spies. He thought it a fair exchange as it gave us a chance to infiltrate their line of information. But this purging of Antyrrian employees is new and worrisome."

"Soldiers preparing for action," Janus said.

"Some of them have families," Bull said. "Antyrrian wives, mistresses, children." It was a pragmatic and oblique solution; Janus thought better of the man than he had in months.

Gost said, "Are you contemplating punishing Antyrrian citizens in hopes that their Itarusine families will be swayed? I doubt you'll see any result beyond rousing the city against you."

"Some men are softer than others," Janus said. "Some lack the stomach for—"

"Murder?" Gost asked, that slight smile touching his mouth again. One word, and DeGuerre and Bull were drawn back into the fold, Janus excluded as the dangerous outsider.

Janus was more relieved than not to hear Evan's familiar scratchy stutter-tap on the door. "Yes," he said, and DeGuerre flung up his hands in exasperation.

"Last, we haven't begun to solve the problems you've raised. Your attention is required. . . ."

DeGuerre trailed off but Janus hardly noticed. Not when Evan came in, all tight shoulders and jaw clenched with silent effort, beneath the weight of the man leaning on his narrow form. Delight petted the boy's tousled hair once, before releasing him to stagger toward Janus. His skirts, ragged and torn, hampered him; he limped as if he'd taken a fall, and his hands were blistered and red. Released, Evan backed out of the door, biting his lips, as if Delight's distress had made itself at home in his own heart.

"Janus—" Delight said. His voice was rough and cracked as if he'd been inhaling . . . It was smoke that trailed in with him, the acrid scent of ruination and flame.

Janus took three steps forward, clasping Delight's forearms, partly to keep Delight upright and partly to assure him of his welcome. He couldn't miss Delight's cringing glance at the admiral.

"What's happened?" Janus asked, though he could guess; a fire at Seahook. What he needed to know was how bad it was. How ruinous it would prove to be.

Delight swayed. Exhaustion and pain made themselves seen in ringed dark eyes, in the careful stiffness of his shoulders as he held himself upright. He stumbled, foot snagging in a skirt draggle, caught Janus's vest, and said, heedless of his near fall, "Did you mean for him to die?"

Janus's mind, usually his best and most reliable tool, blanked. Delight had come to the palace, *Delight*, not Chryses. Come to a place where he was unwelcome and scorned.

"I'm building a future at your command," Delight said, hands tightening on Janus's clothes, though a blister popped and he flinched. "I think you owe me the truth at least. Did you expect him to die? Set him back to spying on Harm as punishment for his actions at the docks?"

"No," Janus said. "I told him to be careful—" He sucked in a breath, shaking the weakness from his voice. "No," he said again, trying to ensure that Delight believed him, but hearing only uncertainty in his own voice. *Had* he meant Chryses to die?

Delight let out a sigh and sagged forward, nesting his forehead against the juncture of Janus's collarbone and chest. He smelled of soot, blood, and sweat; his hair was burned also, frizzled and snarled along his spine. Janus touched it gently, felt the way Delight trembled with the effort of controlling his grief.

"Who's dead?" DeGuerre demanded. "Explain yourself!"

"Hector," Bull said. He put his hands on DeGuerre's shoulders, holding him back when DeGuerre moved toward Delight.

"Damn you, it's my—" DeGuerre broke off, unwilling to claim Delight even in extremity. Like Last, Janus thought, only taking him back when forced.

Janus stroked Delight's spine, the knots of it pressed against his hand. "I burned it," Delight whispered, the sound carried on an upward puff of soot. "I burned Seahook to deny them the satisfaction of firing it themselves. Burned my notes to ashes rather than let the antimachinists take them."

He shuddered in Janus's arms, and Janus raised his head, met Bull's blank gaze, Gost's speculative one, and DeGuerre's carefully turned back.

Delight flinched again in Janus's arms, from a pain purely mental. Fear crept across his face; the exhaustion fading. The man expected recriminations, Janus realized, now that the story was out.

Janus touched his cheek, brought Delight's face from hiding, and said, slow and seriously, "You could have done nothing else. You defended your country's best interest, though it cost you dearly."

Delight shuddered against him, relief as much a burden as the fear, and said, "I let him burn, too. . . ." If the man hadn't been so exhausted, so dried by the heat of the blaze, he would have had tears standing in his eyes, Janus thought.

"Then he'll have a marker more fitting than any gravestone," Janus said. "A marker of slagged metal by the sea."

Delight sagged; his clutching hands loosened. "You won't let him be forgotten. They were his plans, too."

"We'll put his name on every engine we build," Janus vowed. Delight sighed.

He settled Delight in the armchair, poured him a cup of tea, and Delight drank it, heedless that it was cold and overbrewed, having been served several hours earlier during Janus's breakfast.

"The antimachinists—" Janus began.

"Where's Chryses?" DeGuerre said, anger making him do the unthinkable and address his disowned son to find out what had happened to the disgraced one.

"He's dead," Delight said. He covered his eyes with scorched palms, breath ragged behind their dubious shelter.

Janus poured a generous splash of whiskey into Delight's teacup before adding more cold tea. Delight drank it down like it was nectar, and the whiskey sparked heat in his flat, glazed eyes. "*Your fault,*" Delight said. "If you'd allowed us on the estate, we'd have been working in security, where Harm couldn't have—"

"Harm," Janus said. "He was behind this?"

Delight nodded, looking down at the teacup, his burned braid sliding perilously close to the surface, adding the taste of char to an already unpalatable drink. "Four of them," Delight said. "With Chryses's body between them. Two were Antyrrian bullyboys. The other two were Itarusine. The one who killed Chry was Itarusine."

"You know this for certain?" Gost said at the same moment DeGuerre growled something ugly under his breath.

"They spoke Itarusine," Delight said. "Not something you'll find your average man doing." He clutched the teacup in his hands, burned fingers bleeding on the pale china.

Gost spoke into the quiet, his voice so poisonously reasonable. "You were in some distress, surely you were mistaken. Itarusine thugs within our shores? Murdering aristocrats? Even disgraced ones? It seems more likely your argumentative brother quarreled with a man equally hot-tempered—Harm is reputedly foul-mannered—and it followed him home."

"You've always over-dramatized yourself," DeGuerre muttered. "Why else still wear—"

Delight closed his eyes against the weight of their disbelief. Janus thought them not so much skeptical as afraid.

"Whatever they're planning," Delight said when the silence had returned, "they're starting it now. Harm's no longer content to wait for commands. He's gotten them."

Janus felt the hairs on the back of his neck rise. Behind him the open doorway felt suddenly populated.

Psyke peered in at the frozen tableau they made. As she entered the room, the trees outside quaked with the violence of fleeing rooks.

Gost and Bull made way for her, perhaps out of courtesy, perhaps out of that same uncanny sense that Janus was prey to: that it wasn't the sound of argument that had brought her to the door but the aura of death.

"Dionyses," she said, surprise and pleasure warming her voice. "Are you— You're *not* well." She rounded on them all. "And you are simply watching, waiting? For what? Him to fall into shock from his injuries?"

"Countess," Gost said, "once he tells us what happened—"

She cocked her head, hesitated for a moment, and then said, "Chryses is dead, murdered by Nikos the Ax, when he tried to race them to the front gate, to protect Dionyses. Seahook is in ruins. And my husband's engines destroyed but thankfully not in Harm's hands. Now you know. Begone with you."

Janus drew in a steady breath. She'd grown careless with what ailed her: not madness but possession. As he thought it, he shivered, aware of her shadow, nearly a separate thing from her, seeming to shift to gaze on him.

Gost's attention sharpened. Despite his usual dismissal of women's words, he hesitated.

"You won't go?" Psyke asked. "Very well." She gained Delight's side and drew him to his feet. "We'll remove ourselves."

Janus ceded her the field. Why not? He had found out what he needed to know and even grieving and injured, Delight was too rational to be swayed by the duchess's hand-me-down prejudices against Janus.

He turned, interrupting the low-voiced conference between Bull and Gost, Psyke's name on their lips. DeGuerre stared at them both, glassy-eyed and silent, his hands clenched at his sides.

"Bull," Janus said, "set the Particulars on Harm. We've left that serpent loose long enough."

"The charge?" Gost said. "Only hearsay from a man who thinks himself a woman, and a woman who collects gossip on the wind itself."

"Yes," Bull agreed, ignoring Gost. "It's well past time to round up the antimachinists. If they've attacked houses, whether at the behest of Itarusine agitators or not, they've become far too dangerous to ignore. At the very least, our attentions might serve to distract Harm from his schemes."

Janus felt a double serving of triumph at that; Bull agreed with him. Even though it was a small and obvious thing, a first agreement made the next more likely. By the faint pinch to his lips, Gost knew it, too.

Gost, Janus thought, had listened overmuch to his own reputation and believed it all. He was a clever man, an agile manipulator, but he overstepped. Ivor and Adiran were threat enough for the throne. Janus wouldn't tolerate another. Though Janus had meant to concentrate his efforts on thwarting Ivor, he would make time to remove Fanshawe Gost.

DELIGHT WOKE TO THE SLOW, golden light of late afternoon filtering through the inner bed curtains. His bandaged hands snagged on the bedclothes, and he winced, both for the damage he must be causing and for the pain it triggered.

He shifted and the scent of soot and loss ambushed him. He put his hands, bulky but soft in their windings, over his eyes, curled around the pain, his breath ragged. Chryses was gone. He was alone.

A soft hand touched his shoulder, stroked his hair; a weight settled on the bed. He tensed; he didn't want tenderness now.

He shuddered and she drew away; her scent lingered a moment, sweetness underlaid with something sharp, cold, and strong enough to penetrate even the rankness of soot, old sweat, and blood.

It made the hairs on his arms rise, painful tugs against flame-washed flesh. He couldn't hear her breathing; once she had moved away, she might as well have vanished, if she had even been here at all.

He bared his face, let his hands fall, and blinking, picked her out, a shadow in the sunlight. "Psyke," he said. Her quarters, he decided, taking in the sweep of feminine surroundings. Her bed.

He fought his way out of the piled linens. "Gently," she said. "Sir Robert fed you Laudable. You've been sleeping for two days. You're like to be stiff."

"Chryses is dead," he said. "Murdered. My aches are nothing to that." He leaned forward and covered his face again. She fell back to that strange, brooding silence, so unlike the girl he had known, inquisitive and attentive to everyone around her.

Delight rose, limbs aching and stinging, head spinning; he seized the bedpost and swayed, watching the shreds of his petticoat and skirt sway also. Psyke took a step closer, reaching out as if she meant to steady him, but then recoiled.

Delight felt stung, his feelings ridiculously injured over that small rejection from a woman he considered a friend, then he saw the expression on her face and knew whatever her difficulty was, it had nothing to do with rejection.

"Ring for the maid," he said. "I'll need clothes." The skirts hardly mattered anymore; he had worn them as long as he had to offend the admiral. He had bigger priorities now.

"You need to—"

"I need to work," Delight said. "Janus—"

"He's responsible for Chryses's death, sent him into danger. How can you—"

"The antimachinists are to blame," Delight said, "not Janus. He only wants the best for this country."

"So he says," Psyke said. The voice wasn't her own; a commoner's cadence overlaid her diction. The pallor of her face changed to a blush of rage, rare in his memories of sweet-natured Psyke. It shook his careful focus, let him feel something beyond repressed grief and blind determination.

Delight fumbled to the delicate chair before Psyke's dressing table, and sat heavily in it. The wood creaked alarmingly, but after all the time spent in the decaying surrounds of Seahook, the sound soothed his jangled nerves. "You don't believe him?" He unwound his bandages to better assess the damage. Blisters and red swollen skin. He'd heal.

Sweet-voiced again, she said, "Challacombe reminds me of the palace proverb: Janus profits when men die. History defines him as a self-involved killer, hardly the mark of a man who should be in power." Psyke settled down on the bed he had risen from, her bare feet dangling like a child's. But even as a hoydenish child, her skin had never showed the kind of dirt her soles revealed now.

It reminded him that years could turn a friend into a stranger. He would step carefully in his speech, at least until he could assess this Psyke who seemed overburdened with bitterness and despair.

"What does the duchess offer you?" he asked instead. Hadn't he heard Janus bemoan his wife's unsavory association often enough?

Psyke looked away, fingers worrying at a spot of soot on her sheets.

"Is it some oblique revenge?" he pressed. "Does the duchess promise you satisfaction for your murdered mother? Your sisters? For Aris? Vengeance is a poor way to rule a country."

"And murder is better?" she asked.

"What happens if the duchess succeeds in killing Janus? Who will step into Janus's place? Who will lead us?"

"There's no shortage of killers," Psyke said, "if you're partial to such."

Delight threw a bottle of scent at her. Psyke ducked her head, let the bottle disappear into the linens without damage.

"Childish," she said.

"Only in response to someone who refuses to even listen," he said. "I am not denying Janus can be a dangerous man. But this is a time for dangerous leaders."

"Danger begets danger. Your actions at the docks brought us closer to destruction than decades of infighting has. Adiran is the rightful heir," Psyke said. "The duchess will raise him, and in the interim your father and Blythe will continue as joint regents—" Her words seemed rote, something learned but not felt.

"And your chosen role? Why do you not seek the regency yourself? You and Janus together—"

"I'm tainted," she said. It was the first thing she had said to him that felt real. "I believe my reputation grows worse than yours, Dionyses. Or haven't you heard it in the streets yet? They call me the countess of death."

"You know how little fondness I have for the scandal sheets. What have you done that could merit such an insult?"

She drew her knees up to her chest, hugged them close, inadvertently baring white ankles and calves, before her skirt hid them again. Delight frowned, registering again the strangeness in the air. It was simple silence: an empty room when the Countess of Last should always be attended.

Silence in her movements when there should have been the rustle of layers over corsets and boning and lacy petticoats. The loose spill of her hair, unpinned and tangled. The flowers on her tables were withered; her dressing table was dusty. In the midst of the palace, Psyke lived like a leper.

"Janus allows them to treat you so?"

"My knight," she said, sad amusement warming the thin thread of her voice, "ever defending me from nannies, governesses, and bullies. Even now, with all you've lost, you're prepared to demand a reckoning. But my future is death and the palace reflects it."

Delight gaped, fumbling for words before he decided words were perhaps not what the situation needed. He rose, nearly tripping over the dirty remains of a tea tray, and took Psyke by the shoulders, shaking her gently until she buckled into his arms and cried.

Her body trembled against his, and it woke every lurking ache in his body; the burns felt as if they bloomed anew over his hands. Her loose hair snagged on his bandages and he pulled back, dismayed at the resurgence of pain—more, at the worsening of it.

His skin had been blistered and tender as if he had fallen asleep in the sun, but now . . . his palms cracked and bled while the rest of his skin grew clammy with fever sweat.

Psyke jerked away, retreating to the other side of the room, and the shadows there. He blotted his bleeding hands on undoubtedly expensive lengths of creamy lace, and went toward her.

She stepped back. "Have a care, Dionyses. My poor maid, Dahlia, always a sickly sort, found service to me a fatal burden. If you have a weakness, I will winkle it out and worsen it."

"Psyke," he said, "if your maid died, it was no fault of yours—"

Psyke's hands busied themselves at her bodice, unfastening the laces there. "You have studied human flesh, know the ways of it, the ailments it is prone to. But tell me, Delight, if it's not Death that has touched me, what is it?" She let her dress fall, turned as she did, so his startled gaze only collected a white curve of breast, a sinuous twist to her spine, before she caught the gown at her waist.

He swallowed, belatedly hoping her rooms were as abandoned as they seemed. His reputation was such that a charge of adultery wouldn't damage it any further, but Janus was his patron and Psyke, his wife. . . .

"Do you *see?*" She stamped a bare foot, hard enough that he winced at the impact of flesh against stone, though she seemed unaffected. "Tell me what has befallen me."

He stepped closer, warily; a day ago, he understood the world and his place in it—Janus's engineer, Chryses's twin, the reclusive dweller at Seahook, and occasional liaison to a privateer. This, this was as new and as peculiar as a dream, where nothing made sense but felt full of import. "Step out of the shadows," he said. A strange reluctance roused in him.

"I live in shadow," she said, peering over her shoulder at him. Nonetheless, she obediently took a step back.

Even in the heart of the room, in the generous sunlight, her skin held inky shadows. *Mourning cloth*, he thought, *badly dyed, and leaving its mark.* Not an uncommon sight, but perhaps her mind had worked on it, created strange fears and fancies abetted by the aura of despair in the palace.

"Do you see?" she repeated. She shifted uncomfortably, her modesty warring with this need for his judgment. The shadows on her skin . . . Sudden rage roused in him: not dye but something more akin to bruises, layers of black and yellow and green. New over old. Had Janus beaten her?

He squinted, took another step closer; the marks were slightly raised, slightly glossy. He moved closer still, until her spine, sweetly undulant, filled his vision. He reached out, ran a gentle finger up from the small of her back to her nape.

He pressed her head gently forward, brushed her hair out of the way, and *saw.* There were scales disrupting the smooth pallor of her skin, blackest at the crests of her shoulders, branching out, growing translucent as they spread, until he could find them only by their sleek texture.

"When I was a child and full of questions," she said, drawing her gown back into place, "I always went to you and Chryses. Will you aid me now?" She turned, drifted soundlessly across the floor, to sit in the window seat.

"Aid you?" he asked.

"He speaks to me, on rare occasion, but His voice is so great and my understanding so small, it becomes as meaningless as the sound of the tide. Will you aid me? Now that you have seen?"

"He?" Delight parroted, thinking of strange and exotic diseases mentioned in the texts the scholars wrote after visiting foreign climes. Perhaps, some sailor-spread malady carried into the palace on imported cloth . . .

"Haith," she said. "Haith."

Delight let out a breath of dismay. This was madness, the unpalatable result of a diet of murder, pain, and family history that claimed allegiance with the god. No wonder Janus had asked for tracts on the gods. He needed to understand Psyke's illness.

"You don't believe me," she said. She folded into herself, rested her head on the jut of her knee as if she were too weary to keep it raised. "I am the last of the Redoubts, the last of the line that He raised to prominence. Is it so remarkable that the god of death would wish to see something end?" Her voice flattened, lost all warmth, all hope.

Delight heard footsteps in the corridor, a soft shuff of palace shoes on thick carpeting, and prayed for interruption, no matter the damage to his reputation.

"Your observations fail you, Delight. You choose not to see. Others know the truth, either intuited or reasoned out. The duchess, Adiran, Ivor, even Janus. Oh, Janus knows best of all what I carry with me."

She slipped from the window seat like a spill of silk; her hands wrapped about his forearm, claws cold and taut. "Their voices grow greater in number every day; do you know how it galls to use Mirabile's deathless spite to keep the others away? But their voices swell and I—

"*Help me*," she pled, once she had regained control of her voice. She turned her hands on each other, knotted her fingers. "Our families were friendly once. We played together as children. . . ."

Before he was forced to answer, Janus's page entered, his small frame burdened with a double armful of clothes. Psyke took the opportunity to slip away; Evan looked after her, thrust the clothes into Delight's hastily raised arms. "Milord Last's in the king's study," he said. "Meet him there." Without waiting for a response, the boy turned and hastened off in the same direction Psyke had taken.

Janus knows, she had said. With his page tracking her like a small, determined hound it was no wonder she took it for confirmation of Janus's belief.

Delight turned to the piles of clothes and spread them out alongside the bed. Two separate outfits lay before him. One was akin to his usual wear: thick-woven woolen skirts and blouse, awkward to move in but quite sturdy in the surrounds of chemicals and reluctant to burn; the other was men's clothes fit for a day at Parliament. Sober in color and cut, wool also, but of a fineness he hadn't felt in years. He ran a finger down the breeches, admired the simplicity of the lines, the crispness of the black wool, the brightness of the white, the flare of blue in the waistcoat; these came from Last's closet, without a doubt, would be a quiet shield against naysayers unhappy with his return to court.

Delight licked his lips, unaccountably nervous with having a choice presented to him. He missed Seahook, the certainties of the day there, even as he reached for the pants. Janus would have another laboratory set up soon, its focus shifted now from creation to defense. With the Itarusine ships closing in, the privateers became more than smugglers: They became their first and perhaps only line of defense. They would need more cannon and shot, and made quickly. If Antyre meant to drive back the Itarusines, it would have to be soon.

"Dionyses DeGuerre," the guard said, ushering him into the study. Janus looked up from his narrow focus on the letters spread across the table, and had to blink Delight into clarity. Perhaps he should ask Delight to make him a pair of spectacles, if the reading could blur his vision. Or perhaps he had simply been awake too long. The past two days had left him with little recourse.

With Delight playing dead in Psyke's bed, Janus's wife had crept into his. Given what he knew of Psyke's unnatural ally, of her predilection for dying and resurrecting in her sleep, Janus chose to stay awake rather than lie beside her. Dahlia's death had been lingering and painful from all accounts.

"You look tired," Delight said.

"You look . . . fashionable," Janus said. Though Janus had sent the men's clothing along with the women's, he belatedly regretted doing so. Delight, dressed as a man, made sober by sorrow, seemed more a threatening stranger than the eccentric inventor Janus had learned to count a friend.

"I presumed it a veiled request," Delight said, "to not scandalize the delicate sensibilities of the court."

"Dress as you please," Janus said. "Do as you please, only aid me with these encroaching and maddening throne thieves!" He tossed down the latest demands from Itarusine merchants and from the antimachinists who had shown the poor taste to flaunt the destruction of Seahook and sign their names to the parchment. The Particulars were out arresting them now.

Delight stepped back, wariness showing in the line of his body, in the way his hands spread out, carefully held low. "Last—"

"Be easy, Delight. I'm not like to take your head off when I need it to keep Antyre from becoming nothing more than an Itarusine colony."

Delight dropped into one of the wing chairs by the empty hearth and said, "I'm hungry." He gestured toward the tray of sandwiches at Janus's side. "May I?"

"I wouldn't," Janus said. "I didn't recognize the maidservant who brought them, and she seemed oddly unfamiliar with the palace. The wine's quite safe."

Delight gaped a moment, and then said, "You . . . poison . . . how can you live like this?"

"As I've always lived," Janus said. "Cautiously."

A man clad in the oiled, gray greatcoat of a city Particular put his head in. "Begging your pardon, my lord, but the captain said to tell you, we got three of the troublemakers, tossed 'em into Stones. You want us to see them executed?"

"How does the prison fare? When I was there a few days ago, it seemed vile enough to serve as punishment for all but the worst offenders to the crown."

"There's sickness, so we heard. We didn't go in beyond the gates, much," the Particular said. "Sickness is affecting even the guards, which makes the food rounds a little less'n regular, if you understand."

The man reached into his greatcoat pocket, and Janus tensed, hand falling to his sword hilt.

"The jailer gave me something for you." The Particular passed him a handful of papers bound neatly into a square, bowed, and left.

Janus opened the packet and found three thick sheets tucked within, scribbled, smudgy drawings of prisoners in extremis, crouched over food bowls, locked in a cloudy charcoal brawl. *Incorrigible*, he thought, and set the images aside for the words written on the wrapper itself.

It should come as no surprise to you that I've managed to ingratiate myself with the common people. They, after all, understand that I have a care for them. So your punishment falls far short of what you intended, and, as such, you might as well return me either to freedom or to my singular cell.

Janus laughed. Did the man think he was being subtle?

"Good news?" Delight asked.

"Poole," Janus said, "carefully not asking for release though he wants it."

"You locked him up?" Delight asked.

"No," Janus said. "Apparently my father and I had one thing in common after all. Even if it was only hatred of a caricaturist. It's strange how you notice these things once it's too—" He stopped his careless words. Delight's face shuttered. He wrapped an arm about himself.

"Where will I work?" Delight asked. "I want to get back to work. Tarrant . . . Oh! Tarrant won't know about the fire; he's supposed to rendezvous with us—"

"The whole hillside's charred," Janus said. "He'll find someplace else to drop anchor, and send us a message."

"So slow," Delight mourned. "And the roads full of antimachinists."

"They're people, not locusts," Janus said. "There's a finite number of them. Don't borrow trouble; we've quite enough of it as it is." He poured Delight a glass of the wine, handed it to him, though the man eyed it with a mixture of desire and horror.

As if getting the worst out of the way, he took several large swallows, and sighed when he didn't fall dead on the spot. "Who's trying to poison you?" Delight asked.

"Most recently?" Janus asked. "I'd assume Lord Blythe. He was most annoyed that I chose not to respond to his demands."

Delight groaned. "He was a horrible nit when I was a boy. Sounds as if he's only gotten worse."

"The duchess encourages him," Janus said. "Still, his attempts are transparent and virtually harmless. It's Psyke I have to beware."

Delight, leaning back in the chair, started forward, eyes narrowing. "What have you done to her? She's gone mad. You fault the duchess for encouraging Blythe's fancies, but you do the same to Psyke, humoring her."

"Not encourage," Janus said. "Acknowledge the change in her, yes."

"She thinks she's followed by Haith!" Delight said. "You could see her to the physician." The wine in his cup sloshed as he gestured.

"You seem very ready to condemn her," Janus said.

"Madness can be cured, if caught soon enough, if she can be taught what is real and what is false."

"And you know which is real better than she," Janus said. "Is it still mad if the facts are on her side?"

"Yes," Delight said. "The gods are gone, and, if truth be told, I doubt they ever existed at all, beyond men's desire for a greater power to instruct them."

"Ani exists in tangible form," Janus said. He understood Delight's position, had held it himself until Miranda's collaboration with Ani created Maledicte.

"I thought you a rational man."

Janus sighed. He didn't have the time to waste on this. "Rational enough to know that belief is unnecessary in the face of facts. The gods exist, Delight, whether we wish them to or not. I can only work toward a world where they are not needed. To make them disappear as they once pretended to do."

Ruthlessly, he changed the subject. Remarkable how irrational a rational man could be.

"I'll have your new workshop set up in the palace itself. The first and second story of the old wing are taken up with Ivor and his staff, but the ground floor and dungeon might be ideal. It connects to the stables and the gardens for ease of delivery, and, as added benefit, Ivor's men will be less likely to set it afire if it's beneath their feet."

"What's to keep them from viewing my progress?" Delight asked.

"A score of kingsguards," Janus said. "I've so many soldiers following me around, I'm sure we must have a surplus. I'll speak to Rue for you. In the interim, feel free to ring for a meal. If you make clear it's not for me, there should be no trouble at all."

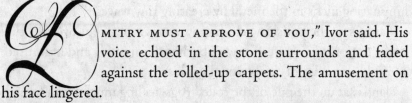

· 21 ·

MITRY MUST APPROVE OF YOU," Ivor said. His voice echoed in the stone surrounds and faded against the rolled-up carpets. The amusement on his face lingered.

"Does he approve of anyone?" Janus asked. "He's always so sour."

"He allowed you entrance, didn't he, pet, when I am most assuredly not prepared for company. Or did you tell him you've come to fence?"

When Janus arrived, he found Ivor's servants had been busy turning the dining room into a makeshift salle, rolling the carpets to bare the smooth stone beneath—better for sure footing—the furniture piled against the wall, a pyramid of dark wood in the dimly lit room. The servants were dismissed, sent off to find Ivor more lamps, the better to light the room. Meals were pleasant in dim surroundings, but blade work was best done in the light.

Ivor raised his saber in a mocking imitation of a dueler saluting his opponent. For a moment, Janus wanted to take the challenge on; the assassination attempt of the week previous had only whetted his appetite, not sated it, and here was an opponent who would not only meet his blade but be eager for it.

The tip of Ivor's blade sketched a quick slash toward Janus's throat at a distance far enough it couldn't be misconstrued as an actual threat, yet it was enough to cool Janus's enthusiasm. Ivor was a strong bladesman, a better duelist, and while Janus doubted Ivor would try to kill him in the Antyrrian palace, a serious wound, meant to slow and distract, could easily fit itself into his schemes.

Janus shook his head. "Another time, perhaps."

Ivor scrubbed a towel through his hair, tossed it aside, letting it land over yet another ubiquitous idol of Haith, and took a seat on the single remaining chair in the room. "Have you come to join me for dinner, then? It'll be a few hours, yet," Ivor said.

Janus shook his head, and Ivor smiled. "Cook will be sorry to hear it. She likes your appetite."

Ivor set down the blade and took up a tin of oil and a polishing cloth. He sent a thin stream of oil onto the blade, let it spill down, illuminating nicks in the metal by creating tiny waves.

Janus saw the polishing cloth grow snags as it swept over the tiny imperfections: Ivor's weapon was both well cared for and hard used, a visible reminder of duels won, lives lost.

Janus sat on the pile of the rolled rugs, feeling much like a foreign dignitary of the Kyrdic court, and said, "I came to see if you would make good on your claims of friendship. I came to see if you would kill a man for me."

Ivor laughed after a moment of sheer, startled shock. Janus prized the expression; he hadn't won many such. "Do tell me you won't ask me to put the blade to my own throat, love. I'd do much for you, but I do value my skin."

"Well I know it," Janus said. He leaned back on his elbows, made himself vulnerable. The man's curiosity would keep Janus secure for the length of the conversation.

"Do you want me to guess?" Ivor said. "There are many I can imagine you would like removed."

"Fanshawe Gost," Janus said.

"The Kingmaker."

"The throne seeker."

Ivor frowned. "And if I do this small favor for you, what do I gain?"

Janus found a smile of his own. Rats take it, but he loved dealing with Ivor, with the mind that worked as his own did. Ivor was well aware of Gost's potential, and it threatened Ivor's bid for the throne as well as Janus's.

"What do you want?" Janus said.

"A throne?" Ivor said, though he smiled. "Or perhaps a night spent with you and your wife."

If that was true, if Ivor had been serious, Janus would have agreed, despite Psyke's undoubted horror. It would be a small price to pay for Gost's removal and carried with it the possibility of Psyke's affinity for death touching Ivor. But it was the request of a hedonist, and, while Ivor enjoyed his pleasures, he was far too practical to trade a murder of such political worth for something as valueless as a single night of intimacy. Ivor said it merely to watch whether Janus would agree or sputter in outrage.

Janus held his tongue.

Ivor sighed. "Fine, my clever one. I want an audience with the prince."

"Guards attending," Janus said. "Half an hour, no more?"

"Stingy," Ivor said. He set the blade back across his knees, drew out a whetstone, and began smoothing the largest of the nicks.

"It will occasion notice," Janus said. "Unfavorable notice. The best we can do is confine it to the stricture of a normal call between acquaintances. A half hour." The rasp of the stone against the blade was really remarkably soothing.

"How do you want him dead?" Ivor said.

"I'd prefer not to be suspected," Janus said. "My reputation's black enough."

"I'd prefer to indemnify myself also. I'll hire someone, if you have no objections."

"None at all," Janus said, trying to hide his sudden triumph. Ivor paused, looked him over quite thoroughly, so much so that Janus worried Ivor had seen more than the surface of Janus's need to see Gost gone, had seen the hope that Ivor would use the same assassin who had killed the king and, in doing so, allow his capture. Allow Janus to clear himself of blame for Aris's murder.

Ivor laughed, a full-throated yelp of amusement, and Janus stiffened. Ivor's laughter stopped as suddenly as it had started, and he reached out and yanked Janus to him. "You are such a fool, pet. You think yourself fit to be Antyre's king when you can't even execute a single man? You run to your enemy for aid and think yourself clever?"

Janus wrapped a hand around Ivor's wrist, tried to pry himself free; but off balance, he lacked leverage. The polished blade touched his cheek. Struggling away, sprawled as he was half across the stones, only meant the blade pressed tighter until a thin rivulet of heat swept down his cheek, blood or sweat. He stilled; his heartbeat roared in his ears, his hands fisted, but he stilled.

He swallowed painfully, the angle rough on his neck. This close, he could see the pale scars on Ivor's throat and the pulse beating hard beneath the skin.

Ivor dropped the blade, put his other hand into Janus's hair. "There," Ivor said. "Don't fight me. It's unnecessary. I will aid you. I simply want my say and to be assured of your attention; you're entirely too practiced at pretending to listen.

"I know Gost's death will please you but is less important to you than your transparent attempt to find Aris's assassin. You may be foolish, but I am not. And Janus—"

The rare use of his given name on Ivor's lips made Janus twitch, garnering a brief spike of pain as Ivor pulled his hair. "A king, even a would-be king, cannot afford to misread the strength of his enemies."

Ivor shoved, and Janus sprang free, panting, enraged, and stung. His hands shook as he wiped his face. Blood after all, the thinnest smear on his fingers. He crouched, all his Relict instinct urging him to fight.

"Oh, do sit down," Ivor said. "You're not an animal. And we have a promise to seal. I'll kill your enemy in such a way that absolves you of suspicion, and you will allow me access to your prince."

"Guarded," Janus said, though his voice was hoarse, as if all the silent tension in his body had convinced his vocal cords he had been screaming in protest.

"Of course," Ivor said.

Ivor danced his fingers down his blade's edge, until blood stippled the tips of his fingers. "So, a deal?"

"Yes," Janus said. Ivor rose in a flash, rubbed his bloody fingers over Janus's mouth and cheek. "There," he said, grinning. "We've sealed our promises in Relict fashion. With blood."

Janus lunged away, caught himself halfway to the door, salt scald in his eyes, in his throat. He shook his head fiercely, felt as off balance and as scoured as he had the day he inhaled the acrid exhaust from one of Delight's machines. "Ivor, make him hurt. I want him to hurt." Someone should share his pain.

He didn't wait for anything further to pass Ivor's lips—amusement, satisfaction, another painful barb. He just wanted to be away.

JANUS STRODE THROUGH THE HALLS, fighting the chill the old wing wanted to press into his bones. His guards, Simpson and Walker, fell in behind him, exclaiming at the blood on his face. Janus tore his cravat free, spat on it, and scrubbed away the blood, throwing the silk at their feet when he was done.

They quailed. Janus didn't wonder at it. He felt murderous, and undoubtedly looked it.

The stairwell beckoned and he clattered down its wide stones; at its base, a young man stepped out to greet him. "Not now, Delight," Janus said.

Delight drew back, disappearing into the rooms beyond with a haste that confirmed it: Janus was in no fit state to be seen.

He ducked out of the old wing at the nearest exit, the servants' doors to the stables. Behind him, he could hear Walker muttering that nobles shouldn't know the back passages as well as all that, and Simpson hushing him with a hiss and a cough.

Not know the back passages? It was his palace. His city. His country. There wouldn't be a part of it he didn't know.

He paused at the stables, contemplating seizing a horse and riding out the last few moments of daylight, or riding into the city and finding a partner to duel at one of the men's clubs; surely there'd be some fool belligerent enough to challenge him, maybe even Savne or

Blythe. . . . His lips drew up in a savage grin; he felt the cool air of the approaching night on his tongue, and it sobered him enough to bypass the stables. Instead, he headed along the length of the old wing's outer wall, the fragrant lure of the king's gardens promising reprieve.

But even they betrayed him, beautiful as they were, the greenery going black with night shadows; the empty maze, blooming with starflowers, proved itself to be peopled after all. He heard the piping voices, sound carried on the still air. Young voices, one higher with a commoner's accent, the other aristocratic. Janus rounded a corner, following the leaping mouse emblem, and found Evan Tarrant and Prince Adiran picnicking in the dwindling twilight.

They fell silent when he burst in on them; Evan leaping to his feet, Adiran blinking up at him.

"My lord?" Walker called from beyond the maze. Janus pounced. Evan yelped, but Janus had the boy's upper arm firmly in his grasp and was dragging him back toward the exit of the maze and the palace. Adiran rose and trotted after, his expression worried as Janus took his friend away.

Walker and Simpson traded oaths when Janus appeared with the boys. "Ensure the prince follows," Janus snapped. Evan whimpered, but Janus hissed at him, and the boy went silent for the long trip back to the nursery. Faintly, Janus regretted hurting the boy, but seizing Adiran would likely get him killed.

The guards outside the nursery panicked at their approach, flinging open the door as if to disprove their eyes, that Adiran was still inside, and drawing their blades when they saw he wasn't.

Janus dragged Evan to the open door, and found his way barred by two lengths of steel. Walker and Simpson drew their swords in return.

A nursery guard said, "Captain Rue said—"

"For the love of sense," Janus said. "It's too late to make a show of duty when you've allowed the prince to walk out under your noses. Go notify Rue of my presence, if you must." He pushed past them, Evan on tiptoes to ease the pain of Janus's grip. Adiran followed Evan, and, once they were all inside the nursery, Janus slammed the door shut behind them and released Evan.

Evan jerked away, his face tear streaked; he rolled up his sleeve, a child's desire to see the wound, and Adiran touched the bruised flesh with curious fingers.

Janus paced the room, for the first time noticing how confined Adiran's world was. Janus had always seen it as a palace in miniature, contrasted it to the rubble of his childhood kingdom, not seeing the cage it was. Forty paces from one side of the playroom to the other, not enough room for even a child to run.

It didn't matter, except that it had probably provoked Adiran's wandering. It was easy to blame the guards, but it was likely the guards were no more to blame now than they had been when Maledicte made his way through the palace, Ani clearing his path.

"I'm sorry," Evan said. His voice was shaky, wary, and Janus felt his temper spark anew.

"I thought you were going to bring Adiran to me if that happened again. Or were you enjoying your playtime so much that you forget there are men who want the prince dead?"

A quick red blush rolled over Evan's face, lingering about his ears. Adiran watched the color spread with apparent fascination. People didn't show much emotion around the boy prince; he might not be mindful, but he was reflective, and those who tended him preferred the boy quiet and calm. Another constraint on an already constrained soul.

It might have been the shadows darkening Adiran's hair, shifting it from tow-headed to a tarnished gold, but Janus doubted it.

Adiran said abruptly, "I'm hungry." Though Janus had heard the two boys conversing in the maze, Adiran's new ability to speak his mind clearly startled him all over again.

"You walked off without dinner," Janus said. "That's what happens. Plan your escapes better next time."

Adiran curled up on one of the floor cushions, sulking as well as Maledicte had ever done. It made Janus wonder how much of Black-Winged Ani's temperament bled through, how much of Maledicte had been Her and not Miranda.

"I could go to the kitchens," Evan volunteered, though he seemed reluctant to leave.

"Please, Evan," Adiran said. "Janus can protect me." Evan got a smile; Janus got something like a smirk, the sweet tilt of Adiran's lips turning sharper.

Janus looked down at the murky shadows moving slowly in Adiran's eyes. There was no gainsaying the progress Ani had made in the boy, changing him from a senseless puppet to a willful child. Evan left the room after another glance at Adiran that made Janus bristle. He commanded Evan's loyalty, not this amalgamation of boy-god.

"What did you do to the nurse?" Janus asked. "She was harder to elude, surely, than your guards."

Adiran wandered away from him, as airy and distractible as ever, but it was all a sham. The all-too-wary glance over a shoulder warned Janus of that.

Janus settled down in the nurse's chair and, when Adiran passed by on another apparently aimless ramble, he reached out and seized the delicate wrist, drew him close.

"What did you ask Ani for?"

The boy tugged wordlessly at Janus's restraint, face wrinkling in consternation. He pushed, pried with his other hand, small sharp fingernails leaving marks, but Janus held fast. "Tell me, Adiran. Did you ask Her for anything?"

Adiran whimpered, all boy now, blue eyes brilliant with tears and confusion.

Janus shook him. Rue would be back with a swarm of guards, and Janus would be chased out like an unwelcome cur. He needed to know Ani's goals, and the boy was the one who had set them.

The boy's hand, digging at Janus's tourniquet grip, suddenly made progress. Janus jerked away, his skin ripped by unexpected talons. Adiran turned a face, blotched red with tears, and hissed at him, one eye gone glossy black as if the prince, along with having a lesser mind, had a body more easily overset by the god's presence.

God or no god, Adiran could not be let free again; Janus reached out to grab the child.

Adiran hissed, *"Release me."* Janus's head erupted in pain; he clenched one hand tight to his skull, remembering that gods' voices were too much for mortals to withstand.

He licked cracking lips, and said, "The boy cannot have bound himself to You. He's made no compact, killed no man in Your name. You merely squat among his bones." His breath was ragged, the pain overwhelming, but he refused to falter, not when She could answer his question.

"You dare," Adiran, *Ani*, said. "Your kind bows to Me, Ixion. Prays for My attention." Blood speckled Adiran's chin as the god's voice forced Her way through fragile tissue.

Janus found himself huddled against the wall of the nursery, knees and palms burning, marking his attempt at escape. "Adiran's asked you for nothing. He's not capable of it."

Ani paced after him, Adiran's head cocked so that the bird eye pinned Janus in place. "*He will be.*"

Janus shuddered, fell; even when Mal had been possessed, raving, fighting without care, the scent of moldering feathers and blood strong in the air, it was only a ghost of this. Like a child cornered by bullies, a man attacked by hounds, Janus curled around his belly, clamped his hands around his neck, tucked his face tight into the dubious shelter of his own bones.

A crash of wings and a scrabbling at the window broke Her concentration, or more likely, attracted Adiran's attention. He drifted toward the barred window, to the rook pinned there, and carefully plucked a feather from its thrashing form.

Love, vengeance, but nothing of mercy in Her, Janus thought, dragging himself to slouch against the door. Not even for Her own creatures. Adiran dropped the feather and reached for more. The bird slowly stopped thrashing.

Janus watched Adiran, watched Ani slowly disappearing, working Her way beneath the boy's skin, like a warship easing its way through the shallows.

By the time Rue and the guards arrived, with Evan hot on their heels, a tray in his hands, it was only Adiran standing there, with a handful of bloody feathers.

JANUS FLED TO HIS CHAMBERS, rinsed the taste of scorched blood out of his mouth with a scouring wash of whiskey, then took a deeper swallow to numb his abused flesh. He fell into the soft chair by the dark hearth, closed his eyes.

He had been foolish; perhaps Ivor was right to assign him such an epithet. He hadn't thought of Black-Winged Ani's presence in Adiran as a direct threat to him. He hadn't killed Aris, after all, was innocent of the crime that brought Her. But he'd forgotten something so basic it bewildered him. Vengeance was far less concerned with justice than it was in sharing one's pain with the world. It mattered less who had committed the crime than who Adiran deemed guilty. It had been so with Mal: Kritos had done the deed, but Ani fixed on the Earl of Last.

Janus now regretted the bargain he had struck with Ivor. The last thing he needed was Ivor in proximity to an eager god. He rose and sought the deeper recesses of his chambers, discarded his coat, hung it neatly over the wardrobe hook, ready for Padget to sponge it clean.

Disturbed, tired, sore, he unlaced his shirt, his breeches, wondering where Padget was. In his bedchamber, he found at least part of the answer. Psyke was asleep on the counterpane, her night rail rucked up to reveal the pale flesh of her calves.

Padget wouldn't have stayed with the countess in residence. Janus could ring for him, but . . . Janus's shadow, wavering in the low gaslight, crawled over Psyke and she woke all at once, like a startled animal sensing a predator's approach.

"My bed linens are fouled," she said by way of greeting and explanation. "Delight left them covered in soot and blood. Will you grudge me yours?" Her eyes were steady on his, clear as they had not been for some time. Her voice, polite even behind the blunt words, was hers alone, the sweet tones familiar.

"There are maids," he said. "You could send for fresh linens and spare yourself my company."

"Ring for them, if my presence disturbs you. I'd rather sleep than wait for the maids to debate belowstairs which of them must serve the countess of death."

"They're cowards all," Janus said.

Psyke smiled at him, bitterly amused. "Then lie with me. You look fatigued, and I've warmed the bed for you."

"I've tasks yet to be done," he said.

"You're nearly undressed." She rose, her gown falling about her legs like the drift of city fogs at night, pervasive, enveloping, unhealthy. She touched the laces undone at his throat, ran a fingertip across his skin in a lover's touch, beckoning him. He shuddered. First Ani, now this. . . .

"Shall I ring for Padget and have him finish the task? Or may I turn my hands to it?"

Janus stepped back, all too aware of the dark scales on her skin; the fine, pale lawn of the nightgown let them show through where they now had crept over her collarbone.

"Perhaps later," he said.

She wove her fingers into his hair and pulled him closer, raised her mouth to his and whispered, "I saw you kiss Maledicte like this once. As if you were drowning, and he the air you sought. I wanted it. Wanted it badly enough that when Aris asked if I would wed you, I agreed."

He jerked away, rubbed his hand over his lips, tasting blood once more.

"You're surprised," she said. "You must have known you were sought after, even given your birth."

"I had no need for a wife," he said.

"I needed a husband," Psyke said. "Sisters who wanted to be wed, a widowed mother with no fortune left to speak of—the sum Aris offered would have seen them live well. Instead, it saw them buried with dignity." She shivered once, eyes closing, not against tears, he thought, but against something more insidious, the encroachment of one long dead.

Her jaw tightened as if she fought words not her own. Janus took her fisted hand, opened the fingers, and kissed the palm. "Psyke," he said, claiming her.

Her eyes opened, blue as forget-me-nots, oddly grateful. "It was your passion," she said. "You presented one face to the court: gracious, assured, bored. You presented another in his arms. You showed depth of feeling—"

Janus shook his head, suspicious of her sudden outpouring.

Maybe this was another ghost after all, or an especially tricky one. He slipped her grasp; her words died away, her face hardened.

"I didn't know then, though Aris warned me, that your depth of feeling was all for selfish pursuits."

"For the country," he said.

She paused in her instant retort, sat again on the disturbed bed. "Not then. Aris was right about you then. It was greed and pride that made you kill your father, along with a healthy dose of fear. I'm not certain what drives you now."

"Aggravation mostly," Janus snapped. He tightened the laces on his breeches, left the ones at his throat hanging. "And, as you've said, a healthy dose of fear. The Itarusines want our country, and most of our people don't care. The poor can't imagine life will improve, and the rich assume it won't change."

He didn't wait for her response, whatever it would be—he had to admit defeat here: She was utterly a cipher to him and would likely stay that way. Instead, he collected his blade, strapped it to his hip, and headed back into the hall, irritably waving the guards back to their posts. "Best watch over the countess. I can care for myself."

It felt good to walk the halls by himself, to hear only his footfalls and not the awkward shuffle of two guards unused to a nobleman who walked at a pace quicker than a stroll.

His peace lasted only for one hallway and a flight of stairs. Bull caught him up as he reached the main floor. "You missed dinner, Last."

"Feared I'll starve? I'm a far better judge of hunger than you'll ever be."

"Easy," Bull said, raising a hand. "I have no desire for argument."

"Then choose your words more carefully," Janus said. "I'm in a brittle mood."

"Then you'll be in a worse one when I'm through," Bull said. He fell into step alongside Janus, and took his arm. "All I meant was that I needed to speak to you and you were nowhere to be found. Or so the pages said."

"If you have need of me, best hunt out my personal page. The others . . ." He shrugged. "Well, they fall under Savne's command,

and he, despite appearances, loves me not. I have been in the palace for the entirety of the day. A very long day. One you propose, if I understand you correctly, to make longer and more maddening." Despite his tone, Janus found himself oddly grateful for the man's stolid and ordinary presence.

"This way." Bull led Janus through the anteroom, gaslights turned so low that they seemed more like distant stars than promises of light. The darkness echoed about them, and Janus rested one hand on the hilt of his saber, kept his footsteps quiet, his breathing quieter, the better to hear any potential ambush.

"Here," Bull said, and opened one of the doors into a tiny meeting room. It was the smallest of the alcoves and the only one that held no servants' passage behind it, no possibility of an eavesdropper.

Bull turned up the gas lamp on the desk, nodded. "Go ahead. Close us in."

Janus shut the door, drew the velvet hangings over it, muffling whatever sound they would produce.

"What is it?" he asked. He leaned against the dark blue curtain, let it close about him like the sky at twilight, restful and intimate.

"Gost's called a session of Parliament tomorrow."

"To name the regent," Janus said. It was the only possibility, and Gost had proven himself quick to seize possibilities. With Aris's death, with the suspension of the usual social season, many of the lords in Parliament had returned to their country estates, leaving only the aimless and the sycophantic.

"That's my assumption," Bull said. "I wasn't informed or invited to attend. Not a lord. No matter that I've been Aris's counselor for five years."

"I wasn't invited either," Janus said.

"But you can attend," Bull said. "They can't bar the door to you." He sank down into the sturdy chair beside the table, no gilt spindles here, only solid craftsmanship. In this court, where appearance was nearly everything, this chamber was too small, too ugly, and too far away from the throne room to be in demand.

"Aris solicited my opinions. First on matters of money, then business, then in his political life. I've grown accustomed to speaking my mind, but doing so has confirmed Gost's fears about my suitability. Rumor has it he intends to have Blythe stand beside him as second regent."

Bull looked gratified at the chuff of disgust this elicited from Janus, more so when Janus allowed himself to drop faint praise in Bull's path. "Gost fears that you might be listened to."

"Last," Bull said, "I cannot attend, but you must—"

"Oh, I'll attend," Janus said. "You needn't talk me into it. Though I think all my presence will mean is that we will learn those who vote for Gost and against us."

"That's something," Bull said. "To identify your enemies." He smiled, reached out and took Janus's hand, shaking it briefly. "Though I believe you have more difficulty identifying would-be friends."

Janus wanted to trust the man, and that worried him. It was easier in some respects, to assume everyone was his enemy, but if Antyre was to change, he would need allies.

"In the interim, rest; you look fatigued. You'll need your wits about you if we're to stop Gost's ambitions."

Janus stifled his retort. Bull smiled at him. "Advice doesn't mean belittlement, Last. Nor does taking it mean weakness." He stepped past him and disappeared into the quiet halls once again, leaving Janus possessor of the room with a slew of new facts to consider.

Three tight-paced circuits of the room later, Janus fled it himself, having decided that whether Bull was an ally or not, his advice was sound.

Janus sought out the old wing, thinking wistfully of his once-hated chamber; it would likely be empty still, if unaired and the feather beds put away. Bypassing a double rank of soldiers reminded him of another option and one that required far fewer stairs.

Fatigue was dragging at his heels, eroding his control, his nerves; and when Delight flung open the door to shout out requests for more paper, Janus jumped back, slamming his shoulder into the wall, saber coming to hand.

"Last," Delight said, "I've not got anything set up yet. Nothing to show."

"A bed?" Janus said. He pressed past Delight, vision narrowing. "Haven't you one of your own?"

"Death's in it," he muttered, and spotting a chaise not yet covered with crates or papers, changed his plans. A feather mattress was nice, but hardly a necessity. The chaise would do just as well. "I've Parliament to attend in the morning. Wake me at seven. I'll kill anyone who wakes me earlier."

$\mathcal{T}$HE PARLIAMENT BUILDING WAS, LIKE so many of Murne's other structures, repurposed from the days of gods and intercessors. Once it had been the shared cathedral of the five gods. At least it had traded dignity for dignity, unlike the smaller temples all too often turned to meet mercantile needs. One of Espit's largest temples lay at the very heart of the Sybarite Street district, her altars turned platforms for beds in Murne's most licentious brothel.

The carriage, a faceless hire coach, circled the building, and Janus slid back the hatch to stop the driver when they came around to Baxit's entrance. Janus stepped through the columns, carved and painted with scrolls recording Baxit's dictates. He could see the tail end of the curving stairs that led to Naga's entrance with its fanged mouth. One dandy ducked his head too late, and lost his high-topped hat to one of Naga's teeth.

Janus entered Parliament's marble hall while the doorman was still calling out his title. He took a quick, vindictive pleasure in the surge of glances and whispers.

The cathedral's inner face had been altered far more than the outside, creating a central open space holding a single podium where the five-sided altar had stood. A new level rose behind the podium, built of painted wood cannibalized from icons sized as tall as the building. Rows of spectator seats crowded tightly into the narrow mezzanine, tilted slightly forward so as to give a better view of the speaker.

Aris had originally approved the addition of the mezzanine to house the most prosperous and influential commoners, to give them a chance to speak. But there had been such an uproar at the idea that Aris had allowed the subject to be forgotten. Janus thought it was one of Aris's better ideas, well worth pursuing in the coming years. In the meantime, the mezzanine held the aristocratic overflow; those without prestige or power, those who came to see their laws passed secondhand.

Chimes rang out, five separate tones blending into a penetrating whole, calling the nobles to order, only an hour later than planned. Gossiping circles broke reluctantly, passing last tidbits of information on whispered breaths.

A furtive motion drew Janus's attention, as well as multiple others'—Savne demonstrating his incompetence once again at playacting. His conference with Blythe was too evident; though he recoiled as if Blythe insulted his lineage and his manhood, the overacting made it clear they had been speaking amiably enough.

Savne headed upstairs like a hound recalled to his master's side. Janus, tracking his progress, met the Duchess of Love's serpentine gaze, glittering with malevolence. Savne sat next to her, bent to whisper in her ear. Janus, watching them, found more of interest in Psyke, sitting quietly in the duchess's shadow.

Janus, well aware of all the eyes on him, of the chimes' echo fading, and of Gost drawing breath to chastise, moved to take a seat. Reluctantly Gost gestured at the ornately carved chair nearest to the podium: the former Earl of Last's seat, Janus's now, by birthright.

Janus said, "Don't trouble yourself. I see my seat."

"Last," Gost said. "What mad start—"

Janus swept by the man without a further word and headed for the stairs. Seeking an upstairs seat was all to the good, Janus thought, taking his time doing so. For one thing, it irritated Gost; for another, it was a pleasant way to ruin the duchess's day. He wove through the crowded mezzanine and fetched up before her.

"Ladies, good morning."

Savne bristled. Psyke, as was newly familiar, looked back at him with an expression not entirely her own.

Janus settled himself comfortably on Psyke's other side, ignoring the duchess's continual, hissed imprecations. He unfastened his sword belt, looped it over the chair arm, hilt toward his hand, boots stretched out before him, and accepted a cup of the bitter coffee a servant brought him. Only after a fortifying sip did he react to the duchess, still jabbering at Savne, muttering about murderers and for Savne to *do something*. Janus ducked his head to murmur close to Psyke's ear. "Do you think I should call the servant back? I fear he's left a kettle to boil nearby. My ears are full of hissing and hot air."

Psyke's face was downturned, focused on the tight knot of her hands nestled palely against her black wool skirt. He had only a view of her cheek, the edge of her lips, but it was enough to see the tiny quiver of rosy lips, the sudden shiver of her fingers as they relaxed.

"If the Earl of Last has made himself quite comfortable," Gost said, standing at the podium. His voice carried with little effort, his fine baritone warming the chill in the room.

"Quite comfortable, though a few cushions might not be amiss," Janus said. He didn't have the benefit of acoustics to help him, but he pitched his voice to be heard.

He hadn't slept well on Delight's chaise, the surroundings bringing to mind his failures—that disastrous demonstration, Chryses's death, even Aris's murder, committed on his watch—but it had also made a few thoughts very clear. Maledicte's popularity—before his bloodshed grew too great to ignore—had been based not only on his supposed wealth, on his pretty face and form, but also on the acidity of his tongue. There was nothing the court appreciated so much as a heckler.

He'd played his role incorrectly, Janus realized, when he'd chosen to be somber, serious, and studious.

"Another mask?" Psyke said, her voice a thin thread of sound connecting the two of them, an act of intimacy with the duchess so keen eared and angry beside her.

"No," he said. "I'm tired of masks. Let them make of me what they will. I'll weather it."

Gost's speech was much what he had expected, an impassioned plea to let logic rule over sentiment, to apply experience over bloodline, to let Gost take the place of first regent instead of Janus. It would have been more effective, perhaps, if Gost weren't forced to praise Blythe as choice for second regent, as well as himself. Or if Gost's cries for experience before blood didn't apply equally to Warrick Bull as to himself.

Janus thought about raising the point, but it would only make him seem grasping. Gost's speech evaded that flaw. There'd be no accusations of usurpation after this speech.

"As sly as a cat," Psyke said abruptly, "that's licked its whiskers clean of butter before leaving the larder. It might rid you of a mouse, but it takes more than it earns."

She ended her comment on a gasp. The duchess had pinched her. Psyke rubbed at the welt rising on her hand with a sulky expression far from her own. Janus bumped her arm, hoping to jostle the ghost within her, and she turned to look at him with a careful calculation he had seen before. It wasn't uncommon to find a schemer behind a woman's pleasant smile, but this one held arrogance and power in it.

"Don't stare. It's rude," she said. "If you never paid me attention before, you can't expect me to welcome it now."

Janus found a name to put with that ghost but kept it tight behind his teeth. Naming her might strengthen her, and the last thing he needed was an enemy returned from the dead.

Gost made the expected suggestion that the Duchess of Love should act as Adiran's guardian, gestured in her direction as if he were flinging the praise he spoke. Gost's grand gesture fell a little short as he found himself gesturing in Janus's direction also. He stumbled, but continued.

The speech wasn't subtle; Janus found himself disappointed. So far, he'd heard nothing but patriotic pabulum and self-congratulation. Then again, Gost was speaking to a room full of stagnant minds. His words needed to be familiar and as weighty as stone to make an impression.

Gost finished with a verbal flourish, so much so that Janus almost expected the man to put his proposition to a vote immediately. But the aristocracy hated to be rushed. Distrusted it instinctively with the luxury of being the ones in charge for generations.

That was going to make the vital difference. Janus could act and act decisively, while Gost had to honor tradition.

Servants stationed at the end of each row of voting nobles began passing folded pieces of paper down the line. One servant, after an irritated wave from Gost, made the climb up the narrow stairs.

Janus watched the crisp paper make its way to him, softening in each successive grasp. He unfolded it, and looked at the incomprehensible script. High Antyrrian. Again.

Psyke leaned in, murmured. "It's a ballot."

"I had assumed as much."

The duchess snapped, "Lady Last."

Psyke traded a long look with the duchess, and she was the first to yield, turning her attention to Savne's sycophantic mutterings.

Psyke leaned close and translated for Janus. It was mostly the same as Gost's speech, though there was an irritating addendum, legacy of the last parliamentary session that Janus had been too busy to attend: a motion exempting nobles from outstanding debts if they were of service to the crown.

Blythe, Janus thought wryly, *still failing to improve at cards*. He took up a pen from a servant's tray, the nib wet with ink, and lined through that motion, scrawling next to it: *Debts must be paid.*

Gost sent a furtive look toward Janus, visibly tensing for Janus to rebut him. Janus hadn't been planning on it; it would be too easy to be drawn into the kind of brangle that showed him to least effect, left him furious and silent, and people about him injured.

Still, if Gost was begging for it, Janus saw no harm in obliging. "Blythe," he said. "Honestly? I thought the difficulty facing Antyre was that our *prince* was mindless. I wouldn't have thought you'd compound the problem by choosing a man with even less intellect than poor Adiran for your second."

Belowstairs, Blythe's hand dropped to his sword. "I'll challenge you."

The duchess leaned forward, a smile curving her lips, as if the young man had the merest chance against Janus.

"And thus my point is proved," Janus said. Psyke giggled unexpectedly—the ghosts again, Janus thought, they were more ruthless than a drowning tide—and set off a slow titter through the room.

Janus left the mezzanine without waiting for any further response, be it from Gost, Blythe, or someone else.

A tug on his sleeve drew his rapid pace to something slower; he looked and found Psyke keeping pace with him. "Best look after me. I left my guards behind." Her words sounded arch, a little flirtatious, still those of the ghost who had giggled at the thought of Janus dueling.

He crooked his elbow and she folded her hand around it, leaned against his side, the better, he thought darkly, to poison him with whatever malign influence dwelled in her.

The duchess called after her. Psyke paused, eyed the duchess coldly. "Once you told me to judge Janus by the enemies he has and by the caliber of his friends. Well, I've judged. Him by his allies and you by yours."

She tugged gently at his arm and set them back into motion. Janus steered Psyke toward the narrow door at the base of the stairwell, framed in wings. The darkness closed around them, marble gone dark with shadow, streaked with distant light.

"It's peculiar," Janus said. "The duchess's sudden insistence on your company. I would have thought her pleased to see you at my side, poisoning me with your presence."

"She thinks me her lost daughter. Or at least haunted by her," Psyke said, shifting easily as a careless lordling nearly fell against her. Drunk before noon, still in his evening wear, having attended the secret parties being held in defiance of mourning strictures; the very example of an Antyrrian lord. "No matter how often I tell her, she will not believe that Amarantha doesn't come to me."

"She doesn't?" Janus asked. That stiff hauteur, that arrogance and disdain; he had thought it Amarantha also.

"No," Psyke said. A clipped, single word; disinclined to annoy her, he let the matter drop.

He stepped out into mid-morning sunlight, to the yielding surface of age-smoothed wood, ducking his head as the doorway extended farther than he had thought, and Ani's wing tips were sharp. They had come out at the back of the building, the long, raised pathway that meandered through the ill-kempt cemetery.

A raw scar of earth, russet against green, signified Aris's resting place. Psyke hesitated; her skirts swayed toward that barren patch, and Janus said, "A dead man needs no visitors. Or perhaps I should rephrase that. You need invite no visitations from dead men. This morning is crowded enough."

Psyke bowed her head, but changed her direction to match his once more.

"Anyway," Janus said, "Aris speaks to you often enough. Or will you tell me I'm mistaken again?"

"Aris meets with me much as he did in life, to complain about you, to urge me not to trust you. To name you his killer."

"Single-minded," Janus said, "before and after death. And still quite wrong."

"So it seems," Psyke said.

Janus tripped over the tip of his own boot, caught himself with a hand flung out to seize the rough-hewn railing. He steadied himself and stared moodily at the splinter in his palm. Even when she agreed with him, it caused him pain.

"Perhaps it should have concerned me earlier that the only one who believed my claim of Maledicte's guilt was Prince Ivor. That aside, I've spoken with the duchess, listened to Blythe, spent an edifying hour with Gost. None of them see anything of the future beyond themselves. The duchess dwells on retribution, Blythe—"

"Least said, best said," Janus murmured carefully, lest she cease this quiet confession.

"Agreed." Psyke took a few more steps in silence, then added teasingly, "Will you ask me about Gost?"

"If you wish," Janus said.

"Gost is a man given over to vanity. He wants to etch his name into history. Himself before all else."

"Does this mean you're allying yourself with me?" Bad form to ask a direct question that put a lady under awkward social obligation, but time was growing short.

The murmur of voices, distantly noticed, began to take on a discernible rhythm and Janus bit back a growl. "Stay close to my side."

"Poole!" the people chanted. "Free Poole!"

"I'm . . . considering it," she said. Her voice was nearly lost in the surge of the angry crowd, many of them waving placards, others sticks.

Janus put a hand on the small of Psyke's back, steered her relentlessly toward the carriages, wishing he hadn't been so quick to leave the cathedral crowd. If he had been able to stomach them for a few minutes longer, they would have exited at the carriage path, ready to duck into the frail shelter of the coach.

Simpson and Walker made an appearance, pistols drawn, coming in their direction. Janus shifted, reaching for his blade, but the guards' eyes were all for the crowd. "This way, quickly," Simpson said.

"We had the carriage brought around," Walker said. "The crowd's mood is ugly. Poole's only an excuse. They're jostling the carriages, overturned one already."

"Thank you for your foresight, gentlemen," Psyke said. She cast her gaze about, watching the bustle of carriages trying to reach the nobles on the walkways. She frowned, raised a hand to shade her eyes, looking for the distinctive blue of the Last coach.

"There," Janus said. "The coachman with the regrettable feather in his hat."

Walker and Simpson waved the man over, and then aided Psyke into the carriage. When Janus joined her, he found her tracing the scars and damages previous passengers had left in the wood.

"Why a hire coach?" she asked.

"Why paint a target on my back?" he countered.

Walker closed the door behind them, stepped onto the footman's post, and waved the coachman to set off. The coach lurched, then slowed.

Walker shouted at the driver to force a way through, to use the whip, his pistol. . . . Janus leaned out. "Too much haste will call attention to us as surely as the Last coach would. Let the driver go as he will."

Walker's lips tightened behind his dark beard, but he nodded.

"Rue said you had a head on your shoulders." As he turned away from the window, Janus heard the man mutter one thing more. "Pity you've no care for ours."

The carriage lurched again, like a ship caught in the first touch of the outbound tide. Psyke rocked with the movement, tucked her skirts tight about herself. Without thinking, Janus leaned forward and caught first her knee, then pushing up the heavy drape of black-dyed wool and black-stained petticoat to reveal her bare feet.

He traced the white arch of her foot, the grit and dust beneath her heel and toes. She shivered.

"Even outside?" he asked. "Even then?"

"I crave the clay beneath my feet." Her eyes on his were sober, testing, as if to ask what would he do with her honesty.

He rubbed at the delicate joint of ankle and foot, the curve of tight-drawn tendons. "Need I prepare quarters for you in the depths of the palace? Have the servants lay down dirt and stone instead of rugs?"

"Challacombe tells me my ancestor disappeared into those secret corridors. Perhaps I could spend my time hunting his bones."

"And speaking to them?" And what was this between them? Gentle teasing or menace so oblique that Janus wasn't sure who threatened whom?

She only dimpled at him, as sweetly pretty as she had been the day he had first seen her, dancing with Maledicte. "Sir, I am a lady. I speak only to those I've been properly introduced to."

"I must say I've missed you," he said. "Your guests lack humor."

She sighed, leaned back, her smile sliding away. He shifted to sit beside her instead of across from her, heedless of the poison that might emanate from her.

Psyke leaned her head against his shoulder, tucking her feet up on the bench. "Well, Aris and Challacombe are dour enough, I admit. But Mirabile finds many things amusing. Unfortunately, I do not. She speaks to me, *through* me, and even while I mouth her words, respond to her thoughts . . . all I recall is waking to find her by my bedside and my sisters slaughtered."

The quiet horror in her voice, the weary pain, woke old memories in Janus, nights when Miranda snugged herself tight against him and listed their friends lost to predation on the streets.

Was it any wonder that the Relicts thrived so? When dangerous women like Mirabile had had free rein in society? Only when Mirabile had turned blatantly murderous, when she turned her attention to the most innocent of the nobility—the debutantes—had anyone thought to stop her. Of course, by then, it was too late.

He idly stroked the curved bones of Psyke's ankle, feeling the skin warm beneath his hand; the pulse fluttering there increased from its slow and steady beat to something quick and light. Her lips parted, palest red and petal soft. He leaned closer, thinking of her saying, *I loved your passion*, thinking of her spurning the duchess's company for his, of her quietly translating the motions Parliament had made. His mouth brushed hers; her lips and breath were cold, but her tongue, pressing against his own, was warm, a lick of flame in the midst of frost.

He pulled away, thinking *poison*.

"You're very accommodating today," he said.

"You brought Dionyses back to the palace."

In her eyes, he saw it was as easy as that. For a woman who'd lost her entire family and friends to a murderous witch, Delight was her family regained.

Our estates marched together, Delight had said. *We were to be wed*.

The carriage halted, nearly pitched them to the floor as the horses whinnied and jerked in the traces, refusing to be gentled.

The outcry in the street took on a feverish pitch. Janus pressed Psyke back to the seat.

Walker dropped off the foot rail, disappeared from sight with a grunt. Janus hissed, bent, pulled the knife from his boot, and put it into Psyke's hands. "Guard yourself."

"I have better weapons than steel at my disposal, though I thank you for your concern," she said. And it wasn't Psyke in her eyes, but the cold superiority of Mirabile. Challacombe would know better than to spurn a weapon of any kind. And Aris? Would he still be turning the blade in his hands, reluctant to admit the need for it?

Janus hastened out of the carriage at another shout and the splintering of wood, the screaming of horses. Not their carriage, thankfully, but close.

The street was a seething mass of packed carriages—horses breaking free and shouldering through, heads raised, eyes white and wild—and in the midst of it all, the antimachinists, hands full of rocks, were laying concerted efforts into destroying everything they could. The chant demanding Poole's release had grown ragged, gone incomprehensible as all unison was lost.

A pistol shot cracked the air, and Janus crouched, hand going to his saber. A guard? Or did the rioters have more dangerous weapons?

A single antimachinist saw Janus, and his eyes widened in fierce exultation. "Ixion!" He plunged toward him, raising a stick studded with broken glass.

Janus fell back. He knew that sticks were far more dangerous than the nobles acknowledged; he had used them to considerable effect himself as a youth. He wasn't hampered by ignorance or surprise, and when the man moved into range, Janus unsheathed his saber into the man's heart. Clean and quick, the best way to deal with enemies in a shifting crowd of this size.

Simpson burst through a small knot of struggling men; common people going about their business who found their morning violently interrupted and were trying to get out of the way.

"My lord!"

Janus didn't have a response for him. His attention had been drawn across the square where Gost's carriage, distinctive with its heavy sun-shading draperies across the doors, was listing, nearly tilted over.

The epiphany burst over him. *This* was Ivor's plan. *This* was the manner in which he chose to remove Gost. A riot, where any death could be deemed accidental, but the damage done. . . . Janus gritted his teeth, regretting the bargain more than ever.

Gost's carriage swayed; the dark curtain billowed into the shape of two men, struggling. Janus kicked a man in the knee; the man—antimachinist or frightened citizen, it didn't matter—collapsed and cleared a path for Janus's next few steps. Simpson called after him, doggedly pursuing.

The carriage door burst open, revealing a heavyset, hawk-face blond wielding a bloody sword, as overtly a murderer as any stage villain. Gost's body tumbled out after him, rolling into the dirt.

The man dropped from the step, landed with an awkward lurch; and Janus found himself suddenly too close to him, in a clearing that hadn't existed a heartbeat ago.

The assassin's face was shadowed by a low-brimmed hat, but his eyes flicked once at Janus, letting the bloody sword shift to prepared-ness again. Janus frowned but echoed it. Not a rapier, but a saber. An Itarusine to be sure, no matter the Antyrrian laborer's clothes.

The man's gaze shifted abruptly to someone in back of Janus; Janus half turned, unwilling to be caught from behind, equally aware that it might be nothing more than a feint. The man hurled himself into the crowd and did his best to disappear.

Simpson drew up beside Janus, pistol still held ready. "Who was that?"

"Harm, I believe," Janus said. He stared at the crowd a moment longer, reliving the moment when Harm landed, that awkward lurch; Chryses had said the man was scarred heavily, but that argued scars that reached into muscle. It stirred small chords of memory, but came to nothing.

"Harm his avocation, also. Gost is dead."

Most decidedly so. Closer inspection revealed the wounds to be ugly, sloppy, and indecisive, as if Harm had dithered between the heart, the liver, the stomach, and finally selected them all.

Make it hurt, Janus had said. Ivor had apparently passed along those instructions, or Harm was just the sort to enjoy it. Gost's face was white and contorted, his eyes bulging, his mouth obscured by a froth of blood.

Hoofbeats and ringing handbells penetrated the shouts and screams, and Janus allowed Simpson to keep him sheltered against Gost's coach while the Particulars cleared the streets of rioters with shot, sword, and spear.

When he returned to his coach, Simpson in tow, he found Psyke sitting on the coachman's bench, face tilted back as if she were enjoying the quiet and the sunshine, her bare feet dangling, while all about her, men lay dead, including Walker. Janus bent, turned him over, but found no wound. Simpson, kneeling over first one corpse, then another, cast a burdened glance at Psyke and made the tiny *avert* against evil.

HEIR APPARENT

23

*T*HE PALACE WAS SILENT THAT night, dinner around the great table, subdued. Servants ghosted about with reddened eyes and unhappy faces: The Particulars' solution to the rioting had been to kill or arrest the commoners in the square whether they declared they were simple merchants or boasted of being antimachinists. Husbands and brothers had been taken to Stones, fathers and uncles had been killed, and still, the servers bent their heads.

Janus watched them and kept a careful rein on his appetite. Poison was too easy to come by, and there was a store of ill will focused on the nobility at the moment.

Harm, of course, had managed to elude the soldiers. Rue swore it wouldn't be for long, and had set the Particulars back to their hunt. Even now, they fanned the embers of the riot anew in their search of houses, shops, inns, and ships. Perhaps they had even braved the Relicts.

Janus turned his gaze from Gost's empty seat, found Ivor watching him. The prince tilted his goblet just slightly, enough so that Janus knew it for the toast it was, but others might see only a temporarily unsteady hand.

Psyke, seated at the head of the table, sat between two empty chairs—Aris's and Gost's. Her eyes were unfocused; her lips moved in constant whispers, and Janus doubted she felt alone at all. The rest of the table was studded with other absences. Adiran—confined to his nursery under doubled guard. The duchess—sealed into her Garden Square residence, behind shuttered windows and locked doors, out of rage at Gost's death, or fear.

Janus sent back his plate, the meal untouched, and excused himself. Bull hastily took a last forkful and stood. DeGuerre grumbled but threw down his napkin and rose also. Ivor grinned, lounged back in his seat, and said, "Time for after dinner drinks already? I knew I was going to like you as regent, my pet."

Janus froze, caught on the points of several different realizations, some of them pleasant, some of them . . . not. With Gost's death, with Blythe's odd absence, with Bull's apparent support, the regency was nearly his; Admiral DeGuerre might grumble, but he knew it. With Gost gone, Janus was the ranking man at the table. When he rose, the meal ended, as did his hopes for a quiet escape. Ivor, damn him, read the surprise on his face all too easily.

Janus refused to sit back down, refused to show he had forgotten such basic etiquette, and so merely nodded before retiring to the parlor. Psyke looked up, her eyes drowning blue, alone at the table with her ghosts.

Ivor followed them into the king's study, settled himself with all the smugness of a cat having gained access to a place it was forbidden to be.

Janus ignored him for the moment, but Ivor's presence cast a heavy pall over the room. Bull looked near to bursting; DeGuerre grew more dyspeptic by the second. The only thing lacking was Blythe sulking like a spoiled child or itching to duel.

"Where *is* Blythe?" Janus asked. It was the only question suited to the audience at hand. Any talk of the riot, Gost's death, or politics would have to wait.

Admiral DeGuerre was the one to break silence and answer, contempt for Blythe momentarily overriding his dislike of Janus. "Fled to the countryside," he said. "Rethought his challenge to you."

"Apparently," Bull said, "he was much struck with your guard's account of how you held your own in the rioting. Simpson tells me you defeated several armed rioters on your own?"

"They had sticks," Janus said. "I had a sword."

"I understand your wife accounted for six men, including her guard, and with no mark upon them," Ivor said. "How does she explain it? Or is it something you'd rather keep secret?"

Janus's neck tightened. Ivor's tone was amused, light, but Janus could read the demand in it clearly enough. Ivor had upheld his end by killing Gost; now it was Janus who had to do the same.

"Bull, DeGuerre, if you'll excuse me. Again. It's been a difficult day, likely to be as difficult tomorrow—"

"Don't worry so, pet," Ivor said. "When the Itarusine fleet arrives, we'll calm any remaining pockets of unrest."

Janus seized Ivor's arm, pulled him from his chair, aware as always of the solidity of muscle and sinew over bone. Ivor was a bruiser for all his cat lounging and graceful mannerism; he rose because he wanted to go where Janus led. Adiran's nursery.

JANUS WAITED UNTIL THEY WERE a safe distance from the study, from Bull or DeGuerre deciding to join them or object, belatedly, to Ivor's tone. Waited until they were in the quiet corridors leading to the main stairwell.

"I asked you to kill one man," Janus said, "not turn my city into a battlefield."

"Some tasks are easier to begin than end," Ivor said. "And it was your error, not mine. You were unclear in your boundaries."

Janus hissed out a breath, but it was true, and he should have known better. Asking Ivor for a favor was more akin to dealing with a wish granter than a man. If the deed could be twisted, Ivor would be quick to see the path best suited to his own needs.

Ivor smiled. "Come now, admit your true irritation. It's not the uprising; you should be thanking me for that. I gave you a clear reason to be rid of the antimachinists. And some of them, permanently, I understand."

"Not Harm," Janus said.

"No," Ivor said, "though you could have seized him, were you not slowed by expecting another assassin in his place."

Ivor moved ahead of him, making Janus take quick steps to catch him up, and each one of them an echo of his inner frustration. They rounded the corner, found the guards lurching to attention, their faces writ with dismay. Janus alone would have perturbed them; Ivor's presence was another level of discomfort.

"My lord," the guard said.

"We've come to see Adiran," Janus said. "We won't be long." That with a meaningful glance at Ivor. Janus waved the guards in alongside them as their unhappy escort.

Adiran sat up as they entered, coming awake all at once. Beside his narrow bed, another slim body rested. Evan, Janus identified, asleep not in the penitential servant's quarters allotted him, but wrapped in furs and velvet as if he were a replacement for the banished hounds.

The boy prince crawled out of his bed, carefully stepping over Evan, and came toward them. Once in the low, yellow lamplight, ever burning, near the door, he raised his face and Ivor shifted behind Janus when he glimpsed the piebald eyes, one gone yellow-black, one blue.

"Janus," Adiran said. In his childish voice lingered earlier reminders of Ani's displeasure with him. It made Janus cautious, made him wish he knew what Ivor wanted of the boy.

Adiran was on that fragile cusp; Black-Winged Ani had improved the prince's mind, no doubt preparatory to striking a compact with him. If Adiran fell—then Antyre fell also, no matter Janus's attempts to hold it. Regent was one thing, a polite lie that the nobles would allow.

A usurping bastard king? Unthinkable.

Adiran tugged at Janus's sleeve, all boy, just a boy, the hope for the kingdom. Janus knelt beside him, ruffled his hair, trying to ignore the tiny stiff prickles against his palm that might be pinfeathers mixed into the blond tufts. "Brought Prince Ivor to see you," he said. "Be polite."

Adiran slid out of Janus's loose hold, walked fearlessly up to Ivor though the guards' hands tensed so tightly on their swords the hilts creaked.

"Prince," Adiran said, a question in his tone. Janus wondered how much lessoning the boy was getting. It was one thing to lock him away, to teach him only how to play when he was mindless. Now, though, perhaps there should be tutors. If Janus could find any he trusted. Adiran could be too easily shaped by information.

As if such thoughts passed to him, Ivor said, "I meant to visit you sooner, your highness. After the death of your father."

Adiran stiffened, tilted his head for a better angle, shifting the crow's eye upward to study Ivor, but he said nothing.

Ivor reached out slowly, allowing the guards time to see his hands were empty, allowing Adiran the chance to step back. But the boy held his position even when Ivor's fingers tucked themselves beneath Adiran's chin.

"Ani's child," he said. "A seed sown by Maledicte."

Rue spoke up from the hall, his voice harsh, his breath coming quick, as if he had run to the nursery on hearing of Adiran's unexpected visitors. He waved the other guards out and they looked grateful. "Prince Ivor, the child can be of no interest to you."

Ivor ignored Rue entirely, and asked, "Do you know who killed your father, boy?"

The question dropped like a stone into water, setting ripples of tension through the room. A rustle and a sigh heralded Evan waking; his sudden, whistled breath heralded his recognizing Ivor.

Ivor's face blanched as Adiran turned to study him more intently. Ivor withdrew his hand, shaking it as if lightning had coursed from Adiran's flesh to his.

Janus, regrettably close, thought something like that might have happened. The boy's human eye began to splotch, dark shapes bleeding through the blue.

"Do *you* know?" the boy echoed. "No one will tell me."

As if to prove the boy's assertion, the silence stretched. Ivor caught Janus's gaze in his own, the battlefield clear between them. Ivor could blame Janus; Janus could lay the blame at Ivor's feet, but the death of Itarus's favored prince ascendant would only bring war faster.

Adiran stamped his foot; the ripple ran across the room, and the toys on his shelves began to dance and stutter. Evan closed the distance between them and said, "They don't know either, Adi. I told you. Now come lie down."

The wildness in the room, a feathery musk that Janus had last smelled when fighting Mal, faded under Evan's small dictatorship. Rue smiled briefly at Janus. "I'm afraid I've commandeered your page."

"Welcome to him," Janus said.

Ivor turned, blindly left the room, hand seeking the wall for support. Janus followed him. Ivor turned, expression savage. "You intend to let him live?"

"He's a boy," Janus said. "The Antyrrian prince, and your words are perilously close to treason."

"He's tainted," Ivor said, but the usual banter was gone from his voice. "He's dangerous. There'll be no kingdom for either of us while he lives."

"Less for you," Janus said. "After all, you killed—"

Ivor hit him, tried to, but Janus had been expecting it and avoided the blow. Ivor wouldn't want him to finish that sentence, not anywhere near where Adiran could hear him. Janus hadn't intended to, but enjoyed that brief show of panic on Ivor's face nonetheless.

The guards rushed forward and Ivor took a few steps back, hands raised. "A misunderstanding," he said. "But if you gentlemen would care to escort me to my wing, I'd be appreciative."

Janus admired it. Even shaken, Ivor remained poised. Far more so than Janus, who felt trapped between the problems Adiran posed and the pressing approach of the Itarusine fleet, bringing Grigor's letter of censure for breaking the treaty.

"Trust me," Rue said abruptly. Janus jerked. "I've done my scholarly studies. If Adiran can be kept from killing anyone, he should stay as he is. Safe."

"For how long?" Janus said. "Until he's grown? Until he learns what anger is? Until we have a mad king with feathers in his skin and death in his eyes?"

Rue's jaw firmed, expressing displeasure or determination. "That's up to you, my lord. You have the plans for the future. You used the god once before to suit your needs. Surely you have a similar plan now."

Sudden bitter amusement swelled in Janus's breast, bubbling up into mad laughter. "But, Rue," he said, "I didn't believe in the gods then."

He left Rue gaping after him, took to the corridors with exhaustion and a mind too numbed to do anything but turn facts this way and that, like a blind jeweler going through the motions when the talent has been lost.

It was only the scent that saved him: a curl of sweet lilac in a dark hall preceding the bitter tang of oiled steel. Janus reared back and took the dagger across the side of his left forearm instead of through his throat.

Over the blade, Savne panted, face going witless in panic, the face of a man who had been relying on a single thrust and the element of surprise.

Janus pushed back hard, giving himself a much-needed space between them. If it were at the cost of the blade slicing deeper into his arm, it didn't matter. The brocade of his sleeve had been pushed in at the same moment as the blade, clinging to the open lips of the wound, staunching the blood flow. Janus punched Savne beneath the join of his rib cage. It was the first blow he'd ever learned, though when he was a child, it involved a stick or stone to add force he lacked. Those days were past and Savne's breastbone cracked, a wet pop; the man folded inward, breath gone, the knife dropping from a hand gone lax.

Janus let him fall, kneed him in the same spot as Savne folded forward. The man wheezed pain, the sound going liquid as ribs gave under the second blow. Janus caught the knife and bent over Savne's huddled form.

Savne rolled to his back, raising his hands to shield his face, but the movement was a mistake. The man's eyes rolled in his head as the shifting bones in his chest caused him to pass out.

Janus cast a quick look down the hall to see if anyone had heard Savne's choked-off cries. The corridors remained empty; the attack hadn't been loud or long, and the carpet was thick, the wallpaper flocked and hung with sound-muffling tapestries.

Janus tapped the knife against Savne's face, leaving delicate wounds in court-pampered skin. He could, of course, slit the man's throat now, but he found there were words he needed to say. He spread the man's hand out and stabbed downward. Savne jerked to consciousness, Janus's other hand over his mouth, and then fell back. Janus pulled his hand away from the man's mouth—it wasn't in Savne to bite, he wasn't a scrapper—but blood washed Janus's palm all the same.

"A word of advice," Janus said, pleased that his breath was no faster than usual, his voice no harsher than his usual pleasant baritone. "If you would ambush someone, best forgo drenching yourself in scent. It betrays your position."

Savne gasped, gasped again, ugly gulps, trying to force air into lungs ruined by the double blow. "But . . . the scent . . . His scent . . . exactly his scent . . . It should have soothed you. She said . . ."

Janus put his hand on Savne's shoulder, leaned in; the man groaned as Janus's weight radiated toward his broken sternum. "Soothed me? When I've spent the past six months learning to associate it with you and your crawling ways, your borrowed mannerisms, and your oh-so-blatant attempts to woo me? Savne, you taught me to loathe that scent."

"Please . . ." Savne gasped.

Janus shook his head. "It was unfortunate that the duchess sent you."

Savne whimpered beneath him, and Janus loosened the grip he had on the man's throat. Savne twitched; a hand flailed at Janus's wrist, manicured nails leaving feeble scratches, but really what did the man think was going to happen? There was no escape. Not for his crimes.

Janus felt the crushing weariness return again. Savne was no challenge; worse, he would never truly understand how he had earned Janus's enmity. Janus dragged the knife blade across the man's throat, digging it deep until he got not only the tide of blood but the quick wheeze of escaping breath after it.

Once Savne was entirely still, Janus said, "Besides, you were wrong. It wasn't his scent. Underneath it all, Maledicte smelled of blood."

And so did he, now, Janus thought; the air was full of wet copper, overriding even the distinctive aroma of dust and lamp oil that filled the palace hallways. He slumped back against the wall and gingerly pried the heavy brocade out of his wound, noting that the blood had spread through brocaded loops and whirls, puddled to the floor.

The slice wasn't long, running the width of his arm, rather than the length, but it was deep enough that when Janus pressed, he could see the creamy shine of bone, the pulse of a vein.

Stitches then, if Sir Robert could be trusted. If not, well, Delight had at least a passing familiarity with medicine, enough to treat him if needed.

On the wall opposite him, a mirror swung slowly back into place, knocked askew by Savne's dying spasm, sprayed with a thin freshet of blood.

Janus forced himself to his feet, misliking the vertigo it brought. A strengthening tonic might not come amiss or, even simpler than the iron and wine tonic, a cup or two of beef broth from the kitchens.

He'd go to the physician's office in a moment. Once the vertigo passed. He leaned forward, rested his hands on the wall, either side of the mirror, panting now as he hadn't during the deeply unequal struggle.

His own gaze caught him, and he stared at his reflection; he wasn't a man given to looking into the glass beyond the necessities of dressing, preferring his internal sense of self. The mirrored glass all too often reflected a stranger.

But now—the man looking back at him was surprisingly young, going gaunt with too many missed meals that might be poisoned, gray with lack of sleep and blood loss. For the first time in years, he felt it was his reflection again. Not some sleek, well-fed, overdressed lordling. No, this young man was a predator, pressed hard.

He laughed, his head spinning again, throat as ragged as if it had been his lungs spitting blood instead of Savne's.

Footsteps in the hall, approaching; Janus turned, the knife held low. If it was more of the same, if it were another attacker, perhaps he would overlook the weapon until it was buried between his ribs.

"Janus!" Rue said. A measure of his shock, that the captain addressed him by his given name.

And a measure of his own shock, Janus thought, that he dwelled on such inconsequentialities as titles and not the simple concern in Rue's eyes. Rue was either his man or a far more able actor than he had ever exhibited.

"He attempted to surprise me," Janus said.

"Ended surprised himself," Rue muttered. He stepped over Savne's body and reached for the arm Janus kept close to himself. "But he did strike you? Some of the blood is yours."

Janus flinched at the man's white-gloved hands, pulled away before there was contact. Rue hesitated. "No?" Assessing him like a damn wild animal.

"Yes, damn it," Janus said.

"You're white," Rue said. "Come on then, lose some of the pride and lean on me."

THE JOURNEY TO THE PHYSICIAN'S offices, once the guards had run ahead to wake Sir Robert, saw the collapse of Janus's pride. He not only allowed Rue to aid him but listened to the man's encouraging murmurs, "Not so far. Just watch this stair. We'll have you put to rights," with a disturbing gratitude.

Rue saw him settled, saw pressure put on the wound, before he rang for Sir Robert.

Savne must have gotten in a lucky stroke and pierced one of the arteries as he sawed downward; the blood still pulsed against the makeshift bandage. But the simple act of sitting still, arm raised high, restored some of Janus's equilibrium.

Sir Robert grumbled as he entered his offices, muttering vile imprecations against those inconsiderate enough to be wounded after dinner. Janus, watching the man weave much as he must have done, coming down the hall leaning on Rue, wondered briefly if he'd have been better off going to Delight for suturing. But Delight's fingers were all too often covered with caustic substances, and Sir Robert's, while shaky, were pinkly clean.

Rue helped Janus out of his coat and shirt, hissing when the bleeding, which had slowed while being held, began to spill afresh. It had an equally sobering effect on Sir Robert.

"Haste is preferable to gentleness, Captain. At least in this situation."

Rue nodded, and Janus laughed as the captain hesitated a moment longer, unwilling to cause hurt. He tore at the sleeve himself, wincing more at the ruined fabric—vanity or not, he had liked that coat—and spurred Rue into slicing the laces tying the shirtsleeves in place.

Sir Robert handed him a blood-thickening drink, gritty with iron. Janus sipped at it, doing his best to imbibe only the warmed wine and spices and none of the metal. He'd been in Delight's workshop often enough to know that metal could pierce soft tissue; he'd had one attempt on his life tonight. It would be unsettling if he were to die of the cure: of the iron filings having been ground incorrectly. Still, the alcohol flushed him with warmth, soothed jangled nerves that twitched every time Rue stepped behind him with his double brace of sword and pistol, twitched every time Sir Robert pushed the curved needle through his skin.

"I want the Duchess of Love arrested," Janus said. "Hanged if we can manage it. But at the very least, arrested."

Rue was silent, and Janus twisted, drawing a slap on the thigh from Sir Robert for moving as he was trying to draw the thread through.

Rue's eyes rose. "I'm sorry, my lord?" He hadn't been listening at all, instead gaping at Janus's skin.

"Question?" Janus asked.

"Who took the whip—"

"My father. The burns? My mother who dropped coals on my skin if she could. The rest? Life in the Relicts. Learning to duel with Ivor as a teacher. Maledicte in a temper. Arrest the duchess, Rue, or my future may be even more arduous than my past. Arrest her or I'll send a man with a blade to see her threat ended."

"As you did with Gost?" Rue's eyes were sharp if not condemnatory. Janus licked wine from his lip.

"The man had no vision beyond his place in history." Janus winced as Sir Robert dug the needle in deep for the final stitch. Janus drank a larger gulp of the wine, the taste as metallic as if he were licking the goblet instead of drinking from it. "The duchess, Rue."

"I'll need more cause than one of her favorite courtiers attempting to kill you."

"Witchcraft," Janus said. He jerked his arm away from the physician who had snapped the thread tight all at once, creasing his skin and yanking the last of the deep wound closed.

"Witchcraft's a way for women to lay claim to power they can't earn," Sir Robert said. "Nothing more. An attempt to make men fear."

"Witchcraft?" Rue said. There was nothing of contempt or dismissal in his voice, dropping instinctively to a whisper. But then Rue had attended the ball where Mirabile left debutantes dying like plucked flowers, had seen houses painted red with shed blood, seen seasoned guards fall before her. "Have you any proof?"

"Psyke will provide it."

"Your wife is friend to the—"

"Psyke has too much integrity to lie when asked a question directly. And too much sense not to see the threat. The duchess runs mad, Rue, and whether she has power or not, she reaches for it. Send men to her house; I think evidence will not be hard to find."

Sir Robert smeared an unguent over the wound, sealing out infectious vapors, and began to wrap gauze about the arm tightly, thickly.

Janus protested, "Leave it to the minimum. I would not flaunt an injury at this time."

"Move your fingers," Sir Robert said. He turned Janus's hand, let the palm face upward. "Push against my hand," he commanded.

Janus attempted to, but found his last three fingers distressingly sluggish and weak, nearly unresponsive.

Sir Robert picked up the gauze again, and said, "No more nonsense. I've heard more than my fill. I'll wrap it tight and dense and you won't bleed out if you rip a stitch or three."

"When the swelling goes down, perhaps matters will improve," Rue said. "And it's not your sword hand."

He said that so easily, Janus thought, *the man who held two weapons at all times.* Didn't he think others might do the same?

"Can we trust Psyke to make a cogent statement? I've seen her, Last, speaking to unseen listeners, seen her bend to smell a bouquet and have it wither."

"I'm more concerned with Adiran than with Psyke. Ivor suggests we kill him, before Black-Winged Ani gets more than a toehold in his soul. Were it not that Adiran's death would benefit Itarus more than Antyre at the moment . . . were it not that I have an instinctive distrust of any of Ivor's suggestions, I would consider it."

Sir Robert fastened the bandage down and left the room hastily.

Rue said, "Consider your audience also, Last, when you discuss murdering the heir to the throne." His tone was mild, his eyes clouded; and Janus thought that Rue had also contemplated what might become necessary.

Janus said, "If Adiran becomes fully possessed, if he sheds blood, he will be bound to Ani's compact. Maledicte was deadly enough, and he possessed his own will to temper Ani's. Adiran is just a boy, with a boy's impetuousness. With Ani's power yoked to impulse, Adiran is the largest danger to our kingdom."

Janus rose, tested his hand again, as if the mention of gods were enough to collect their healing gifts. The fingers stayed recalcitrant, and forcing them only sent a stab of pain through his wound.

Rue said, "You may have a point. Let us hope it doesn't come to that, and take up our tasks to ensure it."

"Tasks," Janus said. He was feeling slow, his head thick, and he wondered if Sir Robert had doctored the wine with more than simple iron.

"I have a corpse to deal with, a duchess to arrest, a child to watch; you—you have a bed to seek."

"I want to see the duchess—"

"It's better done without you. If you come along, it'll be a fight;

she'll curse and scream. If it's only the Kingsguard—she'll be too on her dignity. I crave whatever peace I can find. Go to your bed."

"Psyke's likely in it," Janus muttered. Yes, Laudable in the wine, to loosen his tongue so.

"You trust Psyke."

"I trust her, but she's not always herself." Still, Janus allowed himself to be herded away, sent to bed like a sickly child, and found it . . . comforting.

THE DUCHESS WAS ESCORTED THROUGH the great hall, black clad, her gloved hands tucked before her, dripping jetty crystals. The two guards beside her held their hands on the grips of their pistols, proof that whatever they had found in her home had been disturbing enough for them to fear her. From his position in the counselor's chair nearest the throne, Janus watched her come, chin held high. Her gaze held fury and ice.

Behind her came the gaggle of her personal servants, all black clad, many of them veiled. Cold fingers slipped into his, made him start, and he looked over at Psyke's pale face. She watched the procession without words, or at least, audible words; her lips moved as if she held a whispered conference.

Rumor had spread; the entire corridor leading toward the throne room was thronged with nobles, some showing signs of having risen early, before their valets could aid them; some showed signs of never having been to their beds and swayed where they stood, cup shot or afraid.

For once in the court's history, they were silent, watchful rather than concentrating on creating spectacle. Janus wondered whether it was for the duchess being brought before the throne to face charges of treason or whether it was for the fear attached to the word *witch*.

A stifled moan rose through the crowd, a frantic gasp and whisper, as the guards continued in, carrying on a litter the bones festooned with sea pearls and gemstones, crusted with tallow, soot, and ash.

"Mirabile," Psyke breathed.

Janus found his own pulse a little unsteady. His hand tightened

around Psyke's. "You were a part of this? Even Maledicte never decorated corpses."

The rustle of the duchess's skirts hissed through the room as she
neared the throne, as if the stiff, black silk was releasing all the outrage she refused to voice. When she drew up at the throne, the
guards halted her and she found her tongue and her focus.

"Scared to sit the throne you stole?" she asked Janus.

Admiral DeGuerre said, "Your grace, please. We've brought you
here only so you might explain away these unfortunate circumstances that surround you."

Bull and Rue, standing beside DeGuerre, traded a speaking
glance. It was hardly surprising that DeGuerre would wish to grant
the woman an escape—she had long been his ally.

The litter was laid down beside her, a bright glimmering like a
bed of poisonous flowers against the shadow of her dark skirts. The
duchess took a careful step away from it, ensuring it didn't touch her,
and sealed her fate.

"Celeste, Duchess of Love, you stand accused—"

Psyke spoke up, her light voice carrying like a chill breeze. "Where
is your aide, Celeste? I do not see her among your servants."

Bull hesitated in his reading of the charges.

"Like you, she lacked dedication to the cause." The duchess's voice
was cracked, like a bell out of true; her aristocratic tones exaggerated
until they approached stage art. "I suppose she crept away as she
came. A shadow without a name."

Janus leaned down to Psyke's ear, murmured, "Is this aide dangerous?"

"She understands the ways of gods and magic," Psyke breathed
back. "She wore a veil at all times, hiding either prestige or the lack of
it; her voice was common enough, but her thoughts . . ."

"Wonderful," Janus said. "An elusive and intelligent enemy."

Psyke shivered; her lips took on a more mocking tilt. "Isn't it said
that you will know the worth of a man by his enemies? But then
men are rarely of any worth at all. . . ."

Wonderful, Janus thought again. Just what the occasion required—Mirabile's ghost spitting bile.

The duchess moved all at once, faster than Janus would have believed of a woman of her age and dignity. She leaped over the skeleton, her heavy skirts scattering gems and candles, and her hand came up.

Janus reached for his knife, his saber, but he managed to get only his forearm before his face to divert whatever weapon she clutched so close.

Liquid splashed over him, flung from the flask in the duchess's hand.

The guards shouted; pistols rang out, filling the room with acrid, choking smoke and explosions sharp enough to shatter tile. A whistling heat seared his cheek, sent him ducking, though his injured arm protested the sudden movement.

Psyke stood, Mirabile's vicious amusement on her mouth, as she watched the duchess bleed and die. Janus yanked her out of the way, though he rather thought she'd be immune to pistol shot.

Psyke touched the liquid running down Janus's face, sweeping it away before it could reach that heated tenderness where the bullet had passed. She licked her fingers.

"Mmm," she said—*Mirabile* said—"Precatorious syrup. Mal was fond of it, if I recall. Though the duchess should have known it was useless flung onto skin. It needs blood," she said, watching a tiny lavender drop pearl on her finger. "But then so many things do. Lineage. Prestige. Life."

Janus scrubbed his face hastily with his cravat. He didn't think the bullet had broken the skin, but he had a healthy respect for any poison Maledicte had deemed worthy of use—he preferred not to chance it. Psyke mused, "How Mal must have chafed beneath your leash. All his audacity yoked to common caution."

Janus gripped her wrist, pinched tight. "Psyke," he hissed, "this is not the time to let Mirabile speak."

She yipped beneath his pinching fingers, and the sound, such a tiny hurt in a room full of shrieking and death, seemed to rouse Rue to fury.

"Stop shooting!" Rue snapped.

Too late of course; the duchess was dead, and Janus had new and unwelcome evidence that at least one of the guards, given the opportunity and a likely excuse, would shoot him in the back. His seat wasn't in the path of the guards' bullets.

Bull reached down a hand, pulled Janus to his feet. "Your arm?" Bull asked. "Did the poison penetrate your shirt?"

Janus sighed. "Sir Robert will be so pleased."

Bull raised a brow, but his hands, tightening on Janus's sleeve as if he had been about to rip it away, relaxed. "Will he?" The physician's reluctance to work was legendary.

"He bandaged me so thickly I doubt the Naga-blessed ocean wave that sank the *Redoubtable* could do more than dampen the wound. The duchess never had a chance. Inept to the last."

"Hardly that. Only look what comes of my bones," Psyke said. She wandered forward, untouched by either shot or poison, and knelt to examine a dark splotch spreading over the creamy marble floor.

It wasn't blood as Janus had first assumed; it was a singular pearl, knocked loose from Mirabile's bones in the duchess's rush toward Janus. The floor around it was blackening, the marble flaking, the fine silver veining in the stone going rusty.

"No," Janus agreed, fighting the urge to strip out of his coat and burn it. "Perhaps not inept."

The crowd, made aware of the danger by Psyke's examination, began to push and shove to leave. Small shrieks rang out as the courtiers discovered that the venomous gems had scattered far and wide through the hall. One courtier, the rakish lord nicknamed Gamble, hampered by his evening wear and the lingering remnants of a night spent in dissipation, fell, putting his hand square on a star ruby. He wailed and Janus laughed.

Rue turned from where he was studying the hole the pistol shot had left in Janus's chair, and frowned. "You find this mayhem amusing, sir?"

"It's only that I've never imagined our Lord Gamble, the king of the cardsharps, ever slow to pick up a jewel."

Psyke laughed, bright and malicious, and the courtiers' attempts at flight became a rout. They might not understand it, but they remembered Mirabile laughing as the debutantes died.

Soon the hall was left to those who had need to be there. Rue, Bull, Admiral DeGuerre, surprisingly standing firm, though his hands quivered on his sword hilt as if seeking a more tangible enemy. The guards, eyeing each other suspiciously, remained, as did the duchess's servants, now huddled even more tightly together and weeping.

Psyke approached them and they shied back.

"What will we do with her servants?" Bull said. His attention seemed to be bent mostly on a girl too young to make her own way in the world, likely the cooking tweeny.

"Stones," Rue said, "would be customary for associates of one accused of treason. And they might consider it merciful."

"Stones is finite," Bull said, "and quite full. Given Lady Last's testimony, it seems the women were too afraid to assist and too afraid to flee. Let them find other work."

Janus thought *there* was the difference between the two men. Rue, a nobleman's get, if impoverished, still was quick to sentence the commoners; Bull, the self-made man, saw their faces and preferred to mete out mercy.

Janus said, "I sympathize, Bull, but who do you think will employ them? None in the courts who've witnessed the duchess's handiwork will, of that I'm sure."

"I will," Psyke said. "I will take them all."

When Janus opened his mouth, as reflexive in his denial as any of the courtiers, she said, "You complain that my maids are either lazy or dead. Here are some that are neither and in need of employment."

She turned to the gray-haired woman among them, the one whose face showed only dismay, whose eyes kept returning to the ruin of the duchess's body. "Do you know where the girl went, Charlotte? The nameless scholar who drank tea like a foreigner, stewed with sugar?"

"The spy," Charlotte said. "She pretended to quality, pretended to aid the duchess, but she sent letters to the palace at all hours, wrapped in veritable tubes of wax."

"Likely to Ivor," Psyke told Rue. "Her accent was faintly Itarusine. I think her one of his pets."

Janus growled. Rue and Bull had been so sure that the assassin couldn't escape from the docks, and yet . . . It would be like Ivor to hide his pawn in the heart of the city.

Psyke studied Charlotte long enough to make the woman fidget, and then she said, "Rue, I have doubts."

Rue paused in his gingerly prodding of Mirabile's gem-studded skull. "My lady?"

Psyke closed her arms about herself, rested her fingers, light as thistledown on her shoulders. She said, voice tentative, "I've been thinking on it. Truthfully, I do little but relive it in my dreams. The chapel was dark, and I was afraid, and Haith's hands came down on me. And Aris was dead at my feet, and so sure of himself. Though even he never claimed Maledicte as his assassin, only that he believed Janus was behind it."

Rue said, "You believe something different now?"

Psyke said, "Shorn of terror, of grief, of an attempt at meaning— what I saw was a slim man or tall woman, dark haired, stepping out of the shadows with an unaccustomed blade in hand. Celeste's aide also matches that description."

"Not Maledicte," Rue said.

"Maledicte's dead," Janus said. "As I've said, repeatedly."

"I know the lists of the dead," Psyke said. "He is not among them."

Rue interceded, though his eyes were intent, filing away information that Janus would once have killed him for hearing. "Alive or not, you think him blameless in Aris's death," Rue said. "Where then do we begin the search for the assassin?"

"Ivor's chambers, where else?" Janus snapped, his voice rough. "The missing valet your men failed to locate. A woman, not a man, and one eyed, which would account for the veil. And call back the duchess's servants. They worked for her. They can remove her corpse and her ghastly, cursed jewels as their first task."

ANUS WAS IN THE OLD wing's dungeons, eating Delight's breakfast—venison steaks, soft-boiled eggs, and a second pot of tea—when Delight returned, the morning fog making a curling mess of his hair.

"I've set up the spyglass," he said. "Anchored it to the peak of Seahook's roof, or as high as what remains. We'll see the Itarusine fleet approaching. Did you eat my toast?"

Janus waved at another covered tray. "Didn't bother. By the time the servants climb up two flights of stairs from the kitchens, walk the length of the palace, and come down two flights of stairs, it's cold."

"And if they come around the palace, it's dusty from passing the stables," Delight said. "Amazing how inconvenient palace living can be. Chryses—" He broke off, poured himself a cup of tea with a slowly steadying hand. "*Chryses*," he repeated, defying his grief, "would have been appalled. He thought the palace meant endless luxury. Not cold toast and having no one to send for the broadsheets. I had to run down a boy on my own and he called me names after I tossed him a copper."

"Box his ears next you see him," Janus said. He held out a hand for the broadsheet, and Delight, juggling tea and toast, passed it over.

Janus's provisional content with the day—the duchess disposed of, Ivor discommoded while the guards searched his wing above—

shattered like the teacup the hastily-spread-out sheet pushed from the table.

Poole's caricature was the least of it. Ugly, yes, and the man most certainly had more than one informant in the palace nobles, but as appalling as the portraiture was, the accompaniment was worse. The sketch, hastily done—either Poole had been rushing or his health was failing—showed the throne room peopled by a grinning wolf, the duchess's body spread out before it, and a barefoot shepherdess cradling Mirabile's skull. In the borders of the sketch lay commoners shot or stabbed by palace soldiers.

The accompanying text eschewed the usual coy format of Lady S—— or Lord G—— and stated directly that the king was dead, the country on the brink of disaster, and the palace overrun by a savage from the Relicts and a madwoman. That if there was to be a future, the people of the city needed to jar the complacency of the noble class and make them see sense.

Janus rose, broadsheet clutched in his fist, and went into the hall calling for Bull.

Once he had run the man to earth, still in his dressing gown, though the pile of papers about him suggested he had been working for some time, Janus thrust the sheets at him and said, "Forget Poole. We want the editor. Our circumstances are dire enough we cannot stand for a call to open revolt."

Bull threw off his dressing gown, revealing a workman's linen shirt, open at the throat, and a pair of woolen breeches. "Collect your guards—those you can trust not to shoot you at any rate—and call for the carriage. I'll send a boy to the Particulars and they'll meet us at the broadsheet's offices on Darter Street. We'll put a stop to it."

"If it can be stopped," Janus said. Fear was a motivator that could not be denied, and the people on the street—poor, hungry, expecting the Itarusines to come sweeping in like a vast spring tide—were afraid as much as they were angry. The only thing slowing them was their ingrained apathy wrought by years of gradual decay. Apathy, though, could be overcome.

On the silent carriage ride to the crowded offices in Darter Street—amanuenses, employment agencies, the shops that sold poorly made livery for the middle class establishments, and a slew of cheap solicitors—Janus watched the people making way for the carriage. Not so bad yet, if a palace carriage drew evasion rather than confrontation. At least, as long as it was a palace carriage with a full complement of kingsguards riding alongside, with a crew of Particulars, scruffy and well armed, walking down the street to meet them.

The editor, young and foolish though he was, had evidently had wiser thoughts after the damage was done. The front of the shop was locked; there was a flurry of movement within. The Particulars caught him attempting to scale out the back window into the filthy alley, and dragged him back.

"Don't kill me," he begged at once. "I'll run a retraction."

Janus sighed. "That works when the damage done is a lady's name bandied about, when a lord is called coward. It works rather less well when you've attempted to foment rebellion."

The young man licked his lips. "M' uncle said—"

"Who's your uncle?" Janus asked. "He's given you bad advice."

"Poole," the young man said. He raised his chin, and, yes, now that Janus looked for it, he could see some of Poole in the boy in the shape of the bones.

"Poole never told you to do such a thing," Bull said. "Poole's smarter than that."

"And his correspondence has been severely curtailed besides," Janus said.

"His messenger brought a note. I just did as it said." The boy scrambled for the overstuffed desk, digging through curls of parchment and thin scrap paper in its pigeonholes like a terrier hunting a rat. "Here," he cried, "here!"

Bull took it from his shaking fingers and said, while idly perusing it, "Who's the messenger, then? Who fed you such a line?"

"Harm," the young man said, and Bull traded a slow smile with Janus.

"Ivor's men do seem to have a taste for hiding in plain sight. His assassin at the duchess's home and his agitator making pilgrimages to Stones."

Janus said, "I'd expect little else from Ivor's men."

Poole's nephew watched the exchange with the dawning of hope. "If I tell you where he lives . . ."

"You tell us where Harm lives, and I'll see you on a sailing ship rather than buried in Stones," Janus said. The boy blanched, but scrambled for another piece of paper, scrawling down Harm's direction.

"This time of day, he's likely at the Seadog, talking to sailors," the boy said.

Janus hadn't thought of the Seadog in months, that low dive of a tavern on the edge of the Relicts, though he had spent his last quiet evening with Mal there, drinking *Absente*, drinking Itarusine brandy, until they were interrupted by a man demanding a duel. It had signaled the beginning of the end for Maledicte, and Janus could only hope it augured the same for Harm.

THEY FOUND HARM LOUNGING IN the nearly empty Seadog, a plate of fried bread piled high beside him, as shiny and greasy as the table itself, a cup of ale at his lips. When he saw them enter—Janus, Bull, and the boy, followed by three Particulars—he raised the mug in their direction.

"You've finally caught up with me, then," he said, a man so used to controlling an audience that he pitched his voice to carry to all the dim corners of the tavern. He rousted a pair of sailors from their alcoholic stupor, caused a young lordling to hide his aching head with a groan and a feeble wave to the early bartender to bring him another cup.

"Come to kill me? The poor workingman who was nearly killed once before by your infernal machines?"

Bull waved two of his burliest Particulars forward. Harm chuffed into his drink. "Have the courtesy to let a man finish his drink." It wasn't ale, despite the common mug; the slosh of it left a sweet sting in the air; the plate of bread held sugar also. *Absente*, Janus identified, and no drink for a poor workingman. Then Harm shifted awkwardly on his stool, brought his face into the feeble sunlight ghosting into the tavern, and Janus saw him properly, the first time the man wasn't retreating at speed.

Janus laid his bad hand on Bull's arm, forestalling the command to seize Harm. "I know you," he said.

"And well you should, nearly flaying a man—" Harm said.

"No," Janus said. "I know you. Casmir Marta Grigorian, prince descendant. I know how you truly received those wounds—laid out on the cold slate before Grigor's throne while his guards beat you like a dog. But does your audience know? You're one of Grigor's spawn, so out of favor for killing his favorite daughter that he sent you here."

"That's not true!" Poole's nephew sputtered. "He's an antimachinist who's been punished for speaking the truth—"

"He's an Itarusine prince," Janus said, "albeit a negligible one."

Harm licked his lips and set down his mug. "I remember you as well. Ivor's trained pet."

"I've outgrown that role," Janus said. "While you . . . you'll die in yours, a one-note performer to the last. Bull, hand me a pistol."

Harm stood upright so quickly the chair went sprawling behind him, his fist closing around the saber at his hip. "I am a prince of the blood. You can't execute me." Remarkable, really, that anyone ever believed Harm anything but an aristocrat. It only exposed how willing people were to believe someone who told them what they wanted to hear.

Poole's nephew made a tiny, betrayed sound that Janus ignored. Life dealt betrayal and disillusionment far more often than it dealt anything else. Better the boy learn it now, while he was still alive to change his ways.

"You're a prince descendant," Janus said, "a dead man only allowed to live so long as you're useful. You killed Fanshawe Gost, you killed Chryses DeGuerre, two noblemen of Antyre. I think Grigor would consider it fair trade."

Bull cautiously handed Janus a primed pistol, seemingly uncertain of Janus's intent. Poor Bull likely thought it a bluff. Bull didn't understand the ways of the Itarusine court. Unfortunately for Harm, Janus did.

He aimed the pistol with care, the scent of gunpowder acrid even before firing, the weight of it uncomfortable in his right hand. He preferred to shoot left-handed; it tended to throw off a duelist, but the wound on his left arm was hot and tight, and his fingers trembled.

Harm said, "You'll shoot me for two meaningless lives, lives that I was set to remove by Ivor Sofia Grigorian? Ivor has far worse to his name. Or did you think it coincidence that he was here barely a fortnight before your king died?"

"Causal relations are easily made, and as easily disproved," Janus said, though inwardly he was exulting. This once, Ivor might have outfoxed himself. To use Casmir, his own despised kin, as his stalking horse was clever. To see Casmir killed for playing the role was twice as clever, pleasing Grigor and granting Janus a convenient scapegoat for any lingering deaths. But Casmir was Winter Court enough to try to take Ivor with him.

"And you're a liar by trade, spilling stories among my people, claiming a name and history not your own. Still, your words are . . . intriguing. What think you, Bull? If you heard a man accuse another of murder on the street, would your Particulars count it as evidence or hearsay?"

"It would warrant investigation," Bull said. "I'd imagine Captain Rue would think the same."

Harm relaxed, content that he had a value, and Janus pulled the trigger. The explosion jarred his body and rang in his ears, enormously loud inside the tavern. Poole's nephew shrieked and collapsed as if Janus had shot him instead of Harm.

Bull twitched, taken by surprise. The sullen bartender and the early morning sailors drinking were unsurprised.

"Bring his body," Janus said. "I want to send him back to King Grigor and if we leave it here, it'll be disfigured or stolen."

The burly Particular, lacking a task now that Harm was dead, seized Poole's nephew instead. "Will you shoot him, too, my lord?" he asked. His jaw tightened.

"There's no need," Janus said. "The Explorations is the place for foolish dreamers. Set him on a ship."

"It won't change anything," the young man said. "Matters have gone too far for that!"

"And a good part of that is your doing," Janus said. "Remember, I'm showing you mercy. Do try not to make me regret it."

"You should regret it," the young man said. "You should regret every moment the palace has spent punishing people for their poverty."

Bull growled and the guards dragged the editor outside.

The burly Particular lingered. "Begging your pardon, my lord," he said, "but there's some truth to what he says. The people feel trapped. There's no jobs in the city, and what there is pays nothing. If they don't make money, whole families are ending in jail, and if they turn to thieving, well it's jail again, only with a whipping first."

He darted a glance at Janus, expectation of understanding in his eyes. "You remember, my lord, what it's like on the streets."

Bull shifted uneasily, the sailors at the bar slid away like water before a troubling wind. Janus raised a hand, silencing any protest from Bull.

If the guard thought himself brave enough to throw Janus's upbringing in his face, he would hear it all before he acted. The man did have the sense to wait until the tavern emptied before continuing. "I've been a Particular for near fifteen years. I remember chasing the boy they called the rat king over Relict stone falls until he and his rabble darted into holes too small for a man like me. I remember there were times I chose to stop chasing. When you raided the markets for food instead of coin. It was a hard time. It's only gotten worse."

"What would you have me do?" Janus said. "Until we cast off Itarus's shackles, all our profits disappear into their coffers. Or would you employ the poor as unpaid soldiers, send them off to fight a war?"

"The solution's your problem, not mine, but I'd think twice about letting the nobles skive out of their debts when other families are ruined by theirs. Fathers, mothers locked away while their children starve."

"Peter," Bull said, "remember your audience."

"Is it the families torn apart that worry you? Or the inequality of debt between nobles and commoners?" Janus asked. "Would it please the public if I declared amnesty for those in Stones whose debts are less than fifty sols? Would it please you?"

Peter hesitated, all his bravado washed away by Janus's response, as if he had braced himself for anything but actual interest in what a Particular thought. The man looked to Bull and Bull shrugged, clearly communicating that if Peter was fool enough to question Janus, he would have to be fool enough to answer questions in return.

Bull said, "Last, that's nearly all of them."

"You and Rue constantly remind me how full Stones is. Wouldn't it help if the only prisoners were those who deserved to be there? The ones who actively caused injury to the country?"

"We cannot afford to forgive the debts," Bull argued, dropping his voice and pulling Janus aside. He waved Peter outside. Peter went with the alacrity of a condemned man escaping the gallows. "Explain yourself. Do you mean to do it? You weren't simply playing with my man to relive old times?"

Janus drew up a seat before a mostly clean table, and waved at the bartender. "Luncheon please, and whatever you have to drink that's . . . imported."

Bull dithered a moment and Janus gestured to the seat opposite. "Man must eat," he said.

"Here?"

"I think my meals are better out of the palace than in it," he said. "The public may be outraged, but they're too poor to willfully poison food."

"And you would send more mouths into the streets. In Stones, they are fed."

"On the kingdom's coin," Janus said.

The bartender brought over a plate, laden high with fried bread and a few gamy cuts of sailor's fare, some animal flesh spiced so heavily it couldn't rot.

Two goblets landed on the table, along with a bottle. Bull touched it; his eyes widened. "This is—"

"Imported is the polite term," Janus said. "Tarrant's been using the Seadog as a drop point for some of his sundries."

He took a warming sip of the Itarusine brandy, found it suited the dark, chewy meat well enough and took another.

"Listen Bull," he said. "We can't afford to have the public in utter rebellion. If we release the debtors . . ."

Bull said, "Do you think it will matter? To have freedom when the chains of poverty still weigh them down?"

"It will delay the inevitable," Janus said. "Ivor's fleet won't arrive to find our city softened by internal rebellion."

"Prince Ivor's agitators are quite capable of creating a revolt on his command."

"Given what we learned from Harm—from Prince Casmir—I think we have enough to confine him to his wing under suspicion of acting against the treaty. It'll be up to you and Rue to find evidence enough to prove Harm's words more than hearsay."

Bull sat back in his seat. "You're confident in this path."

Janus hid his smile with the heavy goblet. Of course he was. He'd always intended the release of the prisoners as a part of his plan to thwart Ivor, but he hadn't anticipated such a perfect chance to do so. "For the country, Bull," he said. "Send the Particulars out to Stones and have them release those listed as debtors. Oh, and have them release Poole also. With his nephew gone, he's like to find it harder to sell his drawings. Perhaps we'll find out who's been guiding his pen."

ON HIS RETURN TO THE palace, Janus left Bull to tell Rue the events of the morning and to oversee the display of Harm's body. It was necessary, but he recalled another body that was meant to have been displayed and quailed from watching it done. The rooks would feast.

Instead, he sought out Ivor, taking along a full complement of guards, and found the prince seated in one of the garden bowers, in the midst of a cozy tête-à-tête with Admiral DeGuerre. DeGuerre's face was a picture, distrust warring with pleasure, as Ivor turned his agile tongue to mixing flattery with lies.

"DeGuerre, if you fall for his platitudes, you must be a great favorite with the playhouses, always applauding an actor's turn of phrase," Janus said, unaccountably annoyed. Hadn't he had Gost removed for worsening DeGuerre's opinion? Now Ivor did the same?

"My pet," Ivor said. "When you and I are dining, I don't allow interruptions. Will you not allow the good admiral and myself the same?"

"Perhaps he'll visit you in the old wing," Janus said. "We captured Harm today."

"Did you, then?" Ivor said.

"He said the most damning things about you. Named your assassin—"

"That I doubt," Ivor murmured.

"And claimed you are responsible for Aris's death."

"This again. You've no proof he's Itarusine. Harm's an antimachinist and an egalitarian," DeGuerre said, and seemed puzzled that he had moved to defend Ivor. Janus thought it was only that the admiral was so accustomed to quarreling with him. Perhaps this would teach him better.

"A prince descendant an egalitarian? Hardly likely." Janus turned his attention to Ivor, watched the man's hands. Ivor was armed and Janus was hampered by his wound, by the weakness in his hand. "Ivor, I'm afraid I've killed your brother Casmir."

DeGuerre rose, and without another glance, walked away.

Ivor reached out and stripped a branch of leaves, letting their torn edges fill the evening air with their green scent. "Do you want this?" he asked. "To make me your enemy?"

"You were always that," Janus said.

"And the guards?" Ivor said. "I presume, despite the lack of evidence, you'll see me confined to the old wing? With or without my personal staff?"

"With," Janus said. "Less the one that we're hunting."

"Very well," Ivor said. He rose, walked toward the waiting guards with a composure entirely unruffled. He paused in their midst and said, "One request?"

"Perhaps," Janus said.

"As I'm about to be confined to boredom and indolence, perhaps a single bout of sparring?"

"I might be young, but I haven't been a fool for a very long time," Janus said.

"Ah, don't fret so. We're at a deadlock, you and I, like two school fellows. That is your intention, is it not? To claim to Grigor that I disrupted the peace treaty first, with my alleged assassination of your king? That your arms display was only in reaction . . . Should either of us die unexpectedly, the treaty will be shattered beyond repair."

"All that might be true," Janus said. "It changes nothing."

He turned to go, heard the rush of movement behind him and a guard calling, "Last!"

Janus got his own blade up in time to meet Ivor's descending one, parried the blow though the force of it ran the length of his arm. It shouldn't have been unexpected; Ivor had been remarkably well behaved, only setting others to commit his murders, when Janus knew how much the man enjoyed the work himself. Even his sanguine temper could be chafed by inaction.

The guards raised pistols and Ivor said, "If you fire, our countries will war."

They hesitated, then began spreading out like a net, swords in hand, coming to separate the two men.

It was likely to be a futile attempt, Janus thought, shifting to block another thrust with one of his own. The blades slipped past each other with a hiss of steel. Ivor took two dancing steps back. A guard, more impulsive than most, darted forward in an attempt to disarm Ivor. He received a slap of the blade for his effort, slicing his cheek to the bone.

Janus lunged forward again, and Ivor evaded it. "Always overstepping yourself," Ivor said. Janus had to drop to a knee, roll away from a thrust that nearly took an eye. His heart raced; his mouth tasted of metal—sour and sudden excitement.

"You try for too much," Ivor said. "It blurs your focus. You want to be king. You want Maledicte back. You want Antyre to prosper. You want respect and admiration, though I believe you would settle for respect and fear. I even think you want your sweet wife. How can you accomplish any of these when your focus wavers so—"

Janus lunged upward; the edge of his blade caught Ivor's cravat, ripping it, before the man's blade forced Janus away.

Their blades clashed again, not with the metallic rasp of the Antyrrian rapiers, but a heavy, grinding *screel*. Janus shifted his weight, dug his heel into the soft loam and broken shell beneath him, pushed Ivor off his blade, then danced three steps back, seeking a chance to catch his breath. His wounded arm ached and bled, and he hadn't needed it yet for anything but balance.

Ivor grinned at him, vulpine and openly content.

Janus let his blade hang loosely before him, tempting Ivor to an unconsidered strike. But Ivor had had the training of him and knew how easily that careless seeming stance could be turned against an opponent. Ivor simply waited, and frustration bit into Janus's belly. Ivor was always just that much ahead, leaving Janus to scramble to catch up.

Janus's breath came faster, fed by the desire to defeat Ivor in even this littlest of fashions. "Do you think man is such a poor creature as to hold but one thought at a time? Do you think I am so simple?" Janus drove forward, blade angling in from the side, and had the brief satisfaction of watching Ivor's blade slowed for a moment. Then Ivor batted his blade away with the irritated languor of a great cat.

"You don't listen. Let me explain it again," Ivor said. "A man's wants are often contrary and force compromise. And a compromised dream is bitter."

"And your dream is simpler?" Janus growled. "Tell me what you want."

"I want my throne," Ivor said, slamming his blade forward, his considerable body weight behind it. Janus raised his blade in time to take the force on his shoulder, though he slid backward under the power of it. "And I want it *now*."

They traded fast slashes at and about each other, stirring the air, and creating a current of steel scent and sweat laced with blood. The stitches in Janus's arm gave, the seam of his flesh going slack beneath the bandages.

Another round of thrust and slash and Janus's blood made a tiny, first foray to slick the grass with crimson. The guards tensed. Their pistols came out again.

Time ran away from them. Soon, a guard would shoot, and that single guard's control over a notoriously awkward weapon would send them to war. Janus knew it. By the wildness in his eyes, Ivor knew it, too, and craved time enough to put Janus in his place, reestablish his superiority. He moved closer to Janus, taking the fight quick and dirty, a matter of brawling as much as swordplay.

"Better hope the one that shoots isn't one who wants you dead," Ivor gasped, "or I'll have your throne with no effort at all."

His hand wrapped over the hilt of Janus's sword, attempting to wrench the blade away by force. Janus, prepared for such a move, forced Ivor back with a sudden jut of his elbow against Ivor's jaw. "Then go back to Itarus," Janus breathed. "Grigor's throne waits."

Ivor fell back, shook his head, and said, "Father's as hard to remove as a barnacle and as malevolent as a stoat. I could remove every one of my fellow princes, and he'd manage to sire another litter of princelings before he died. Fratricide does grow dull. So, I compromise."

"Meaning you'll take my throne until yours comes available," Janus said.

"Not an ideal solution, I own. I am, after all, as loyal a son of Itarus as can be found," Ivor said. His quick bow was a dare, and Janus took him up on it, charging forward, all his weight committed, and slammed his blade against Ivor's.

"Loyal, right enough. Loyal enough to continue Grigor's plan. You *want* a war between our countries."

Their blades caught at the hilt; their eyes met for a long moment; and Ivor's face, even behind the grimace of effort, relayed only sincerity as he replied. "I think you would want the same. Nothing clears out the deadwood so well as a war, and I feel both our countries are overburdened with such."

Janus disentangled their hilts with a quick jerk, catching Ivor off guard and disarming him. Janus seized Ivor's hilt, though it trembled in his hand, the weight nearly too much for his injured arm. He crossed both blades before Ivor's chest, high enough to be a threat, to make it clear this duel was done. "But, Ivor," Janus said, "wars are expensive, for both victors and the defeated. Plague, on the other hand, is cheap."

Ivor flinched. For the first time in their edged friendship, Janus had the advantage, and it had little to do with the steel he wielded. Janus backed Ivor toward the thick hedge of boxwood and thorny roses, and when Ivor ceded the ground, Janus dropped the blades.

The guards surged forward, and Janus waved them off. "There's no need, gentlemen. He'll come quietly, now that I've won. Won't you?"

"Have you won?" Ivor murmured.

He fell silent when Janus reached out, touched the sweaty divot of skin exposed where Ivor's cravat had been ruined by that one quick thrust of Janus's blade.

Ivor swallowed, but turned his head, allowing Janus's fingers to find what he sought: the tiniest run of scars, the only stain on that otherwise well-kept hide. Janus leaned closer, the better to admire it. It wasn't so much; but for Ivor, it represented the one battle he had nearly lost. The one thing he had been powerless against.

Janus touched that tiny scar, and murmured up into Ivor's ear. "All a plague costs are lives and, as you say, Murne is overfull of useless life."

"What have you done?" Ivor breathed. He shoved Janus off him.

"Thrust," Janus said, allowing himself a smile. "Parry. Counterthrust. The second useful thing you taught me. And, better still, you said, if parry and counterthrust could be one movement. Your ships might approach our borders, but they will never be on our shores."

"What have you done?"

"Slipped the plague from its chains," Janus said, still in that confiding whisper. "I think it will prove a better barrier to your plans than months of diplomatic maneuvers. I doubt even your loyal Itarusine ships will brave such."

"Plague once survived, can be survived again."

"True," Janus said. "But will *you* trust your life to that?"

Ivor licked his lips; his eyes, wider than usual with shock, narrowed suddenly. A smile took shape, a ghost of his usual self-satisfaction leaking back. "An elegant bluff, my pet, well aimed, but ultimately unsustainable. Plague, despite your metaphor, is no dog, waiting to be summoned on demand."

"No," Janus agreed, and allowed Ivor's face to brighten for a single heartbeat, before he continued, "but it can be *stored*. Aris made a mistake when he turned on Maledicte and sent her to Stones. Ani hated it so much she tried to erase it and all its denizens. She set loose plague, and it's been biding there, fed and nurtured, growing more potent, waiting to be set free."

Ivor sucked in a breath. "The prisoners' pardon . . ."

"The prisoners' pardon," Janus agreed. He nodded to the guards, and they came forward, circling Ivor with wary respect. Janus handed the saber to a guard and said, "He carries a dagger as well. Be watchful."

They led Ivor away, and Janus settled down on the grass where he stood, blade across his lap, the aftermath of a successful duel weakening his knees. He wondered how Maledicte had stood it, how he had been more fiercely alive after a battle than before. Confronting Ivor left him feeling as if someone had seized him by the throat and shaken him. Wrung out and oddly guilty. Ivor, for his own purposes, had aided him over the years.

Rue's voice drifted across the lawn, coinciding with the sudden fall of petals from a rose above Janus's head. "I came, hotfoot, to see if Ivor had managed to kill you. I'm relieved he's failed."

"He allowed me to win," Janus said. "He's a more accomplished duelist than I am." He brushed snowy petals from his hair, plucked them from his sleeve where they clung to the slow-welling blood. "We must be more cautious now," Janus said. "Until now—"

"Until now, we could claim we still honored the treaty," Rue said. "Imprisoning Ivor and killing Harm sends a different message." He held out a hand. "Come, there's something I want to show you. Your man Delight's been industrious."

After a pause to have one of Sir Robert's assistants rewrap Janus's wound—Sir Robert refused to do so, called it rewarding foolishness—Rue led Janus onto the tower roof overlooking the city and the sea.

There were rooks lazing about, and Rue picked up a loose piece of coping and threw it into their midst, sending them shrieking off the roof and into the laden trees below.

Janus bent his head to the spyglass, fixed in the direction of the sea. The ocean waters gleamed red in the setting sun, sending sparks of painful color into his eyes. He stepped back, sun dazzled and too close to the edge.

"It's the Itarusine fleet," Rue said, "waiting a mile outside of our harbor. But what we're interested in is . . ." He swung the spyglass in its cradle and focused again. "There."

A single ship in his vision this time. A heavy prow, a series of spiked figureheads. An Itarusine icebreaker making slow headway against the waves. "Grigor's messenger ship, the *Icebear*. Delight said the *Bear* will reach the fleet in two days."

"Too soon," Janus said. He needed time. Time for the plague to spread, time to make the city unwelcoming, time to prove that Ivor had killed Aris.

"Tarrant will harry them," Delight said. Janus leaped away from the spyglass, heart hammering at the man's near-silent approach. Back to his skirts today. DeGuerre must have irritated him again.

"Jumpy," Delight said. "But I heard you killed a prince today. I suppose I'd be a trifle nervy also."

"Tarrant," Janus said.

"He sends me a message," Delight said, pulling out a scrap of paper from one of the voluminous pockets sewn into his skirts.

"He is a clever man," Delight said, smiling a little. "Clever enough to find a way ashore when the Itarusine fleet rings us, more clever still to find me in the palace."

"He came himself?"

"Sent a sailor," Delight said. "One who was wounded and no longer fit for piracy. Tarrant thinks he can delay the *Bear* one full day, perhaps two."

Janus calculated. Still not enough time for the plague to be a genuine force. But enough to pretend. "Delight, I need large signal flags made."

"Flags are rarely useful in land-to-sea communication," Delight said. "Sea fogs and wave reflections—"

"Plague flags," Janus said. "I want them flying from every rooftop. I want the Itarusine sailors feared to take a single step ashore."

"Plague?" Delight asked. He swallowed. "A bluff?"

"No," Janus said. He turned to look over the edge of the roof again, this time not out to the sea, to the avowed enemy, but to the crowded streets spiderwebbing away from the palace. "Murne suffers from a rat's tangle of dilemmas. Too much of our profits go to Itarus. Too many people are unemployed. Too many people starve. Until we've redone or cast off the treaty with Itarus, there can be no resolution. But even with it gone, there will be too many people. Problems cannot resolve themselves like a candle being blown out. Rather, they smolder and recur.

"We have too many people? We have too many unemployed? Plague is as good a way to winnow the chaff as any. The weakest will die first," Janus said. "The strong will survive, and there will be jobs aplenty burning and burying the dead. The aristocratic lines that die—their estates will revert to the crown and replenish our coffers."

"That's madness," Rue said. "You could not have done this deliberately. . . ."

"I can, and have done," Janus said. "But, remember, Rue, you chose to follow me. If you have doubts, only ask yourself, would Black-Winged Ani treat our people any better?"

· 25 ·

$\mathcal{P}$SYKE WATCHED HER NEW MAIDS flutter about her rooms in a smothering cloud of black cloth, their faces drawn. The duchess had trained them well enough that Psyke need say nothing, only sit like a sculpture while they set right the neglect that had been slowly eroding the gentility of her days, made it all too easy to be lost in the strangeness of having other voices in her mind. With each plumped pillow, each dusted shelf, each dress shaken out and ironed, Psyke felt more herself, the Countess of Last, and less a vessel for the dead.

Perhaps not a sculpture of a woman, she mused, but a spider at the heart of her web. She waited patiently and was rewarded, as night drew in, as the other maids sought out the evening chores, by a single maid coming in to dress her for dinner. The girl was tall, slim, and kept her face downcast, her hair arranged in an improbable Kyrdic fashion.

"I suppose the long fringe hides the eye patch," Psyke said, and the woman stopped pretending. She sat sideways on the chair before the dressing table, facing Psyke.

"You expected me."

Psyke felt a surge of indignation touch her, and it took her a moment to realize the outrage was her own. She reined it back, and said, "Where else would you go when Prince Ivor is no shelter any longer? His rooms scrutinized, and you so ardently sought on the streets. Judging by your accent, you're a long way from home. The Explorations?"

"I have no home," she said. "Nor name. That much is true. Also true: I can aid you . . . teach you how to resist the gifts of the god or to use them. If you shelter me. If I'm found, then Ivor will be disgraced or killed. I would not cause him hurt."

"*You killed Aris,*" Psyke said, and the woman fell silent, as if she had forgotten that death lay between them.

The girl collected Psyke's face brush, spun it in her fingers, transferring a dusting of powder to her nails. She wiped her fingers on her gown, leaving ghostly streaks against the black.

"You offer me nothing of use," Psyke said. "Knowledge I have already gained, and your bargain benefits only you. If you wish me to keep you from the gallows, to keep Ivor safe behind his shield of privilege, I need something more."

The girl gnawed her lip, denting its full red with white teeth, feral yet determined. "I can help you with Black-Winged Ani," she said. Her voice flatted out, all musicality stripped bare by evident fear.

"How?" Psyke asked. All her ghosts were in concert in the question, though the tones were different. Mirabile, drifting about the room in a cloud of pale feathers, roused to scornful fury in a heartbeat. Challacombe pressed forward in a puff of smoke; and Aris, pallid, wraithlike Aris, remembered he had once been a scholar and took an interest.

"I know what drives Her—"

"As do we all," Psyke said. "Love and vengeance."

"In the abstract, yes." The girl brushed her hair out of her face, knotted her fingers in the dark tangles. "In the specific? Do you know that—what She wants?"

Mirabile assayed a cool breath in Psyke's ear. *She gives herself airs.*

"So what does Ani desire, then?"

The girl smiled, flashing charming dimples entirely at odds with the thick black cord and solid leather of her eye patch. "Can't share all my secrets right away. Find me a safe harbor, and I'll be at your beck and call."

Psyke said, "I think I'll keep you at my side. I need a lady-in-waiting."

The girl's jaw firmed, arrogance in her face. "I can't stay here. It would be remarked upon." Her tones were barely civil, and Psyke smiled. Even without a mirror, she knew her smile was Mirabile's cruel one. It might be Mirabile's inspiration that fed sly tidbits of petty viciousness into her mind, but the intent was all Psyke's.

"A servant," Psyke said, "is invisible." She'd seen how the girl had bridled when the duchess ordered her to a task. "All servants are, even one so distinctively marred as you. For you to be recognized or discovered, first someone would have to want to look. But servants are nothing and no one looks. I'm sure your beloved Prince Ivor counted on that."

The girl's hands scrabbled aimlessly among the detritus on the dressing table, knocking aside perfume, eyeblack, plucking pale hairs fitfully from Psyke's brush. "I'm his lover," she said. "The only one he trusts."

Psyke let her silence answer for her, after the girl's protests died away. "Feel gratitude and loyalty to him, if you must," she said, "but don't confuse your emotions with his. There's advice for you and more useful than anything you've offered me."

The girl hurled the brush at her; Psyke ducked. It hit the wall, denting the plaster.

"I had seven sisters," Psyke said, "including one brat who was the despair of six governesses and four nurserymaids. Tantrums do not disturb me. Recalcitrance does. You've made your offer and I've made mine. Have you any objections?"

The girl was too long used to being masked or veiled; her expressions shifted like clear water, every emotion evident. For all her intelligence, Ivor's little assassin was remarkably naïve. A wiser woman would have understood that Ivor was sacrosanct, no matter his actions. A wiser woman would have fled the country when the duchess was arrested. Or, at the least, met Ivor's allies in Murne, not made this desperate attempt to stay near him.

"Won't you be frightened to have an assassin at your back?" the girl said.

"Aren't you frightened to serve the countess of death?" Psyke countered.

The girl rose, paced the room. "I prefer to live. To return to Itarus with my prince. But death would free me from a danger you can only begin to imagine."

"If that's the case, I will oblige you," Janus said, appearing in the doorway like a specter. There was blood on his sleeve and blood in his eyes. A moment later, his blade was in his hand, and then at the assassin's throat.

Psyke said, "Janus, no!"

JANUS WONDERED WHEN HE HAD become so accustomed to his wife speaking to ghosts that he was startled to find someone responding to her voice. Startlement gave way to quick disbelief and finally rage as he overheard enough to identify the speaker; Ivor's girl, Ivor's assassin.

He backed the maid against the wall, her eye wide and panicky. Psyke's protest was a mouse squeak to a cat, only furthering his predatory instinct.

The girl slid a dagger from her skirt, snaked it upward in an underhand blow meant to split his belly and spill his intestines. He twisted, heard the steel rasp against the buttons on his waistcoat, and tried to grasp her wrist with his left hand. He delayed the second blow before his hand failed him, and she used the moment not to strike again but to duck away from the blade near her throat.

That decision told Janus all he needed to know. She might have had training—he imagined that under her gown, her skin was as marred as his from Ivor's blades—but she lacked understanding of battle. It would have been better by far to risk his blade for the certainty of a strike while he was weak. As it was, she darted away from him. He lunged forward, stepped deliberately on the black trail of her hem; and, when she sprawled, brought the blade down again.

Psyke's shove, slight and small though she was, prevented his blade from doing the assassin a fatal injury. The blow meant for her neck skittered upward, gashing her cheek open to the bone and ripping off her eye patch.

Janus pushed Psyke back, hardly an effort at all, and turned to find the assassin crouched before him, her dagger used to cut her skirt free of his restraining weight. She hissed at him, but her face, beneath the splash of blood, the scarlet ruin of her exposed eye socket, was skull white and terrified.

Psyke hung on his blade arm with a tenacity that appalled him, wrapping her arms about him as inexorably as a sea siren. "I promised she would live."

"As your maid?" he said. He kept a careful eye on the assassin, even while he began the efforts of detangling himself from Psyke. "You tried to kill me when you only thought I had a hand in Aris's death. The actual assassin you choose to spare?"

"If you kill her," she said, breath perfectly even in his ear, despite her exertions, "will anyone believe that she was Aris's assassin without her confession?"

"I won't betray him," the assassin spat.

Janus caught sight of Psyke's face and some of his killing rage faded at the expression on it: a cold rage of her own and a healthy dose of contempt.

"You love him so much, you'll die for him?" Janus asked.

"I would," the assassin said, as defiant as a debutante declaring her love for a most unsuitable mate, aware of the romance of it all.

Janus said, "I tell you, if he had word that we'd captured you—"

"You haven't," she said. She sat back, dusting her skirts. "Despite all your men hunting me. I came to you—"

"—he'd deny you and send a new assassin to kill you without any more thought than he'd give to disposing of a broken weapon." Disgusted, Janus stalked back through Psyke's sitting room, and flung open the door to the hallway. He startled the two guards on duty, looked them up and down, searching for that dark ribbon about the sword hilt, and when he found it, said, "I've an assassin in my wife's bedroom. Come and remove her." He gestured to the guards farther down the hallway at his own door, and said, "You two—fetch Rue."

After far more roundaboutation than Janus thought his head could bear—where would she be imprisoned now that Delight had spread his mechanics throughout the dungeon? Could they put her in Stones? No, Rue wanted her accessible and the streets were dangerous enough that she might escape them on the way—the guards swept the assassin off to the little-used dowager's tower above Aris's rooms, there to be watched by a rotating complement of kings-guards.

Psyke sighed once the assassin had been removed, righting small things jostled during the unequal struggle, and drawing Janus's attention.

"Your *maid?*" he asked.

"I thought to keep her close at hand, the better to coax her to turn on Ivor."

"Whatever your intentions," Janus said, "you might be comfortable with a proven assassin at your back. I am not."

"Do you think imprisoning her there is wise?" she asked. "Such an unusual cell will garner attention, will reveal her presence to Ivor. He'll see her dead."

"It would be less wise to leave her free. We have problems enough in the palace. Delight's spyglasses showed us Grigor's fleet approaching. Its arrival will be a matter of days. Ivor took his confinement too calmly and likely plots ways to free himself. Our best hope is to have your assassin . . . coaxed into betraying Ivor, so that we might greet Grigor's emissary with proof of the prince's wrongdoing."

"You intend to torture her?"

"I neither know, nor care what Rue intends. Only that he get results," Janus said.

"I admit I thought to turn her, but I also doubted my chances. She loves him, will hear no wrong said of him."

"Love ends and turns to betrayal more easily than you might think," Janus said.

*J*ANUS HAD BEEN ON THE roof of the palace for nearly three hours, watching the incremental progress of the enemy ships, when Evan coughed behind him.

The day had been so far remarkably free of interruption. Bull was scouring the city, trying to separate profitable merchants from Itarusine ones. Ivor sent missive after missive from his confinement; it kept the palace pages hopping, intercepting them for study before allowing them onward. So far, the letters had been useless, harmless drivel, designed solely to keep the palace guards busy investigating their recipients. DeGuerre, aggravated past endurance by the new alliance between Bull and Janus, had retreated to his city home, where Poole joined him soon after. And Rue . . . Rue sought to make the assassin speak.

"What is it, Evan?"

"Note. From Rue." The boy's voice was thin, strained, a casualty of two events in quick succession. The boy had overheard Rue and Delight discussing the spreading plague and Janus's attempt to harness it for his own purpose. When the boy had rushed to Janus's side, breathless and aghast, saying Janus couldn't have, not deliberately, not just to keep the Itarusine fleet away, not when Murne's citizens would suffer first and worst. Had he truly released the *plague* to keep away the Itarusines?

When Janus had admitted to that—leaving off his desire to decimate a troublesome population—Evan's pale eyes had clouded over. "My ma," he said, "my ma was a plague pigeon. And died of it." Before Janus could decide how best to respond to that, Evan had backed away. "Adiran's probably woken up by now. I'm going to him."

Like that, Janus had lost Evan. A careless discussion overheard by a boy whose mother had been a do-gooder with a scented mask. Janus had seen one of them as a child, braving the rubble in the Relicts. The gray-cloaked figure had been unmolested—the adults shying away from the dangerous miasma that might surround the physician, the children wary of the beaked mask that smelled of roses and camphor.

The plague pigeon had spotted Janus and Miranda, leaning against each other in the shelter of a fallen shop, and stopped. Were they sick? he had asked, a stranger expressing muffled concern from behind a nightmare mask. Were they hungry? He offered bread and cheese wrapped in cloth.

Miranda and Janus had fled, too wary to reach out, and when they found another, safer viewpoint, they saw a second pigeon chastising the first. "It's the Relicts," the man said. "There's nothing to be done. Come away from here and help those worth helping."

The plague pigeons were walking the streets of Murne again, summoned from their own lives by the flags Delight had unearthed; fabric marked by a densely coiled serpent, glittering blue and green, with an open, fanged mouth. Naga, the god of avarice and health.

Only in extremity were the gods remembered, Janus thought. Only in extremity were they summoned.

He peered through the spyglass on the palace roof, shifting it another five degrees. Tarrant's harrying hadn't slowed the icebreaker much; the ship was simply too big to sink, too heavy to stop, and too heavily manned to burn successfully. He'd watched one such attempt, cannons firing, juddering the smaller privateer through the waves, the unheard report of pistol shot and cannonball, none of it enough to pierce the icebreaker's thickened hull. When a sail caught fire, a quick line of traveling crimson and orange, like the sunset, the crew of the *Icebear* had moved with practice, and extinguished it.

For a moment, looking at the *Icebear* churning its inexorable way to Murne's beleaguered shores, he found himself tempted toward prayer. Or to something more active. The streets began to see men dying or dead; no street seemed exempt. Even the noble houses— that had to open their doors to deliveries, to servants, to the plague—had found themselves with their own share of the sick. Surely there was death enough in the city. He thought he might ask Psyke to wake Haith and entreat Him to destroy the Itarusines.

Hadn't her ancestor bartered with the god for his victory? But Redoubt, for all the god's favor, had ended alone, powerless, lost in his own city, in the heart of his kingdom.

The gods' bargains, Janus thought, were best left unaccepted. Ani hadn't bettered his life any, for all Maledicte's attempts to channel it so. Last could have been killed without Her aid, and more subtly, without rousing the frenzy of fear and suspicion that had led to Maledicte's fleeing the kingdom. Without Ani, Janus would have Miranda by his side still, a wildly eccentric wife for a nobleman— the image that came to mind, though, wasn't Miranda but Psyke, wandering barefoot and mercurial through his rooms.

He wondered if Psyke would say the same. Haith had gifted her with immortality of a type, the ability to die and rise again. But He had also left her head mazed with ghosts, left her body altered by His touch.

No, on the subject of gods, Psyke and he were likely in rare accord.

Evan thrust the note at him, still at arm's length, and Janus reached past it, seized the boy's wrist, and drew him closer. "Hold still," he said. "You're always darting off before I can respond to messages these days."

Evan stopped working his wrist in Janus's grip. Janus plucked the note from the boy's grip with his bad hand, flipped it open. Unsealed. Rue was either in a hurry, or nothing much of importance was contained within.

It proved to be the latter: The note was a simple message that could have been delivered verbally, were it not that Janus would distrust any such message.

Last, meet me at the dowager's tower at your convenience. Callan Rue

Perhaps Rue had finally gotten answers from the assassin.

"There'll be no need for a return message," Janus said.

Evan tugged, trying to free his wrist. Janus said, "Don't you want a reward? You used to ask me for candy." He passed Evan a handful of hard candies stored in his pocket—much to Padget's frustration—for this occasion. Janus wasn't fool enough to think Evan's affections could be recovered so easily, but he was one of the few pages who could be relied upon to send Janus's messages to the ones he meant to receive them. "Share them with Adiran if you want."

The boy looked at the candy, translucent green with syrupy pink and gold liquid centers gleaming through and said, "They have Laudable in them."

"Only the gold ones," Janus said. "And it's a child's dose. To soothe away nightmares. You might have need of them if you continue to sleep in Adiran's rooms. I often had nightmares near Maledicte. I have them near Psyke."

"Lady Psyke?" Evan asked, as if he couldn't credit it.

"The god touched make difficult friends," Janus said. "Still, if your dreams are pleasant, perhaps Adiran's are not."

He finally released the boy, felt cheered when Evan didn't back away immediately but studied Janus's face as if his childish experience could explain adult motives.

"Thank you," Evan said. A bit curt, and his leave-taking abrupt after that, but Janus was pleased. He'd win the boy back yet.

He took a last look through the spyglass; there had been no miracle, the *Icebear* bulled onward. Janus went inside, the quiet halls dim and silent after the whip of the wind at tower height, the mutters of the rooks, and the brightness of the sun on the sea.

He gestured one of the guards back outside to keep watch on the *Icebear*, waved off the ones who attempted to fall into step with him. Ever since he was shot at in the throne room, Janus had eschewed private guards, preferring not to have his wariness dulled by the presence of men who might not aid him should he need it. He carried his blade openly, loosely sheathed, and had foregone the tight coats currently in fashion for a looser style that allowed greater ranges of motion.

Rue leaned against the door to the dowager's tower, in conference with a mixed group of Particulars and kingsguards, reporting from the docks.

Delight had decided that the docks could be made more secure if they ran brass gates between the quays in the shallower waters. Admiral DeGuerre had opposed the idea even as Delight had finished explaining it, objecting that it wouldn't stop the icebreaker, and arguing that it would be tantamount to declaring that Antyre had no intention of honoring the treaty with Itarus.

Janus had been set to interrupt the battle between father and son, but Delight, resolve firmed, had simply shaken his head. "The waters are too shallow for the icebreaker; we'll slow the smaller boats, making them vulnerable to our cannons should it come to that; and as for not honoring the treaty—well, if the city is beset by plague, is it so improbable that we would seal our harbor?"

From what Janus overheard now, the gates had been fed into the waters on long brass wires, entangling one or two of the boats that were installing them.

Rue waved everyone off at Janus's approach, reminding them to keep Delight under careful escort.

"Last," Rue said.

"Anything from her?" Janus asked.

Rue shook his head.

"She won't talk?"

"Oh, she talks," Rue said, "but nothing useful. Not even her name. She seems more afraid of giving us that than she fears the whip. As for Ivor's complicity in Aris's death—she won't even admit she knows him, all evidence to the contrary."

"How can one woman cause us so much grief?" he said. "A single confession from her, and Itarus would have to withdraw its strongest charges. We'd be back to our careful stalemate."

"I don't think we can count on her confession," Rue said. "She doesn't fear physical violence. And she's clever. She's convinced half my men that if they mistreat her she'll call Ani down upon them, swearing bloody vengeance."

"The gods again," Janus said. "I wish they'd never returned. Speaking of which . . . Adiran is being watched?"

"A series of guards changing on the hour—if he sneaks out, he'll be missed quickly—and the back passageways watched also. Your page Evan's the only one who's allowed in, takes him his meals, reads to him, though sometimes Adiran tells him stories instead. And it's enough to freeze your blood, the words that come out of our prince's mouth."

"They can be no more disturbing than what Psyke mutters in her sleep," Janus countered.

Rue shook his head. "Last, I don't like this. Black-Winged Ani is threat enough, even muted as She is. To add the Countess of Last's troubles to the mix—"

"Psyke seems to have gained confidence and control," Janus said. "Adiran is supervised. My concerns currently are all for Ivor."

"Yes," Rue said. "He's been—"

"Entirely too amiable at being relegated to prisoner. His people have been contained also?"

"The servants and guards he brought with him, yes. Any others he may have suborned within the palace are still free."

Janus slumped, feeling as if he were shouldering a stone. Even knowing it would be heavy, the weight was still surprising and unpleasant.

"He won't bide much longer," Janus said. "Make her talk. If she intimidates the guards with her blather about Ani—if she could summon Her, Ivor would have had her do so at once, always greedy for power—we'll send her someone unlikely to know fear."

"You have someone in mind?"

"Psyke," Janus said. "She claims to speak to ghosts. If the assassin will not talk, perhaps her ghosts will."

TONE WALLS, IVOR SOFIA GRIGORIAN mused, looked impregnable, soothed nervous hearts, and generally made effective prisons. Generally. It all depended on who was trapped inside, and what they were willing to do in the name of freedom. Ivor studied the piles before him with wary satisfaction.

Dmitry tapped on the door to Ivor's dining room-turned practice salle, and came in. "The palace delivered foodstuffs to our cook, unprepared, as you asked, and fresh as the city could provide."

"How accommodating," Ivor said. "Janus's need to be civil will be the death of him. The news?"

Dmitry held out a long curl of waxed paper, still spattered here and there with blood from the cuts of beef that had concealed it. Ivor set it on a chair, wiped it once more, the better to read the notes his agents had sent him.

It *was* plague in the streets, or something much like it; Ivor supposed the answer would lie in how many people died instead of recovered. His lips thinned. Janus had surprised him there, shown a broader focus and more decisive hand than Ivor had expected.

Gates were being strung between the harbor docks, spikes just below the surface, traps for any small vessel trying to make its way ashore. "Now that," Ivor said, "is shortsighted. Once the Kyrdics hear Antyre has taken to laying snares in the waters, they won't want to trade. It's dishonorable. Ixion listened to the wrong advice there."

"In the interim, sir, it leaves you without escape," Dmitry said. "And the city is too insalubrious for me to recommend hiding in plain sight—"

"Ah, but this is Antyre," Ivor said. "And the waters are warm. A fence meant to snare inbound boats is not much of an obstacle to an outbound swimmer. Still, my little assassin's lazy and hates expending effort. She'll complain for days about having to swim."

Dmitry stiffened, his square-set shoulders going fractionally more so. His eyes flicked to the note and back again.

Ivor let out a breath, interpreting Dmitry's expression as bad news and related to her. He skimmed to the bottom of the note, where the news was added by his palace informants. "They've captured her."

"She might speak—"

"She won't—" Ivor murmured more to himself than Dmitry. "The dowager's tower is on the central wing, is it not?"

"You're not considering rescuing her—"

"I was planning on visiting Adiran on my way out. What's another few flights of stairs?" Ivor tapped the note thoughtfully.

"With respect, sir, you should have killed her once she had accomplished the task you purchased her for."

Ivor said, "What man discards a tool when it's still of use?"

"She *will* speak, sooner or later."

"No," Ivor said. "She can't. I hold her name. Should I speak it, well, it would garner her the attention she least desires. She'll hold her tongue to the death."

"Still, our father will be displeased that you let so distinctive a tool fall into enemy hands. Your secrets may be sacrosanct; she may not care about revealing others."

"Grigor won't know. Unless you intend to tell him?" There were benefits, he thought, watching the man shake his head, to having new tools. Old ones often had old agendas. Dmitry, with a single damning phrase—"our father"—slipped and revealed more than he had intended. Grigor hadn't sent Ivor to Antyre on his own after all.

Ivor bent his attention back to the note, skimming the intervening messages his agents had thought pertinent. The antimachinists, it seemed, had drawn back in disarray, confused by their leader's unmasking and drowning in the influx of released prisoners. It was only to be expected; Ivor hadn't anticipated any further use for them. The antimachinists were unable to burn a single house without outside encouragement.

Ivor lit a match, let it fall to the stone beneath his feet, and while it sputtered and flickered, he fed the note into it until it was greasy ash on his fingers.

He smudged the stone with a booted foot, watching the ash turn to a darker streak on a polished floor. Stone was challenging. One not raised in Grigor's Winter Court might not think it possible to defeat. But Ivor had vivid experience reminding him otherwise.

He'd been a boy still, just given his first real blade as a prize for recovering from the plague when so many of his brothers had sickened and died.

Grigor feared lingering miasma and ordered his mistresses to burn out the rest of it, claiming the palace was their domain.

Ivor had followed as his mother, Sofia, painted the stone walls with an oily paste, smeared it thickly into chinks in mortar, directing a small army of servitors to do the same. Anya, his aunt, had found fuel by the simple expedient of tearing down all the portraits of courtiers she disliked or despised. Ivor helped roll tapestries, and pile them like logs in doorways and near heavily draped windows. Then they lit fires, careful of their long skirts, heedless of those who were still too weak or too ill to leave.

The fires had raged until the stones glowed nearly black with heat and the ice fields on the mountainside ran thick with melting ash and soot.

Rather than wait for the plague to take its toll, Grigor had claimed a victory over it by defining the extent of its spread, by saying here and no farther.

Perhaps, Ivor thought drily, he should have been more cautious when urging Janus to read the Itarusine histories and learn from them. Janus was nothing if not retentive. Murne, unlike the winter palace, could not be scoured from within. Too open, too many wooden structures, too much soft-baked brick, and the water so near.

Still, Ivor intended to try. Grigor wanted Antyre for its ice-free waters, for its rich soil—the cities were of lesser interest to him.

Twilight was settling in; a slow weight in the stones, a drift of shadow through arrow slits, and Ivor rose to begin his work. His mother would have been scornful of the tools he had to hand, an assortment of discarded lamps he had drained for their oil, the fat from the kitchen, coals.

Stone didn't burn, this was true. But the furnishings would, and nicely.

"The servants?" Dmitry asked once Ivor had made a lazy circuit of the hall that connected the rooms, passing bedrooms, dining hall, sitting room, study, library—he took extra time with the library; the paper would feed the fire—and ended back at the salle.

"They're irrelevant," Ivor said. Dmitry was silenced.

Once the blaze had begun, seething in a dozen places, Ivor gestured to Dmitry who took up a stance near the double doors into the main palace.

"What if they don't release us?" Dmitry asked, showing a distressing lack of trust in Ivor's plan.

"They will," Ivor said. "The difficulty lies in escaping this prison but not being shuttled into another." He dipped another cravat into a water basin, tied it loosely about his face. The smoke twined its way down the hall, wispy but blackening, creating the start of thunderheads beneath the high ceiling.

Ivor lay back on the chaise, his cravat filtering the air, and waited. Dmitry fidgeted, his composure fleeing. Ivor supposed this was another thing he could lay to Janus's account: the revelation of Dmitry's character. He had thought the man imperturbable, as solid as icebergs in a winter sea. Now, he saw only that the man had never been pressed beyond the known, saw the man was as brittle as rime, all polished sheen and nothing of substance beneath.

When the tickle in his throat grew nearly breath stealing, Ivor said, "Now, Dmitry, if you would."

Dmitry pounded on the double doors, shouted, "Fire!" and coughed. Ivor didn't think the coughing was deliberately added for verisimilitude but rather an involuntary reaction to the thickening smoke.

The scrape of the outer bar being raised was a sweet sound: It was the one variable Ivor hadn't been able to judge with certainty. Janus might have issued orders to prevent such an escape, ordered them to keep the bar in place for any request out of the ordinary, but Ivor gambled. If the palace was still playing the part of civil host, trotting deliveries and meals in, he thought it likely that the bar would be raised.

The first guard stuck a wary head in, got a mouthful of smoke, a cindery wash of heat, and stumbled forward. Dmitry brought his dagger into play, stabbing the man in the throat.

Too soon, Ivor thought, crouched below the worst of the smoke. He risked the door being shut again, leaving them to their fate. But the second and third guards were committed, already partially through the door, and perhaps, in the rush of smoke and flame, they hadn't seen what happened. The door remained open.

Cooler air swept into the foyer, made twists of the smoky clouds, set them dancing through the marble hall, shattering against drawn swords.

The doors were still impassable, at least for one bent on escape instead of rescue.

Ivor picked up a second basin at his feet, the one he'd been chaperoning most carefully, though not for the reason Dmitry assumed. Not a desperate splash of water should straits grow grim. Instead, the basin held the hottest-burning oil in the palace. Without hesitation, he flung it over the guards and Dmitry alike, then snatched a burning book and tossed it after the oil.

The men ignited in shrieking unison, writhing and twisting, as if they could strip themselves of flame as easily as a man shed his clothes. They fell, rolled, beat at each other and themselves, but the carpets had been saturated in fats and oils, in pomades and perfumes—some of it made a lovely scent as it burned—sage and lilac—mixing with the stench of singed hair and leather.

Ivor slipped by, impeded briefly by Dmitry's clutch on his boot. He kicked back, then left unscathed save the print of a bloody hand on his heel.

He heard approaching footsteps: The alert had gone out. He followed his planned route. Catching up a lamp on the wall, he hastened down the stairs toward the stables and Delight's lair. He shattered the lamp at the base, urged the fire to spread. If Delight's machines caught, the blaze would burn long and hard, and likely take the palace with them.

The burning oil spilled down toward the next flight, laying a thin rivulet of flame that just kissed the base of the stairwell and the straw there. It was the stable entrance, and, no matter how often it was swept, wisps of straw remained.

He kicked the smoldering straw into the stables ahead of him, marveling as always at the sensitivity of beasts. Already horses were moving uneasily in their stalls. Ivor pulled his cravat back over his face and shouted to the stable hands, "Fire in the palace! Move out the beasts and the carriages!"

The stable men, hearing no more than the aristocratic voice and the tone of utter conviction, swore and began leading out the horses.

Ivor left with one of them, coughing, shielding himself behind a stallion's bulk. He ducked away before the guards got more than a glimpse of him—it was easy enough; the guards' attention was all for the smoke trickling through the stables and the white-eyed horses dancing in controlled panic.

Against that spectacle, one man walking briskly toward the king's gardens was nothing to worry about. Ivor quickened his pace to a steady run when he judged himself out of sight. Time was short. Soon the guards would summon Rue, summon Janus—both of whom would recognize the blaze for what it was, not only an escape, but a distraction.

The sharp scent of boxwood rose in the night, pungent, unpleasant, letting him know he was close to the maze; from there, it was only another minute's walk past the rose-studded terraces below the nobles' ballroom, past the tree-laden grotto outside the king's ballroom, and then to the lawn leading to the heart of the palace.

He'd done it quickly enough; the rapid pace his heart set told him so. Usually, there were six or more guards stationed near the wide, glass-paned entrance doors, and once Rue and Janus had their say, there'd be six again. But currently there were only two guards, looking as lathered as the horses, as if they expected smoke and flame to come rushing in on them at any moment.

They got Ivor and his blade instead. Two quick slices; he had the first guard's spine cut through before the other turned, and then he opened that man's belly. He left them lying there, and sought out the servants' stairs, allowing himself a moment to regain his breath in the quiet stillness between the dark walls.

Adiran was on the third level. His guards would still be there: Ivor doubted they'd move for anything less than total cataclysm.

He had two choices now: to take them on, by himself, or to take the time—possibly too much time—to collect his assassin from the tower.

He realized, not without a little regret, that she, too, would be guarded, and fighting off her guards would attract attention that would make collecting Adiran, even with her aid, that much more difficult.

Ivor climbed, counting steps; the servants' stairs ran half floors occasionally, to make space for linen cupboards and dumbwaiters.

He slipped through the narrow, concealed door into the hallway, and the influx of fresh air made him aware of the scent of smoke, burned flesh, and horse sweat he carried with him. He shucked off his coat, tossed it back into the stairwell, hoping to leave most of the scent behind. He would prefer not to rouse the guards sooner than he must.

Ten steps down the silent hall, heart thumping, a smile on his lips—it all came to this moment. *Janus, my pet,* he thought, *it would have been wiser to join me. Adiran will hunt you to the ends of the earth once I name you Aris's killer and Antyre will be mine.*

DEFENDER OF
THE CROWN

*T*HERE WAS NO DOUBT THAT Ivor had set the blaze deliberately, Janus thought, looking in at the wreckage, at the
bleeding, burned men being carted away, nor that he had
done it to aid his escape. The question was, had Ivor had more purpose than simply escape?

Fire was classic distraction, Janus thought. It was also a weapon.
Perhaps it was meant to do only as it had, free Ivor, and burn Delight's—

Delight let down his skirts, wiped at the soot streaking his fair
skin, and said, "We kept it out of the engineering wing. He failed
there."

Rough laughter came from one of the men slung between the
arms of two guards. "Failed?" the man wheezed, through a face raw
and pitted.

"Dmitry," Janus said. He recognized the man only by the chain
around his neck and its great silver locket that held a picture of the
royal family.

"He burned me like I was of no more account than the maids,"
Dmitry choked out. Janus waved a hand at the nearest guard, then
when the man only gazed back in blank dismay—exhausted or
shocked—Janus said, "Delight!"

Delight swayed over at once, dropped to his knees beside Dmitry
and Janus. "Have you charcoal?" Janus asked.

"Rather too much of it, I think," Delight began, and then under-standing dawned. He patted at his pocketed skirts, finally pulling out a stub of charcoal and, better still, a leather-bound notebook.

"Dmitry," Janus said, "will you have your revenge on him?"

"I will." Dmitry coughed, left blood on his lips and teeth; his eyes rolled up in his head, his sclera yellow.

Janus reached out, pressed the stub into the man's burned hand. Dmitry stiffened, neck arcing, jaw going rictus tight, then when he eased, Janus said, "Sign your name."

"Dying, not a fool," Dmitry gasped. "Write first. I'll not sign a blank confession. Don't trust you, either." His free hand clutched Janus, left hot, wet circles on his already heated skin. "In Itarusine, mind you."

Janus took the charcoal stub back, wrote as neatly as he could, though the situation was hardly conducive to calligraphy, the book propped unsteadily against his thigh. *Ivor Sofia Grigorian sent the assassin, X, to kill King Aris of Antyre. Witnessed by Dmitry . . .*

"Your surname?" Janus asked. Dmitry roused himself with a jerk and a groan.

"Grigorson," he said on a breath. Grigor's son. Dmitry's mother must have been wildly ineligible for him to be denoted a bastard in a court full of children born out of wedlock.

Janus added it, wondering if Ivor had known. Or cared. He pressed the charcoal into the man's hand a second time, and Dmitry made his signature on the page before he died.

Janus folded the book closed, passed it to Delight. "Don't write over that, please. No matter how clever you are or how much paper you need."

Delight sighed but made no other retort. Instead, he reached over Janus's shoulder and closed Dmitry's eyes. Delight leaned against Janus, rested his face against Janus's back. "It's over, then," Delight said. "You've proof that Ivor sent the assassin. We can greet Grigor's missive with one of our own, and when Rue catches Ivor—"

"Failed," Janus murmured. Dmitry had *laughed*. "Rue! Where's Rue?"

"The stables, my lord," a guard answered. "Seeing if Ivor's steps can be traced through the mess the horses made."

"Get him back to the palace," Janus said. He felt cold and sick, all his triumph draining away. He knew now why it had felt unearned. It was. "He's after Adiran."

Delight said, "Are you sure?"

"A boy with a god waiting to be roused inside him? A boy who's a weapon waiting direction? Ivor doesn't need Grigor's support, doesn't need anything but Adiran and Ani."

"He'll accuse you of killing Aris," Delight said, understanding finally what Janus feared.

"I should have understood before. Always at least two purposes," Janus said. "Succeed at both and when you've mastered that, try for a third." He hesitated a moment, turned back to a guard, and said, "Increase the guards around the assassin's cell—if she's still within."

"You think he's capable of overwhelming the guards?" Delight said. He tripped over the rough hem of his skirt, but Janus shot out a hand, and yanked. Delight stumbled but stayed upright.

"Much as it pains me," Janus said, "I must admit him capable of nearly everything."

They took the carpeted stairs in silence, their footfalls leaving soot stains and blood, and as they reached the landing Delight said, "Why not Grigor?"

"What?"

"Why not tell Adiran that Grigor killed his father?" Delight asked. "Why involve you?"

"Don't be stupid," Janus snapped. "Not now. Even should Adiran, guided by Black-Winged Ani, kill Grigor, there'd be brothers and sons and ambitious women left behind. Ani, sated, would withdraw Her aid, and the god is not so biddable as to work through all those obstacles first, saving Grigor for last. I could barely hold Maledicte in check and he was ever on my side."

Delight fell back, either out of breath or startled by Janus's implicit admission. It didn't signify much. Not when Ivor could be whispering poison into Adiran's ear, dooming Antyre. If Adiran came after him, Antyre would lose both of them and be easy prey for Itarus.

Janus skidded as he reached the top of the stairs; his boot slipping on the marble. He thought it was soot, until he saw the guard lying in blood beyond it. A bruise blacked his temple, but he breathed.

Ivor was hurrying, indeed, Janus thought, *to leave the man alive.* It gave him a brief spurt of hope. Perhaps he could catch Ivor with the boy, confuse the situation, though Black-Winged Ani, given the choice between killers to seek vengeance upon, would probably take both their throats.

Still, the living guard was evocative. If Ivor was in so much of a hurry, it was likely he meant to make his stand elsewhere.

The ships, Janus thought. He'd take Adiran to the ships if he could, learning to corral Ani's power to best effect.

Janus's hopes dwindled as the silence of the hall struck him. If Ivor were still present, there would be struggle. A boy's pained whimper caught his ear, coming from the prince's nursery. He hesitated a moment, drew his blade. One-armed wasn't the ideal way to face Ivor; out of breath and agitated would see him dead.

Correction, he thought drily. Black-Winged Ani could see him dead no matter his state, no matter his weapon. Terror washed over him like the flux, like the icy water of the winter sea that he had been forcibly bathed in. As then, Janus refused to let it shake him.

He wished, however, that he had Psyke at his side.

The boy's whimper sounded again, the choked-off sobs of a child in pain. Janus stepped into the room and dropped his blade.

"Evan," he said. There was a tangle of guards at the far wall, one groaning, the other sporting a broken arm, whose bone jutted free of flesh.

Janus afforded them only a cursory look—they'd live—and bent over Evan. "J-janus," the boy whimpered, his hands clutched over his belly.

"Shh," Janus said, "hush, let me look." His heart throbbed; his throat felt thick.

"Adiran stabbed—" Evan's face ran wet with tears. His cheeks should have been blotchy; instead they were bloodless. He grabbed at Janus. "I want my da—" and suddenly Janus was holding a limp child. He gathered him up, though his bad arm trembled, and he had to roll the boy closer to his chest. Blood wet his shirt and skin.

No guards, Janus thought wildly. There were always guards. He had spent cumulative hours bemoaning the fact, and now . . . he was on his own.

He headed for the stairs, trying to peer over the boy's jutting shoulder, the limp fall of his neck. "Rue!" he shouted and, by the gods, the man was there.

Rue swore. "The prince?"

"Gone with Ivor," Janus said. "Help me get Evan to the physician. He's been gut stabbed."

Rue winced. "Kinder perhaps to let him go—"

"No," Janus said. "He *has* to live. Antyre depends on it."

He took the stairs with a stride that tried to combine the nearly impossible mixture of haste and care, remembered the guard at the landing, and stepped over him. Rue caught up, his face white and set.

"Run ahead," Janus said. "No matter who Sir Robert's helping, this boy must come first."

Rue shot him a look mingled of horror and doubt, but he darted ahead, unimpeded by any burden but fear.

Janus, watching him go, nearly slipped. A quick shoulder under his steadied him, though his rescuer, Psyke, protested the effort it took. Janus checked Evan's security in his arms, tilted the boy's head back so his shallow breathing cooled the sweat on his neck.

"His mother's frightened," Psyke said.

"His mother's dead."

"She still knows her child," she said. Her voice was serene, her expression not. "What's happened? I heard shouting and there's the stink of blood in the halls."

"Ivor."

"Did he strike Evan down?" Her fingers, wound into his sleeve, knotted. "Did he take Adiran?"

"He took Adiran. But Adiran dealt Evan's blow—"

"The compact," she breathed. "Ani's compact."

"Can you slow his death?" Janus asked.

"I . . ." For a maddening moment, he thought she meant to deny it, but she finished, "I only deal it." As if in emphasis, the boy's breathing stuttered, his body twitched and spasmed, and Psyke nearly sent Janus down the stairs as she recoiled.

"Forgive me," she said, backing away, taking the stairs one at a time, her eyes on him. "Save the boy."

"Psyke—" Janus called. She paused. "There must be something you can do."

"Haith brings *death*," she whispered. "I can do nothing." She turned and fled, bare feet soundless, sure-footed even in the spilled blood.

Janus found Rue coming to meet him, and though the man offered, refused to give up his burden.

"Do you know where Ivor will go? Delight said you thought the docks, but the gates will slow—"

"Ani will not be slowed, should she choose otherwise," Janus said.

Sir Robert came out, blanched, and said, "Just a child!" He took Evan from Janus's arms, asked tersely, "Is it your blood or his decorating your shirt?"

"His," Janus said.

Sir Robert hissed when he saw the wound.

"Will he live?" Janus asked. Rue leaned close to hear the answer.

"It's not so bad a wound," Sir Robert said, after an investigation that had Evan whimpering, even unconscious. "It's shallow and untutored, a narrow wound, dealt by a weak man or—"

"A child," Rue murmured. "The prince." Dawning realization showed in his eyes; he drew a hand over his face and leaned back against the wall.

"On a man, I'd say he'd heal and well. But it's a foul big wound on a child. . . ." Sir Robert's face went grim and set; he called out to his aide to bring Laudable and plenty of it.

Janus laid a hand over the man's wrist, tightened his grip. "Evan has to live."

"Oh, his father's one of your privateers, I understand, but—"

"If he dies," Janus said, "if he dies, then Adiran has given his soul into Ani's keeping. If he dies, Antyre's future goes with him."

Sir Robert's lips thinned, and he bent over the boy, determination replacing the pity in his eyes.

THE NIGHT WAS DARK, FULL of lingering smoke that clung to the greenery around the palace. Ivor's flames had burned hot, had succeeded in getting a foothold in the stables, and the soft grasses of the gardens were hummocked and pitted with the marks of horses being hastily led away from the flames. Janus stumbled over one of the ruts, saved himself from falling by catching at a thorny climber. He didn't know whether to be grateful or dismayed that his grip failed, sending him to a knee but sparing him a palm studded with thorns.

A form ghosted out of the night, and Janus shifted his weight, trying frantically to get to a stance where he could draw his blade, its sheath grating against the dirt. "My lord," Simpson said, and Janus found himself pathetically grateful that it was a familiar face. Then he remembered the pistol shot aimed at him during the duchess's arrest: Simpson had been among the guards in the throne room.

Still, Janus took the hand held out to him, allowed the guard to pull him to his feet. And if his hand fell again to his sword hilt, Simpson said nothing but merely slid his gaze over it, then took a judicious step back once Janus had his feet again.

"We need horses for riding," Janus said. "Steady tempered. I need an escort to the docks."

Simpson—his hands stained with soot, exertion painting darker streaks along the sides of his shirt, his coat long ago discarded—looked as if he wanted to protest, but stifled it.

Instead, he nodded. "I'll inform Rue."

FULL NIGHT WAS ON THEM now, moonlight seeping slowly through the sea fogs, the smoke that blanketed the city. The sounds of their horses' hooves were muffled, and they went slowly, despite the lanterns they carried, despite the lamps lit along the streets. The guards' faces were grimly set, and Janus's heart echoed it. The night sky settled heavily upon him: the raspy flutter of wings as the rooks sought their destination; the swelter of fire pits that burned in the poorer neighborhoods—dug deep, cheap burials for those who died of the plague.

Janus shivered; his mind felt empty, all his cleverness stripped away. He had no plan, at least none he could feel any certainty of, surely nothing Ivor would laud, only a tangle of fear, desperation, and the drumbeat rage in his blood that Ivor would not have his country for the asking of it.

If Sir Robert saved Evan, then perhaps Adiran could be turned from the precipice, from committing his soul to Ani's cruel guidance. The boy had always been sweet natured and biddable. If Evan survived, if Ivor could be separated from Adiran—perhaps matters could still be saved.

Likely though, Janus thought, his mood going grimmer, Ivor would have Adiran blooded again, simply to be sure the compact was sealed. If the boy had been willing to injure his only friend— Ivor would have little trouble beyond the limitations of Adiran's strength. Ani gave nothing of Herself until She had been fed Her bloody measure of devotion.

A single plague victim, lying in a feverish stupor, would prove no difficulty even for a weak child to dispatch, given a sharp enough blade. But Ivor feared the plague . . . perhaps he would trust to Evan's death now, escape the city. . . .

The fragility of his hopes appalled Janus. He had never held to anything so delicate, preferring the security of careful planning, of sure knowledge and countermoves.

Instead, he was left with this, depending on Ivor's fears of the plague, on a child's good nature being more intrinsic than his hatred, and on the only certainty he had left: that if all else failed, if he and Adiran fell, and Antyre after, he would take Ivor with him so that he would be shorn of his triumph.

At least he could pride himself on that much, that even in despair and failure, he would attempt to take his enemies with him, rather than retreat into the apathy that Aris had nurtured so long.

They left behind the wide streets of the merchants' shops and homes, the horses filing into lines of two or three abreast. Simpson guided his steed to Janus's left, and a red-bearded soldier took his right as their little procession of guards and soldiers headed into the Relicts and the piers beyond. There were other paths, but the docks that jutted out from the Relicts were the ones that had the clearest path to the sea, the deepest waters where the deep-bellied, long voyaging ships made their beginnings and ends.

The Relicts were silent as they rode through; and the soldiers, younger, less seasoned than the Kingsguard, were visibly uneasy. These soldiers had never fought for anything other than their own prestige, had never used their blades and pistols for anything other than show.

One of the soldiers behind them started at some imagined movement, jerked his horse to an ungainly halt, bumping into another soldier, the whinnies of two protesting horses as a result.

Janus said, "If you're imagining ravening hordes of Relict rats leaping out at you, stop. We're armed men on horseback, hard pickings for men with sticks. They're far more like to be scavenging the city for dead men's possessions."

"You're certain?" the man asked. His gloved hands pulled at his reins; his horse tossed its head.

"Quite," Janus said. Simpson turned in his saddle to shoot a glare that reminded the soldier exactly why that might be an unwise question.

Janus was pleased to have Simpson's company even if he was waiting his chance to kill him. Riding through the Relicts woke painful memories of fifteen years of hardscrabble living and willful neglect, his desperate struggle to keep Miranda and himself alive, and it woke later memories also. The slow, stumbling gait of his horse reminded him of the night he had followed Maledicte out to the pier to watch him kill Last.

He wished he were riding out to that moment again, when they had wrung victory from a man who had discarded him without a second's thought. Would he have done things differently? If he hadn't interfered, if Ani had left, the compact completed, and Maledicte freed of Her madness, would he still have Miranda at his side?

If he had her beside him now, he knew she would bare sharp white teeth and growl, "Stop thinking and *act!*"

He wondered what advice Psyke would have offered had he stopped to ask. He doubted she would ever advocate action over thought; she was as moodily introspective as Aris had ever been, though she at least could be roused from it.

The young soldier danced his horse again, and Janus spurred his own mount in reaction; he felt as nervy as a winter wolf come down into the city. At this rate, he thought, listening to his heart race in its bone cage, he'd be grateful to face Ivor. At least then his impetuous nerves would serve more purpose than to sour his mouth and his belly.

The sound of the sea lapping at pilings reached out to him, brought a tang of salt rot to his senses, and raised the damp hair at his nape. There was a new and unfamiliar sound as well, a gurgling suck as the night tides crawled over and through the brass gates strung across their domain. Janus heard hushed voices carried on the breeze, a tease of meaning that swirled away without ever granting more than a single word here and there. But it was close enough, the words heard were important enough—*palace, guards, boat, escape*—that Janus said, "Dismount. We'll try for surprise, leave the horses here."

"They'll be carved up for horsemeat," Simpson said, squandering the fragile goodwill he had earned with Janus.

"Then leave a man behind, or do you fear the city's savages will devour him also?" He swung down from his mount hurriedly, using the reins to stabilize his uneven descent, his weak arm useless. Janus unsheathed his blade the moment his feet touched ground, and walked forward, choosing not to wait for the others, not wanting to get caught in the mass of jostling horses unhappy with their surroundings.

Instead he moved on through the rubble, treading a path into his past. He'd nearly forgotten how oppressive the nights could seem. Even the bobbing pole lanterns the soldiers carried seemed swallowed, surrounded by a blackness as unrelieved as the grave. He licked his lips, tasting salt.

When Maledicte stalked Last, playing at predation as if that could make the intent to kill any less real, when Mal had come to the docks, he had drawn the night fogs about him like a cloak.

Janus let out a steady breath as he passed yet another pile of shadowed rubble, a leaning window frame holding a half-tilted wall. Adiran, with Ani's wings sheltering him, could be anywhere.

Janus shook his head; he was letting fancies rule his mind. While Adiran might very well seek a nest in a small cranny of stones, Ivor would not. And Ivor held the boy's reins; Ivor would want, as Janus had wanted, to watch his enemy die.

Ahead, Ivor was on the pier at the heart of a strange mélange of men, obviously some of his agents collected in his trip through Murne. There was a baker, called away from his ovens, three clerks who had apparently been working late, merchants called from their homes—all armed with pistols or swords. The shadows and the lanterns were deceptive, made an army out of what was—Janus squinted, trying to count people instead of light dazzle—only seven of them.

"The prince isn't there," Simpson whispered.

"No," Janus said. It felt like false reprieve, something meant to lure them into what could be a well-set trap.

"Do we have any other option?" Simpson said. "Should we wait for Rue?"

Janus repeated himself. "No. Listen."

"They're not speaking," Simpson said after a long pause where he stood on point as well as any hunting hound. Any untrained hound.

"Listen to the water," Janus said. "A boat's coming in. Small." If he opened his eyes wide, let the darkness shape itself, he could almost see it, a shadow against the glitter of the water, a dinghy coming in without lamps to lead the way. "They'll be gone before Rue arrives."

"The sea gates."

"His men will open them." Janus shook his head, infuriated. "For all we know, some of his men helped set them up. There will have to be a thorough purging of our streets after this. I will not have Murne a breeding ground for spies and saboteurs."

He took a breath, said, "Leave Ivor to me. If it can be avoided, we want him alive, as hostage against Grigor if nothing else." Janus chose not to share his worries about Ivor's guidance of a god-touched prince; they knew only that Adiran had been kidnapped, that this part was meant to bring him back.

"Ivor's men?"

"Kill them all," Janus said.

He strode forward out of the Relict's sheltering darkness, unsheathing his blade. It hissed against the leather, and he found his breath echoing that serpentine sound.

He heard the scuffle of men following, and heard Simpson dispatching one of their men to guard the latch that held the gates in place. That left them with only four to occupy Ivor's men, and Janus to face Ivor.

Ivor turned as if he felt himself in Janus's thoughts. His dark eyes narrowed; Janus knew they'd be discovered momentarily—the soldiers wore white beneath their blue coats, the shine of metal in moonlight.

"Such a very good pet," Ivor said. He pitched his voice to carry; it didn't take much effort. Unlike the night when Maledicte had brought blanketing silence under Ani's wings, this night, so far, was ordinary enough. "Come to find his master."

"No more badinage," Janus said.

Ivor stripped off his coat. "I regret it's come to this, Janus. I am as fond of you as I can be fond of anyone."

"You talk too much," Janus said. He rushed in, savoring the quick startlement in Ivor's eyes at what appeared a suicidal lunge. Ivor, after all, was barricaded behind his loyal men. But the man who moved to confront Janus was blown backward with a roar and the stink of gunpowder. Simpson stepped out of the rubble, tucking the first pistol away and aiming a second.

Ivor nodded. "Very well then." He unsheathed his saber, and, after a smiling glance at Janus's nearly useless left hand, pulled out his dagger. "You're outmatched."

"I've always been outmatched," Janus said. "In the Relicts, in the Winter Court, in the Antyrrian court. Yet I'm still alive."

Ivor urged his own men out of the way. They were reluctant to do so, not only out of protectiveness, but self-preservation. They had to know that their lives were only obstacles in the Antyrrians' path to Ivor.

The moment they moved, the soldiers engaged them in pistol shot and blade work.

Janus decided, as a ball sped by, leaving him wincing reflexively from a danger that had already passed, that Simpson hadn't been the one aiming at him in the throne room. He was apparently the only one of the men with him now who had any ability to aim a pistol.

Ivor closed with Janus, taking advantage of his distraction; Janus barely raised his saber in time, blocking the slash meant to open his throat. He twisted, taking himself out of range of the second blow, the follow-up with the dagger that normally would be intercepted by a dagger of his own.

Instead, he twisted, dropped to a knee, and came up with a loose handful of grit, tossing it into Ivor's face. The man ignored it, too confident in his own body and too knowledgeable of Janus's training to fear the momentary blindness. Ivor pressed forward and Janus shifted, slipping under the blade, putting a shoulder into Ivor's sternum and shoving him back. Janus got himself out of Ivor's blade's reach, chastising his own instincts; time was not his ally. The longer he fought Ivor, the more certain he was to lose. He was hampered— one blade against two, one man against his mentor—and Janus knew with certainty that Ivor hadn't taught him everything. Ivor always kept some secrets.

Ivor smiled again, showing his teeth in wolfish enjoyment. "Well, that was bracing. Again?"

Janus circled Ivor, two full rotations while he tried to think; but all he could think was that he couldn't beat Ivor and that he *must* beat Ivor.

"I am surprised you came yourself," Ivor said, "when you have others, more . . . able . . . to send instead—"

"Some tasks you want to see done yourself," Janus said. He flicked a gaze beyond Ivor when a single groan cut through the sounds of steel meeting steel. One of the palace soldiers sagged, a dagger in his throat. The clerk tugged it out, wiped it free of blood, and chose another target, all the while limping.

"You intend to kill me?" Ivor said. "Is that wise? To thwart Her? I thought you capable of learning from the past, Janus."

Ivor grew impatient, took three graceful steps forward, blades moving, and Janus found each of his thrusts turned back, sweat trickling down his spine.

Ivor frowned, dark suspicion in his eyes. "I trained you better than this. Of course, I wouldn't have thought you'd let that sycophantic fop of the duchess's maim you either."

Janus changed his footwork, shifting to the Antyrrian rapier fighting style, hoping for a moment's advantage. He didn't get it. Ivor shifted fluidly, knocked Janus back and down. Janus groaned as his bad arm took his weight. The flesh around the sutures tore again, but he scrambled to his feet instead of curling around the pain. That was for later. If there was a later.

A pistol shot exploded and sang between them, making Ivor jerk back; Janus made it to his feet and out of the range of Ivor's sword before he even looked to see Simpson holstering a spent pistol.

Simpson had saved his life. Janus put that startling thought aside for another time and dealt with Ivor.

His plan had seemed simple enough at the palace: capture Ivor; recover Adiran before the boy's path was irrevocably set.

But Ivor had no desire to be captured, or even slowed, and Janus's skills had deserted him. He might, with Simpson continuing to distract Ivor, get in a killing blow, but what of Adiran? What of Antyre?

"My poor pet," Ivor said. "You look at me as if I'm the solution to all the difficulties facing you. While I'm not one to belittle myself, let me tell you, should you kill me, your problems will only increase—"

Janus growled, lunged forward, concentrating on a move Ivor couldn't expect, going back to the days when he was a rat and facing boys better armed than he. He swung at Ivor, and at the point of highest impetus, he let go of the blade.

Ivor's eyes widened; he ducked the sharp edge. Even unguided, even falling, the heavy blade could wound, and Janus caught Ivor's right wrist, yanking it back and around, disarming him. If it had been the Relicts, Janus would have stayed close, beaten his victim down with the stolen weapon. As it was, he merely kept Ivor's arm pinned behind his back, kept himself leaning close, his weight his only weapon left.

This close, Ivor should have been hampered, unable to use his dagger for more than feeble half strikes, but he flipped the blade in his palm, shifting its direction, and stabbed, underhand and backward toward Janus's belly.

Janus released him, flung himself away, and thought it was done. He had lost. Ivor shook out his arm, collected the blades at his feet, his own and Janus's.

"You gambled," Ivor said, "but games that defeated children will not defeat an experienced duelist. Still, if you'd had the use of two arms—who knows?"

Simpson staggered to Janus's side, put his blade before Janus.

Ivor said, "I should kill you," and there was such a strange reluctance in his voice that Janus faltered. It wasn't fondness, almost sounded like fear.

Ivor's saboteurs, the three left standing, said, "Your highness, the boat—"

During the skirmish the boat had made it beyond the gate. The oarsmen stroked toward them. Janus knew it meant another of his soldiers dead. On Janus's side, only Simpson lived.

"Sir?" Simpson said.

"Kill him," Janus said. He would have to trust that Dmitry's confession would be enough to overset the murder of the prince ascendant of Itarus, that Adiran could be turned from his vengeance without Ivor confessing his lie to the god!

A sudden wind rose, blowing toward the sea instead of from it, with a silence beneath it—the sound of the world taking notice of a predator moving through—and then a skirl of black against a black sky, blinking the stars away.

Rooks, Janus realized. Adiran come to help Ivor at last. He whispered quick and low to Simpson, "Do not engage Adiran—do not go near him. If he kills—"

Simpson nodded. His eyes were wild, the whites visible all the way around, and Janus thought his might be the same. Black-Winged Ani's presence filled the air and froze men's blood as if they were caught in nightmares.

The rooks swirled closer, their wingbeats audible, a cyclone of them, and walking at their base, a child-shaped figure with a dagger in his hand.

Two words insinuated themselves into the churned air and carried to the cluster of men on the dock. Two words that rasped like feathers and seethed with rage. Two words that filled Janus with despair, with the certainty that Evan had died.

"Found you."

Beside him, Ivor began to laugh.

*P*SYKE SLOWED HER STEPS AS she reached her quarters; she paused with her hand above the handle. Mirabile said, startlingly vivid in her ear, *Hiding again? That's what you did while your family died. Will you do the same now when the stakes are greater?*

One of the kingsguards stationed by her door reached out and opened it for her, never meeting her eyes; they both knew she was meant to be caged, a potential danger neither Janus nor Rue had the time to deal with, but Psyke knew also that the guard feared her.

She passed him, into her rooms, dwelling on need. She needed to aid Janus, aid Antyre. Her husband had won there; the two were inextricably linked in her mind. To save him was to save the country. But what could she do? She had spoken as true as she knew to Janus, startled by the despairing way he clutched that child so close: She brought only death.

Even now, she feared it was true. Ivor had set fire to the west side of the palace, and men were dying putting it out. On the streets of the city, men were dying of plague. In Sir Robert's offices, a boy was dying, his whimpers growing softer as he weakened. It felt like pressure in her head, as if she had fallen into a cave and the earth weighed upon her. Haith's voice surrounded her, faint whispers she could try to ignore. *Give me . . .* He said. *Give me your—*

She plugged her fingers into her ears like a child.

Hiding like the mouse you are. A waste of a god's attention. Mirabile's voice, shrill, penetrated even that defense.

Psyke moved away from the door, away from the guards who might hear and suffer yet another spasm of panic that their lady talked to the dead. Once she had reached her sitting room, turned up the lamps to drive out the shadows, she said, "You might offer me advice instead of censure."

As always, speaking to the ghosts seemed to encourage their existence, clothed them in something close to flesh. It eased the stiffness in her spine and neck, to not have to brace herself against a sudden voice, from here, from there, from within her head.

You mistake me for someone who has advice to give, Mirabile said. She sat in a rose pink chair that did nothing flattering to her scarlet hair. *I never heeded it when alive, so I have no words now. You do know he'll die.*

"Who?" she asked, but Mirabile, viper tongued and smug though she was, was correct. She did know. *Janus,* she thought.

Janus, Mirabile echoed. *He's proud and possessive of what's his. He claims Antyre and he'll fight to the death for his chance to keep it.*

"Can I help?" she asked. "You bartered with Ani. Surely you must know how to ask Haith for aid."

Mirabile said, *You don't listen well. I have no advice for you. I thought I understood Black-Winged Ani, but Maledicte knew Her better than I ever did. What makes you think I paid any attention to the lesser shadow Her brother cast?*

"Then leave me alone," Psyke said. She threw a book at Mirabile; the ghost faded and the book thumped to the floor, creasing its pages.

Psyke knelt, collected it, smoothing the damage. Aris had given it to her, the old genealogy of her family from the time her ancestor was king. Before Haith had taken his family from him.

She flipped through the pages, paused at the portrait of Thomas Redoubt, wondering if he had felt Haith's touch, if his skin had rearranged itself to reflect the god. If he had felt as drowned as she did.

He couldn't have, she thought. Not and fought as he had, not and shaped the kingdom as he had. He had had Haith's aid, not merely His presence.

Her hands balled themselves into fists, fury lancing inward. Difficult to make a choice to act when every action she took seemed to be the wrong one. She had sought the duchess's aid, a woman who threw her allegiance to their sworn enemies. Psyke had aided the assassin she sought. She had accused her husband of a crime he hadn't committed, worked against him when she should have worked with him. Now, she was going to let him die because she couldn't act?

You might stop wallowing, a new voice said, *and listen. Learn. Hark above.*

Psyke watched Challacombe fade as silently as he had come, ghostly in life, silent in death.

She opened the door to the hall, ignoring her guard's suggestion that she withdraw into her rooms where she'd be safe.

Instead she headed toward the sound of argument and complaint drifting downward. "Nowhere's safe," she said and passed the guards unhindered. She left them watching an empty room, more empty than ever, since its ghosts followed her.

She climbed the stairs, hunting the sounds of quiet argument, following a deeper sound, a distant thumping like the beat of a distressed heart.

She found herself at the base of the dowager's tower, the guards' voices coming clear. "We're not leaving the door. Rue said—"

"But he'd want to know she's talking—"

Psyke stepped up; the guards fell silent; and, as if the assassin had sensed her, she stopped pounding on the door and said instead, "Ani's come. Let me free, Lady. Let me free and I'll aid you. I'll tell you anything you want to know."

She sounded as if she had pressed herself against the door, as if the urgency in her words had pressed her as close to egress as possible.

"Open the door," Psyke told the guards.

"Not for anything, Rue said," the guard objected. Psyke merely held out her hand, waiting for the key.

So sure of yourself, then? Mirabile asked.

"Go away," Psyke said. "You're not wanted or needed. Do not try my patience or we'll find out together what Haith enables me to do."

The guard blanched and dropped the key into her palm, startling her. She'd nearly forgotten the men were there. Nearly. She supposed there was a small part of her satisfied with the way they hastened to do her bidding.

The old key's iron scrollwork was heavy and uncomfortable in her palm. The key turned easily enough; perhaps Rue had greased the lock once they decided to hold their prisoner in the tower. The door sagged, a monstrosity of old oak and iron, and it took Psyke resting all her weight on the handle to open it. She half expected the assassin to bolt past her, and Psyke was braced, ready to fling herself at the girl if needed.

The assassin crouched at the base of the stairs; she looked up at Psyke with an expression that was as mutely miserable as Psyke felt herself.

"How will you help me?" Psyke asked. "Are you even able to? I will close the door again, leave you to your fate—"

"Ani will kill Ivor," the girl said. "She'll kill your husband, and She'll destroy your prince. Vengeance only leaves its users hollow, and your prince was an empty shell to begin with. There'll be nothing left."

Psyke stepped back, took a deep breath preparatory to shutting the heavy door.

The assassin scrambled to her feet, put her hand out against the edge of the door. "You can stop Ani. *We* can stop Her."

"You are imprisoned," Psyke said. "I hardly think you can do—"

"You need me," the girl said. "Or do you think to save Janus on your own when you can barely stand?"

Psyke straightened hastily, took her weight from the door, but her body missed its support, wanted to sag into its strength again.

"Haith doesn't work as Ani does," the assassin said. "Black-Winged Ani makes constant trades as one gains Her favor by killing more and more. Haith . . ." She turned, as if to go up the stairs, though Psyke knew it was only a bluff. The woman wanted out, wanted to aid Ivor with an intensity Psyke could nearly taste. She let the woman walk the stairs, and was rewarded when the assassin abruptly turned and huffed at her.

"Haith," Psyke murmured, and, oh, the sound of His name on her lips pleased the world. She felt the foundations quiver far beneath her feet, a little shudder of pleasure. "What does He want, then? How do I woo Him and gain more of Him than I have? While being safe from death benefits me, the ghosts do not—"

The assassin flew down the stairs, clutched at Psyke's sleeves. "Let me out and I'll tell you. We don't have much time."

"We have too little time for you to play games with me," Psyke said. A quick shimmer of movement in her vision, and there was a ghostly bird rushing toward the window, impacting it in silence and vanishing. Psyke reluctantly called Mirabile back. Confronted by her angry presence, the ghosts that were beginning to appear fell back. Mirabile's mouth turned down—shunned in death as in life.

"You don't petition Haith or trade with Him. You don't entice Him into favoring you. You command Him by strength—"

Psyke shook her head. It was ridiculous—but the girl leaned closer, her eye fever bright, her lips trembling with urgency, looming over Psyke like a raptor.

"*Listen*," she hissed, just as Challacombe echoed it. *Listen*. "Why do you think Haith bows His head in every representation of Him?"

"Out of mercy," Psyke said, repeating nearly forgotten catechism. "To spare us the death in His gaze."

"No," the girl said. She shook her head for further emphasis, stamping a foot. "You're Redoubt's kin and you don't know! Your ancestor knew. It's why he killed his family."

"*Haith* killed his—"

The girl shook her head again. "Thomas Redoubt rose to power on the death stored in the battlefield, rose to a throne and ushered in peace. When a new enemy emerged, Redoubt commanded Haith to rid him of his foe, but to no avail. The ghosts had worn away, you see, tired of dogging Redoubt's path, no longer interested in the world of the living. So Redoubt made new ghosts. He killed his wife and his children, one by one, sparing only the daughter who was wedded and away. Then, with their ghosts in tow, he commanded Haith to kill his enemy.

"Haith did as commanded, but when the urgency was

gone . . . when Redoubt realized what he had done . . . he became a ghost himself and faded away into Haith's domain.

"Haith doesn't bow His head for mercy. He doesn't bow it out of sorrow that all creatures fail and die. Ani doesn't call Him Her crawling brother because He's part of the earth. Haith is a subservient god. And all it takes to command Him is strength of purpose and an army of the dead."

Psyke shuddered; the world shuddered with her, Haith's dismay at being stripped so bare. The windows warped and grew ragged cracks. Plaster sifted down like snow, and the tower swayed.

The girl clutched Psyke, hanging on to her as if Psyke could echo Haith's urge for flight and leave her. The shaking slowed, and Psyke pushed free, pushed harder until the girl was pressed against the wall, half falling down against the stairs, all torn skirts, wild hair, and one glittering eye. "I can command Haith? I can do more than kill with my presence?"

"It's not killing," the girl babbled. "Not you. More like you're *encouraging* the death they would have—"

Psyke borrowed a movement she'd seen Janus use on Savne once, when he was goaded past discretion. A tight hand on a slender throat. Mirabile leaned close and whispered. *I stopped your youngest sister's breath like that. She squirmed and thrashed, but the poison had made her weak and I held on until I felt her last breath leave and the heaviness of dead flesh.*

Psyke's hand flew back.

The assassin, rubbing her neck, skirted Psyke warily and headed for the open door, her back tense as if she expected Psyke to stop her at any moment.

"Where will we find them?" Psyke said.

The assassin stopped. "You have to promise me you won't use Haith to kill Ivor. Or I won't tell you the last of it. How to command Him."

"You've told me enough," Psyke said. "Strength of purpose, ghosts. There are ghosts aplenty waiting without the palace."

"You need His attention first—"

"Your scholarship fails you," Psyke said. She caught up with the assassin, taking quick steps, seizing the girl's sleeve, fought vertigo for being so far from the earth. "I've had His attention from the very beginning. It's always on me."

The girl's face hardened; Psyke held her sleeve and said, "You needn't look for a weapon. I have no great desire to see Ivor dead, only gone from these shores. I prefer peace to war."

The girl hesitated; the hardness dropped from her face, leaving only a girl who had been roughly treated. Psyke's fingers, pressed into the assassin's arm, were collecting the sticky residue of old blood.

They whipped her, Mirabile said. *She didn't scream.*

Psyke said, "Come with me," to Mirabile, to Challacombe.

The assassin's body was one long knot of tension against Psyke's side. She muttered, "Collect your ghosts if you must, only remove your elbow from my side."

"Won't you take the pain for a chance to save your precious Ivor?" Psyke said. "Or should I go alone, and leave you locked away, wondering . . . ?"

The assassin shifted, wrapped her arm around Psyke's waist, supporting her. "I'm the injured one."

"I'll be better once there's earth beneath my feet." Psyke could feel the lure downward, an anchor on her flesh, drawing her toward Haith, toward the dead. She raised her head. The palace ghosts were filing toward her: Challacombe; Mirabile; murdered Savne; the guard who had tried to kill Janus; and Psyke's poor stupid maid, Dahlia, who looked bewildered even in death.

One missing, she thought, and deliberately focused her will. "Come, Aris, your kingdom has need of you. Your son has need of you." He wisped into being but barely, his eyes blue flames and resting on the assassin. Psyke thought briefly that it was good the girl couldn't see the ghosts, or even her nerve might fail under that seething gaze.

Instead, the assassin only strengthened her grip on Psyke and together they led the ghosts downward. The guards on the floor below said nothing, but cleared their way. It was the first indication Psyke had that perhaps the ghosts were no longer invisible. The way the men drew back, long after she passed, suggested they felt some presence beyond her own. Captain Rue joined her and the assassin at the main door; before he could make the obvious offer to join her, she shook her head.

"Stay here, Captain. Keep the palace secure. Should we succeed, we'll need a safe harbor."

She held his gaze, tilting her head back to meet his eyes, and finally, he dropped his, bowed. "Yes, my lady."

The assassin murmured, "Finally," and tugged. Psyke stepped out onto the streets of Murne, and all around, those dead or dying, took notice.

· 3 0 ·

*I*VOR'S BREATH RASPED IN HIS throat; Janus took a moment's distracted pleasure to think that at least he had given the man a bit of a fight, before all his attention was riveted on the approaching figure, and the death he might carry.

Adiran had always been the very image of an Antyrrian child, hair like gilt, sky-colored eyes, and skin as pale as winter milk. The child approaching them was studded with shadow. The sunlit hair was tousled and tufted with dark feathers, the pale eyes were mottled black and blue, as piebald as any of the northern horses. His translucent skin . . . seemed as full of movement as the sky was full of rooks, a shifting, pulsing wingbeat.

Surely with all these changes, Janus thought, despair washing over him, surely Evan was dead and Adiran was well and truly wing-bent, his vengeance as much a need as breath.

Ivor's men swore, and they stepped forward, swords at the ready. A single, simple action, and it changed *everything*.

Janus shuddered with new understanding, how close he had come to throwing it away, and it seemed the city shuddered with him, a vast exhalation of relief.

"*You* didn't wake him," Janus said, still numb with relief. "He's not coming to aid you. He's coming *for* you. The blame apportioned correctly. Ani's sworn to kill you."

Ivor let out a breath of his own. "I'm not certain. Are you? If I didn't set him on, and you didn't—who does he blame?"

"Too late to muddy the waters," Janus said. "All I need do is stand aside."

"If I die, Grigor, loathsome father though he is, will turn your streets red with blood," Ivor said. "He's lost too many prince ascendants these last few years."

"At your blade—"

"And yours, my pet, and yours. That alone would give him the excuse."

Their argument broke off as the rooks darted and fell like arrows. Janus flung himself away from Ivor, rolling out of sword's reach, out of the way of the plunging birds. Adiran dropped to a crouch, watching with head-cocked interest. The birds made no distinction between Ivor and the other men. Simpson passed Janus a blade from one of the fallen soldiers, and they hunched and swung and batted while beaks tore at their clothes and talons left bloody stripes on their hands and faces. Rooks fell to their swords, but others kept coming.

Janus wondered grimly how Ivor fared, and sliced a sharp-edged wing away from a bird seemingly determined to fly directly through him if it had to carve a path with its beak.

A shriek reached his ears, a man screaming in agony, followed by a splash and more shrieking. Janus turned, shielding his face and neck, and looked out over the water. A man thrashed and flailed, pinned on the spines of the water gate, while a cluster of swarming rooks made nest material of his face and hair.

Ivor cursed, his escape cut off. The boat the man had been in drifted slowly away from the pier. Adiran moved for the first time since the rooks had begun their attack; he giggled and walked forward, the dagger held loosely before him.

If Adiran weren't possessed, the scene might have been amusing, watching Ivor's face as the untrained child came toward him. But in the midst of slashing wings, beaks, talons, with a kingdom at stake, with a man screaming and drowning . . . Janus thought again of Ivor's claim that if he died, Grigor would declare war. It was more than possible. Grigor wanted Antyre badly.

"Adiran," he said, though he had to force the breath out. He felt more like a Relict rat than he had for years—at the mercy of instincts that urged run, hide, seek shelter, and wait for this to pass.

Simpson hissed warning and disapproval, and Ani's rooks swept over him in a flurry of stabbing beaks that pierced his throat. Janus watched his only ally die. Shaking, Janus raised his voice, tried to project the same confidence that Maledicte had sometimes responded to; but Maledicte had been his lover, their shared history a leash on them both. "Adiran," Janus said again and again, until the boy slowed, turned those light-dark eyes on him.

"I know you," he said. The voice was wrong, not the prince's, not the boy's who had giggled as men died, but something more disturbing. A voice that made Janus's head hurt and Adiran's lips gloss dark with blood. "I warned you not to think to use Me again."

Ivor shuddered, his hands coming away from his face. In the slick shadows on Ivor's palms, Janus thought the man bled from the eyes at the sound of Her voice.

One of Ivor's remaining men—the baker, his white coat gone dark with blood, feather, and gunpowder—narrowed his gaze at the closing distance between Ivor and Adiran, between life and death, and darted forward, blade slashing.

The rooks confused the air; the baker bulled through, and Adiran threw the dagger into the air. The glittering blade disappeared midtoss; the rooks' wings took the shine for themselves, and the baker began screaming as the newly razor-edged wings ripped him apart.

"There's a machine for you," She said, the words ragged in Adiran's young voice. "Do you like it?"

Janus decided not answering was probably wiser than misspeaking and drawing Her ire. Ivor looked at the dark water, considering his chances. If he could swim out far enough, would he be safe? Janus doubted it. Being out of Her chosen element would annoy Her—it had made Maledicte violent and crazy while in the underground cell at Stones—but not slow Her.

The razor-winged rooks took to the air again, the chime of their wings as dangerous a harbinger as the sound of acid bubbling in Delight's laboratory.

"I didn't kill Aris," Ivor said.

The rooks shivered, their smooth flight stuttering a moment, as if Ani's attention had faltered, as if the unnatural thing She had done to them made them less creatures of air than they had been before.

Adiran came forward another step, his hands empty, his eyes full of hatred. "You did. I heard the guards say so."

Ivor licked his lips, took a step back, to the very edge of the docks. "Men can be mistaken. Men are not as infallible as gods."

Ivor was a fool, Janus thought. Only a fool argued with gods, and only a fool thought Ani capable of reason. Whether or not Adiran chose to believe, Ani would see everyone on the docks dead, just to slake Her temper.

"You did, too," Adiran said again. His own voice this time, a child's argument. And only a fool argued with a child.

The rooks rose, circling higher, gaining speed, spreading apart until it was evident that when they stooped again, the only one left standing would be Adiran. Everyone else would be shreds of flesh and bone.

Janus clutched the sword tighter and tried to decide if it were better to go out fighting or, just this once, accept that he had been beaten. He had never expected his life to end due to an over-abundance of years, but this was too soon.

The rooks descended all at once, but it was in an uncontrolled fall; limp bundles of feather, metal, air-touched bone, and eyes gone white with old death. Adiran whirled, his attention shifting.

"See to your prince," Psyke said as she stepped out of the Relicts. A pale, luminous fog tumbled after her, like swirls of fog blown over ice. A black-clad shadow detached itself from her side, darting toward Ivor.

Adiran let the assassin pass, let her join Ivor, his attention all on Psyke. "Why do you interfere?"

"Why do You?" she countered. "You were not summoned. Adiran knows nothing of hatred."

"It's love that engenders vengeance. I know love," the prince said. "I know my father was taken from me by Ivor Sofia Grigorian." The boyish treble sank to a crow's low mutter under the weight of his grievance. He turned away from Psyke, reminded of Ivor's presence.

"You're mistaken," Ivor said, "misled by gossip or outright slander. Do you have no care for the truth? Your father was a stickler for it . . . for proof of wrongdoing. Are you his son? Or Ani's?"

"I want my father avenged!" Adiran cried. "I killed my friend to give me strength to see you die."

"Evan's alive," Psyke said. "And fretting for you."

The vise that had fastened itself around Janus's heart eased. They could be clear of this madness, if they could only keep Adiran from killing Ivor. They could save Antyre.

An overwhelming surge of gratitude shook him as he watched Psyke standing calm in the face of what must be an echo of all her fears—Ani, taking flesh again.

The boy shook his head, his hands flailing about his face, as if her words had unleashed an unexpected storm of wasps. Psyke took a step closer to the boy, held her hand out. "Come back to the palace, Adiran."

"Where you'll pin me in the earth? Cage me in stone? There are bars on my windows. Wings want to fly."

Janus shivered. Hadn't he heard that before? Maledicte, half crazed from being locked away in Stones, leaning up against him, Ani murmuring through his voice, wistful paeans to the sky.

Psyke's serenity shifted, a quick overlay of Mirabile's petulance and impatience on her face; she snatched at Adiran and he disappeared in a rush of feather swirl, as swift as flight, and hissed at her from a safer distance. Feathers snagged in the air, caught by the roiling, cold fogs surrounding Psyke, the shape of fingers surfacing and fading. Psyke wrapped her arms tight about herself; her lips moved, her brow furrowed. Containing her ghosts.

"I'll not be caged again," Adiran declared.

"No reason you should be," Ivor said. He shifted the blade in his hand to reflect moonlight, to catch both the boy's attention and the crow god's. Janus made an attempt to silence Ivor, lunging forward, blade in hand, and found himself blocked by the assassin.

"You won't win this time," she breathed.

Janus pushed back, using his weight against her. She wasn't Maledicte, wasn't god touched; though she was quick and his shielding arm hampered, she was hampered herself.

The mad determination in her eye reminded him of Miranda in the Relicts. She loved Ivor beyond sense, and would die for him. Janus meant to give her the opportunity to do so. He took a step back; she danced forward, trying to keep him too close to use his saber, but he gained enough distance to knee her in the hip, sending her reeling backward. He followed her retreat with a sideways slash; she swept her skirt into his face, and retreated behind it.

". . . you've been misled," Ivor continued, his voice as calm as lake water, as smooth as cream. "Fed deliberate misinformation by the guards. I didn't kill your father. You need look closer to home for your vengeance."

Adiran cocked his head, either listening or confused. Janus doubted many of Black-Winged Ani's targets stopped to argue with Her.

The assassin's blade ground against his own, and he lost track of Ivor's storytelling; his nape prickled, waiting for Adiran's attention to veer to him. It was, after all, where Ivor was heading, whether Adiran understood it or not. Janus gritted his teeth and hoped there was more of Adiran than Ani, more of that sweet faith and incomprehension of the world, than Ani's fury.

"Your prince is a fool," Janus said. He elbowed the assassin in the throat, not a hard enough blow, curse it, but enough to buy him a moment's reprieve. She brought her saber around, kissed his shoulder with it, a shallow caress that added the tang of metal to the sea air already overburdened by scent.

He shook it off, ignored the shiver than ran through his bones. "Ani might listen to him, but it would only broaden Her list of enemies, not spare him. Once She has chosen Her target, She will not be swayed."

Janus had expected to instill a tiny seed of doubt. Instead, her eye filled with the complete certainty that he spoke truth. Her free hand rose to touch her eye patch, and he moved in, blade arcing for her heart.

He would have killed her while she was lost in whatever memory he had woken, save Adiran screeched like a tortured soul; and, in her haste to ensure Ivor's safety, she ensured her own, turning as the blade chased air.

She flung herself between Adiran and Ivor, her blade wavering.

Ivor spoke more quickly, more plainly, the better to make a child understand. "*Janus* killed your father, not I. Turn Ani's gaze to him. She can tell you, if you choose to hear. Ani knows he's a kin killer."

Adiran shook his head, instinctive denial, and Janus let out a slow breath, his heart rocketing in his chest.

"He killed his own father," Ivor said, but his voice grew ragged. Even Ivor's iron nerve had its limits.

"He reads to me and brings me sweets."

Janus laughed. It bubbled out of him like hysteria. All Ivor's cleverness meant nothing when faced with a child's innocence and Black-Winged Ani's obsessive focus.

Ivor closed his eyes for a bare moment, something he wouldn't have dared to do, were it not for his bodyguard. When he opened his eyes again, for the first time since Janus had met him, Ivor looked . . . broken. He pulled the assassin to him, kissed her brow, and then flung her into Adiran's arms.

"You want the killer? She is within your grasp. My words might have set her on, but it was *her* blade that carved out your father's heart."

Adiran pushed her aside and she skidded away and fell, her skirts tangling about her legs, her hands clawing at the rough stone and wood of the dock as she fought to get back to Ivor. Psyke took a quick step forward, knelt, and spoke quietly in the girl's ear, restraining her with a single hand.

Adiran scooped up the assassin's fallen blade; the silver edge tarnished, then went black, feathery wisps coiling, flaring and fading.

Ivor watched Adiran approach—a rictus stretching his cheeks like some demented doll—then bolted into Janus's shadow.

Adiran paused, cocking his head, and staring sideways like a raven deciding where best to begin scavenging.

"If I die, Ixion," Ivor warned.

"I'll give my condolences to your country," Janus said. It was pure bravado. His throat dried, and it wasn't all for the god-touched boy watching them, as if deciding whether a blade through Janus would be the simplest way to strike Ivor dead.

Janus thought that while Adiran's blade might be long enough, his strength was unlikely to push it through two sets of rib cages. Janus would die just the same, though.

"See to your lord," Psyke's voice rang out. "Rise and protect him!"

Janus felt a sudden sting of betrayal, that Psyke encouraged the assassin. . . . Then his blood chilled as if winter had come early. Psyke hadn't been speaking to the assassin. Fog streamed across the dock, given some terrible purpose, and Janus jerked as a cold tendril of fog touched him briefly, carrying a whisper, a familiar voice thinned to nearly nothing. *Trust Psyke*, Chryses murmured, and then the fog had moved on, leaving Janus shaking.

It was not fog, nothing so natural as that, Janus realized, but Antyre's dead, clustering so closely that the intangible had become physical. The fog swept over the docks, cradled the corpses left from the skirmish between the Antyrrian soldiers and the Itarusine saboteurs, and sank inward, giving Janus quick and disturbing glances of ghostly limbs struggling like those of sailors from a scuppered ship.

The dead Antyrrian soldiers jerked to their feet, skin gleaming like wet fish scales, their weapons held in tightening grips. One of them saluted Janus, his hand held up, a ghostly eye surfacing in the dead man's palm for a moment.

Trust Psyke, Janus thought. How, when he didn't even know what she was anymore? Ani's motives were ugly and violent but comprehensible, built out of the depths of men's souls. Haith, on the other hand, was as enigmatic as the face He hid beneath His hood.

Adiran swung 'round, shrieking words that burned through the air, ate away at the ghost fog that Psyke hastily drew about her. Janus and Ivor dropped as one, shielded their ears at the sound of the language of the gods.

"I am immune to death," Psyke said. "Can your avatar say the same? The boy is fragile, mortal, and unblooded." Despite her brave words, Janus noticed the fog about her thinning, as if the dead were being destroyed or dispersed.

"Not for long," Adiran said. He tore into the dead soldiers with skill born only of savagery and borrowed hate.

The assassin inserted herself into the fray, still attempting to save Ivor, when it became evident that the corpse soldiers could not hold Adiran back. Indeed, Adiran's hesitance faded, as if they granted him the practice he had sorely needed, that Black-Winged Ani needed to learn what the boy prince was capable of.

Dodging a strike, the assassin danced away, turning Adiran from his path toward Ivor. The boy checked himself almost immediately, and the assassin shouted. "Boy! Ivor spoke nothing less than the truth. If you wish to strike down your father's murderer, you must strike me."

Adiran darted toward Ivor. Janus intercepted the boy, Ivor still sheltering behind him, cursing himself even as he did. His own death was no part of the plan, but Ivor—

Janus shuddered. If Ivor died, Antyre would war. If Janus died . . . if Psyke could stop Adiran . . . bitter as it was, Antyre might survive without him. But would it want to? Was Haith any better as a ruling god than Ani?

Janus ducked Adiran's first angry slash—a boyish flailing, instead of the more focused destruction he had turned on the guards. Ivor pushed Janus forward, nearly doing the work for Adiran. Janus abruptly found himself besieged on two sides.

"Bastard," Janus hissed.

Ivor said, "Survival first." He grinned a wide, wild thing, seized Janus by the shoulders, and hurled him into Adiran's blade.

Janus groaned; the blade tip bit in, just above his hip, shallow but painful. Adiran yanked the sword back, let Janus stumble out of the way.

The assassin pushed herself back into the fight. Janus fell to his knees, clutched the wound, the blood warm between his fingers. He took a few ragged breaths, trying to gain the energy to stand, to pick up his blade again.

Psyke knelt beside him, her fingers cold on his hands. "Rest a moment," she said.

"Rest too long and I'll be dead," he grated. "If Adiran doesn't kill me, Ivor will."

"No," she said. "I won't allow it."

"If you have the ability to prevent it, I wish you would, or are you waiting for a more threatening wound—"

"Hush," she said. She laid a cold hand over his lips; in the fog behind her, Janus thought he saw Aris looming toward him and flinched.

"I shot him and he didn't fall," the assassin said. "I gutted him, and watched his blood spread over the floor."

Adiran's face crumpled, a small, bloody fist came up and knuckled at one eye, smearing tears across his skin, but his other eye stayed fixed on Ivor.

The assassin said, "So *you* won't look at me, boy? Will *Ani?*" Her voice cracked; her hands shook. She cast a quick look over her shoulder at Ivor, and her resolve firmed. "I am more an enemy to you than you know. I killed your father, yes, but first— Have you truly forgotten me, Ani? When you sought me so assiduously? Killed my parents, my village, everyone around me, until I gave up my name. Surely you remember me. . . . Maledicte put out my eye on your behest."

Adiran froze, the feathers in his hair fluffing outward like a startled raven's. Ivor slipped farther along the dock, his eye on the dinghy that bobbed along the brass gates.

The assassin shook, the blade held out before her inscribing looping arcs, translating her fear.

"Your name," Adiran demanded.

Janus's breath pained him; he watched the assassin lure Ani closer, goad Her into adding another target, and wondered what this would gain them. The assassin would die, but Adiran's vow had been shaped by the guards he had overheard: He'd sworn vengeance on Ivor Grigorian.

Hopeless, he thought, found he'd whispered it aloud. He couldn't defend Ivor from a god, even were he willing to die for it.

"Not hopeless, not yet," Psyke murmured. Her hands on his shoulder tightened nearly to the point of pain. Her lips moved in what he thought was prayer; whispers of it touched his ear, pulses of warm breath and the soft aspiration of Haith's name. The ghosts swirled about her, brushing over Janus's skin. He felt the effort they were putting forth, and knew, whatever it was they were attempting to do at her command, they were failing. . . .

"Not enough," Psyke said. Her eyes were tragic. "How can it not be enough? When the dead line the streets? When I hold the king in my grasp? How many more deaths do I need to command You?"

The assassin backed away, calculation and terror vying in her face; her lips were bloodless, her eye fever bright.

Adiran followed in a bird hop, the blade led before him like a beak.

"Your name," he demanded.

"*Nadiyeh*," she said. "Nadiyeh—"

The name meant nothing to Janus, but Adiran's small form went still so quickly it left a tangible vibration in the air. Janus swallowed hard, struck by the taut lines of the boy's body. There were moments when he saw beyond position and rank, looked beyond a young prince and recognized kin. So it was that he recognized what froze Adiran, knew what it felt like when blood turned acid with rage and breath strangled itself in his throat.

Nadiyeh whimpered low, a sound stifled by an animal desire to be unheard. Soft as it was, the sound carried, amplified by Ani's desire to hear it. Adiran's lips curved in a fashion that had nothing of boy in it and everything of an unexpected satisfaction. Perhaps not a new addition to Her roster of vengeance, but an escaped one, reclaimed.

Nadiyeh hurled herself toward the water, as if she thought such shallow depths could protect her from Ani's beak and wings. Adiran lunged; his blade pierced her skirt and leg, pinned her in place.

The assassin screamed, her voice rising high and thin; she grasped at the blade through her thigh, clawed her way up it, hands going bloody, to seize Adiran's tightly straining wrists. "Ivor, flee!"

Adiran yanked away, the sword slipping from her leg, from her hands. Blood spurted, washed the docks.

Psyke flew from Janus's side, tried to intercede with Ani, but she was countered by Adiran, moving as quickly and far more violently. Psyke's skin striped itself red in places, as if Ani's talons had made themselves felt. Psyke healed, the wounds sealing shut, leaving paler stripes on her fair skin.

"Countess," the assassin said. "Countess." But her voice was weak with pain; her hands pressed tight to the gash in her leg were unequal to the task.

Janus staggered toward her, urged on by the fogs, all whispering, *Trust Psyke.* He didn't know what Psyke had planned, but the assassin was part of it. Though it galled him to succor the assassin who might have cost him his throne, she was better left alive until he knew why Psyke had brought her here.

He took off his belt, rolled the assassin's blood-sodden skirt higher, and turned the belt into a tourniquet. She grasped at his shoulders, leaving her blood staining against his, and said, "The countess must hold to her bargain. . . ."

"With Haith?" Janus asked. Panic seared him. What could Haith ask of Psyke, but death and more death?

"With *me*," she said.

Adiran, flustered and frustrated, all his sallies against Psyke stymied, turned back to his original goal: Ivor.

Janus panted, panicked, wondering where in hell Rue and the rest of the guards were; a glance back gave him an answer. The city burned; streamers of smoke clogged the night sky, billowing gray-black thunderheads that hung heavily overhead.

Ivor's saboteurs, taking advantage of the chaos Ivor had made at the palace. Janus rose, wanting badly to get to Ivor before Adiran did, to exact his own vengeance on the man who had dared to burn his city. The stab of pain in his side, the assassin's clutch at his leg, held him back.

Ivor had taken advantage of the lull in Adiran's attention to slip down one of the piers, attempting to get to the dinghy.

Adiran halved the distance in a single flurry of movement, and the assassin groaned beneath Janus's hands. She forced herself upright, took a labored breath; blood tinged her teeth, her lips, found a final strength.

Nadiyeh said, "Is a boy's desire for vengeance greater than yours, O great one? And a boy's mistaken desire at that? Or do you forget that I slaughtered the king. . . ."

Adiran shuddered, two desires manifesting in him at once, two conflicting hungers for blood. Ani's insult, and his vengeance. His shirt tented, a ripple against the darkness, wings straining beneath.

Psyke moved to interfere, and Nadiyeh said, "Countess, your answer is *one*. One more death. But remember my bargain. . . . If you cheat me, I'll turn your commands to dust in your mouth."

Adiran chose, lunged toward Nadiyeh, and she rose to meet him. She stepped into the blade, letting the sword press home, easing its way in beyond the sheltering ribs. She clutched the blade, pulled herself along it, and made a tiny sound that could have been a whimper or a laugh, a sob or a cry of triumph.

"Now," she whispered. *Now*, and her voice spun into nothingness as her eyes closed, as she pulled the blade downward with her dying weight. Silence rang on the pier, the silent pleasure of Ani's gloating, the weight of the compact between Herself and Adiran snapping into place. Whether Evan lived or died, Adiran's course was set, Ani's chosen victim used to fuel Adiran's quest for vengeance.

Janus felt defeat roll over him like the tide; his city burned, and it would burn more once Grigor learned of Ivor's death.

Adiran licked the blade tip, tasting the death he had dealt, and smiled when he found it palatable. He raised his head, and said, "Now, Ivor." The voice was a terrible blend, the rasp and rattle of the god overlaid on Adiran's childish sweetness. Janus knew he should rise, knew he had to do something to prevent Ivor's death. If Ivor died, they lost Antyre, and more, they lost Adiran—Ani was a harsh intrusion into any mortal host. How much worse would it be for a child, mostly mindless to begin with?

Janus staggered to his feet, thinking at least, if he killed Ivor instead of Adiran, the compact would hold; Adiran could be used to protect the country. As he had used Maledicte.

Ivor had found a boat hook and was trying to snag the dinghy. Now he dropped it hastily and took up his blade again, facing Janus, facing Adiran.

Psyke took a deep breath and said, "Haith, I summon you." It was nearly conversational, save for the waver in her voice, that fragile uncertainty.

A shadow emanated from the earth, flowing through the fog like a serpent and rose to stand three times as tall as Psyke. He inclined His head toward her, waiting patiently as only stone could wait.

Give me your command, and I will obey.

"I command you," Psyke said, her voice gaining strength. "By your people that I hold to me, I command you to do my bidding."

Haith fell to his knees before her, His hood falling forward and shadowing even more of His face. "Command Me as you will, Lady of Redoubt. Name your victory."

Janus cringed, his hands flying to his ears, but where Ani's voice was glass shard ruin to Her hearers, Haith's was the quiet whisper of a last sigh before death.

Adiran's feathers bristled; his eyes burned blackly, and talons now tipped his fingers, clicked against each other around the steel sword hilt. "Begone, Brother Worm. Crawling *thing*."

Haith's attention never veered from Psyke. Her hands trembled; her eyes tore themselves from the kneeling god and found Ivor.

Janus's own hands were knotting, tacky with his blood and Nadiyeh's, wondering what Psyke intended. If she set the god on Ivor . . . If she set Him on Adiran . . .

There was no chance for victory that Janus saw.

Psyke's eyes flared blue; her voice rang out: "Haith, rid us of Black-Winged Ani!"

Ani shrieked outrage; Haith's head rose, His hood fell back, revealing furrowed scale and twisting horn. Psyke's gaze never faltered. "Backed by the dead, I command You."

Haith rose, stiff now where He had been fluid before, like a man gone old before his time with a sudden shock. "We are connected," He said, "kindred all. . . . Kill one of Us, and the others tumble into the grave."

Psyke said, "We have no need for gods."

Haith exhaled the scent of incense, old woods and leaf rot, of the cold that came on a first winter morning. "As you will—"

Adiran's body shuddered, swelled, burst into strange flesh, becoming a creature of multiple talon-tipped wings, with a beak grown long, curled, and sharp edged. Black-Winged Ani birthed god's flesh out of mortal clay, and aimed Her rage at Psyke.

Psyke never quailed, trusting Haith, trusting that her command would be obeyed. Janus's belly clenched; if Haith dallied, went reluctantly to Psyke's command, Ani would free Him of the need to do so.

But Haith's shadow enveloped Black-Winged Ani, dragged Her screeching into the stone, pinning Her wings, and holding Her back.

"Brother!" Ani screamed.

Janus fell to his knees, the sound echoing in his head, savaging tissue in its path. His face was wet; his vision red tinged, and all his senses were overlaid by blood. Distantly, he saw Ivor curled on the dock.

Haith hissed, tightened His shadow about Her, like a coiling serpent. His hands fastened claws into Her wings, piercing the membranes, spilling feathers along the docks, turning the ocean waters black with sodden feathers and red with blood. Janus spared a moment to mourn Adiran, trapped beneath Her skin, and Haith's eyes turned toward him, green as grass and slitted.

"Never mourn one who is not gone," He said. "It only tempts Me to take notice. . . ."

Ani shrieked again, Her wings batting at His face, and Haith plunged a sharp-scaled hand into her breast. She quivered, but fell silent.

Dead? Janus doubted it; love and vengeance seemed as immutable as death. Haith hissed in pained satisfaction, and began to sink into the stone with a susurrus of scale, dragging the dark ruin of Ani's manifested body after Him, sweeping blood from the docks as neatly as any wave. Perhaps not dead, but defeated nonetheless.

When He had gone completely, there was a pale glimmer left, a child curled up, eyes closed as if sleeping.

Psyke sighed softly and collapsed, leaving Janus wobbling on his feet, and torn in two directions: See to his wife? See to whatever remained of Adiran? A wave of heat, a stinging swirl of smoke reminded him that there was still Murne to see to, the plague and the fires to recover from, if possible.

A scrape of metal heralded Ivor rising to his feet, using his saber for balance. The two men faced each other across a dozen feet, and Ivor raised his blade after a moment. "Well then? Shall we duel for the remains of the dead?"

Janus staggered forward, every bone aching, and thinking bitter thoughts about Maledicte, about Adiran, about Psyke, who had a god's healing touch on their wounds, and never knew what it was like to be burdened by exhaustion and pain and still have a task to do.

He shouldered past Ivor, ignoring the blade, and taking up the boat hook. The dinghy was close enough; the inbound waves urging it onward. The boat pole thunked against the solid edge of the craft, jarred his bones.

Janus said, "Return to your ships, Ivor: your ships, and your kingdom. You are not welcome in mine."

He dodged the blade Ivor sent toward his neck. Ivor's face burned with rage, all his poise stripped. "I will not go home a failure," he hissed. "I would rather die here—"

Janus stumbled, fell back, and when Ivor tried to close on him, curled up and kicked out in a Relict rat's last-resort attempt to be rid of an attacker. Ivor took the blow in his belly, skidded into the water with a splash and a groan. Janus clambered back to his feet with every bone protesting.

"I'll unwind the gates," Janus said. "Grigor's ship approaches. If you're not feeling energetic enough to row yourself out to him, you can wait for the tide to go out. Explain to him that the treaty was broken by your assassination of Aris. We will not accept censure. And we will expect an apology."

Janus leaned over the side with the boat hook, watched Ivor splash out of the way to cling to the other side of the dinghy, and then he pushed the boat farther from the dock. Ivor cursed, and clambered aboard rather than be rubbed against barnacle-studded pilings. "I've left you a kingdom of rubble," Ivor said.

"I've begun there before," Janus said. "I know how to rise above it. Can you say the same?"

Ivor went silent and the boat slowly moved away, guided by a single oar and Ivor's pained exertions.

A faint whimper roused Janus from his contemplation of the lightening sky, and the sails on the horizon. He crawled to his feet, and found Adiran sitting up, knuckling his eyes, and beginning to sob. Janus held back, blade at hand, wary. If Ani were not gone—

"I had a bad dream," Adiran wailed. "I want my father! I want Evan!"

Janus collapsed beside the boy, studying him in the dawning day. There were still dark tufts in his hair, though whether the feathers were merely matted in by blood or growing outward was unclear. And when Adiran shot a frightened glance up at Janus, one eye was still mottled black and blue. Janus felt the hilt of his dagger in his hand.

No one could say it was murder, now. Not with the marks of Ani's possession still so clear on the boy; Rue would support him. As would Bull. A single blow—the child all unwitting; even now, he leaned against Janus's side seeking comfort—and the throne would be his. There'd be no palaver about regency, about acceptability; he'd be their only choice.

Adiran pushed himself more urgently into Janus's arms. *Then again*, Janus thought. Adiran was himself once more, sweet natured, simpleminded, hardly a threat to Janus's ambitions. The boy twisted in his arms and looked up at him with such weary intelligence that Janus remembered Adiran had shared his misery in complete sentences, a feat he had been incapable of, before.

He patted the boy absently, and tried to think. Everything that had once been so clear was muddled now. Maledicte—his spur, his purpose—was gone. The throne was one blade thrust from his reach, and he hesitated.

If he chose to leave Adiran alive and improving, he would only ever ascend to regent. Adiran would grow, take the throne, have children, and the opportunity would pass. Would he miss it? Janus rested his chin on Adiran's head, smelled blood and feathers and thought of Maledicte crying, *When is it enough?*

In the beginning it had been only about rising faster, rising higher, securing a future for himself and his lover, beyond the capacities of the world to take it away. But now—the future he wanted secure was for his country. If he were king, surrounded by guards, tethered by propriety and rules, could he accomplish enough? Even as regent, would he accomplish anything, or would his days be lost to petty political maneuverings?

He raised Adiran a little, let the boy's head loll back on his shoulder, baring his throat. It wouldn't be a bad death; the boy had fallen back into a fitful sleep. Adiran would simply never wake. There'd be a single, startled cry, nothing more.

His gut spasmed; a cold chill ran his spine. The infant hadn't cried either and yet it still haunted his dreams. He lowered the blade. He didn't want the throne—not like this. Not under duress and suspicion, not with the rest of his life spent guarding his back. How little would he accomplish if his every moment was spent ensuring his own safety?

Ivor had once offered him a position as king's knight, and though it had been for a country not his own, the idea had appealed. Perhaps he could make a new place for himself in Antyre. Not useless regent, not hated king, but something else. Someone who held power and used it for the betterment of the country. There'd be profit in it for both him and Antyre if he was clever. And despite Ivor's schemes nearly snaring him, Janus knew himself to be a clever man.

He flipped the dagger around, considering the idea one last time—this moment would not come again—and then dropped the blade to the blood-washed dock.

"I'm pleased to see your judgment improves," Psyke said behind him. A breeze touched his neck, and he heard the rustle of steel falling away.

He jerked around, waking Adiran to fretful crying, his startled gaze all for the blade Psyke was lowering. How long had she stood there, silently waiting to play executioner? Perhaps she had told herself the same stories he had told himself: that he would never notice, that no one could object. . . .

She held out a hand to him—small, soft, aristocratic even with blood-rimmed nails, everything Maledicte had never been—and he took it in his, let her help him to his feet.

Miranda had been his heart, his purpose, but she was also his past. Psyke, Adiran, Antyre . . . these were his future.

She sighed, looking back toward the palace, to the fading streamers of smoke going hazy in the morning light. "So very much damage," she said. "Death and fires and plague. Despair and distrust. So much to repair."

"Not to repair," Janus said, mind already working. "To *improve*. We're moving forward for the first time in generations."

Some of the strung-wire tension in her shoulders eased; a tiny smile blossomed at the corners of her mouth, a barely there tilt that once he would have mistaken for either no expression at all or a sneer.

Adiran tugged Janus's sleeve with cautious fingers, still wary, still uncertain, and said, "The ship's leaving."

It was true. The scarlet sails thinned themselves in the corona of the rising sun, as the ship tacked onto a different course.

Janus watched it for the space of two heartbeats, then shook his head. He draped an arm over Psyke's shoulders, shifting his weight to relieve the pressure put on his wounds, trusting her support would be freely given. Adiran watched, brow furrowed, and then he pressed himself against Janus's other side. Together, bound by need and loss, they moved forward into the city.

About the Author

LANE ROBINS was born in Miami, Florida, the daughter of two scientists, and grew up as the first human member of their menagerie. When it came time for a career, it was a hard choice between veterinarian and writer. It turned out to be far more fun to write about blood than to work with it. She received her BA in Creative Writing from Beloit College, and currently lives in Lawrence, Kansas.

www.maledicte.com